The Organisation

BY THE AUTHOR

THE COUNTDOWN CHRONICLES
Kiss of the Mandarins
The Warehouse
Never Go Back
The Deception Covenant
Endgame

THE ORGANISATION

ORIGIN TALES
The Brotherhood
Rise of the ACF

VLADIMIR SERIES
Vladimir's Diary
Red Empire
Fifty Years to Paradise

THE VAV CHRONICLES
Vampires And Victims

OTHER WORKS
The Prophecy Illusion
Trinity

The Organisation

Martin M. McShane

The Book Guild Ltd

First published in Great Britain in 2023 by
The Book Guild Ltd
Unit E2 Airfielod Business Park
Harrison Road, Market Harborough
Leicestershire, LE16 7UL
Freephone: 0800 999 2982
www.bookguild.co.uk
Email: info@bookguild.co.uk
Twitter: @bookguild

Copyright © 2023 Martin M. McShane

The right of Martin M. McShane to be identified as the author of this
work has been asserted by him in accordance with the
Copyright, Design and Patents Act 1988.

All rights reserved. No part of this publication may be
reproduced, transmitted, or stored in a retrieval system, in any form or by any means,
without permission in writing from the publisher, nor be otherwise circulated in
any form of binding or cover other than that in which it is published and without
a similar condition being imposed on the subsequent purchaser.

This is a work of fiction and is entirely a product of the author's imagination.
Any resemblance or similarity to names, places, characters, incidents or events
or to any actual person, living, dead or undead, is entirely coincidental.

Typeset in Adobe Garamond Pro

Printed and bound in Great Britain by
CPI Group (UK) Ltd, Croydon, CR0 4YY

ISBN 978 1915853 141

British Library Cataloguing in Publication Data.
A catalogue record for this book is available from the British Library.

There is nothing
More difficult to carry out,
Nor more doubtful of success,
Nor more dangerous to do,
Than to initiate
A new order of things.
#Unit

PROLOGUE

The Organisation doesn't have an official name because it doesn't officially exist. It began life seven hundred years ago as a Brotherhood whose noble mission it was to defend and protect ordinary folk against an avaricious Aristocracy. However, over the centuries, the Brotherhood became just another criminal enterprise. Time and again Brethren rescued their beloved Order from those who would subvert it only for it to return to bad ways.

Those who lived through the Bonaparte betrayal doubted their Brotherly Society would survive. Elder Brethren worked tirelessly to restore their precious Order but the wounds of division ran deep. They eventually succeeded but things were never the same. A new name was needed; *The New Brotherhood*, for a new era! For half a century the Organisation went by that name but it fell out of use for reasons which will become apparent.

Reigning supreme over the Organisation is the Chancellor. The Chancellor of the late twentieth century went by the name of Margaret Rotheram. At the start of her reign, the Organisation numbered north of 1.1 million globally, of whom less than forty knew its true mission. She was not one of them.

BERLIN

In the spring of 1928 Frederik Noelle-Neumann was appointed Managing Director of Noelle-Neumann Industries. The vote was unanimous despite him having married, against the family's wishes, a Russian Jew. They had wanted him to marry somebody from '*the list*'. On Frederik's sixth birthday the family had consulted the list for new-born females. Four potential future brides were selected; child mortality being what it was they didn't want to back just one or two horses.

By 1936 many in Hitler's Germany believed war was inevitable. Companies like Noelle-Neumann Industries often benefit from war but with Jewish blood running in their veins the majority of the family were for quitting Germany. Some considered heading to Russia, their ancestral homeland, but most didn't want to take the chance of a cold reception from the Bolsheviks. They ultimately agreed that Switzerland was probably the best place for them to sit out a war but they clung on in the hope war could be averted.

*

Dynasties, especially European dynasties such as the Noelle-Neumann's, believe they are something special but they are not so very special at all. They consider themselves to be powerful, important and influential and to a degree they are but only to a very small degree. True power, importance and influence lies with organisations which few have ever even heard of. While the Noelle-Neumanns of this world are busy with the day to day running of their grubby little empires they don't have time to raise their heads and look around and see what is really going on. They never get to see the machinations of the Mandarins or the Organisation or, more relevant to them, the manoeuvrings of The 400. Noelle-Neumann types are of natural interest to The 400 and indeed many such of them are their unknowing servants, brushing up against them in the worlds of finance and commerce as they do. If only the Noelle-Neumann types could recognise things for what they are and not what they believe them to be then they would realise that they are but bit players.

Occasionally, very occasionally, The 400 inducts new members. The 1920s was the perfect time to recruit as many of The 400 had been slaughtered by the Bolsheviks but they procrastinated. Things got desperate. With war inevitable, the 1930s was perhaps not the right time to recruit. It was put to a vote. While it was a close-run thing the risk averse carried the day and The 400 slid back into the shadows to await the outcome of the coming conflict. Not so the Organisation; they were gearing up to make pots of money.

By chance, in the distant past, an ancestor of the Noelle-Neumanns had been a Disciple of the earliest incarnation of the Organisation, known then as The Brotherhood. She had acquitted herself extremely well, but since that time they had not spawned anything worthy of interest or mention or recruitment.

*

Frederik Noelle-Neumann was about to call his father to inform him that his wife, Anastasia, had been taken by the Gestapo the previous evening when a brisk knocking came to the front door. When the family's English butler answered the door he was confronted by a Gestapo Officer flanked by men in long leather coats. He asked them what they wanted. The Officer said they had come to speak with Herr Noelle-Neumann. The butler disdainfully asked what it was they wished to speak with his master about and was told it was none of his business. He was ordered to bring Herr Noelle-Neumann before them at once.

Hearing the commotion, Frederik hung up the phone and asked the Officer what he wanted. He replied, "You need to accompany me to Gestapo HQ to answer some questions about your wife's links to Bolsheviks residing in Berlin." In response, Frederik said, "There must be some mistake, my wife fled St Petersburg in 1917 to escape from the Bolsheviks. They slaughtered her entire family and would have killed her too if she hadn't—" The Officer held up his hand to silence Frederik. "It's just routine, nothing to worry about. I'm sure you'll both be back home before you know it," he said with a reassuring smile.

The previous evening Frederik asked if he might accompany his wife to Gestapo HQ and had been told that was not possible. They had walked together hand in hand to the ornamental gate at the end of the drive. As the gate shut, Anastasia looked back over her shoulder at Frederik. There were no tears in her eyes but her face wore a haunted expression. It was only then that he understood the danger she was in. A handsome young Gestapo Officer clicked his heels together, saluted, and opened the door for Anastasia to get into the car. After they drove off Frederik raced back to the house to call his father. Just then his daughters came running into the room shouting, "Where is mother going? Where are they taking her?" They had seen Anastasia being driven away. Their eyes had momentarily met through the car's rear window but their mother looked through her children as though she didn't want to be associated with them. The girls were in floods of tears. Frederik stayed up all night to console his daughters as best he could but they were inconsolable.

*

Frederik met Anastasia in March 1925 at the British Ambassador's birthday party ball. She never did explain why she was there alone, or why she was even there at all. Frederik couldn't take his eyes off her. She looked so beautiful "in that dress". Not wanting to let such an opportunity slip by, Frederik, a dreadful dancer, asked Anastasia to dance. After crushing her toes he asked her to take a walk with him, "in the night air." She laughed. "What? In this temperature? Are you crazy? Look at how I am dressed? I grew up in Russia and we know to stay indoors when not dressed for such weather." Her English was so impeccable that Frederik assumed Anastasia worked at the embassy and so asked her what it was she did there. She laughed. "Frederik, darling, I don't work for the embassy. Let's dance." Her voice was mesmerisingly husky. The way she said "Frederik darling" melted Herr Noelle-Neumann.

They danced and talked and drank and drank through the night. The party was still going strong when they left arm in arm in the early morning light. Frederik took Anastasia to a small café on K'dam where they breakfasted and arranged to meet the following Wednesday. That was it. That was how it all began.

Though Anastasia was a few years older than Frederik it didn't put him off. If anything he found the age difference… comfortable. After only a few months he proposed but Anastasia turned him down. She did it in such a way that he didn't feel rejected, he was just left feeling that the time was not yet right. He proposed again two months later and this time she accepted. He wasn't sure what the difference was that second time of asking but he didn't care, they were getting married. All he had to do now was break the 'good news' to the family.

Frederik thought of his family as a European quasi-aristocratic dynasty; of which there were many at the time. The Noelle-Neumanns weren't the oldest family but they were amongst the most successful. They had fingers in dozens of moneymaking pies right across Europe and into the Far East. There was always talk about expanding into England and the Americas but so far there hadn't been a reason to do so. That was about to change.

*

Waiting to be interviewed, if interviewed was the right word, Frederik sat bolt upright on a high-backed wooden bench just inside the entrance of Gestapo HQ. People were milling about, coming and going, all round him; some in handcuffs, many wearing the same expression Anastasia had worn the previous evening; "like when somebody is not going home again…"

"Herr Noelle-Neumann," called the handsome young Officer who had taken Anastasia away the previous evening, "come with me." Then, speaking to the Sergeant standing behind a high desk, he whispered confidentially, "There is no need to record this one. We won't be keeping him but if things change I will let you know."

"Where are we going?" asked Frederik in a panic. "Where are you taking me? Where is my wife? When can I see her? When will you release her?" He realised he'd asked a lot of questions without giving the Officer a chance to answer; though, through his expression, Frederik could tell the Officer didn't seem inclined to give him any answers.

"Come with me," he repeated.

Frederik followed the Officer into a small office furnished with one desk, two chairs and an angle poise lamp. A solitary bulb dangled from the ceiling. The enamel shade covering it concentrated a cone of yellow light onto the desk.

"Herr Noelle-Neumann, read this please and if you agree then sign it." The Officer handed Frederik a single sheet of paper which he refused to acknowledge as a futile demonstration of defiance.

"What is it?" inquired Frederik casually, still not deigning to look at the sheet of paper.

"Look at it Herr Noelle-Neumann. Read it. If you agree then sign at the bottom of the page where it says 'signature' and put the date next to it."

"What is there to agree with?" replied Frederik glancing down at the document. It appeared to be a list. He glanced at the paper again, harder this time. The heading at the top of the page read 'The Personal Effects of Anastasia Noelle-Neumann [nee Abrankovich] – Jew.' "Why have you given me a list of my wife's jewellery? Isn't she allowed to wear it while she's in here? Where is she? Can I speak with her before I sign?"

"Herr Noelle-Neumann, this is a list of your wife's personal effects. If you agree with it then sign it and they can be handed over to you."

"But I want to see her. She must be so—"

"Herr Noelle-Neumann, your wife is dead." That word rung in Frederik's ears. He shook his head in disbelief of what he thought he'd heard the Officer say.

"What? What did you say?"

"Your wife is dead, Herr Noelle-Neumann. I am sorry for your loss."

The word sunk in second time around. The vision of Anastasia looking at him over her shoulder came back to Frederik. He pictured the haunted look on her face; how well named the look was as Frederik knew it would haunt him for the rest of his life. He hardly knew what to say next. *Why aren't I crying?* he thought.

"Herr Noelle-Neumann, I realise this must be a shock for you but you need to…"

"I need to what?" responded Frederik with rising anger in his voice.

"Herr Noelle-Neumann, I advise you to carefully consider what you say next. I strongly advise you to sign the paper, pick up your wife's effects and leave this building while you still can. You married a Jew for God's sake. Not only that, a Jew with Bolshevik friends. What did you expect would happen?"

"She barely escaped with her life from the Bolsheviks… they murdered her parents… I told you all this… she would never… she was a gift from God and I…"

"Sign and leave! This is your last chance!"

"May I at least see the post mortem report?" asked Frederik calmly.

"A post mortem has not yet been carried out."

"How did she die? What did she die from?"

"I do not know, Herr Noelle-Neumann."

"How can I find out how she died; find out what happened to her? I don't even know when she died for God's sake."

"Call back in a few days and check if there's a post mortem report."

"Which mortuary will she be… has she already been taken to… I can't think… I…"

"You are right, Herr Noelle-Neumann, you need time to think. Go home and have a think and come back in a couple of days when I'm sure all your questions will be answered." Frederik stood and left the room in a daze.

At the front desk, Frederik was handed a pathetic little bag with his wife's name scribbled on it in pencil. He stared at the bag and then at the desk Sergeant. Before Frederik could open his mouth to speak the Sergeant gestured for him to leave the building.

As soon as Frederik was on the street he thought of a dozen questions he needed answers to. He walked on for ten paces and then, turning on his heels, made his way back to Gestapo HQ. Guessing that was what Frederik would do, the handsome young Gestapo Officer wedged his foot against the inside of the revolving doors. He stared at Frederik through the glass and shook his head. Frederik turned and told his Chauffeur that he was going to walk home, he needed time to himself.

"How did he take the news of his wife's… passing?" asked Gestapo Major von Stieffel.

"Not as badly as some. He just sat there most of the time hardly able to string a sentence together."

"He is probably in shock."

"What did you expect?" interjected the handsome young Gestapo Officer overstepping the mark.

"Later he'll get angry and most likely do something stupid. We were at Heidelberg University together, you know. We weren't friends exactly but I'm sure he'll remember me should we ever meet again."

"He'll most likely return tomorrow demanding to know the details."

"Yes, probably. If he does be sure to let me know. Dismissed."

"Jawohl Herr Major!"

*

During his walk back to the family home, Frederik considered not telling his daughters that their mother was dead but how could he keep it from them? They must know, they deserved to know, they had to know. He shoved open the ornamental gate and slowly trudged, shoulders slumped, head bowed, up the path toward the house. As though his legs wanted to spare everybody hearing the sad news they resisted him moving forward. Out of the corner of his eye he saw a curtain move followed by the front door flying open. Running toward him were Frederik's daughters, Lilliana and Henrietta. The girls slackened their pace as they neared their father. By the look on his face they could tell that something terrible had happened to their mother. They both threw themselves to the ground. Lilliana beat her fists on the rough path in rage only stopping when Henrietta held her close. Frederik, paralysed with grief, watched his daughters' shoulders rise and fall in deep guttering sobs, incapable of reaching out to them to provide fatherly comfort.

As the servants emerged from the house they ran toward Frederik. He dropped to his knees and screamed. The Chauffeur had already told the staff of the day's events. Though he could not know for certain their mistress was dead he believed there could be no other outcome of a visit to Gestapo HQ that resulted in his master's desire to walk home alone. The staff, respectfully and gently, scooped up their master and his daughters in their arms and carried them into the house. It was only then, in the privacy of his own four walls, that Frederik held his daughters.

As the longest-serving member of staff, the cook asked Frederik if she should call his father. He thanked her but declined her offer, asking instead that she take care of his daughters while he made the call himself.

As good news travels faster than bad, Frederik's father was already on his way to Berlin to see his son. When the Noelle-Neumann Patriarch arrived at the house in the small hours the two men grabbed hold of one another and held on tight. Frederik Snr assured his son that he would do everything in his power to find out what had happened to his daughter-in-law. Frederik told his father how much he loved… had loved… Anastasia and how he knew she was not what the family had wanted for him but he hadn't cared what the family wanted because he loved her so. Frederik Snr said he understood; "We've grown to love Anastasia, she'll be sorely missed by all," he lied.

After talking throughout the night, father and son, exhausted, dropped off to sleep just as dawn was breaking. They were woken at nine-thirty by the cook gently shaking them by their shoulders.

"There's a phone call for you sir," the cook whispered to Frederik.

"How many times must I ask you to call me Freddie?"

"Not while your father's in residence, sir."

"Who is it on the phone?"

"He wouldn't say," replied the cook.

"Shall I take the call?" Frederick asked his father. Even though he was the head of a massive business empire, Frederik lived in the shadow of his father, always seeking his approval.

"Of course, son," replied Frederik Snr in an uncharacteristically gentle tone of voice.

"Hello," said Frederik into the mouthpiece.

"Frederik Noelle-Neumann?" the caller asked in a formal tone. Frederik feared the worst; was it the Gestapo calling, ordering him to present himself at their HQ?

"Yes, this is he, what do you—"

"Listen to me carefully, Herr Noelle-Neumann, you are in great danger but your daughters are in even greater danger. They know you and all your family are part Jewish… but your daughters are half Jewish… more than half Jewish. They will come for you all. You must leave Germany if you want to live." The caller hung up.

Shaken by the call, Frederik stood motionless for half a minute before the cook asked if he was alright. He didn't reply, he just hung up the receiver, put on his coat, picked up a set of car keys and left the house muttering, "They don't scare me! They just want to steal my business! I'll show them!" Twenty minutes later Frederik parked outside Gestapo HQ. He was prevented from entering the building by four armed guards. After stating his business, the handsome young Officer who seemed to be central to all that had gone on turned up in the company of a Major who Frederik thought he recognised.

"Ah, Herr Noelle-Neumann, I see that you remember me," said the other Major.

"Heidelberg?"

"Precisely. Now, my old university friend, please follow me to my office and we'll find out what we can do for you." The men entered the building together and after walking in silence along a labyrinth of corridors they halted outside an office that had *Major K. von Stieffel* written on the reinforced opaque glass wire window of the door. Frederik spoke as soon as they sat down.

"I want to know what happened to my wife," he said coldly.

"Of course you do… Freddie. May I can call you Freddie? That's what they called you at Heidelberg… Freddie. Very… English."

"Karl… please… just tell me what happened to my wife… I'm begging you."

"I had a feeling you would return after you'd had a chance to think things over so I made it my business to get to you before you did anything stupid. You know what I mean don't you Freddie?" Frederik made no answer. "As I said, I had a feeling you'd return and so I asked Leutnant Meier here to look into matters and get back to me. I'm afraid that your wife… Anastasia? suffered a heart attack. It appears she had an hereditary heart problem and it was only a matter of time before…"

"She had regular medical examinations. None of them showed she had any…"

"Advances in medicine are being made all the time, Freddie. What one doctor says today another will say differently tomorrow. Freddie, your wife died from a heart attack."

"May I see the results of the post mortem examination?"

"I'm not sure if one has been carried out yet."

"Then how can you be sure my wife died from a heart attack if you haven't seen the post mortem results?" interrupted Frederik.

"That is what our doctors told me."

"Herr Major, I understand that a post mortem examination will be carried out this afternoon," interrupted Leutnant Meier. The Major glared at him for his unwanted interruption.

"Very good, thank you Leutnant Meier. See Freddie, a post mortem will be carried out this afternoon and I can assure you that you will receive a copy as soon as it is ready. You know Freddie, your family is very powerful, very influential, not everybody gets treated so courteously as you. You should be grateful."

"Thank you Karl, I appreciate your kind help." Frederik felt like biting off the end of his tongue for his words stuck in his throat. "I'll be on my way. It was good seeing you again Karl."

"Before you go Freddie, I have to speak with you on a delicate matter. Leutnant Meier, leave us, go about your duties."

"Jawohl Herr Major." The young Leutnant left the two men to their business.

"Coffee? Schnapps?"

"Neither for me thank you."

"I understand, you're not in the mood for any social niceties. Here you are, sitting in grief in the building where your wife died, speaking with one of the servants of the organisation responsible for her death. Why should you follow the conventions of polite society?"

"You said my wife died from a heart attack."

"Don't be naïve Freddie. She was a Jew and a Bolshevik sympathiser. She was double damned. When she wouldn't confess, things went too far, she was not meant to die, we wanted to turn her. I understand she was threatened that her daughters would join her here and even then she refused to give her Bolshevik friends away. She must have been very dedicated to their cause."

"Karl, Anastasia fled Russia in 1917 to escape from the Bolsheviks. They murdered her family... they—"

"Very convenient story that, don't you think? The Bolsheviks murdering all her family and her escaping Russia... all by her little self... making her way to Paris all alone... without any help."

"Paris? Nonsense, she came straight to Berlin. She..."

"That is what she told you but we have other information. No, Freddie, your wife first went to Paris and then London and then here to Berlin. She was a Bolshevik, Freddie, and was spying on us and reporting back to Moscow."

"That is a lie! A ridiculous lie! How could she? How could she be a spy? How could she be reporting to Moscow when she had people around her all the time; me, the children, the staff, her friends? You must have her confused with somebody else or you are playing a game with me."

"It is no game Freddie, I can assure you of that. But we digress, let me be clear with you. Some of your business enterprises are of interest to the party. We want you to do some work for us. I would rather you did so willingly but I am afraid that if you need persuading my superiors have authorised me to tell you that your daughters will be arrested unless you co-operate." The thought of his girls being arrested by the Gestapo dizzied Frederik. He went to stand in defiance of the threat made against his daughters. A panic attack set in. He began to hyperventilate. "Calm down Freddie, calm down. Sit back down. Take some water."

"I can't breathe. I can't breathe…" gasped Frederik. The room spun as he passed out.

*

When Frederik came round he was lying in a hospital bed. On a cabinet next to him was a pot of pills with its top unscrewed. Looking down at him was Major von Stieffel. "You are in good hands," said the Major smiling. Von Stieffel told Frederik that he was going to Munich for a week and would speak with him upon his return but in the meantime he was free to go home to his family. The Major stretched out a hand for Frederik to shake, which he took reluctantly. Von Stieffel picked up on Frederik's reticence but made no remark, he simply departed the ward after whispering something to a doctor standing by the door.

As soon as the Major was gone, Frederik raised himself to get out of bed. The doctor who the Major had whispered to came racing across the ward. He grabbed hold of Frederik's shoulder and told him that he had to remain in hospital for at least the next two days and would take no argument about it. The doctor informed Frederik that his family had been advised of his whereabouts and they were due in to see him. Twenty minutes later Frederik heard voices he recognised in the corridor outside his room. As he called out the curtain around his bed was pulled back to reveal Lilliana, Henrietta and his father. They were wearing worried and concerned expressions on their faces. Frederik told them he was feeling fine and would not be there at all had he managed to get to his pills in time. The twins looked at one another; they had no idea their father was dependent on medication though Frederik Snr showed no sign of surprise even though he too did not know his son had a heart condition.

Frederik made no mention to his daughters of the threat they were under, preferring instead to discuss it with his father as soon as he was discharged from the hospital. Lilliana picked up the brown bottle on the cabinet beside her father's bed and looked at the label. She couldn't read a word of it. "Typical doctor's handwriting," she muttered and put the bottle back down. They wanted to talk about their father's medical condition but he wanted to talk about anything other than that and Anastasia's death. It was neither the time nor the place for such words.

As they were about to leave, Frederik Snr asked for a few minutes with his son so the twins left them alone. They both knew what the conversation was going to be about.

"I know you went to Gestapo HQ. That was a stupid thing for you to have done. Did you find out anything about how Anastasia died?"

"Nothing of any use."

"You're a terrible liar, Frederik." Whenever his father called him '*Frederik*' in that way it brought back memories of an unhappy childhood.

"This isn't the right time or place, Father." Whenever Frederik called Frederik Snr '*Father*' in that way it brought back memories of disappointment.

"Are you or the girls in any danger?" Frederik Snr could tell by the expression on his son's face that he had hit the mark. "What did they say? I assume they made threats? Do you want me to take the girls to Frankfurt?"

"No, don't do anything that might attract attention. An old university friend… he wasn't a friend exactly… but he's now a Major in the Gestapo…"

"You know a Major in the Gestapo?"

"Yes. He wants me to do something for the Nazi party. I didn't get to find out what it was because I fainted. He's going to be in Munich for a week but wants to speak with me upon his return."

"How much trouble are we in?"

"A lot. We'll need to make plans. Switzerland?"

"Let's not discuss it now. We'll talk properly once you're home. You just concentrate on getting well again and don't worry about us, we'll be fine. I'll see you tomorrow. Goodbye son." For the first time in Frederik Snr's life he almost told his son that he loved him.

The conversation between the Frederiks was bugged. The listeners recorded everything and ordered SS guards to pick up Frederik Snr before he exited the hospital. Lilliana and Henrietta became concerned after their grandfather had not showed up for over half an hour and so re-entered the hospital only to be ushered out at the end of rifle butts by armed guards ordering the "*little Jew girls*" to go home.

*

At nine o'clock that evening Frederik Snr appeared back at the house. The girls rushed to greet him, wrapping him up in their arms. He seemed okay, there was no sign of any mistreatment but he didn't want to discuss the day's events. Instead he said it was time for them to go to bed and that Frederik would back home the following afternoon. Overjoyed at the prospect of their father returning home the twins didn't argue with their grandfather and went to their room. Despite the family home having twenty bedrooms the girls shared a room; they said it was because they were twins and couldn't bear being apart. They talked about what they thought was going on and where it might all lead, especially in light of the guards at the hospital calling them "little Jew girls" and threatening them with shoves from the butts of their rifles.

The following afternoon Frederik Snr picked his son up from the hospital and drove him straight home even though he wanted to drop in at the office as he had some things to do that just couldn't wait. Back at the house Frederik was surprised to see a dozen senior members of the Noelle-Neumann clan there. After the briefest of inquiries as to Frederik's health the family convened an extraordinary board meeting. Frederik asked if they were aware that he had just lost his wife… that Anastasia was dead.

"Of course we're aware, Frederik but, terribly sad though the news of Anastasia's passing is, we cannot afford to dwell on that for unless we act quickly we may all be doomed. Did you know your father was taken by—"

"I don't even know how she died," interrupted Frederik as if not listening to his grandmother. "They said it was a heart attack. The morning I returned to Gestapo HQ I received a call warning me of the danger we are all in…"

"Who was the phone call from?" asked the grandmother.

"He didn't say and I didn't recognise his voice. I don't even know how she died. At Gestapo HQ I met somebody from my time at Heidelberg University. He told me Anastasia was double damned; she was a Bolshevik agent according to him. He said things about Anastasia that were just—"

"Frederik, your father was interrogated by the Gestapo after visiting you yesterday. They had obviously recorded your conversation with him. Think Frederik, think. Think about what you said while you were with the Gestapo and while you were in the hospital. Did you, could you, have said anything that might endanger you? Endanger us?"

"I don't think so. One of the doctors came and sat with me for a long time after father left. We talked about all sorts of things but I can't recall any of our conversation. I… I felt odd at the time, like I was dreaming but it wasn't a dream."

"Christ Frederik, they must have drugged you, you might have said anything!" cried several relatives in unison.

"What shall we do?" asked an uncle.

"We'll do what we've always done," answered the Matriarch, "we'll run away to fight another day. Let us discuss our course of action."

*

Conversations had by the Noelle-Neumanns of this world can affect the lives of so many people in so many ways. Those mentioned seldom find out they were discussed until they are subsequently surprised in some unpleasant or unexpected way. This can be anything from getting fired to missing out on things you were in line for, like a promotion, or, in exceptional circumstances, being killed. So, if you have ever found yourself the victim of some malign fate here is how it came about; you were discussed where you would not have wanted to have been discussed and a decision was made concerning your future.

*

The family meeting was drawing to a close.

"For your own safety and for the safety of your children, Frederik, you must leave Berlin immediately."

"But England? Are you sure?"

"We are unanimous!"

"We've long wanted to establish the family business there and now seems… sorry Freddie, I don't mean to sound heartless but I—"

"Stop blithering Rufus. It's not a matter of being heartless it's a matter of survival, our survival and the survival of those lovely girls of Frederik's, the business opportunity is secondary," lied an aging aunt.

"Then why don't we all go to Switzerland?"

"The Swiss can't be trusted. As soon as war starts they'll tip all those with Jewish blood into the hands of the Nazis. No, we must go to England. The strip of water that separates Britain from Europe has played many vital roles in history and I have a feeling it will do so again."

"You are wise as you are beautiful Grandmother," said Frederik. The Matriarch smiled a snake smile at the back-handed compliment.

"What shall we do about—"

"That is none of your concern, Peter. We will take care of matters before we leave!"

"All vendettas must be settled!" exclaimed an aging aunt with a grimace.

"Yes, we must settle all vendettas before leaving!" repeated mad old Christabel.

"Yes, thank you for that, Christabel. Have no fear, we shall take care of those that need taking care of before we leave."

"Last man… or woman… out, turns off the lights, eh?"

"Why do you say things like that Wilhelm? Do you imagine it makes you appear humorous… or intelligent perhaps?"

"No, I just wanted to… never mind," whimpered Wilhelm.

"It is settled then. Frederik leaves for London tomorrow night and the rest of us will follow on as agreed. Good luck everybody. God watch over us and keep us all safe, we put ourselves in His guiding hands."

The next day Frederik went looking for his father to give him some last-minute instructions regarding a business deal he was putting together but Frederik Snr was nowhere to be found. He called around everybody who might know where his father was but couldn't locate him. That evening, as Frederik and his daughters were saying their goodbyes to the staff, the telephone rang. On the other end of the line was the same voice that had warned Frederik of the danger he was facing. The message was short. "Your father won't be joining you in England. To save your lives and the lives of his granddaughters he's sold his soul to the Nazis." Message over, the line went dead.

LONDON

Following their arrival in London, the Noelle-Neumann clan set about establishing the family business. Expensive elegant offices, befitting people of their status, were leased in the most desirable commercial and banking districts and were furnished to impress. The family worked tirelessly to recruit staff, acquire companies and set up new contracts. Each took on extra responsibilities to remove the burden of the day to day running of the business from Frederik's shoulders to give him time to grieve the loss of his wife and spend time with his daughters. They were all in it for themselves, of course. They saw London as a new beginning and thought a new beginning needed new leadership. The more time Frederik spent with his daughters the better they liked it.

Shortly after his arrival in England Frederik received a letter from Major von Stieffel. It said that his father was now reporting directly to the Reichsminister for Aviation, Hermann Göring. The letter did not say what role Frederik's father was playing but it wasn't difficult to work out. Frederik replied to the Major's letter in the hope that he might find out the truth about his wife's death, or murder as he had come to regard it as. The family begged him to break off contact with the Gestapo Officer but he was convinced that somehow, some day, Major von Stieffel would tell him how his wife had met her end. Not knowing how Anastasia had died was eating Frederik up inside. The longer the not knowing went on the worse he got.

Instead of taking time to settle himself and his daughters in their new home, Frederik worked night and day; "driven by self-pity" the family said behind his back. He worked slavishly to keep thoughts from his mind of what might have happened to his beautiful Anastasia at the merciless hands of the Gestapo. For their different reasons, family members implored Frederik not to neglect his daughters; "take them on a nice family holiday." Frederik correctly interpreted these acts of apparent concern for his children as them wanting to take the business away from him. To remain in control, Frederik doubled and redoubled his efforts meaning he saw even less of his daughters. Through working such long hours seven days a week Frederik became ill. With all he'd been through and all that he was still going through, unsurprisingly, he collapsed at work one day and was rushed to hospital where he was diagnosed with extreme physical, mental and emotional exhaustion. He was an empty shell of a man.

A Noelle-Neumann family conversation.

"At least in hospital he'll get some much-needed rest," said an ancient aunt feigning concern for Frederik.

"We can have the girls come and stay with us, they'll like that," suggested Audrey Rotheram née Noelle-Neumann.

"We're dancing around the edges. What are we going to do about Frederik?"

"What do you mean?"

"You know very well what I mean. He's incapable of running the business."

"Oh, don't take that away from him too, not at a time like this," said the ancient aunt while considering who she would vote for to take over the running of the company.

"I, for one, will not hear of it," lied an uncle.

"Over my dead body," lied another.

"Have it your way for now but if he—"

"We'll demand he takes a holiday and decide after he returns," proposed the Matriarch grandmother. All agreed with her.

The family elders visited Frederik in hospital and presented him with an ultimatum. He either took a holiday with his daughters or he'd be removed from the board. He recognised they were partly doing this for his own good and so agreed to take some time away from the business. *Where should we go on our family holiday?* he wondered. His eventual choice surprised everybody, especially Lilliana and Henrietta.

Right up until the time of departure the trip was almost cancelled as being sheer madness to undertake such a journey. Frederik's little Noelle-Neumann family were going to go travelling in Anastasia's Russian homeland. It was more of a homage and a pilgrimage than a holiday, the girls later recalled, but they had a wonderful time despite being arrested four times by Bolshevik fanatics. The girls had their father back and he had his daughters back and to keep the family together Frederik decided to leave the family business. He'd all but lost interest in running the firm anyway and so resolved to resign from the board upon his return to England. He thought they might go to America where he felt confident they could all make a fresh start.

Upon his eventual return to the London, Frederik was pleasantly surprised to discover that the business was thriving all thanks to somebody he hadn't previously noticed. She'd been hired as an administrative assistant in the first days of setting up the London office and had been promoted to office manager around the time he'd left for Russia a year earlier. Now, after only a comparatively short time, she was running the whole show. Celia was smart, educated, diplomatic and kind; instinctively knowing how to get the best out of people. Her way was to have things appear to be run by consensus so people willingly fell in behind her. Frederik was astonished and enchanted by this straight-talking Northern Lass.

Having seen how well everything had been run in his absence, Frederik promoted Celia to financial controller. The two worked closely together and as they did so their feelings toward one another grew. In the spring of 1937 Frederik took Celia to meet his daughters, telling them a fine tale as to why this lovely young woman was walking in Regent's Park with them. The twins were not so naïve as to think there was nothing going on between their father and his financial controller. They were happy for him. He announced his engagement to the new love in his life in the autumn of 1937 and they planned to marry early the following year. They talked about having a child or two to make their married life together perfect.

A Noelle-Neumann family conversation.

"What do you make of Frederik's announcement? I'm very happy for him myself," lied an uncle.

"Oh, it's wonderful news isn't it? I hope the girls aren't feeling too put out by it all though," whined Audrey Rotheram.

"I don't know what you lot are talking about. It's a disaster. She's not from one of the old families. Her father is a factory worker for goodness' sake!"

"He's a factory owner, Uncle Harold, there's a big difference," piped up one of the younger Noelle-Neumann generation.

"What does it matter what her father does for a living if they love one another?" said her sister in support.

"What does it matter? What does it matter! Don't you ever go doing anything similar or you'll find yourself cut off. The very idea! Who the hell does she think she is marrying a Noelle-Neumann? She'll never be one of the family. She'll never be a Noelle-Neumann in my eyes."

"The world is changing Grandma."

"Grandma? Grandma? Who is this Grandma you are referring to? If it's me then I'm your grandmother. Do you see what's happening? Do you? The whole world is collapsing. There are no standards anymore. Everything is so vulgar!"

"Come on Grandma, get with the times. It'll soon be 1940! I love you, Granny, but you're such an outrageous old snob."

"I'm not a snob, ask any of the servants, see what they say. I am simply unwilling to lower my standards nor will I accept into the family riff-raff such as Frederik's fiancée. She's only after his money you know. She'll never get a penny of it if I have any say in the matter. She'll never be a Noelle-Neumann in my eyes!"

"She's good for Uncle Freddie. And she's very smart too. Look at what she's done for the business. We've all benefitted because of her and there's no denying it."

"What? Rubbish! Total rubbish! How can you believe that a woman, a woman of all things, could do it all by herself, even with a hundred like her? A woman! Pah!" yelled Uncle Friedrich in disgust.

"Women can do all sorts of things you know Uncle; we can vote, go to university, travel, climb mountains, fly aeroplanes and drive cars; race them even. On top of all that we can have babies. So there."

"Where do you get all this from child?" asked several exasperated Elders.

"Times are changing and I think Celia is perfect for Uncle Freddie."

"She'll never be a Noelle-Neumann in my eyes!"

*

On the first of September 1939, Frederik and Celia Noelle-Neumann welcomed a daughter, Alice, into the world; the same day as the Leforts' second set of twins were born in Paris. The same day Hitler invaded Poland, after a Faction of the Organisation gave him a nudge to get things started. It was beginning to appear as though the war was not going to start on time, some nonsense about Göring wanting to develop super-weapons to make the Nazis invincible before kicking things off. The Faction, led by a minor Royal, needed the war to start on time as hundreds of millions of pounds of contracts had already been signed with the MoW. Any delay meant they'd all be ruined.

The main body of the Organisation was against war at that particular time and had set up measures to try and delay it starting. When their measures failed they adopted some innovative strategies to ensure Hitler would lose the war. More on that another time.

*

What a life, what a world of privilege and luxury little Alice was born into. Just as with her twin half-sisters she would have the best of everything and want for nothing. Frederik was determined that she would follow in their life's path. Celia was more for keeping Alice's feet firmly planted on the ground, though she had to admit that the life Frederik had given the two older girls hadn't spoilt them in any way; they were both charming, considerate, intelligent and modest. At times Celia thought they were just too good to be true.

From the moment it was announced that Celia was pregnant, the family machine went into action. Alice's name was entered onto the rolls of the same schools her elder half-sisters had attended and the list was consulted for suitable male children born from 1930 onwards, ready for when the time came for Alice to marry. She'd have some say in the matter, of course, so long as her future husband was from the list she could marry anybody she wanted.

Frederik, Celia, Alice, Lilliana and Henrietta soon settled into the suburban Surrey lifestyle of their stockbroker belt community. Despite Celia being born and raised in a grimy industrial town, she fitted right in with the Surrey set. She loved family life with her husband and child in leafy Surrey. Though neither Frederik nor Celia were great party goers, they enjoyed all the culture, society and entertainment that London had to offer. It was cleaner and purer entertainment than the decadence of Berlin and not gaudy like Paris, which somehow manged to pass itself off as chic. Life was as perfect as it could be for Frederik, Celia, Alice and the twins.

*

During the early months of 1940 the fortunes of the Noelle-Neumanns changed dramatically as they faced internment despite their Jewish blood. This was in no small part due to Frederik's old pals back in Berlin being amongst those who were running the Nazi war machine and Frederik Snr working for Hermann Göring. It was a brave, selfless act by Frederik who, to prove his loyalty to Britain and to keep the Noelle-Neumanns out of the internment camps, came up with the idea of him spying on the Nazis for the British. He hated the Nazis for obvious reasons and was glad to do it.

On the 8th of June 1940, under cover of darkness, Frederik Noelle-Neumann came ashore at Antwerp docks and made his way to a house the family owned in the Berchem district of the city. When he arrived he was surprised to find a relative living there. This cousin was the black sheep of the Noelle-Neumann clan. He was from the branch of the family who had removed the 'Noelle' from the family name and simply went by Neumann. The cousin was immediately suspicious. *How could Freddy have gotten out of England?* he asked himself and, more interestingly, *Why did he leave his family?* Frederik confided in his wayward cousin, telling him that as he'd been under threat of internment he'd escaped England by stealing a small fishing boat and sailing to Antwerp. His intention, he said, was to make his way to Berlin to assist the Nazis in any way he could. He said he felt certain the Intelligence Services could find a use for him. All the cousin was interested in was whether he would be allowed to remain in the house as he had nowhere else to go.

This unexpected turn of events was just the lesson Frederik needed to make him aware of the danger he now faced and how carefully he'd have to tread in future. He'd heard the expression 'expect the unexpected' and thought it an absurd and stupid thing to say but now he felt he understood exactly what it meant. Frederik left the house in his cousin's care as he prepared to travel to Berlin.

Shortly after Frederik departed for Antwerp railway station, the cousin went to the Gestapo and alerted them to Frederik's presence and his concerns about his story. He was picked up two hours later. A search of Frederik and his belongings turned up false papers and maps secreted in the turn-up of his trousers. He was taken away by the Gestapo and was never seen again.

The Gestapo allowed the cousin to remain in the house in Berchem. They made it clear he would have to act as an informant for them if he wanted to retain his freedom. Vigilant locals, ever quick to spot the tell-tale signs of collaborators, made plans to rid themselves of the traitor in their midst.

Eight days after the cousin sold Frederik out, he was walking between buildings along the quayside of Antwerp docks. As he neared a junction with a side road, four men moved to block his path. His guilty conscience immediately guessed why they were there and what their business was with him. He turned and quickened his pace. Before he made the thirty metres to the opposite end of the road another group of four men appeared and blocked his path. He thought of crying out but in his moment of hesitation the first group had closed on him with one of the men placing an oily hand over his mouth.

The men didn't speak a word. They just stared at him. He heard the clanking of a metal chain behind him followed by a crushing blow at the back of his head. When he regained consciousness he found himself wrapped in chains and lying on the floor of a warehouse. He made to speak but only a muffled sound came from his gagged mouth. The oily gag was removed as a priest entered the room.

"I know all about you Monsieur Neumann and what you did to your cousin, Frederik. I have my spies too," said the priest coldly. "When you went to the Gestapo to sell your cousin out, who did you speak with? What did you say to them? What did you tell them? What did you hear while you were there? Who did you see while you were there? Who can you name as a traitor?"

"I don't know what you're talking about. You've made a mistake. I'm no spy."

"Monsieur Neumann, you're a collaborator. Don't bother denying it. I already know this. You went to the Gestapo of your own free will and told them about your cousin Frederik Noelle-Neumann. Don't bother lying to me, I know everything!"

"Then you don't need anything from me," responded the cousin defiantly.

"I want to hear it from your own mouth, my Son. Tell me what you know. I am your Father Confessor. I want you to confess everything to me. It'll be good for your immortal soul to cleanse your conscience in my presence." After a minute's consideration the cousin began speaking what would turn out to be his final words.

"Forgive me Father for I have sinned, it has been eight months since my last confession…"

Once the cousin had given up all he knew he was carried, grunting in terror through his oily rag gag, to the edge of the Hansadok and tossed into its freezing waters. The cold shock on hitting the water caused him to gasp. Wrapped in chains as he was he rapidly descended to the muddy, sludgy floor of the dock. When he hit the sea bed his body turned to face toward the surface. He saw sunlight dancing on the water above. Before he passed, the cousin counted seven heads peering down through the ripples his body had made as it entered the water.

*

Word of Frederik's death at the hands of the Gestapo was passed back to England via a network of brave Belgian and French resistance fighters. Once confirmed, the Ministry of War passed the tragic news onto the family. They didn't even bother telling them personally, which would have been the decent thing to do under the circumstances. They just sent them the usual telegram containing the words; 'missing in action, presumed killed'.

The family never found out how Frederik had met his end nor did they ever get to know of the cousin's part in it. Life for them all would never be the same again. Celia feared the plans they made for Alice would never be realised.

The thoughts many people have running through their heads in such terrible and tragic circumstances can seem inappropriate to them. But there's nothing wrong with them no matter how practical or pragmatic, rather than grief-stricken, they are. The future is something which figures highly on the list of the living for obvious reasons: Where shall we live? How shall we survive? What shall I do with his clothes? Do his debts die with him? Was he having an affair? What if she wants to come to the funeral? What if...? Such thoughts following the death of a loved one shouldn't make the thinker feel guilty. Everyone has them.

Immediately after Celia received the telegram, relatives began dividing up the family business. Piece by piece they took everything from Celia. "She's not in any fit state to run the business," they said to justify their actions. "We can't let all Freddie's hard work go to waste, can we?"

A Noelle-Neumann family conversation.

"She's not a real Noelle-Neumann, she only married into the name. Frederik was a Noelle-Neumann and so are his children but she is not."

"But Frederik loved her. That's why he married her. If I take your argument to its logical conclusion then I'm not a Noelle-Neumann either."

"Nonsense, darling, of course you are, you have breeding."

"We cannot allow the children to suffer. I won't hear of it," said a schemer.

"He was going to leave her you know."

"Rubbish. You're just saying that to—"

"Let's leave Freddy's wanderings out of this. In all conscience we cannot let Celia or the children suffer any more than they have already. Little Alice is so sweet and she deserves the life she was born to. If nobody has any objections I'll take Alice into my care until things have settled down," suggested the childless Audrey Rotheram.

"You just couldn't wait could you? Hasn't she suffered enough? Now you want to take her children away from her."

"Not children, cousin, child; Alice. The other two are quite grown and will be leaving the family home shortly anyway. It'll give

Celia a chance to rebuild her life with no children under her feet. I never liked the name Alice," added Audrey absentmindedly.

"She's taken to drinking you know. Quite heavily so I hear."

"Can't say I blame her. She was so in love with Frederik but he's gone and she's alone."

"No, she's not alone. She has the children. Remember?"

"Yes, but how will they cope with a mother who's an alcoholic? No, it's better this way."

"What way?"

"Haven't you been listening? The two older girls will attend finishing school in Switzerland and young Alice will go and live with Audrey. It's for the best."

"Who mentioned anything about attending a finishing school in Switzerland?" asked an aunt who wasn't at a previous family conversation.

"Who'll talk to her? Who'll tell her?"

"Me, I'll talk with her. It's best coming from me. I've gotten to know her quite well you know. We're practically neighbours so it won't be that much of a wrench when Alice comes to live with me. I'll tell her she can come and visit Alice any time she pleases. She'll be much better off living with me. Imagine the education I can give her."

"What about the authorities?"

"I don't think we'll have any trouble with the authorities with the mother being a drunkard."

"Best to make it official though, don't you think? I'll speak with the company lawyers tomorrow and get the ball rolling on the paperwork."

"Please don't do this."

"Do what, darling? It's for the good of everyone. You'll see."

*

Alice Noelle-Neumann went to live with Mr and Mrs Cyril Rotheram at their family home on the outskirts of Reigate in Surrey.

The house was large and surrounded by lawns which were so perfect they resembled bowling greens. Beyond were shrubs and beyond the shrubs were acres of woodland. In all the house sat in eight acres of fine Surrey countryside.

With no fight left in her and having lost everything she loved and held dear, Celia Noelle-Neumann went to live and work in London to help with the war effort.

*

With Christmas approaching, and though there wasn't much cheer to be had, everybody in the land was determined to celebrate as best they could under wartime conditions.

Churchill was constantly on the radio bolstering the morale of the country with rousing speeches delivered in his growling style. He'd even been out and about among the ordinary people of London and other cities that had been bombed in the blitz. While in Liverpool he was photographed atop a mound of debris that had recently been the middle four houses in a terraced row. Cigar in hand and making a V for victory sign with the other, he'd shouted defiantly to the gathered crowd, "They shall never defeat us! We can take it!" A mother who'd lost all but one of her eleven children in the bombing raid shouted back, "You might be able to take it, mate, but we're fed up with it!" The woman was forcibly removed by Churchill's bodyguards.

Opinions about the war varied between the Factions of an increasingly fragmented Organisation. They ranged from jubilation that the war had finally gotten under way to bewilderment as to how another war could have started so soon after the last one and finally to one of anger that it had not stopped Hitler when it'd had the chance. Once again, the world was in turmoil and that was just how many in the Organisation liked it.

*

Just before Christmas, Celia wrote to the Rotherams about her visiting Alice on Christmas day. They ignored the letter and it being wartime Celia assumed it had gotten lost so she wrote another. The reply she received devastated her.

Dearest Celia

Thank you for your letter of the 17th inst.

We are all so proud of what you are doing for the war effort. We all do our bit, of course, but what you are doing puts the rest of us to shame. You'll be delighted to learn that Alice is in fine health and thriving under our careful supervision.

She said her first word a couple of days ago. She called me Mummy and Cyril swears she called him Daddy, though I have my doubts about that. Now that she's started talking there's no stopping her! She rabbits on and on in a language we cannot comprehend one word of. We try to correct her but she either doesn't seem to understand or she is just plain stubborn. Oh well, not to worry, early days yet!

She crawls along on the floor and pulls herself up on the furniture, leaving sticky hand marks all over the place. We put a stop to that with the use of cotton mitts from the local hospital. Apparently they use them on children who might otherwise scratch themselves.

Just took a break from writing as I was interrupted by the Nanny. Apparently Alice just took her first step and she wanted me to see. Only four I understand but it's a start I suppose. She fell in the end and cried a little but the Nanny soon soothed her.

Now, about you coming here for Christmas. I'm not so sure that is such a good idea. Alice is just starting to settle properly and I feel seeing you will unsettle her. Perhaps we could pencil in Easter? The Easter holiday isn't too far away so it should not be any great hardship for you.

All our love.
Audrey and Cyril

After reading the letter for a fourth time Celia walked back to her digs in a numb daze. As she neared her lodgings one of many stray bombs dropped by the Luftwaffe that night exploded near her. She lingered for days before passing. Lying in her hospital bed she drifted in and out of consciousness and as she did so her mind re-read the contents of Audrey's letter. "Alice is thriving under our careful supervision." But what of love? Was there any love in Alice's life? "Alice spoke her first words. Alice took her first steps..." She was Alice's mother. She should have been there for the things mothers should be there for in their children's lives. Celia didn't want to think such thoughts but she couldn't control them or empty them from her head.

Just before she passed, Celia suffered the cruellest of thoughts. Had she not noticed Audrey's letter sitting on the hallstand that morning she might never have read it at all. She only spotted it after another lodger had scattered a pile of letters on the floor and returned them with Audrey's letter on top. For a moment she had considered leaving it until she returned to her digs after work. Instead, she put it in her handbag and took it with her. "If only I hadn't turned to complain about the letters being knocked off the hallstand. I wouldn't have seen it. If only..." Tears rolled down Celia's cheeks. She heard a nurse call to the Ward Sister telling her that the patient was crying. "She can't be crying, my dear, she's dead and the dead can't cry."

*

On hearing of Celia's tragic death, Audrey became frantic at the thought of Nazi bombs taking little Margaret away from her. She'd stopped calling the child Alice two days after bringing her home and had already set wheels in motion to have her name legally changed to Margaret Rotheram; a proper name in her opinion. The company's lawyers were told to handle it.

With a child now resident in the house, the Rotherams were just like all the other families in East Reigate. They ignored the vicious rumours that had begun to circulate about the circumstances surrounding how they'd come by the little baby girl that had come to live with them.

An invitation only Noelle-Neumann family conversation.

"Shocking… and awful. Just awful." The aunt who said this really didn't give a damn.

"Poor Celia. Poor, poor Celia," wept another aunt though no tears were in evidence. "At least it was quick."

"What? Quick? It wasn't quick at all. She lingered for very nearly a week."

"I understand she didn't suffer at least."

"How do you know? What do any of us know? None of us went to see her and don't you dare say you didn't know she was in hospital! She put you down as next of kin with her job at the ministry. We knew. We all knew. We just didn't go. Guilty consciences, I say. Guilty consciences one and all."

"With the benefit of hindsight, what we did was possibly wrong but—"

"But nothing. It's occurred to me, as I'm sure it has to you all, that if we hadn't done what we did then Celia would still be alive today and living with her daughters."

"They're not all hers."

"I'm not going to argue with you. It's daughters, plural. She was Frederik's wife and the older girls loved her. We killed Celia as surely as if we'd dropped that bomb on her ourselves." Several Noelle-Neumann heads bent to the floor, faking remorse.

"And what do you propose we do about it? We cannot undo what has been done!"

"We must take care of little Alice. The first thing to do is to take her away from Audrey and send her to live with relatives on Celia's side of the family. It's the natural thing to do."

"Audrey will fight it. You know what she's like. Let's leave the child with her for now but we'll…"

"Are you insane? That poor child has suffered enough! We must take her from Audrey as quickly as possible. The mad old bat thinks she's dealing with a dolly not a baby. Have you seen her with her? The way she dresses her? She's not fit to be a babysitter let alone a 'mother'."

"It's settled then. We'll have a word with Audrey and—"

"We? Who's this we? I'm not going anywhere near her, you know what's she's like."

"I'll go by myself then."

"Good, but leave my name out of it, dear."

"And mine," cried another.

"My advice to you is to leave well enough alone. You know what Audrey's like and what she'll do to anybody that attempts to take the child from her. She won't hold back. She'll drop us all in it with the authorities!"

"In case you hadn't noticed, there's a war going on, the authorities have got better things to be getting on with."

"But that won't stop them prosecuting criminals otherwise there'd be a free for all. We'll end up in prison for certain and in times of war I dare say some of us will be executed for what we've done… what we've been involved in."

"I'm still going to see her."

The subsequent conversation between Audrey and the niece went very badly. Audrey threatened her with what she could expect if she did anything which might cause her to lose Margaret. "Who?" asked the niece puzzled. "Margaret," replied Audrey, "I never liked the name Alice so I had it changed… to Margaret."

The niece wrote to child protection leagues about Audrey and even met with representatives. That was a mistake, a very big mistake. One of them was a Rotheram family acquaintance who contacted

Audrey about her niece's activities. Audrey followed through on her threat. The niece was arrested on trumped-up fraud charges and held on remand. While in prison, she was turning gun parts on a lathe to help the war effort. She somehow became entangled in the machine and was torn limb from limb by it.

This 'unfortunate accident' was the last straw as far as the family was concerned. Doing the things Audrey had done to others in the past was one thing but to do it to a Noelle-Neumann was quite another. The family broke off all contact with the Rotherams; they referred to this as an excommunication and left little Alice to her fate as Margaret Rotheram. In truth, the family's action was to salve their own consciences for what they had collectively done to Celia.

RAISING MARGARET

Things began going badly for the Rotherams. Everything and everybody, it seemed, were set against them. They damned the memory of their deceased niece, blaming her for all their misfortunes. Uppermost in their minds, however, was how best to protect little Margaret from the nightly bombing raids over London. They couldn't bear the thought of losing her or of sending her away on evacuation with the local riff raff.

*

With the war hotting up, things were going rather well for the Organisation but not so for poor old Britain. With the surrender of the French, the gutsy British were forced to fight on all alone against the might of Nazi Germany as, politically, America didn't want to get involved in another 'European' war and the Soviet Union were collaborating with the Nazis through the 'Trade & Credit Agreement', thereby supplying Nazi Germany with the raw materials necessary for making war. Added to this despicable underhandedness was the reprehensible Molotov/Ribbentrop non-aggression pact making the trading partners allies and permitting the Soviet Union to invade certain countries under the secretive 'Spheres of Influence' clauses within the M/T pact. The Organisation was, quite naturally, growing concerned over losing its assets in Europe, just as The 400 had lost theirs at the hands of the Bolsheviks. Scheming how best to deal Hitler's ambitions a fatal blow thoroughly occupied the minds of the Governors of the Organisation. Fortunately, they eventually came up with the perfect solution.

*

Audrey and Cyril argued day and night about how best to keep Margaret safe from Nazi bombs. They were both opposed to the idea of sending her away on the evacuation programme but it seemed like it was the best, perhaps the only, viable option. Audrey, however, was for keeping Margaret as close to home as possible because she, as a so-called parent, couldn't bear to be parted from her so-called child.

"None of the other parents have sent their children away on evacuation. They say it's more for inner city children as that's where most of the bombs are falling. But I'm scared that a stray bomb will fall on Reigate. What are we to do?"

"Build an Anderson shelter?" suggested Cyril.

"Far too flimsy!" scolded Audrey.

"A proper air raid shelter then."

"A target for the Luftwaffe!"

"Not if it were buried deep underground in the woods!" responded Cyril. Audrey stopped to think before speaking which was unusual for her.

"With all that weight on top of it what if the roof caved in?"

"It wouldn't if it were made from reinforced concrete and steel."

"And where are you going to get concrete and steel? There's a war on!"

"I know a few people," replied Cyril, tapping the side of his nose with his forefinger.

"Then stop dithering and get on with it!"

Cyril didn't waste a second. He acquired thousands of rock-hard engineering bricks along with hundreds of bags of concrete and gravel and tons of steel meshing; all on the black market. He paid a local builder a small fortune to construct the bomb shelter on the QT. It took four men just over two weeks to complete the work. The *pièce de résistance* of the shelter was that it had its own electricity supply and running water. When the work was completed the Rotherams held a grand opening party, something that was quite out of character for them. The Nanny had recommended they do it because it would help dispel the "horrible rumours" that were flying around about how Margaret had come to live with them.

The whole of East Reigate came to the grand opening of the Rotheram's Bomb Shelter, which the Nanny lit with candles, creating an atmosphere of adventure for the children. Carrot cake was served with real, genuine, orange juice to drink. Again, the Nanny's idea. Audrey thought the Nanny was having a few too many ideas lately and she didn't like the way she looked at Cyril either.

The Nanny's ideas worked wonderfully. The rumours about Audrey and Cyril ceased almost completely and parents even got involved in decorating the bomb shelter to make it as homely as they could. They brought along toys, including a massive doll's house complete with miniature furniture. The bomb shelter became the play HQ of the local children. For the first time, Cyril and Audrey Rotheram socialised with people who had nothing to do with the Noelle-Neumanns. They recognised the potential this presented and vowed that in future everything they did for Margaret they must benefit from.

Very few bombs landed on Surrey during WW II and of those that did none landed within miles of the Rotherams' bomb shelter.

*

All throughout the war, the children of East Reigate played daily in the bomb shelter and the woods surrounding it. In 1944, Cyril got the builders in again. This time to dig a swimming pool. Margaret became the most popular child in the neighbourhood. Naturally, Audrey and Cyril benefitted from Margaret's popularity. They no longer needed the Noelle-Neumanns. The children that came to play at the bomb shelter were a socially diverse lot, from the poorest and least educated to the most privileged and privately educated. The kids just mucked in with one another, oblivious to the pressures felt by those parents mixing above their socioeconomic station. The Rotherams did their best to make the socially inferior parents feel uncomfortable and unwelcome. They eventually disappeared off the scene along with their socioeconomically inferior offspring. Margaret missed the kids who disappeared, preferring most of them to most of those who stayed.

Living in Reigate in the county of Surrey meant lots of children had ponies. One day, one of the Pony Club gals rode her fourteen-hand Piebald to the play HQ. Margaret had seen horses trot by the house in the lane outside her bedroom window but had never been allowed near them. Audrey had told her they were dangerous creatures, "Likely to kick out at any moment!" While snooping on play HQ that day, Audrey was horrified to find the children dressing a pony in hats and coats. She demanded the young gal and her pony leave immediately. For the first time in Margaret's life she answered Audrey back, "No, Mummy, I want the pony to stay!" The other children froze. They were more than a little wary of Mr and Mrs Rotheram. Truth be told, they were scared of them. Some believed the days of the play HQ were over and were stunned when Mr Rotheram told the gal that she and her "delightful pony" were welcome to stay while dragging his wife away by her elbow.

"Don't you see?" whispered Cyril frantically.

"See what?" replied Audrey through gritted teeth and rubbing her elbow despite it not being hurt in the slightest.

"Ponies! Girls and ponies! Perfect for Margaret, socially speaking, wouldn't you say? And for us too of course. Plus they'll keep her away from boys!" Audrey liked the sound of Margaret being kept away from boys.

"But they are so dangerous, Cyril. One hears all the time of dreadful accidents involving them. They throw their riders on purpose! They hate being ridden you know."

"Nonsense!" exclaimed Cyril. He hadn't said such a word to Audrey in a very long time. "We see people riding in the lane all the time and never has anybody got thrown or hurt. We should get Margaret a pony."

"But she's too young. She's—"

"She's a Surrey girl and Surrey girls and ponies go together. How about this? We take her to a riding school and see how she gets on. Who knows, she might hate it. But at least we'll know and she'll know and she'll be safe in the hands of experts." Cyril glanced at his worried-looking wife and whispered, "If Margaret gets a pony, we'll get to meet the right sort of people. People who can do us good."

Audrey wasn't entirely convinced but agreed that Cyril could take Margaret to the local Pony Club to see if she liked riding. What neither of them recognised in Margaret answering Audrey back was the start of their precious daughter rebelling. It would become a battle of wills and in that respect Margaret was very much her birth mother's daughter.

*

After the war, Audrey enrolled Margaret in a prestigious private school close to Reigate, naturally, so she wouldn't have to board. She couldn't have abided Margaret boarding. The school took girls from four to fourteen. Academically speaking the school was middle of the road but socially and sports wise it was top drawer. Margaret represented her school at most sports, including hockey and netball, while also becoming the Surrey schools under-sixteen record holder at cross country, 440-yard hurdles and the mile. Many of her records lasted well into the 1990s.

Outside of school, Margaret was a member of the Pony Club and was discovered to be a natural born rider. Between Pony Club, athletics, hockey and netball, Margaret seemed to lead the perfect life. "Perfect," Audrey used to always say. "Perfect in every way." And indeed she was, from the ribbon in her hair to the shine on her shoes. If the slightest speck of dirt landed on the child, Audrey would whisk her away for a change of clothes or a flannel and spit wash. For Pony Club competitions, Audrey would pack four changes of clothes, "just in case." The one aspect of Margaret which Audrey was disappointed with was her total lack of musical ability.

Audrey constantly tutored Margaret to act in a civilised and polite manner to make herself and Cyril feel proud of her. They couldn't have chosen a better child. However, had they witnessed her language and behaviour when she was with her school or Pony Club pals they would have been thoroughly shocked and appalled. Margaret knew well enough to keep those sorts of behaviours out of the line of sight of Audrey and Cyril.

The Rotherams seemed intent on moulding the young Margaret into another Audrey. They took her with them to garden and dinner parties where she'd enter into polite conversation with all manner of people. *A good foundation for her future*, thought Audrey and Cyril. And they were right but not in ways they could possibly have foreseen. While socialising with the right sort of people, Margaret came to the attention of somebody that would change her life forever.

*

For Margaret's fourteenth birthday, Audrey and Cyril bought her a Palomino pony to make her little Surrey girl life complete. She could have been in danger of becoming a spoilt brat but she was made of better stuff than that. The teenage Margaret filled her time with school and study and ponies and plans for university and conversations with her closest female friends about boys. They each had one boy in particular in mind, not the same boy in every case fortunately. Love was in the air and the Reigate Pony Club Christmas Fair was just round the corner.

Audrey wanted the Pony Club Christmas Fair to be in the grounds of their home. By then the bowling green lawns had been destroyed by horse boxes being driven over them. Paddocks and stables had been built on the back lawn and an outdoor arena installed with jumps. All the wear that comes with Horsey stuff totally wrecked the once immaculate lawns and gardens. But Audrey and Cyril could not have been happier as they'd benefitted so much from the contacts they'd made through their daughter. They'd long since given up any hope of a reconciliation with the NNs and though Margaret had been the cause of their break from the family she'd been the source of them making a new and far better life.

*

It could never be said that Audrey and Cyril were ever cruel to Margaret but they weren't loving parents. In her early years they were overprotective in the extreme, treating Margaret as though she were made of sugar glass, thereby instilling anxiety into the forming character of the child. Cyril getting Audrey to agree to Margaret having riding lessons was a big step for her to take and whenever Margaret got hurt around horses she'd give Cyril hell, telling him to tell Margaret there'd be no more riding. Cyril never delivered Audrey's messages. How could he? He could see the sheer joy Margaret got from being around horses and the delight in her eyes whenever he dropped her off at the stables. He would give Audrey a few days to level out again, making the most implausible excuses as to why Margaret couldn't leave the riding school at that precise time. Audrey would shake her head and scowl at him, her eyes telling him that she didn't believe a word he'd said.

Audrey's controlling nature suffocated the young Margaret but the older she got the more she came to recognise and resent it. Neither Audrey nor Cyril saw the changes taking place in their daughter as they were far too busy taking advantage of the situations she created for them. For Margaret, though, something always seemed wrong in her relationship with her parents. She couldn't put a finger on it but there was something in the back of her mind, something from the distant past that kept nagging at her.

*

As much as Audrey was determined that the Pony Club Christmas Fair would be held at their home, Margaret was more determined that it would not and so made her own plans. Plans which included boys. Margaret knew plans including boys wouldn't go down well with Audrey so she was secretive, cunning and conniving with the arrangements and was determined to have her own way in the matter.

It was becoming apparent, particularly to Cyril, that the older Margaret got the more rebellious she was her behaviour; "She gets that from her father," they'd say out of Margaret's earshot. Slowly, slowly, they realised they were losing control but didn't know what to do about it. Whenever they were losing a battle, out came Cyril's cheque book. One would have thought they'd have seen the flaw in that approach, but no.

With a good deal of prompting and prodding from Margaret, the Pony Club committee decided that its Christmas Fair would be held in the field next to the cricket club; which, in turn, was next to the rugby club. All the boys Margaret and her friends knew played cricket or rugby or both and she was determined to get them involved in the Christmas Fair as she had her eye on one of them. Margaret was besotted with a gangly six-footer called Timothy and being tall herself felt it was a match made in heaven. There were lots more popular and hunky boys around than Timothy but she only had eyes for him.

Everybody said of Timothy's father, Rex, that he was an 'interesting individual'. Nobody was quite sure what he did for a living. When asked, "What line of country are you in old chap?" he'd simply tap the side of his nose with his forefinger as if to say, "Sorry old chap, can't say," and that would be the end of the matter as far as Rex was concerned. This side of the nose tapping irritated the hell out of everybody, and he knew it. Inside he was smiling and thinking, *If you only knew.* It was widely rumoured that there were a large number of Military Intelligence spook types living in the Reigate area so everybody assumed Rex was 'one of them'. Which he was, but just not in the conventional sense.

*

An Organisation briefing.
"It's me," said the Governor over the phone. These were the usual words spoken to alert the recipient that the call was Organisation business.

"You're a little early aren't you?" replied Rex.

"Yes but with the time of year and all that… you know? Got to get ready to get off to the slopes! How about you? Going skiing with the family for the Christmas hols this year?"

"No, we're going on a cruise of all things; the wife's idea."

"What about young Timothy? What's his preference? Skiing or Cruising?"

"It's girls at the moment actually. Well, a girl actually; singular. He's smitten with a rather sweet young thing from the village. From what I can tell it's reciprocal."

"Oh, to be young and in love again."

"Yes. Quite. Shall we get on with it?"

"Indeed. Look, to speed things along, old love, can you just give me the highlights rather than going into all the detail? We can do the full thing at the Easter briefing. What do you say?"

"You're the boss. As I don't have any pressing concerns presently I'll go straight to prospects. The young girl who's taken Timothy's heart is somebody I'd like to include on the lists. She's about the right age, a little young perhaps, right background and as bright as a button. Interesting thing about her is her parents are not her biological parents."

"Adopted?"

"After a fashion. It's all rather sordid actually. I won't go into detail just yet but suffice it to say she's a Noelle-Neumann."

"Really? Now that is interesting. Are there any familial connections currently?"

"None currently I understand. A few generations back there was one but that should be okay shouldn't it?"

"Perfectly fine old love. Write your recommendation on her. List A would you say?"

"Yes, she's perfect for list A."

"Well, if there's nothing more?"

"No, nothing old thing. Have a lovely Christmas."

"Same to you old love."

And so Margaret Rotheram had officially come to the attention of the Organisation and was added as a Potential on list A, which is where fast-track Operatives begin their journey.

*

From its inception in the early fourteenth century, when it was known as the Brotherhood, the Organisation implemented a flat structure. Consequently, the Organisation of modern times has only five levels, four if you ignore Operatives; a Chancellor at its head. The next level down are Governors, then Controllers, then Counsellors and finally Operatives. The Chancellor, Governors and some Controllers have so-called personal assistants, PAs, at their disposal. They do not have job descriptions and do whatever their bosses order them to do, up to, and including, espionage and assassinations. They call them so because murder is such an ugly word whereas assassination has a certain *je ne sais quoi* about it.

To maintain order, exert control and limit the possibility

of exposure as a result of, for example, treachery, Operatives are often only aware of three or four other Operatives in their Unit. Outwardly, it might appear as though Operatives are lowly servants of the Organisation but this is not so. It can cost the Organisation a great deal in terms of time, effort, money and resources to get an Operative to where it needs them to be and it doesn't like them moving around. Counsellors and Controllers come and go but the Organisation places great value on its Operatives.

Finally, there's a group which operates across the entire Organisation, one which you hope never to come to the attention of. They are called Sentinels. It is unclear exactly who they answer to but logically they can only be under the control of those who run the Organisation. It is rumoured that the Chancellor places Sentinels in the guise of PAs close to Governors and Controllers so they can be swiftly dealt with should their ambitions get the better of their senses.

*

Margaret's first alone time with Timothy was in the pavilion of the Reigate Cricket Club during the Pony Club Christmas Fair. She found it all very disappointing after the build-up everybody had given it. Was kissing meant to be like that? He'd wanted more but that was out of the question as far as Margaret was concerned, mainly due to her not wanting to run the risk of adding to her disappointment.

After what Margaret felt was her fault at not being able to kiss properly, she gave up boys to focus on her studies. Her improved grades delighted Audrey as she'd become concerned that her daughter wasn't doing well enough to get a place at a top university. The private tutors helped with grades as did the educational holidays they'd taken as a family, particularly to Greece, Egypt and Italy. Audrey had great ambitions for Margaret and it again looked as though she was back on track to fulfil them.

*

As part of Margaret's school's outreach programme, she began teaching underprivileged children to ride and all that came with it: cleaning tack, feeding and grooming the horses, mucking out stables and so forth. Much to Audrey's chagrin, the charity work took up more and more of Margaret's time. Audrey foresaw her and Cyril's social life going up in smoke after all the hard work they'd put into it. To restore things more to her liking, Audrey bought Margaret a top-class eventer which she entered into competitions. What Audrey and Cyril failed to notice was that it was time their daughter spent with them that was sacrificed as her charity work and riding continued undiminished. All they noticed was her success and popularity introduced them into the right social circles. Increasingly, their socialising turned into over-socialising as their consciences wouldn't let go of what they'd done to Margaret's mother, Celia. When they were drunk, guilt laid heavy on them with each blaming the other for Celia's death.

Being heavily involved as she was in charity work and eventing, the local newspapers always seemed to have articles about Margaret Rotheram in them. Her photograph regularly adorned the front and back pages of local rags. Her long honey-blonde hair and strong facial features meant Margaret was extremely photogenic. Friends suggested that she should do some modelling work. Then a school friend, who was already a photographic model, told her bluntly that she was "too athletically built" to be a model. *Too athletically built?* she thought. That night, Margaret stripped off to look at herself naked in a full-length mirror and had to agree with her friend. She was a fine figure of a young woman, well seated as they say in horsey circles, but she was no skinny model. She hoped and prayed that the puppy fat would burn off one day.

STREET-KID LIFE

The Organisation depended heavily on the old ways of maintaining control; the ways of fostering despair, desolation and desperation among the masses through their political and trades unions familiars but times were changing. The old ways had allowed it to function as it pleased because ordinary people needed to work hard to keep their heads above water; they didn't have time to look around them and see what was really going on in the world. Which was exactly how the Organisation liked it.

Results-wise, the Organisation's performance for the first half of the twentieth century was good[ish]. The Wars had been profitable and, with the help of the Russian Splinter, the Bolsheviks had won a great victory, overthrowing Kerensky and slaughtering the Romanovs to boot – which seriously hacked The 400 off. They were even more hacked off when most of their members in that part of the world were wiped out by the Bolsheviks for being "politically unreliable class enemies". The good old Bolsheviks could turn a phrase when they wanted to. They had high hopes for a chap in Germany but he didn't work out, being a puppet of the German Faction as he was.

Financial results apart, Governors were congratulating one another over the recruitment of somebody they'd saved the life of during the Boer War and had high hopes that Mr Churchill would achieve his potential and have a long and illustrious career in politics. He was tipped for the top and with the Organisation behind him he'd get there.

Come the end of WW II, the Faction of the Organisation which had started the whole thing off were furious at the cancellation of Its MoW aluminium fabrication contracts. But their production lines soon adapted to produce beer barrels and other products essential to post-war Britain. At the time, the old enemy, the French Splinter, was suspected of being behind the cancellation of the MoW contracts as intelligence indicated they were making plans to marginalise the Organisation from future prosperity across an open European Market. An open market is a dangerous place as far as the Organisation was concerned but not wanting to miss out it planted Doublers inside the French Splinter to keep matters in check.

*

Whether times be good or times be bad, times are always good for the Organisation. Not so the coopering industry though, which, following over a millennium of existence, was wiped out overnight by the Faction's move into aluminium beer barrel production. This led to Joseph Frost being made redundant, the implications of which the Organisation could hardly have believed.

*

While little Margaret Rotheram was playing nice Surrey gal games with her friends in her lavishly equipped bomb shelter deep below the Rotherams' wood, hundreds of thousands of ordinary kids were being evacuated to places of so-called safety. For the kids of Liverpool this meant North Wales. The vast majority of these children were street urchins who'd never seen green fields or farm animals. Many of them, including Joseph Frost, were reluctant to return home to Liverpool after the war. Mary Hughes, on the other hand, couldn't wait to return home and leave behind her the cruelty she'd suffered at the hands of her evacuation family and local children.

Shortly after Joseph returned to Liverpool he got a job, through a family friend, as an apprentice Cooper. In those days families were large and consequently there were lots of friends about. Families, especially of the poor, had to be large in order to survive the alarmingly high child mortality rate. Joseph was one of fifteen children but by the time he turned five the last of his brothers, Gerard, died. Every one of Joseph's brothers died but all his sisters survived.

Joseph's forebears had immigrated to Liverpool from Southern Ireland during the potato famine. They'd been bound for America but never managed to get past the public houses along Liverpool's dock road. As happened to thousands of Joseph's countrymen, they got caught up in a way of life and stayed where they were. In the eighty years that followed, Joseph's ancestors progressed from the starvation line to the poverty line.

*

Joseph Frost met Mary Hughes in the Grafton Ballrooms in the summer of 1950 and following a courtship lasting a year they married in the summer of 1951. It wasn't unusual at the time for newlyweds to set up home in one or other of their parents' houses so Mary and Joseph went to live with Mary's parents in poverty-stricken Everton, an inner-city district of Liverpool. The house was large and as Mary's siblings had left home by the time she'd married there was plenty of room for her and Joseph.

On the 7th of October 1952, Michael Frost was born. Joseph and Mary so loved living with Mary's parents they discussed living with them permanently and Michael going to Mary's old school right opposite their front door; something Mary wasn't entirely happy with as she'd been cruelly teased due to her being almost completely deaf. Thankfully, there was one child, Eveline, who'd been kind to Mary and took her side in playground fights. The pair remained friends throughout their lives.

The amateur social engineers of Liverpool's City Council, however, had plans that would shatter the Frost's dreams. Every house in Everton was bulldozed flat before Michael reached school age. Everton became a pile of broken bricks and, in the process, Liverpool's centre was cut off from the rest of the city, effectively killing it stone dead. These amateur social engineers did a better job of destroying that proud city than the Luftwaffe had. The Organisation was happy though with the outcome when contracts to build new houses, shops, offices and factories came its way.

*

At age eighteen months Michael contracted whooping cough. He whooped and whooped and whooped, wracking his poor little malnourished body around the clock. After a week of non-stop whooping, Michael's nana intervened with an old wives' remedy of him breathing in hot tar fumes as she held a damp tea towel over Michael's head. It was a long shot but the old woman felt she needed to try something, anything, as he was very weak and getting weaker. Neither she nor Michael's parents realised that he was already on the mend or that the hot tar treatment would have long-term consequences for Michael's health as the old wives' remedy caused a thinning of the lining of the nasal passages, making him prone to heavy nose bleeds, as well as damaging his developing lungs. In the fighting streets of Liverpool's docklands having a nose that bled easily was a big disadvantage when it came to sorting out differences street-kid style.

Relieved at Michael coming through his whooping cough scare, Mary and Joseph discussed concerns they had about their son. He was eighteen months old and yet hadn't spoken a word; nor had he ever laughed or cried. The boy just went about his life in his own little world. They didn't think he was deaf as he looked at people when he was being spoken to but nobody could gauge what he was thinking through his blank stare.

To get to the bottom of what was going on with her son, Mary took him to see a specialist. Nothing wrong was found with him that would explain his lack of speech or anything else. Physically, Michael seemed fine, so why wasn't he talking or laughing or crying? When asked something he'd nod his head or shake it, so he understood what was going on. Recalling the dreadful treatment she'd suffered at the hands of cruel children, to keep Michael safe she kept him indoors for over a year.

After Michael was born, the doctors had told Mary that he would act as her ears. He'd be able to listen out for the things she couldn't hear. A knock at the door… an oncoming bus. These thoughts comforted Mary but what did it mean in light of his lack of speech, especially as she and Joseph were thinking about having another child? Would number two turn out to be the same as number one? Little did they realise but Mary was already pregnant so the point was moot.

*

On the 5th of December 1954 the Frosts welcomed their second son, Thomas, to the world. By comparison with Michael's birth weight Thomas was scrawny at 5lb 2oz. During his first year of life Thomas was in and out of hospital a half dozen times. He finally came home to stay on the 4th of December 1955 just in time for his first birthday the following day.

The whole family were excited as, infant mortality being what it was in Liverpool's docklands, few expected Thomas to survive. They gathered at Mary's parents' house to celebrate the day many doubted they would ever see. There were enormous amounts of presents bought for Thomas, most of which the givers could ill afford but it was a special birthday for a special little boy and, besides, being poor meant they knew how to suffer through financial sacrifice to demonstrate their love and devotion.

After a rousing chorus of 'Happy Birthday to You', Michael walked over to his little brother, kissed him on the cheek and said, as clear as a bell, "Happy birthday Thomas." The whole house fell into stunned silence. Had Michael really just spoken? Mary, being almost totally deaf, hadn't heard a thing above the noise of the singing but she was aware something was going on judging by the looks on the faces of the family. Joseph grabbed her by her elbows and, looking straight at her, spoke with exaggerated mouth shapes so Mary could lip-read him, "Our Michael just spoke. He said happy birthday to Thomas." Mary didn't believe him. All the family nodded to her to confirm the fact but part of her said that they were just playing one of their cruel jokes on the little deaf girl. Those thoughts washed away as she saw with her own eyes how shocked everybody was. Michael refused to repeat his act despite the urgings of relatives and by the look in his eyes he showed no sign of recognition of what he'd done. "Leave him alone! Leave him alone!" cried Mary, scooping Michael up and carrying him off to the cellar kitchen, away from the crowded parlour.

Mary sat Michael down on one end of an old threadbare, faded, burgundy-coloured sofa. Its rusty springs poked through the fabric. In its day it had been a very grand sofa but that was decades ago. It was the same sofa from which Michael had first seen the Demon as he lay recovering from whooping cough. He had watched It make Its way down the last of the stairs; hungry… snarling… drool dripping from Its foul maw… rotting flesh hanging from the gaps between Its broken fangs… never taking Its yellowy golden eyes off Michael for a universal second… Its head turning to keep him in Its sight… never stopping on Its journey before finally disappearing into the dark, dank, damp of the coal cellar. Mary grabbed Michael's shoulders and looking directly into her number one son's eyes said to him, "Can you hear me Michael? Did you just speak son? Did you just wish Thomas a happy birthday?" Michael returned Mary his typical blank stare. There was no sign of recognition in his eyes as he hopped off the sofa and returned to the parlour to get a slice of birthday cake before it disappeared.

For the next several minutes everybody tried to get Michael to speak. Each wanted to be the one he would talk to. But there was no more speaking from him that day and even though he wasn't looking in the least bit upset by the urgings of his relatives, Mary decided enough was enough, and anyway it was Thomas' special day, so she kept Michael by her side for the rest of the party, shooing away anybody that approached him.

*

Two weeks later, Thomas came down with whooping cough and already being weak from months of hospital treatments it nearly saw him off. Mercifully he was spared his nana's old wives' 'hot-tar-and-damp-tea-towel' cure. He made a full recovery and had a comparatively medically incident-free rest of his childhood.

*

Just before Easter 1958 the Frosts heard of a terraced house that had become available. It was actually a condemned property but due to the chronic housing shortage brought about by the amateur social engineers they had no choice but to move in. Its previous occupants had been moved out by those same amateur social engineers to a new housing estate in Runcorn; a desolate place twenty miles from anybody or anything they knew. People did not thrive under such conditions.

The little terraced house was located just twelve yards from a busy main road called Great Homer Street, known to all as Greaty. During the previous four months, two children, being unable to stop their homemade steering carts from crossing Greaty, had been run over and killed by busses. Such is the fate of street kids when left to their own devices.

Next door to the Frosts' was a yappy little Jack Russell which took an instant dislike to Thomas. Whenever it was on the doorstep he would call for Michael to come and escort him past it as it never seemed to bark at his big brother. In fact as soon as it caught sight of Michael it would run up to him, roll over onto its back, inviting Michael to tickle its tummy. Thomas once tried to join in the tummy tickling but the dog went rigid, bared its teeth and growled until he withdrew his unwanted hand.

Being from an enormously large Liverpool Irish family, it was no surprise that four families in the street were related to the Frosts, including their immediate neighbours, the Mulhalls. They had seven children, all of whom were older than Michael.

One morning during his walk to school, Michael was confronted by the notorious Sharkey twins. They both set on him for no other reason than they liked attacking kids to show how tough they were. Michael just stared at them as they punched him. Several punches landed on Michael's nose which started bleeding, the flow of blood being exacerbated due to the lining of his nasal passages having been thinned by his nana's old wives' cure for whooping cough. Passers-by intervened in this one-sided battering of a little boy in short trousers. The Sharkey twins took off before they could be collared. Michael's nose continued bleeding, his pullover becoming absolutely saturated with blood. On reaching school his class teacher took him home straightaway.

Mary went into a blind panic when she saw her number one son covered in blood. She'd never seen so much blood. Michael was very pale and so Mary laid him down on the settee. She grabbed a wet flannel from the kitchen and wiped away the blood from his face and neck. The flannel was soon blood sodden. Mary went to the kitchen sink to rinse it out. When she returned to the lounge there was a man sitting on the edge of the settee pinching Michael's nose closed.

"Excuse me, love, who are you please?" asked the ever-polite Mary.

"I'm Doctor Kirwan, I was next door at the Mulhalls' when I heard about your son's nose bleed. Michael isn't it?"

"Can you speak up please? I'm a bit hard of hearing." Mary used this expression throughout her life because, according to her, she wasn't deaf, she was "hard of hearing". She could lip read but was nowhere near as good at it as she thought she was because she had so few reference points for words grownups use. Despite her being almost totally deaf, Mary never sought assistance for her condition. In her mind this was admitting she was deaf which, of course, she wasn't, she was "hard of hearing". Thereafter, Doctor Kirwan mouthed his words clearly to Mary.

"Your son has a very bad nose bleed."

"He's alright, it's just a bit of a nose bleed, that's all. He'll be okay."

"Mrs Frost, this is a very severe nose bleed and could be dangerous for your son."

"Don't be daft," replied Mary who immediately felt embarrassed at what she'd said as in those days you didn't disrespect, question or doubt Doctors. "I'm so sorry, Doctor Kirwan, I meant to say he'll be okay after he's had a lay down."

"Mrs Frost, Michael needs hospital treatment. His nose needs cauterising to prevent serious bleeds from happening in the future. I'll write a note for you to take to the hospital."

After writing the note, Dr Kirwan read it out aloud to Mary, asking her if she understood everything. She replied that she did and thanked him for his help. A week later Michael had his nose cauterised. After scar tissue built up in his nasal passages he never again suffered bad nose bleeds, which was an advantage in the fighting streets of Liverpool's docklands.

*

The Frosts were all very happy living in their little terraced house and on July 1st 1958 the Frost boys were joined by a little sister,

Rose. From the moment she arrived Joseph was besotted with his daughter. He swore she would want for nothing from him throughout her life. While the boys were clothed by charities, little Rose 'Queenie' Frost was always dressed in new clothes and new shoes and given toys that were the envy of the street kids. Thomas grew up resenting the treatment lavished on Queen Rose by his father but Michael was oblivious to it all as he simply didn't think in those terms.

*

Following his run-in with the Sharkey twins, Timothy 'Timbo' Mulhall, one of Michael's cousins living next door, offered to teach Michael to box so he could defend himself. Even though he was only nine and a half years of age, Timbo Mulhall already had a bad street reputation. He was big for his age, fast and mean, and could hit hard with both hands and was not averse to throwing in a head-butt when the opportunity presented. A natural boxer and a great street scrapper, Timbo began instructing Michael in the art of boxing. Every morning during school holidays Michael showed up at exactly 9.30 a.m. and sparred with Timbo for precisely one hour. In the beginning he showed no sign at all of having any boxing ability whatsoever. However, over the weeks of the summer holiday of 1958, Michael, after minutely observing Timbo's technique, learned to box through mimicking his cousin; eventually improvising combinations of punches by the end of August, just in time for the start of the new school year. What impressed Timbo most about Michael's boxing was that he was comfortable in either the Southpaw or Orthodox stance. Timbo coached Michael to be a busy boxer, switching stance every couple of punches to keep opponents off balance.

*

It was a month after the start of the new school year when Michael came across the Sharkey twins on his walk to school. This time though he was in company with cousin Timbo. The Sharkey boys well knew of Timbo's reputation and didn't fancy their chances picking on Michael with him around.

"Hey you Kevin Sharkey, our Michael wants you out," shouted Timbo at the twins using the traditional words to challenge somebody to a fight. "An' you too Colin Sharkey."

"Nah, yer alright Timbo, we're on our way to school so we don't want to get into trouble."

"Never mind 'nah', you were on yer way to school when you hit our Michael so what's the difference now, eh?" The difference now of course was that Michael was in the company of Timbo Mulhall from whom they'd already taken a couple of hidings both in and out of the boxing ring. The Sharkey's became even more concerned when a large crowd of kids formed a fighting circle around them.

"Ye scaredy-cat chicken ye!" directed a girl standing in the fighting circle at Kevin Sharkey.

"Get lost you Maureen Dring," yelled Colin Sharkey at his twin's taunter.

"Maureen Dring'd burst you Colin Sharkey," yelled another of the kids in the fighting circle who all laughed at him.

"C'mon Kevin, what are you scared of mate?" Timbo asked in a friendly tone of voice. "Why don't you 'ave our Michael out?" he added in an insistent tone of voice.

"If we fight your Michael then you'll join in and batter us," replied Kevin Sharkey.

"Honest a God I won't; honest. Look, youz can fight him one at a time and I promise yez that I won't join in." All knew that promises such as this from Timbo were worthless but nobody could say that to him.

As Kevin Sharkey removed his overcoat Timbo whispered to Michael, "Go on our Michael, get stuck in there, burst him. Kick him in the plums if ye get the chance. Remember all the sparring we did? But this time it's for real so burst him!" Motivational talk over, Timbo retired to the inner edge of the fighting circle. As soon as his coat hit the floor, Kevin Sharkey, who was two years older than Michael, launched himself toward him with fists and feet flailing.

Michael regarded the oncoming blur that was Kevin Sharkey with total calmness, he simply stepped back out of the way of the initial onslaught and assumed a Southpaw stance. Kevin Sharkey stopped dead in his tracks.

"What's all this then, eh Timbo?" shouted Kevin. "Have you been teaching your Michael boxin'? That's not fair that's not," whined Kevin Sharkey.

"Put yer dukes up!" shouted Timbo in reply, which Kevin Sharkey immediately did, a stance Michael recognised as the start of the fight and so moved to within punching distance.

One punch was all that Michael threw before the fight was declared over according to the rules of street-kid fighting. As soon as his punch landed, Kevin Sharkey began crying. He turned, put his overcoat back on, and walked away holding his cheek. "Okay Colin Sharkey, it's your turn now," announced Timbo but Colin was already running across the road to shouts of "Chicken!" and "bock, bock, bock" noises from the fighting circle. This is always the way with bullies, stand up to them and they have nothing.

"Ye did well there our Michael but next time try and keep the fight goin' so everybody can see what ye can do… let them see how good ye are… show everyone what yer made of."

Michael continued with his boxing lessons from Timbo and also joined his school's boxing team. He quickly earned himself a reputation almost equal to that of his older cousin. By the age of eight Michael was winning almost all of his fights both in and out of the ring.

ONE LAST SUMMER HOLIDAY

Final exams came around and, as hoped, Margaret did well in them. With the contacts Audrey and Cyril had made through her, interviews were secured at both Oxford and Cambridge.

While Margaret was waiting to hear back from colleges she decided she would go on a holiday abroad with some girls from school but it turned out they were all going on "one last holiday with Mummy and Daddy before I go off to uni, sorry Marg, but they insisted… plus, they're paying." Margaret hated being called Marg, though didn't object to being called Margot, which people sometimes called her. Not willing to give up on the idea of going on a summer holiday without Audrey and Cyril, Margaret got in touch with a few of her old Pony Club pals even though they were a few years older than her; one or two of them even smoked. Margaret couldn't stand smokers but was determined not to go on another boring Audrey and Cyril-type holiday. When she gave them the news, her so-called parents were horrified that their only daughter wanted to "go on holiday alone".

"I'm not going on holiday alone, as I told you, I'm going with some of my old Pony Club pals. You remember Zuzhanna, don't you? You always liked her and her family. Her father and you were great friends, Daddy."

"I wouldn't go so far as to say we were great friends," Cyril lied to keep the truth away from Audrey. "I like Tom and Alice but they're—"

"They're… they're…" interrupted Audrey. "We've moved on, haven't we Cyril dear? I mean to say, they're rather… common, dear. There's nothing wrong with them per se but they are rather common. Don't you agree Cyril dear?" Cyril hesitated in supporting his wife which earned him a scowl.

"It's not that we don't want you enjoying yourself darling because we do. Don't we Audrey dear? It's just that a trip abroad is—"

"I've been abroad dozens of time so it's nothing new," snapped Margaret.

"That's not what we mean and you know it. It's not safe for young girls to go on holiday by themselves… without an adult."

"I'm not a little girl anymore. In case you hadn't noticed, which you obviously haven't, I'm a young woman now. What's more I'm off to university after the summer hols and I'll be living in Cambridge. You know, where the spies came from."

"Now Margaret, no need to go upsetting your mother like that," pleaded Cyril. "Please, darling, won't you reconsider this ill-thought plan of a holiday abroad with your friends? I know, why don't you come on holiday with us darling? We'll go anywhere you like. How about America? You always love it there."

"Daddy, I'm too old to be going on holiday with my parents."

"Nonsense," Audrey chipped in. "Your little friends still go on holiday with their parents."

"Little friends? How old do you think they are? Two of them are married and two are engaged to be married. Some already have children."

"Well, we know why that is don't we so we won't be going down that avenue!"

"What avenue is that Audrey?" Margaret had never called her mother Audrey before. Her doing so, especially in such strained circumstances, produced a deathly silence in the room.

"Please don't call me Audrey darling. Call me Mummy. Please?"

"Sorry 'Mummy' but I'm going on holiday with Zuzu and the others."

"I didn't want to say this but you've forced my hand! You can't go on holiday by yourself, I forbid it! And, what's more, I won't sign for you at the bank so you can't get any money to go on holiday, so there!"

"Mummy, darling, I've been signing for my own money for ages. Daddy arranged it at the bank so I could do it whenever I liked." Audrey tossed Cyril his second scowl of the evening. The arguing went on for hours.

"It seems you're not going to change your mind but let's not let this come between us."

"You're far too soft on the girl. She's always been able to wrap you around her little finger."

"Nonsense dear, that's not true is it darling?" Cyril asked his daughter.

"Of course not Daddy," Margaret replied casting a sly grin in Audrey's direction. "You do what you do out of love for me, don't you Daddy. And if you love me you won't stand the way of my going on holiday with the gals."

"Look! See? Do you see? She's doing it now you fool."

"Audrey, darling, we're just going to have to accept that Margaret is a young woman now, and well capable to make her own decisions and live her own life. She'll be going away to university after the summer for goodness' sake," said Cyril unexpectedly. Audrey stormed out of the room. "I'll go to her later. You tell your friends that everything is alright and you'll be going on holiday with them."

"I know. I love you Daddy."

Unable to get her way, Audrey ran upstairs, stomping down hard on every tread as she went and slamming the bedroom door shut behind her. Cyril followed two minutes later.

"Get out! Leave me alone you swine!"

"Audrey… petal… pumpkin, if we alienate her we'll lose her forever. She's growing up so we'll have to play things differently from now on. After university she'll most likely get a job in London and will probably want to live there and…"

"Surely not?"

"Surely so, darling. Then she'll meet some man and get married. Have children. That will open up a whole new world for us so please don't do anything to mess it up."

"I'm not sure I can bear it. You don't know how a mother feels."

Neither do you! thought Cyril. "I know this is hard on you, darling, but it's hard on me too. I was hoping we'd get introduced to a lot more people on the eventing scene but that doesn't look like it's going to happen now. We must support her through university… and afterwards too, no matter what she does. We'll visit her regularly in Cambridge, or wherever she ends up. We'll be the type of parents other students will envy her for having. We'll make contacts of her friends' parents just like we have through her eventing and stuff. It'll be a new direction for us. You can see that can't you dear?"

"I suppose you're right. But I'm right too! That girl wraps you around her little finger. She grinned slyly at me when we were arguing."

"It's only natural in the circumstances. She wants to show that she…"

"There you go again, always taking her side. There'll be men all around her while she's on holiday and you know what that means don't you? Or don't you care?"

*

The atmosphere in the Rotheram household in the days leading up to the holiday were frosty to say the least. Margaret was flouncing about the place and giving Audrey and Cyril the silent treatment. She knew the effect that would have on her father. Over the years, she'd learned the best way to get something out of Cyril was to keep schtum. She knew that sooner or later he'd say something to her advantage rather than endure her continued silence. He eventually asked her about the hotel she'd be staying at; what it was like and how many stars it had. She said she thought it had, "one star, I think, perhaps none, I really don't recall." Cyril begged Margaret to reconsider. When she said she wouldn't he said, "Let me give you some holiday money so you can at least have proper accommodation. There's no telling what might happen to you in a one-star hotel." Margaret replied saying that £150 should do the trick. She knew Audrey was listening and when she passed her in the hallway she threw her a sly grin. Cyril got it in the neck for that one.

*

During the flight to Kos the Pony Club pals caught up on old times before discussing holiday plans.

"I've heard that if you get blotto on Ouzo all you need do the following day is have a drink of water and you get blotto all over again. Apparently it stays in your system for at least twenty-four hours," claimed Zuzhanna.

"Really?" said Lavinia sceptically.

"God's truth I swear!"

"I know what I'm drinking then!" laughed Lavinia. Arabella lit a cigarette.

"Oh God, you're not still on those things are you? What type are they anyway? They stink."

"They should ban smoking on aeroplanes in my opinion."

"Well, Marg, when you're president of the world you can do that but in the meantime I'm smoking all the way to Kos."

"Don't call me Marg… Belladonna."

"Meow!" screeched Zuzhanna. The girls laughed nervously.

"No nicknames, okay?"

A truce was agreed; only their proper names were to be used during the holiday.

As soon as the girls checked into their luxury five-star hotel they stripped off, pulled on swimwear, grabbed a bunch of towels and set off for the beach. Right on the beachfront sat a Taverna. Serving at the tables were four of the most handsome men the girls had ever seen. They looked at one another, winked and then laid their towels as close to the Taverna as they could get them. One of the waiters shouted that they should take care of their beautiful pale skin otherwise it would get sunburned. He ran to them with a beach umbrella, driving its pole deep into the sand.

"Pretty ladies, that will keep the sun off you until your skin gets used to it. Don't try to get a suntan too quickly, we Greeks are used to it but you… English? you are not. My name is Nakis." The girls were dazzled by this stunning-looking Greek God.

"Hello, I'm Zuzhanna… Zuzu to my friends." Zuzhanna held out her hand, which Nakis took, kissed and held. It appeared he wasn't interested in the other girls.

"Zuzu… that sounds Greek! Do you have you any Greek in you?" Zuzhanna shook her head. "Have you just arrived? I think so otherwise I am sure I would have noticed you before now. How long are you here for?"

"Two weeks," Zuzhanna replied as Nakis kissed and released her hand.

"I should get back to the Taverna," he said uncertainly. "Perhaps you will come and eat there later?"

"Hey Romeo, are you trying to get us to spend all our money at your grotty Taverna or what?" Arabella said joking.

"No! No! I… I… I only…" Arabella and Lavinia laughed at Nakis' gibbering.

"It's okay, just teasing," said Arabella. Nakis smiled. He liked being teased. "Tell you what, we'll pop in later for a bite to eat and something to drink. Ouzo perhaps?"

"I think you will prefer one of our special Ouzo cocktails but, whatever you do, don't try the Retsina, it's an acquired taste and you won't be here long enough to get used to it," laughed Nakis who then offered to put suntan lotion on Zuzhanna's back before finally going back to work. She accepted his offer.

"Good oh Zuzu, that's right, play hard to get," mocked Lavinia slightly jealous.

Arabella lit a cigarette, passed it to Lavinia and lit another for herself. Margaret was surprised to see Lavinia smoking too and tutted at them both. They told her that they were on holiday and she was not their mum. Zuzhanna asked if anybody was hungry. "Christ Zuzu, take it easy, we've got fourteen days to go yet, he'll be all the better for the waiting." The girls laughed and told Zuzhanna to try to play harder to get.

*

For the next week the girls hung around the beachfront next to the Taverna and when their handsome waiters finished work for the day they went on beach walks with them, holding hands, laughing and kissing. It was a real holiday romance for the girls. The waiters tried everything to be alone with their girl but their tried and tested ploys failed one after the other; one of them would pretend to have lost something or have something in his shoe, anything to let the others get ahead of them. No chance. The other girls would stop and wait for the trickery to be over and then continue on together. Zuzhanna was keen to be alone with Nakis and would slip out of sight until the others backtracked to locate them. Nakis didn't mind having their plans frustrated, he seemed genuinely happy just to be with Zuzu. The other waiters, however, were starting to lose interest as they wanted more than just kissing.

At the start of the second week of the holiday, Margaret persuaded the Pony Club gals to explore Kos with her. As soon as they made it back to their hotel from the excursions, Arabella, Lavinia and Zuzhanna showered, changed and ran to the Taverna. Upon their arrival one evening, they spied women, "some of them are old enough to be their mothers for God's sake," paying their handsome waiters far too much attention for their liking. They slinked up to the waiters to show the older women that they were theirs. As Margaret was at the hotel they took the opportunity to say what was on their minds about her and her excursions.

"She's such a bloody goody two shoes with all her 'cultural crap'. Where is she anyway? What's she doing? Why isn't she here?"

"You know what, I don't think she fancies Marcos in the slightest."

"I've noticed that too. It's almost as though she doesn't like men at all," said Arabella, giving the other girls a knowing sly glance.

"What are you saying Bella?"

"Nothing really. Well, it's probably nothing but, you know, she doesn't seem to want to… you know?"

"What?"

"Have sex with Marcos, dimwit!" hissed Arabella loud enough for everybody to hear.

"Have you had sex with Dmitri?"

"No, not yet at least," admitted Arabella. With the mention of sex, racy thoughts ran through their minds. "What about you Zuzu? You spend far more time alone with Nakis than we do with our chaps, have you and Nakis… you know?" Arabella enquired.

"No, of course not!" she blushed. Not wanting to continue with this line of conversation in public Zuzhanna changed the subject. "Anyway, don't you think Marcos is a bit short for Margaret?" The girls laughed.

"Tell you what."

"What?"

"Somebody should have a word with the virgin Queen. You know, get her to loosen up a bit… or a lot! Maybe encourage her to have sex with Marcos even though he's a bit on the small side. He only comes up to her chin when she's in flats," sneered Arabella.

"I've heard he's not small at all; if you know what I mean!" The girls gasped and giggled.

"You never know, she might actually like it. It might even do her a bit of good!" said Arabella.

"Who'll speak to her?"

"Me!" volunteered Arabella. "I'll do it!"

"No, not you Bella; you and she don't exactly… you know… you don't exactly get along so if it comes from you she'll—"

"You're right. So you'll do it?" smirked Arabella pointing at Zuzhanna.

"Okay, I'll do it. I'll have a word with her."

When the girls arrived back at the hotel they sought out Margaret and nudged Zuzhanna toward her.

"Oh hi."

"Hi. Had a nice time at the Taverna?"

"Yes thanks." After a short pause Zuzhanna continued. "Margaret?"

"Yes?"

"We were talking."

"Oh yes."

"Yes… and we were thinking…"

"Go on!"

"Look, why are you behaving like you're on holiday with your parents? Going on bloody excursions for God's sake! What's that all about?" Margaret thought for a moment and had the good grace to laugh rather than be angry at her friend.

"I see. So, who's been talking?"

"All of us!" butted in Arabella.

"I might've known you'd be involved!"

"Look Margot, we're friends so I say this to you as a friend; you don't know how to be young."

"What do you mean?"

"Your parents… well, they always keep you on such a tight rein that even when you're not with them you're with them… know what I mean? I don't want to be disrespectful but your parents are… bastards… to you I mean, not literally of course," babbled Zuzhanna.

"Stop! Just stop! That's too much!"

"No, we won't stop. We've started so it's best out. Your parents use you."

"Use me? How?"

"Yes, they use you! They always have! They're always right behind you, making the most of the contacts they meet through you. Everyone can see it so why can't you?"

"You're crazy."

"No, no I'm not. Ask anybody. Your parents are creepy. Aren't they girls?" The other girls nodded. "Sorry to say this but it's been a long time coming."

"Where are the rest of your family?" asked Lavinia. "Your relatives, where are they? You don't have any aunts, uncles, cousins. You do realise that you're nothing like your parents don't you?"

"I admit the family resemblance isn't strong but—"

"We didn't mean your looks!" interjected Arabella.

"But—"

"No 'buts' Margot, it's time you broke the mould and we've got just the thing. Haven't we girls?" The girls nodded.

Arabella, Lavinia and Zuzhanna told Margaret that because their gorgeous waiters had been such 'good boys' they were going to be given a reward and they wanted Margaret to reward Marcos in the same way. After a moment's consideration Margaret agreed and a pact was made. On their last night in Kos they were going to have sex with the waiters. Anticipation built up inside the girls only for Margaret to recall the disappointment of kissing Timothy that night in the Cricket Pavilion in Reigate.

*

On the last day of their holiday, the girls sat down and wrote postcards. Up until then, they'd been busily doing all the things they'd never had the chance to do while on holidays with their parents. To their friends back home, Arabella, Lavinia and Zuzhanna wrote that the highlight was, of course, having a holiday romance with handsome Greek waiters; "what a great time we've had on Kos; we've been sunbathing topless, drinking, staying out all night, sleeping late... meeting men." To their families they wrote; "what a great time we've had on Kos; visiting ancient monuments, swimming in the sea, reading lots and lots and getting early nights to charge our batteries in preparation for university." On receiving the postcards the girls' girlfriends were envious while their parents were proud of their daughters; "what good girls they are", they bragged, "they have repaid us the trust we placed in them."

That night the girls went to the Taverna for their last meal on Kos. They were nervous and excited about the pact they'd made to have sex with their handsome waiters. Inside, they each, except Arabella, wanted to back out of the pact but felt that if they did so the others would ridicule them.

So, after a night of drinking and dancing with their handsome waiters, the girls were in the mood to take things further. Margaret was the most apprehensive at the thought of having sex. She'd heard so many stories which had left her feeling nauseated and she was not at all keen on doing the things she saw girls doing in the photos Arabella had brought to the stables. At the time she had wondered, *Do people really do that?*

The couples split up, going their separate ways for privacy's sake. The evening was starlit, the breeze warm and the surf rolled softly along the tidal margins. The atmosphere was perfect. The time was right.

Margaret wasn't sure how Marcos had managed it but after only a few minutes she found herself naked and lying on her back with only a small sand dune for cover. Where her clothes were she had no idea. Her pants, at least, hadn't gone far, they were caught up on her big toe. Marcos' muscular hairy chest was bare and he was trouser less. All he had on were his underpants. Margaret's eyes wandered over Marcos' body. She laid back invitingly. As Marcos slid his underpants down his thick thighs Margaret noticed the elasticated waistband straining against the bulge of his penis. As his underpants passed over the end of Marcos' cock it sprang violently erect, slapping his stomach then waving in the air as though in victory.

Margaret had never seen an erect penis in the flesh before. She was shocked at the size of it and became hesitant as she'd heard so many tales of first-time sex from the girls at school. Tales involving pain, tearing and bleeding. Looking at the size of Marcos' penis she believed the stories.

Marcos laid on top of Margaret and forced her legs apart with his knees. She loved his raw strength. Reaching down she grabbed his penis to guide it inside her; she'd been told by the girls at school that was the thing to do.

"Margaret? Margaret? Where are you?" It was Zuzhanna shouting.

"What the hell do you want?" shouted Margaret in a voice she didn't recognise.

"Where are you?" cried Zuzhanna tearfully.

"We're over here." Zuzhanna followed Margaret's voice, coming upon both her and Marcos naked and entwined.

"Oh God, put some clothes on," yelped Zuzhanna averting her gaze.

"Why? So you can have him?" cried Margaret still using the voice she didn't recognise and wondering why she'd asked her friend such an obviously irrational and stupid question.

"Eeeeue, no thank you," squirmed Zuzhanna. "You'll thank me for stopping you making such a dreadful mistake after you've heard what I have to tell you."

"Tell me what?"

"These bastards have made arrangements to meet up with some girls after seeing us. What do you think of that?"

"Zuzu, they probably meet dozens, or possibly even hundreds, of girls during the summer. You weren't thinking of marrying yours were you?"

"What are you saying?"

"I'm telling you to get lost and leave us alone. I'll see you back at the hotel."

Zuzhanna thought for a moment before walking back along the

beach to the spot where she'd left her beautiful Nakis in the hope he was still there.

Marcos assured Margaret that he had no plans to meet any other girls that night. The night was hers and hers alone as far as he was concerned. The couple re-entwined.

Margaret's only reservation about her handsome muscular waiter was that he was so very much shorter than her and while they were making love she pictured him as a mountain climber. No matter how hard she tried, she couldn't shake that image from her head. Though Margaret went on to have lovers who were shorter than her, she shuddered whenever diminutive men came on to her.

Back at the Taverna several sad-looking forty-something women were sat at tables waiting and wondering where their handsome young waiters were.

*

After the girls returned to England they remained on friendly terms, meeting up regularly. After a few drinks they would reminisce about that warm night on the beach with their handsome Greek waiters. On one such night, Zuzhanna asked Lavinia a question.

"Are you, erm, writing to yours?"

"Oh God, no. Why, are you?" Zuzhanna's blushes answered Lavinia's question.

"What about you Margaret? Are you still in touch with… whatshisname?"

"Too busy getting ready for uni. I have so much to do before I go up to Cambridge you wouldn't believe it," answered Margaret.

Oh, she's "going up to Cambridge" is she, lah dee bloody dah, thought Arabella bitchily. "No time for men then, Marg?"

"I've enough on my mind at the moment, thank you Belladonna. Though I've had some… never mind. Hey Zuzu, don't forget to invite us to the wedding."

"Ha, ha, ha, very funny," giggled Zuzu.

*

Zuzhanna married her handsome Greek waiter eighteen months later. They went on to have four children and lived all of their married life in Surrey. She died from cancer at only fifty-five years of age. Margaret attended her funeral but sat at the back of the church wearing a heavy black veil to cover her identity and didn't make herself known to any of the mourners. She was a different person then and merely recognising her would be extremely dangerous for all concerned.

*

An Organisation conversation.

"Well, Rex, that all sounds very interesting, very interesting, well done... well done. Now, let us proceed to the lists and see where we are with them."

"Indeed Madame Governor. Firstly I'd like to discuss the Margaret Rotheram case."

"Ah yes, I remember you mentioning her. Odd that you refer to her as a 'case' though. I hope she and Timothy are no longer seeing one another?"

"You will be pleased to hear they are not. I too am pleased as she's showing extraordinary promise. She's at Cambridge you know?"

"Jolly good. Much better than Oxford. What a complete dump Oxford is!"

"I'm an Oxford man."

"I, of course, know that Rex, I was teasing you. What's she studying?"

"Politics and economics."

"Excellent. Things have changed since I was a young gal; they have so much more choice nowadays... so many more opportunities. I can't say that I find either of those subjects of interest personally;

but for an Operative? Perfect wouldn't you say? How will you recruit her?"

"Rather cruelly I'm afraid. Do you remember I told you that there was something sordid involving the family?"

"Of course I do, I'm not very likely to forget something like that."

"I'm slightly concerned that when she finds out the truth about her so-called parents her reaction to it might send her over the edge but with time against me it's necessary if I'm to recruit her."

"Tell me all."

Rex told his Governor the Frederik Noelle-Neumann story and how the Rotherams had taken his youngest daughter, Alice, away from their mother, who died shortly afterwards in the blitz.

"Are you certain there is no other way? I mean to say, this really could send her off the deep end. We're okay with a nice line in blackmail to trap recruits… but this? I'm not so sure that your plan is a good one I'm afraid."

"It's too late. I tracked down Alice's sisters and told them where they could find her. They'd been told she'd died in the blitz alongside her mother. Their reaction to the news that Alice was alive was, naturally, rather mixed; shock, disbelief, scepticism and so on but after they spoke with relatives they accepted it. 'Imagine,' the relatives said to them, 'what might have happened had we not taken charge of the situation?' But they would say that wouldn't they?"

"Well, as you say, it's too late now. When will they meet?"

"In four days' time."

"Let me know how it goes. Next…"

THE LEAFY SUBURBS

While waiting to be rehoused by Liverpool City Council's amateur social engineers, the Frost children were busy going about their street-kid lives.

Right opposite their house was an open area, called an Oller, which was created after a Nazi bomb hit Christ Church, completely flattening it. No damage whatsoever was done to the surrounding houses in either Anderson or Aughton Street. Everybody in the area was upset at having their church bombed but a secret Faction from within the Organisation, known as the ACF, were delighted as it was further proof, as though further proof were needed, that God, as rendered by mainstream religions, did not exist.

The Anderson Street Oller was totally covered with black cinders. At its northern end was a metal tubular 'monkey-bar' playground while its southern end was fringed by three advertising hoardings; the largest of them ran parallel with Greaty with two slightly smaller hoardings, one at either end of the larger hoarding, set at an angle, like wings. The hoardings, or '*tins*' as they were known locally, were over twenty feet high and supported from behind by two-inch angle iron, the ends of which were concreted into the ground of the Oller to brace the whole structure. Not only could the angle iron support the weight of the advertising tins they could also carry the weight of over thirty kids playing War or Cops and Robbers on them.

The rules of Cops and Robbers were simple but the same could not be said for the game of 'Back-Jigger Shimmy'. By pressing their hands and feet against the walls of the entry-ways between houses, Back-Jigger Shimmyers would raise themselves up to roof level before descending. Simple enough but dangerous. This wasn't so much a game as a test of nerve as well as a feat of strength, daring and bravery, or possibly just plain old street-kid stupidity.

Some kids, Michael included, would shimmy-race up the back-jigger walls, touch the guttering and race back down again. The really 'brave' kids went one step further but this was often a shimmy too far. Instead of lining up to touch the guttering at the lowest part of the roof they'd line up to touch chimney pots at the highest part of the roof. This added well over a dozen feet to the shimmy. With the chimney stacks having been subjected to repeated heating up and cooling down for over a century and a half, the mortar between the bricks had become crumbly and when disturbed by shimmying a dusty, talcum powder-like substance was deposited over the bricks, lubricating them. Also, at that height, the chimneys were covered in a slippery, slimy, mossy residue making them doubly treacherous to a Shimmyer. Once a Back-Jigger Shimmyer lost his grip he was done for unless he was really strong or lucky and managed to slow his descent before hitting the ground, or the observers, over thirty feet below. Girls seldom, if ever, took part in this game. Survivors of falls who went home crying to parents and telling them what had happened got their backsides dusted for being so stupid.

*

July 1961 was the beginning of Michael's last summer holiday on the Oller before the Frosts moved house to the leafy suburbs. Neither he nor Timbo had any idea where these leafy suburbs were. "I'll miss ye Michael. Promise me you'll keep yer boxing up after ye move away. You're a good little boxer, you know, and, who knows, you might be able to beat me one day," said Timbo before stifling a muffled laugh at the idea of little Michael Frost ever beating him at boxing, but he felt he had to give his protégé something to shoot for. In actuality, after three years under Timbo's tutelage, and being a veteran of a dozen boxing tournaments, Michael was good enough to give his cousin a run for his money. In that time he'd TKO'd an American Golden Gloves champion called Victor Christian during an exhibition tour. What was impressive was that after backpedalling around the ring for two and a half rounds, Michael switched stance and landed a punch which brought his much larger opponent literally to his knees. None of the kids had ever seen anybody hit so hard. A one-punch KO is not easy for anybody to produce, especially not a boy of Michael's age or build. Not only was Michael having success inside the ring but outside of it too with his street-kid fights. Mary was extremely concerned over Michael's street fighting and begged him to stop. Seeing how upset his mum was Michael promised her he'd only fight in the ring in future. He meant it every time he said it.

When not boxing, Timbo was constantly in trouble with the Police and to get him away from the crowd he was running with his mum sent him to live with relatives. "Oh, by the way our Michael, I'm gonna live with me Aunty May so we won't be that far from one another after ye move. That's good news isn't it?" said Timbo. Michael nodded.

*

The Frosts moved house in time for their children to start the new school year at their new school. Settling in is hard for kids after they move away from their friends and everything that is familiar to them and particularly so for Michael. The terrifying visions of his yellow-eyed Demon became more and more frequent. Now, though, It was accompanied by a legion of horrifying looking tormentors. He'd stopped talking for a time but after he settled down in his new school his speech eventually returned, much to the relief of Mary and Joseph.

One Saturday morning, Michael, Thomas, Rose and a few of their new friends were hanging around a local wood when they saw Timbo running toward them being pursued by a gang of kids. Leading them was a teenager known locally as '*Buckhead, King of the Kids*'. Timbo, Michael and the others were quickly surrounded. Buckhead had heard about Timbo's reputation and wanted to fight him to demonstrate that he was the local hardcase. Timbo couldn't back down in front of his cousins and so agreed to fight the older, and much larger, Buckhead. As Timbo was removing his coat, Buckhead head butted him in the face. Timbo fell to the ground with blood streaming from his nose. Buckhead was about to send the boot in when Michael pushed him over.

"Go away and leave my cousin alone," said Michael in the monotone voice he used when angry.

"Piss off you… you… you… you…" Buckhead's gang laughed at his inability to finish a sentence. "Shurrup youz lot or I'll burst yez," screamed Buckhead.

"Go away and leave my cousin alone," repeated Michael in a voice now lower, clearer and laced with menace.

"Fancy yerself do ye, mong boy?"

"Leave our Michael alone ye big turd ye," said Timbo, "he's not even ten yet and he's… well, you know, he's not right in the 'ead like. He's not all there," Timbo said pulling a funny face.

"What do you mean, Timbo?" Michael asked, puzzled.

"Nothin' Michael… nothin', it's just tha'… well, you know… you're a bit slow in the 'ead like, aren't ye?" Michael had no idea what Timbo was talking about.

"C'mon then big mouth, 'ow about it, eh? Fancy yer chances do ye?" screeched Buckhead challenging Michael to a fight.

In response to Buckhead's challenge Michael raised his fists and took up a Southpaw stance. Buckhead laughed and comically mimed rolling up his sleeves, like Popeye did when getting into a scrap with Bluto. Bending down as if to scratch his leg, Buckhead, from his crouching position, rushed full speed onto Michael. Reacting by instinct, Michael took a big step to his left and sent a lightning-fast punch across Buckhead's jaw with a precise eighty percent impact and twenty percent travel and follow through. The punch was a doozy. Buckhead was out cold before he hit the deck. Everybody gasped at Michael's punching power. They'd never seen anybody hit so hard. Buckhead's gang quickly dispersed, leaving him lying motionless in the dirt.

As the kids arrived back home, Mary emerged from her front door. Rose couldn't wait to tell her what had gone on. "What? Have you been fighting again have you Michael? What have I told you about your fighting? What are we going to do with you, eh son? Get inside… now!" As ever, Mary was quick to dish out punishment, slapping Michael hard across the back of his bare sticklike legs. As with every occurrence of this punishment, Michael didn't cry and Mary was sorry five minutes later. "You're going to have to learn not to get into fights son, especially now we've moved house. We don't want our new neighbours thinking we're common."

*

After school one day, Michael, Thomas and some of their school mates were sitting on a wall, kicking their heels, when they noticed the notorious Sparrow Hall gang heading their way. Michael hopped off the wall and walked toward the 'Sparra' boys.

"Alright Timbo?"

"Awright our Michael. What you up to?"

"Sitting on the wall over there," he said pointing.

"How are ye gettin' on at yer new school? Are ye doin' any boxing there or wha'?"

"They don't do boxing."

"Wha'? No boxin'? Are they fruits or wha'?"

"They do cricket and football and sometimes country dancing."

"Yeah, thought so, fruits. Tell ye what, why don't ye come with me to my new boxing club. I'll call for ye at five next Tuesday and we'll set off."

"Okay," replied Michael.

"Are you jokin' Timbo, takin' that little fruit boxin'?" sneered Baz, who'd taken a dislike to Timbo from the moment he'd joined the Sparrow Hall Gang.

"I tell you wha' Baz, he'd burst you," replied Timbo in defence of his cousin.

"Get lost. You're dreamin' mate!" snorted Baz, sceptical of Timbo's claim.

"Listen. When I was gettin' me head kicked in by some big turd called Buckhead our Michael KO'd him. One punch was all it took. An' in a boxing match with some American lads he put their best fighter on the deck, again with only one punch."

"Do you think I'm soft in the 'ead? 'Im? Get out of it. If he's so good then I'll take him on."

"I'm warning ye Baz don't do it." But Baz was in no mood to listen. Baz saw the chance to hammer one of Timbo's rellies to get back at him and he was not going to miss it.

"Listen Michael, you don't have to fight if you don't want to," said Timbo not wanting to get into trouble with Michael's mum for getting him into a fight.

"Shut up Timbo, let him speak for himself," interjected Baz.

"Leave the lad alone Baz," chorused the Sparra boys. "He's doin' no harm."

"Piss off youz lot. Are yez his ma or wha'?"

"Listen Baz, let's forget it, he's not all there in the head if you know what I mean. Sorry Michael," said Timbo.

"What do you mean, Timbo?" asked Michael.

"You're erm… different to the rest of us… you know… different like. A bit, erm… slow like," sputtered Timbo using the words he'd heard grownups use when describing Michael. Michael still had no idea what Timbo was talking about.

"Look Baz, he's only ten so leave him alone."

"But accordin' to you he's the next Rocky Marciano." Without warning Baz punched Michael on the nose which started it trickling with blood.

"You sneaky twat Baz. Are you alright our Michael?" asked Timbo, concerned.

"My nose is bleeding."

"C'mon then Micky Frost, put yer dukes up or are ye chicken or wha'?" taunted Baz, bobbing up and down on his toes boxing style.

"My name is not Micky, it's Michael and I promised Mum I wouldn't fight any more."

"See Timbo, he's just a chicken," cried Baz making bock, bock, bock chicken noises.

"Let's go bridge dropping," said Michael to his mates, ignoring Baz's taunts. The two groups of boys went their separate ways.

"See you next Tuesday then our Michael?" yelled Timbo.

"Okay," Michael shouted back.

"Christ Michael, are you alright?" asked Stevie Newcombe concerned that Michael's nose would never stop bleeding.

"Yes, I'm okay, it didn't hurt much."

"Ye did the right thing not getting into a fight with that Baz Grogan, he's a right bastard."

"I'm not scared of him, it's just I promised Mum I wouldn't fight any more."

As they walked away from the Sparrow Hall gang, Michael's mates kept looking over their shoulders until they were certain they were safe.

As arranged, Timbo turned up at Michael's house at five o'clock the following Tuesday and every Tuesday for the next five years.

*

The rules of Bridge Dropping were simple. The Bridge Dropper worked his way, girls were not interested in playing this game, along one of the girders holding up the railway bridge as it passed over a road twenty feet below and hung there to attract the attention of passers-by before dropping to the pavement. If a Bridge Dropper wanted to receive the adulation of his peers he would add style to the drop. For example, synchronised dropping with a buddy or two and/or rolling, paratrooper style, on landing. Points were deducted for blood or ends bitten off tongues.

*

The time eventually came to sit the eleven plus exam for entry into Grammar school. It was common for parents, such as Michael's and his mate's, not to get involved in their children's education; homework was seldom checked and they were left to get on with things by themselves. Of all the kids in the area only Michael passed the eleven plus exam and won a place at a Grammar school. When the other kids heard the news they taunted him mercilessly, saying he'd be better off going to the same school as them instead. It was just the same in Mary and Joseph's day and for generations before; if you look like you're going to advance, get ahead, make something of yourself, your so-called mates do all they can to hold you back. They do this out of fear of being left behind. To set Michael up for Grammar school Mary and Joseph made lots of sacrifices, including cashing in an endowment policy to pay for his school uniform. They willingly made the sacrifices because they were so very proud of their number one son. This pride, however, didn't stop Mary and Joseph divorcing two years later. Thereafter, Michael and his siblings received free school meals and free bus travel too. Mary used to say to the kids, "fill up on your school dinners as much as you can and see if you can bring some pudding home if any's going spare."

After Joseph left the family home, neighbours, so-say concerned about the Frost children, contacted Social Services, claiming Mary was neglecting them by leaving them home alone while she went out to work. The way Mary saw things was simple; they were her kids and she was going to pay her way and didn't need charity. She could do it. At least she hoped she could. It was an almighty effort but Mary kept her children despite the best efforts of the amateur social engineers of Liverpool's Social Services department to take them away from her and split the family up.

REUNION

Margaret Rotheram was hurrying back to her student digs to change her clothes and get to her bar job at The Mitre public house when she heard a female voice call out, "Alice?" She paid no attention but something inside made Margaret slow her pace. "Alice? Alice!" shouted the female voice but louder this time. Margaret turned in the direction of the caller; an elegant, well-dressed woman older than herself. Next to her stood a similarly elegant, well-dressed woman. *Twins?* thought Margaret. They were looking straight at her, "Alice? Alice, is it you? It is you!" Though strangers to her, the women looked familiar to Margaret. With their thick honey-blonde hair and strikingly handsome features they both looked remarkably like her.

"Excuse me ladies, are you referring to me?" Margaret asked.

"Yes, yes we are. She looks so like Father doesn't she Lilly? It's the hair… and the eyes too of course."

"She does Hen. Alice, please don't be frightened. We're here to… please let us go somewhere we might talk in private."

"I'm sorry ladies but I think you've mistaken me for somebody else, my name is Margaret and I'm in a hurry, so please, if you don't mind?" Margaret turned to walk away.

"I think you will want to hear what it is we have to say to you."

"Look, I've told you, my name is Margaret and I don't know who this Alice is you are referring to." Even as Margaret spoke she knew she should listen to the familiar-looking strangers.

"Okay, have it your own way but there's something we need to tell you that you need to know. But, as you're in so much of a hurry we'll tell you who you really are on the street if you like!"

"Don't be so heartless Hen, she can't know, how could she? She was just a baby when—"

"Your name isn't Margaret, it's Alice, Alice Noelle-Neumann… and you're our little sister," blurted out Henrietta, Lilliana's twin and Margaret's half-sister.

After the woman spoke, teardrops formed on the lower lids of Margaret's eyes. Her head was in a spin, she couldn't breathe, her chest felt like it was in a vice. Instinctively she knew the woman was telling the truth. "Look, let us go somewhere to speak in private," said Lilliana. "We have a car. Come… please. Come with us, we'll explain everything." Margaret walked trance-like across the crowded pavement toward the car door opened for her by a man in a Chauffeur's uniform.

Cars are the perfect places in which to hold difficult conversations. They provide a confined, secluded, private space in which one can talk freely and, as they are often on the move, it is hard to avoid difficult topics.

*

The sisters began by introducing themselves; "I'm Henrietta, Hen, and this is my twin sister Lilliana, Lilly." They weren't identical twins but very nearly so. They were obviously older than Margaret. Henrietta explained that their father, Frederik, married Alice's mother, Celia, in 1938 after he'd come to England following the death of their mother, Anastasia. "Father believed she was murdered by the Gestapo," said Lilliana in little more than a whisper before the story continued.

"The family decided it was best for them all to get away from the Nazis and so they set up the family business in London. But Father simply couldn't forget his 'beautiful Anastasia' as he called her. He spent all his time at the office; wallowing in self-pity, according to the family. The truth be told, he neglected us. Eventually, it all became too much for him and he collapsed at work one day and was rushed to hospital where he was diagnosed with extreme physical and emotional exhaustion. To recover his health, he took some time away from the business which we spent travelling in Mother's Russian homeland. It was more of a pilgrimage than a holiday. Away from the business Father was a different man, we had a wonderful time together. He talked about leaving the business to make a new start in America.

"After we returned to London, instead of going to America, Father returned to the office. He expected to find the place in a mess but instead he discovered the business was flourishing all thanks to somebody called Celia. They worked closely together and, over time, they fell in love, I suppose. He brought her to meet us for lunch in Regent's Park one day. We were not so naïve as to think there was nothing going on between them… we were happy for him. The most difficult thing, he told us, was going to be telling the family that he intended to marry Celia. He said they'd been disappointed by his choice when he married our mother and probably more so in marrying Celia."

Next came the part of the story concerning Alice. The twins asked Margaret if she wanted them to go on. She said she did. They told to her that after war broke out the authorities were going to put them all in an internment camp. To prevent this from happening their father volunteered to spy for the British Secret Service. The plan was for him to travel to Berlin and join up with his old friends who were running the war for the Nazis and pass information back to London. The twins said Celia told them that they were held hostage in case their father double-crossed the British Authorities. "Which, of course, he never would have done," said Lilliana proudly. The twins paused in silent remembrance of past events.

"Celia got a telegram saying father was dead; it read 'missing in action presumed killed' but she knew what that meant. As you can imagine, she was devastated. The family decided that it would be for the best if we went away to Switzerland while you remained in England with Celia."

"We actually ended up in Lincolnshire with the women's land army for a while and then Lilly got a job intercepting Nazi signals and passing them on to a place called Bletchley Park. Do you know it?"

"No," replied Margaret even though she did.

"It wasn't long after we arrived in Lincolnshire that Aunt Eugenie came to see us with the news about you and Celia being killed in London by a bomb. I don't know how she can have been mistaken."

"What if she wasn't mistaken?" asked Margaret.

"What do you mean?"

"Nothing. Carry on."

Henrietta and Lilliana continued their tale, which involved them attending a finishing school in Switzerland before going to work in the family business in Italy before eventually returning to Germany. They told Margaret they were both married, with each of them having a daughter named Alice.

"How did you find me?" asked Margaret, her senses on high alert.

"It was all very peculiar. We were contacted by a lawyer from Bern who said that he had information about a relative living in England who we thought had perished during the war. We wanted to meet him but he refused, saying it was a 'trifling matter' which didn't require a meeting. Over the next two months he contacted us four or five times before finally confirming your identity and giving us your address here in Cambridge."

"My address in Cambridge? Not Reigate?"

"No, Cambridge. Why Reigate?"

"Because that's where I live with my... parents."

"Who are your parents?"

"Go on with your story please," said Margaret ignoring the question.

"That's it really. There's nothing more to add except we are wondering what your story is."

"I'm wondering that myself."

"Who are your parents, Alice?"

"It odd but when you call me Alice… it seems right." Margaret thought for a few seconds before continuing, "My name now is Margaret Rotheram. My parents are Audrey and Cyril Rotheram. We… they live in Reigate."

"We lived in Reigate with Father when we first moved to England and… oh dear." Lilliana stopped speaking as she realised something was not right. She and Henrietta were visibly upset and shaking. Holding back her tears Henrietta continued.

"The Rotherams are relatives. Before she was married, Audrey was a Noelle-Neumann. Oh, it's all starting to make sense now!" Henrietta and Lilliana began to sob uncontrollably.

"Take me back to Cambridge please," ordered Margaret without the slightest trace of sisterly compassion in her voice.

The sisters didn't talk or even look at one another on the drive back to Cambridge, each opting to stare out of the car's windows. When they arrived at Margaret's student digs Henrietta asked if they could meet that evening for a meal, "a family meal, to get to know one another." Despite her not being in the mood for socialising, Margaret agreed to meet up with her half-sisters because, she thought, they'd done nothing wrong plus she needed more information to piece things together. There was another reason, however. Margaret had family… sisters! She wasn't alone in this world if she had sisters. And they had children! Margaret was not alone in the world. She wanted so much to call her mother; no, not her mother, Audrey, call Audrey and find out what the hell was going on. *No, not yet. I need to find out who is behind my sisters' coming here. There's something terribly wrong with all this.*

*

That evening the sisters met for dinner and had a tearful but pleasant time together. Diners sitting close to them felt uncomfortable with some of the things they were overhearing and so asked to be moved.

A sister's conversation.

"What will you do now?"

"I don't know," Margaret lied.

"It must have been as big a shock for you as it was for us when we found out. At first we didn't believe it. When we decided to travel to England to check if the story was true we weren't sure what we'd do if we found you. How should we approach you? Perhaps through a lawyer as we'd been approached? Write you a letter? We weren't sure. But when we saw you walking along the street we knew. It had to be you. It had to be, so we called out your name and then there was no going back."

"Yes, we were very concerned why we'd been told that you'd died along with Celia in the blitz and now, suddenly, you're there, right in front of us. We knew it had to be you because we share our father's looks; his hair… his eyes. He was such a handsome man. We're so alike we three, even though we have different mothers."

"Did you like my mother?" asked Margaret.

"We adored her."

"Did you love her?" The twins looked at one another before Henrietta answered.

"Your mother… Celia, was a wonderful woman and father was very much in love with her. If anybody was to replace our mother we were glad it was Celia."

"What will you say to Aunt Audrey and Uncle Cyril? Will you mention anything? It might be best not to mention anything."

"How can you say that Lilly?"

"Digging up the past might lead to… who knows where it might lead but nowhere good that's for certain."

"I don't know what I'll say to them," Margaret lied again.

The twins reminisced about their lives in Germany before leaving Berlin for London and what Margaret was like as a baby.

Then it struck her. Audrey and Cyril had hardly mentioned anything about when she was a baby. She hadn't thought it odd up until then but it was now crystal clear why that was so. When the evening was over, the sisters kissed and held each other close before making arrangements for the following day. However, Margaret left a note at the twins' hotel four minutes later for them to pick up in the morning informing them that she had to go away.

As Margaret left the hotel she bumped into Rex, Timothy's father. Had she been in a less fragile state she would have thought it all just too much of a coincidence but she wasn't thinking straight. They greeted one another with the now popular Kissy Kissy face dance, ensuring not to touch cheek with lip. Rex asked Margaret what she was doing out so late, "Shouldn't you be studying young lady?" He laughed to show that he wasn't being entirely serious. Margaret made up a lie on the spot as to tell him she'd been to dinner with her sisters would require lengthy explanation. Rex asked how her studies were going before casually mentioning that he had a new job which involved him awarding funding to students of underprivileged families and handed her his card. To excuse himself, Rex said he had an early start the next day and, at his age, he needed to get to his bed. After they parted Rex shouted from the door of the hotel, "Give my best to your parents when next you speak with them."

*

Early the next morning Margaret travelled to London to stay with her old Pony Club friends. They knew there must be something amiss but didn't want to pry. Zuzu was shacked up with her handsome Greek waiter and the rest all had boyfriends so they had little time for Margaret, but what should she say if they asked? They all assumed it was man troubles so Margaret concocted a suitably sad story of infidelity. She couldn't possibly tell them the truth. Margaret supposed that the news of her going missing would soon get back to Reigate and that her overprotective parents would panic. She didn't want the Police involved so decided to meet with her so-called parents face to face and have it out with them. No, she didn't ever want to see them again. She called them instead that evening.

"Hello, Reigate 655…"

"It's me."

"Oh darling, where are you, we were so worried about you. Lorraine called to say you weren't at your lectures today and you'd been seen getting on a train for London. Where are you?"

"In London," answered Margaret coldly.

"Are you alright my darling? Is anything the matter?"

"There is as it happens. Who are my parents? What happened to them?"

"What do you mean darling? What's this all about?"

"Stop lying Audrey, I know the truth." There was a long silence on the other end of the call.

"Come home to Reigate my Angel. We can talk about it when you get here. I'll make you your favourite—"

"I'm never coming home again. I never want to see either of you ever again. If you try and contact me I'll go to the Police as I'm certain that what you did was illegal." Margaret wasn't sure if any crime had been committed but mentioning the Police couldn't hurt in her view.

"Please don't do this Margaret darling. We love you. We… come home, please. Don't do this to us, Margaret. It'll kill your father."

"My father is already dead, Audrey, but you know that already, don't you? Goodbye Audrey. Remember what I said about not contacting me. I mean it. Never ever try to get in touch with me… ever. If you do you'll regret it. By the way, my name is Alice, Alice Noelle-Neumann; but you know that already, don't you?" Margaret unnervingly gently and calmly placed the handset back on the cradle of the phone sending a click and a humming sound to Audrey's earpiece.

After ending the call Margaret felt a rush of relief, satisfaction, elation almost, but she also felt empty inside. Her life thus far had been a sham. She now fully accepted what her friends had said to her on Kos, her parents had indeed used her for their own benefit. Having no reason to remain in London Margaret caught a train back to Cambridge early the next morning. When she arrived at the station, she went straight to the hotel to see her sisters. They were preparing to leave Cambridge as she'd disappeared, leaving them only a note. They were both extremely upset. She told them she'd called Audrey. They asked how the call went. Margaret ignored the question, instead she asked them not to mention anything of their visit to Cambridge to other family members. They told her that they'd already told various relatives about their trip before they'd left Germany. Margaret begged them to lie when they returned home, saying that the information from the lawyer was incorrect and the person he'd traced wasn't Alice. As far as anybody was concerned, Alice was dead. The twins agreed to keep the truth a secret. Margaret promised to contact the twins after she'd had time to adjust to the reality of her situation. Seeing how upset Margaret was they were concerned that they'd never see their sister again. "Now that I have sisters I don't want to lose them," she replied. The sisters spent the rest of the day and evening together. Before leaving to return to Germany the twins gave Alice photographs of her namesakes. They said they'd write regularly to let her know how they were doing at school and send frequent photographs as "they change so quickly". They each instinctively knew they'd probably never meet Alice again.

*

As Margaret was waving goodbye to her sisters as they drove away, Rex appeared standing next to her at the hotel entrance. He waved too.

"Who are we waving to?" he asked.

"Oh, just some German tourists I got friendly with. They came into the bar where I work and we got talking. My German isn't half bad and I'm always looking for somebody to practise with."

"I hope you don't mind me saying but you bear a remarkable resemblance to them. Remarkable. You could almost be sisters."

"Do you really think so?" replied Margaret with a cold calm in her voice. "I don't see it myself."

"Really? Well, I never was much good at things like that… you know, faces, names, ages and so on. But you do look so much alike. Will you keep in touch with them, they seemed rather nice. I had a chat with them yesterday. They were concerned that you'd gone missing."

"I wasn't missing. Why does everybody keep saying that? I went to London on urgent business."

"Well, they thought you had. They seemed rather upset. Strange behaviour wouldn't you say for people you'd only just met? And you were here with them rather late the night before. You must have gotten on like a house on fire to have had dinner with them after so short an acquaintance."

"What do you want Rex?" demanded Margaret bluntly.

"You and I need to talk old thing. But not here. I know your secret," he whispered. "I've an interesting proposition to put to you." Margaret looked at Rex in a knowing way that only a woman can. "No, not that. This is business. This is about your future."

"I'm not sure I know what you're talking about Uncle Rex."

"Oh I think you do. You called your… you called Audrey last night."

"Enough! What the hell do you want Rex?"

"I told you, I've an interesting proposition to put to you. You know I have a new job and I have it in my gift to finance your education… as your sponsor if you will. What do you say Alice, will you listen to what it is I have to say?"

"Alice? Who's Alice? My name is…"

"Stop it Alice. Do you think I pulled that name out of thin air? I told you, I know your secret. And I know you'll never go back to Reigate ever again. You can't complete your studies on what a part-time bar job pays so let me do a favour for an old family friend."

"If you think this will get Tim and me back together again, you're mistaken."

"This has nothing to do with you and my son. In fact a condition of my sponsorship will be that you will never have anything to do with my son ever again. You look confused. Let me be frank with you. You're an exceptional, a very exceptional, young lady and I think I have a suitable career for you after you leave this place."

"People say you're a spy. Are you a spy Uncle Rex?"

"No Alice, I'm not a spy. Have a think about what we've talked about and call me on the number on the card I gave you when you decide you want to hear what it is I have to say to you."

"Oh, can I have another card please Uncle Rex, I seem to have misplaced the one you gave me," smiled Margaret coquettishly.

An Organisation conversation.

"It's me."

"Oy, I'm supposed to say that. This is highly irregular."

"You wanted to know how things worked out with Margaret Rotheram."

"Well?"

"I spoke with her after she met with her sisters. I told her that I knew that she knew that her mother wasn't her real mother… if you get my meaning?"

"I think I do. Carry on."

"She didn't go over the edge as you feared she might. Quite the opposite in fact. I suggested she consider my offer to fund her education and to give me a call when she's ready to have a meeting. She called me not two minutes ago and we're meeting tomorrow afternoon."

"Be careful Rex old love, she may be more fragile than you think. What are you going to offer her?"

"I'll offer her a grant to complete her education with the proviso that she does some bits and pieces for me during her studies. That'll draw her close to us and make it hard for her to leave. I'll make it sound cloak and daggery to feed her suspicions about me. She'll believe she's being recruited by MI6, in the way previous students have."

"What about her parents… or whatever they are?"

"Sadly, the chap, Cyril, doesn't have long to live."

"Does he not? Is he ill?"

"Not that I'm aware of."

*

The following afternoon Rex and Margaret met up at a pub outside Cambridge. He'd dyed his hair and was wearing a trilby hat.

"You're looking very smart today Uncle Rex," Margaret lied.

"Thank you. I've come straight from… the… erm… office," said Rex, trying his best to sound cloak and daggery. "Have you had time to consider my offer?"

"I have."

"Well?"

"I'd like to know more. I'll start by asking if you're behind all this."

"Behind all this what?"

"My sisters showing up in Cambridge… and Audrey and Cyril… you must have known!"

"Things come to our attention but that doesn't mean we're behind everything. No, I learned of your circumstances second hand," Rex lied.

"From who?"

"Sorry, old thing, can't say; security and all that," replied Rex accompanied by his customary, and very annoying, tapping on the side of his nose with his forefinger.

"Fine. This meeting is over. If you can't tell me what I need to know then—"

"Alice. Please. Sit down. There are things I can tell you today and things you will learn over time. I just can't go round telling people what is in my head. I've signed certain covenants and if I break them I could go to jail," said Rex, laying it on thick for effect. "Please, Alice, listen to what it is I have to say today and be assured there will be more to come tomorrow."

"But tomorrow never comes though, does it Uncle Rex?"

"Young lady, I'm not here for an existential philosophical discussion with you, I simply want to talk with you about funding your education and, if you pass muster, I might have a rather interesting job for you after you graduate."

"I have no intentions of becoming a spy."

"There are more jobs than spying, Alice. Look, for the time being just accept the funding I'm offering you as a favour from an old family friend. There are no strings attached, I promise. You need the money and I need to show that I'm doing my job by funding impoverished students. I assume you are impoverished now that you've broken ties with your parents?"

"They are not my parents Uncle Rex. My parents are dead."

"So, Alice, do we have a deal? There's nothing to sign, all I need are your bank details and we're all set to go. Simple. What do you say?"

"Give me some time to think about it."

"Certainly. You have twenty-four hours from… now," said Rex tapping his watch.

*

Even before she arrived back in Cambridge, Margaret had made up her mind to accept Rex's offer but, not trusting him, she'd be extremely cautious and the minute she saw something she didn't like she'd… what? What would she do? She needed money to complete her course and graduate. Yes, graduate. Then she'd be able to make her own choices in life. Take up a career of her choosing. Politics? Economics? She already knew she didn't want a career along either of those paths.

The minute Margaret got back to her digs she called Rex to tell him that she was prepared to accept his offer, but with certain conditions. Rex replied that there were no conditions on his offer and he expected likewise from her. He added that if at some future time she wanted to walk away then she could but in the meantime he required her to attend certain functions to demonstrate that his choice of candidate was appropriate. She argued that, contrary to what he'd said, he was imposing conditions on her to which he replied he certainly was not as what he required of her was normal for any academic grant. "Besides," he said, "you might enjoy it. By the bye, there's a little departmental get together this weekend which you should find interesting and not a little fun. It'll be perfect for building up your network of contacts." Margaret saw the sense in what Rex was saying. Having been brought up knowing there really was no such thing as a free lunch she agreed to attend Rex's little departmental get together. She wouldn't enjoy it though; she was determined not to enjoy it. Before the call ended, they talked money.

"We haven't actually talked about the money side of things yet."

"You're right, we haven't. What would you like to know?"

"Well, for starters, I'd like to know the size of the grant and how much I'll be getting and what date the money will hit my account. I'm a little behind with the rent you see."

"We can't have that. We can't have our little star out on the streets."

"Are you mocking me Rex?" asked Margaret in the tone of voice she would soon become famous for. A tone that could lower the temperature of any room in an instant.

"You're very firm aren't you? Strict even. I can see why Tim liked you. No, Alice, I'm not mocking you. I'm just trying to be a bit jovial. I'm not all about work you know. I do have a sense of humour."

"I see," Margaret replied smirking. "Uncle Rex, in future, please promise me you'll let me know when you're being humorous," she said in a mocking tone of voice. Rex liked her ways.

"I will, and thank you for the suggestion," he replied sarcastically.

"You'll receive enough to cover your rent and your studies plus an allowance of two and a half thousand a year for personal expenses; clothes, entertaining and the like. No need for receipts."

"That's very generous. My rent is—"

"We know how much your rent is, it's pretty standard for Cambridge. Oh yes, you'll be reimbursed any expenses incurred while on little departmental get-togethers and the like."

"I see. And where is the one this weekend by the way?"

"Paris. You do have a passport?"

"I do but it's at Reigate and I have no intention of ever going there again so that's a bit of a problem."

"Not to worry, I'll arrange for a nice fresh new one for you. Your tickets, itinerary and your new passport will arrive in the post tomorrow. You can catch a taxi Frogside to the departmental get-together."

"Tomorrow? That's quick to arrange a new passport. Are you sure you're not a spy Rex?"

"Please Alice, this line isn't secure!" hissed Rex but thought he'd better stop laying it on thick otherwise Margaret might catch on. "By the way, that is the last time I will refer to you as Alice."

"Why? I'm going to use my proper name from now on; Alice Noelle-Neumann."

"Ah, about that, your passport will be issued in the name of Margaret Rotheram. We can talk about changing your name later but for now it will complicate things with the funding and all that. Is that okay Margaret?" She hung up the call without answering the question.

*

And that is how it happens for the vast majority of the Organisation's recruits; isolate, integrate, initiate, manipulate and, finally, control. Margaret would be sucked deeper and deeper into the Organisation with each thing she did for it. Every act would be recorded and filed away to guarantee her compliance and loyalty. She was a fly stuck fast on the Organisation's web and to struggle would only attract the attention of the spider at its centre. It would become Margaret's family and in turn she would become one of its most obedient children, doing whatever it ordered her to do. No job would be off limits for her; not even the job of Avenging Angel. The Organisation does not like to attract attention to its activities and only sanctions assassinations as a very last resort. At least that's what Its Governors like to believe.

Margaret was one of the few who entered the Organisation as a willing recruit and with Rex behind her she would rise rapidly through the ranks. On her upward trajectory she'd come to the attention of the Mandarins, but that was always the plan. Rex knew they were looking for somebody like Margaret. Somebody with fresh, new ideas. An idealist, a naïve idealist; someone to change the Organisation to the Mandarin's design. Somebody to preside over its doom.

Promotions would follow quickly, one after the other. Those around Margaret had a choice. Hang onto the coat-tails of the rising star and go where she goes or languish in mediocrity and receive her judgement.

TROUBLE IN PARADISE

Quite unexpectedly, Michael settled into his all-boys Grammar school from day one. There were, of course, a few fist fights between the first formers to establish the pecking order but Michael didn't get involved. He did, however, go along to watch them and learn. Apart from the normal school team sports of football, rugby and cricket, Michael's school had sports clubs for archery, fencing and boxing. Michael was not interested in team sports but readily applied to join the sports clubs as he liked the idea of fencing and archery and assumed he would be chosen for the boxing team.

At the start of his second week at school, Michael went along to join the fencing club. As so many students applied for membership, the fencing coach asked the students if any of them had any experience with swords.

"I was in a pantomime once as Peter Pan," shouted Steve 'Spike' Smith from the middle of a cluster of students, having already established himself as the class clown. All the kids laughed.

"Yeah, very funny, very funny," the coach replied dismissively.

With the twenty best getting places on the fencing team, five at a time, the students picked up a foil and copied the exercises shown them by one of the older boys so the coach could see what they had. He was looking for balance, speed, strength and aggression. If the first lot were anything to go by things were not looking good. Then came Michael's turn. When he took hold of the foil for the first time the coach said, "Oh good, you're cack-handed, we need some lefties. You're in if you can do the exercises." Michael completed the exercises and then repeated them using his right hand. "Ace, you're an ambi," cried the coach. "You're definitely in!" None of the pupils had any idea what an ambi was but if it got them on the team they wanted to be one. They hadn't noticed Michael switching hands, they just thought he was showing off and anything he could do…

"No, no, no!" screamed the fencing coach. "Just do what you've been shown, you divvies. None of this fancy stuff, you're not Errol bleedin' Flynn. What's up with you lot?"

"You picked Frosty after he did fancy stuff so we're doin' the same," shouted Spike from the middle of the crowd.

"Frost didn't do any fancy stuff, as you call it. He did the exercises using his left hand and then repeated them with his right hand. He's an ambi. Ambidextrous? Have any of you lot heard that word before? It means he's as good with his left hand as he is with his right."

"Our kid's like that when he plays with himself," grunted Spike in an attempt to disguise his voice. The kids in the fencing class doubled up with laughter.

"I know that was you Spikey boy. Come on down, let's see if you can fence as good as you talk."

Spike, as it turned out, was already experienced with a foil, having previously had fencing lessons with his Scout Troop. He was on the team. The following day Michael went along for boxing club selection. His reputation had preceded him. The boxing coach was excited at the prospect of having 'the' Michael Frost on his boxing team.

*

The first year at his Grammar school flew by for Michael. He was freakishly good when it came to languages and was exceptional at mathematics but languished in all other subjects apart from metalwork and woodwork because "he's good with his hands," as Mary always said.

In their second and third years, pupils could choose to drop some subjects, replacing them with others from a list. It became a choice for Michael to drop either Geography or History and replace it with another subject. He chose to continue with History as he was good at remembering dates. Goodbye Geography, bonjour French.

For Michael, the passing of school time was neither boring nor enjoyable, it just 'was'. He continued to do well in languages and mathematics and in his third senior school year Michael was one of only eight pupils invited to join a specially sponsored Russian language class. As with German and French, he was the best of the students in Russian too.

Outside school, Michael spent most of his time studying alone in libraries. It was impossible for him to study at home because of the constant noise Rose made. One day, he came across a book on military strategy which had been left in the languages section. He was on his way to take it to the librarian's desk when some words on the back cover caught his eye; they fired his imagination so he added books about military strategy to his reading.

Apart from spending much of his time in the library, Michael kept up going to the boxing club with Timbo every Tuesday. This routine continued until the autumn of 1967 when Timbo, along with four other members of the Sparrow Hall Gang, were sentenced to between three and five years in prison for a series of robberies. During one of these robberies a bystander had been stabbed by one of the gang and there being a strict code of 'no grassing' they each got stiffer sentences than they would have otherwise received had they pointed out Baz Grogan as the knife man.

With having no Timbo to go to boxing club with, Michael's head became seriously out of kilter. His visions became more frequent and more terrible, producing feelings of despair as he couldn't share his torment with anybody. He was boiling up inside and it wouldn't take much to set him off. It was only a matter of time.

*

Thomas was playing in the street outside the Frosts' house when he attracted the attention of a local thug who set upon him for no reason. While little Thomas was being attacked by this much larger and older kid, he shouted, "I'm gonna get our Michael onto you." The thug's answer was, "Go and get him then. I'll burst that college puddin' if he comes out 'ere." Michael heard all while observing proceedings from the lounge window and went to Thomas' aid.

Without uttering a single syllable of threat or warning, Michael set about the thug with a ferocity he had never before shown. Kids ran to form a fighting circle but slowed their approach when they saw the pounding Michael was handing out to the teenage thug with the big street reputation. Most of them were secretly enjoying watching this bully getting his just desserts. One of the crowd, however, was the thug's best mate and he jumped on Michael's back causing a separation between the fighters. *We'll do this div now*, thought the joiner-inner until he saw his so-called 'best mate' legging it down the street leaving him to face Michael alone. The joiner-inner leapt off Michael's back.

"Look mate, I was just tryin' to break up the fight in case you got yerself hurt like," said the quick-thinking joiner-inner.

"Yer a liar you are John Divine," shouted one of the girls from the fighting circle which then began making bock, bock, bock, chicken noises. The girl continued, "You were joinin' in the fight to make it two onto one ye lyin' chicken ye."

"Honest mate, I wasn't, she doesn't know what she's talkin' about. I just didn't want ye gettin' yerself hurt sort of thing. An' you, Daisy O'Dwyer, you want to learn to keep yer gob shut an' stop stirrin' it." After speaking those words, the joiner-inner went to attack little Daisy O'Dwyer which was his biggest mistake that afternoon. Michael grabbed him by his hair, dragging him backwards, causing his feet to leave the ground and his head to hit the kerb. Immediately blood streamed from an open head wound. It looked very serious. "Quick, somebody dial 999 and ask for an Ambulance," shouted one of the fighting circle.

Mary emerged from the house after witnessing what had happened while passing the lounge window. She pushed her way through the group of kids to see a lad laying on the ground, his head in a pool of blood. It was all too much for her. She began crying and dragged Michael into the house by his shirt collar. Once inside Mary sat Michael on the settee.

"Are you going to smack my legs Mum?" Michael asked.

"No son, no, I'm not going to smack your legs. I think you're in real trouble this time with your fighting. What have I told you? Eh? What have I told you? Haven't I told you a thousan' times not to fight?"

Through lip reading, Mary couldn't tell that the word thousand ended with the letter 'd'. There were many misspoken words in Mary's vocabulary and some relatives used them to make fun of her. She never caught on to what they were doing. But Michael did. He knew what shits some of his relatives were to his mum because she was deaf.

*

After the Ambulance Medic patched the joiner-inner's head up, who was nowhere near as hurt as first feared, he was sent home to lay down. But that wasn't the end of the matter. Answering a knock on the front door, Michael came face to face with Police Sergeant Bill Huggard.

"Are you Michael Frost?"

"Yes I am."

"Is yer mum home please son?"

"I'll get her for you." Mary soon appeared at the front door.

"Oh good Jesus, who called the Police?" she exclaimed on seeing the Sergeant's uniform.

"Now don't panic luv, I'm just here to have a little chat with you and Michael about what happened this afternoon. I've already spoken to some of the kids in the street and though what Michael did was wrong he's a bit of a hero for what he did to those bullies."

Sergeant Huggard and Mary had a long chat about Michael after she'd explained that he'd have to speak up as she was hard of hearing. It was time to have a word with Michael.

"Now then Michael, yer mum's told me you've been going to boxing for the past few years and that yer pretty good."

"I used to go with Timbo until he went to jail."

"Yeah, yer mum said. Tell yer what, though, we don't have a boxing club here but we do have a Karate club run by the Police Association and I'd be glad to take you along if you like? We even have lessons in Japanese sword fighting, ye know, like Samurais and stuff. I hear you're on the school fencing team so that might be interesting for ye? This lot use wooden swords mind you, not the metal ones. Ye wouldn't want the kids round here getting their hands on real Samurai swords," joked Sergeant Huggard. "And once a week I run a minibus down to Bootle for the Royal Tank Regiment Cadets. How do ye fancy givin' that a go? They do all sorts of stuff and they go away to Altcar out by Southport for weekends. It'll be fun for ye goin' away with lads yer own age."

"I like fencing," was all Michael said in reply.

"Okay then, we'll start you off at the Dojo and see where we go from there, eh? I've left the address with yer mum. There's no subs so it's free. I'll see you tomorrow night then young man?" said Sergeant Huggard. Michael gave no reply.

During his first visit to the Dojo, Michael kept glancing over toward the Kenjutsu class practising with wooden swords. "You can have a go at that some other time," said Sergeant Huggard noticing Michael had become preoccupied. One of the swords wasn't wooden though. One of them was a beautifully decorated Katana held by the Sensei. "Nice sword," whispered Michael to the yellow-eyed Demon standing at his side. "If I had a sword like that I could cut your head off!" The Demon evaporated. Karate lesson over Sergeant Huggard introduced Michael to the Sensei.

"Sensei, this is Michael, the lad I told you about."

"Hello Michael, Sergeant Huggard told me you're quite the boxer and that you are on your school's fencing team. Is that garden fencing?" joked the Sensei.

"We use foils," replied Michael not getting the joke as usual.

"Yeah, I was just making a little joke there Michael. Never mind."

"Is that what ye call it?" mocked Sergeant Huggard. "That was rubbish, no wonder the lad didn't laugh."

"I like your sword," said Michael mesmerised by the beauty of the Katana.

"Here," offered the Sensei. Michael took hold of the Katana and instantly felt at one with it. A fire took hold of him. His eyes reflected the silver of the blade. Michael posed with the Japanese sword as he'd seen the Sensei doing and performed several exercises from memory.

"Wow, he really likes my Katana," whispered the Sensei to Sergeant Huggard. "Would you like to join our Kenjutsu class next time you're here Michael?" suggested the Sensei.

"Hey you, not so fast, I need him for my Karate class," Sergeant Huggard protested.

"Yes p... pl... please," sputtered Michael. This was the first time in his life that Michael had ever spoken the p word. He found it hard to say as it stuck in his throat. No matter how many times friends, relatives, teachers or family had tried to get Michael to say please he'd never spoken that word until then.

"Okay Michael we'll get you in early next week so you can do both classes. Karate first and then some Japanese swordplay after," suggested Sergeant Huggard. Another first that evening for Michael was he was looking forward to something without it occupying all of his mind. Instead, thoughts of the Dojo gave him a warm feeling of contentment in his stomach.

During each subsequent visit to the Dojo, Michael practised with the Sensei's Katana at every opportunity, blending Japanese swordplay with traditional fencing techniques; a combination which would result in his own devastating and unique style of sword fighting.

*

The following week, Sergeant Huggard took Michael, and a whole bunch of troubled Huyton kids, to the barracks of the 1st Royal Tank Regiment in Bootle. The evening began with a bit of good old fashioned square bashing. Michael took to its routineness like a duck to water, especially as it quieted the voices inside his head.

"Squaaaaad… aboooout… face!" screamed the Cadet NCO.

"Check. T. L. V. Check," shouted the Cadets as they performed an about face.

"Squaaaaad… halt!" screamed the Cadet NCO. The Cadets' feet thumped the ground as they came to a halt.

"Squaaaaad… stand aaaaat ….ease!" screamed the Cadet NCO. The feet of the ranks of Cadets thumped the ground in perfect unison. "Stand easy," called out the Cadet NCO calmly. With the Cadets stood at ease, the shoulders of Leading Cadet Tommy Munroe were going up and down like pistons and tears were streaming from his eyes.

"Corpwal," said the duty Officer, "who is that Cadet and why is he waffing." On hearing the Officer's speech impediment the Cadets had to fight to stifle their laughter.

"That's Leading Cadet Munroe, sir," answered the Cadet NCO.

"Why is Cadet Munwoe waffing Corpwal?"

"I don't know sir. Shall I ask him sir?"

"No thank you Corpwal, I'll ask him myself. Munwoe!"

"Sir?" answered Leading Cadet Munroe.

"Why are you waffing Munwoe?"

"I think it's because of the name of the Cadet next to me, sir."

"What's so funny about his name Munwoe?"

"It's Bates, sir. Somebody called him Master Bates, sir, and it made me laugh, sir."

"Well Munwoe, I think Munwoe is an even funnier name, don't you Munwoe?" suggested the duty Officer, his face barely an inch from Munroe's ear.

"Yes sir," agreed Leading Cadet Munroe biting his inner cheek to keep from laughing. By this time all the Cadets were almost peeing their pants holding in the laughter building up inside of them. *Please, no more, please!* they silently begged.

"That Cadet doesn't appear to be waffing Corpwal. What's that Cadet's name?" asked the duty Officer, pointing at Michael.

"I don't know sir, he's new tonight. What's your name for the Officer, Cadet?"

"I don't know but some of the Cadets said his name is Rupert, Corporal," replied Michael misunderstanding the question.

A gasp came from the ranks of Cadets followed by an expectant hush. They held their breath. Unable to remain standing at ease the Cadets rocked backwards and forwards on the balls of their feet in an attempt to restrain the laughter building up inside them.

"Captain Wupert, eh?" echoed Captain Jones while peering hard at Michael. "And what's your name, Cadet?"

"Michael Frost."

"Say 'sir' when addressing an Officer, Cadet Frost," interjected the Cadet NCO.

"Michael Fwost eh. I'll wemember that name. Cawwy on Corpwal." With that, Captain Jones left the exercise yard. The Cadet NCO spun round to face the ranks of the Cadets, his face beetroot red through holding in his laughter.

"Stone me Frosty, I thought I was gonna piss meself there with you calling the Captain a Rupert! You're a case you are, Frosty… a case!" cried the Cadet NCO with such a strong Brummie accent that Michael could hardly decipher what he said but as everybody was laughing he attempted to join in the laughter with mixed results. Before returning to Sergeant Huggard's minibus, Michael told the Cadet NCO that he didn't appreciate being called Frosty and asked him not to do so again.

*

Leading Cadet Munroe was in his late teens and worked alongside his father as a 'wharfie' on Liverpool's docks. At his age, he should have been in the Tank Regiment's Territorial Army, TA, but the strict discipline imposed on TA Soldiers being what it was he was determined to remain a Cadet for as long as possible; something which would prove to be his undoing.

*

While at Cadets especially, life became blissfully routine for Michael, which helped keep his head in kilter. Though he still enjoyed lessons in foreign languages and mathematics at school, he lived for the Huyton Dojo and evenings at the barracks of the Royal Tank Regiment. During his fourth week at Cadets, Michael fired a Lee Enfield .22 at the indoor shooting range. Unlike the other Cadets, Michael enjoyed cleaning his rifle afterwards and would clean those of the other Cadets too if they wanted.

Leaving the barracks one evening Michael passed a small group of TA Soldiers. He recognised one of them. It was Buckhead. Buckhead didn't notice Michael but he knew it could only be a matter of time before they would come face to face.

Rising Star

Following her graduation in 1961, where she achieved a double first and was awarded a generous economics prize of £15,000 from an anonymous source, Margaret Rotheram joined a firm in the West End after a friend of a friend recommended her for the job of PA to a partner there. She was told that being a PA was the fast track to a top job.

The firm was a typical *'do very little while charging enormous fees'* Advertising/PR Consultancy. Margaret's role was approved by Rex but to keep the job she had to rise to a position where she could be of use to the Organisation. In those times it wasn't easy for a young woman to carve out a career in such a firm, especially as Margaret had been hired for her looks not her qualifications. She'd have to work at least twice as hard as the men to get anywhere plus she had her duties to the Organisation to fulfil. She was going to be a very busy girl.

Thanks to circumstances engineered by Rex, it didn't take Margaret long to commence her climb up the corporate greasy pole.

*

Once in a suitably high position within a company, the Organisation likes its Operatives to stay put as it *'invests enormous amounts of time and resources in placing and monitoring Operatives; thereafter combining their outputs with those of other Operatives to achieve synergy and drive efficiencies.'* Few knew what that meant but that's the way things were. Operatives like Margaret had to stay put and little by little make small, almost imperceptible, changes at the behest of the massive machine that is the Organisation. That way, over time, nobody questions the Operative's actions and that's just the way the Organisation likes it.

*

A secret Mandarins Supreme Council conversation.
 "I say it's taking too long. Far too long!"
 "If we rush things we risk everything we've achieved so far."
 "What about you? What are you doing?"
 "I'm doing my bit… thank you."
 "Ladies and gentlemen, let us not argue amongst ourselves. We knew the road would be long when we began our little endeavour."

"When will we see some action… some results? We're doing a lot of talking and spending vast amounts of money but—"

"I will not see our plans go up in smoke for the want of a little patience. I implore you, look at the progress we've made over the past five years, let alone the previous thirty. We are on the brink of destroying the Organisation, and Its seven hundred-year history, and if it takes a few extra years to achieve our goal then so be it. We almost succeeded with Bonaparte but we were betrayed. We will not make the same mistake this time. So, I beg you all—"

"It's okay for you, you have time on your side. What about me and Sophia and Raphael? We won't be around for the big day if things carry on as they are. Please, let me implore you… get things started!"

"I can assure you all that we are entering the final phase, the players are in place and we just need to let time do our work for us as it always does. We can't just go changing Chancellor with a click of our fingers!"

"I don't understand why on Earth we need to change the Chancellor at all. He's in our pocket isn't he?"

"He's an incompetent fool who can't even—"

"Didn't you put him where he is?"

"He doesn't have the confidence of Controllers, let alone Governors. If he attempts to implement the plan we will have wasted the last five years!"

"Then what do you propose we do about him?"

"Isn't it a bit late to be having these discussions now? Allow me to—"

"Be quiet all of you. You're acting like a bunch of squabbling children. I am not concerned with whether you or you or you will be alive to see the great day. Others too have worked to achieve our goal and have passed along the way without complaint. We will only make our move when the time is right for us to do so and not a minute or even a second before. We all want the same thing, don't we?" All heads nodded in response for to contradict Max would've been dangerous to life and limb. "Good, then let us carry on with our meeting. Recorder, read the next agenda item."

The Recorder read aloud the final agenda item. It was an update report on suitable candidates to replace the Chancellor of the Organisation. Unfortunately, two of the candidates had recently died in road accidents. The circumstances had been fully investigated but nothing suspicious had been found. The investigators should have looked deeper. There were now only four of them left plus Rex's recently introduced outsider, Margaret Rotheram.

"Rex's outsider should be withdrawn. The remaining candidates, any of whom would make an acceptable Chancellor, are all capable of executing the plan and, what's more, they are already Governors. Your candidate is a mere Operative."

"You call her an outsider but I see her coming up on the rail to become the favourite."

"Your horse-racing analogy is as pathetic as your candidate."

"You've only introduced her so you can run things in the background."

"I can assure you all she's no patsy." Rex took a moment to cast a glance at those seated around the table. "Unlike the four remaining candidates, Margaret Rotheram was a willing recruit. Plus she has a tragic personal history… which works in our favour. She's full of self-doubt and regret and is ambitious and naïve enough to believe she can achieve some sort of validation through hard work and success. She will see her promotions as just reward for her efforts… and we will see to it that she rises. What's more, she genuinely believes change is necessary for the survival of the Organisation. She'll be even more convinced when she learns about the mission. She already believes that the Organisation is run as an old boys' club and has previously undermined her Counsellor on a couple of occasions. So much so he's threatened to have her officially reprimanded. He doesn't realise he's got a Tigress by the tail," laughed Rex. "She's the one. Believe me, she's the one."

"Yes, hmmm. Thank you for that Rex. Looking at my watch I believe we've run out of time and so this meeting is officially over. Thank you Recorder for a job well done. I will make arrangements to meet with each of you individually over the coming six months." Several around the table thought, *Who put him in charge?"*

"Six months is good timing, it fits in with our next gathering," said Sophia.

"Yes I know it is, that's why I suggested it."

Not everybody survived their one to ones with Max.

*

From her very beginnings in the Organisation Margaret was for changing it. In her early days she established a cell of Blind Operatives in key political positions right under the nose of her Counsellor. According to Margaret her Counsellor was a member of the old farts' club and was therefore part of the problem, especially as, in her opinion, he wasn't controlling his Units as he should. It was the swinging '60s but Beethoven was playing in his head in an era driven by the music of the young.

It should be explained that a Blind Operative is one who is unknowingly directed to do the bidding of the Organisation while never having been recruited by it. Some 'Potentials' who drop off the lists become Blind Operatives. This is good business. Having invested so much time and effort in the Potentials it would be a waste to simply cut loose those who didn't make the grade. Better to use them for the benefit of the Organisation. The thing that originally brought Potentials to the attention of the Organisation was probably still there inside them and it's the job of Counsellors to find it and direct it. Blind Operatives, just like Operatives, are not on the payroll of the Organisation which makes them cost effective as assets.

Some of those that dropped off the lists were recruited as Sentinels. Some of those who blindly followed orders became

Sentinels. Those that kill without compunction become Sentinels. Psychopaths become Sentinels. Margaret's future had been discussed during personnel reviews and had been recommended for the Sentinels for her red work but Rex blocked the move. He said she was far too valuable to the Organisation where she was.

*

In the absence of control Margaret assumed control, while operating under the premise of; "It is better to beg forgiveness than seek permission, do what you need to do to get the job done." It was so in Machiavelli's day; "in the absence of power a Prince must take power". It's exactly the same thing… in principle. For this to work, Margaret's background, upbringing and education came to bear. Taking control is second nature to people like her. They feel they are born to it and in many ways they are. She'd led others all her life, from the time in the bomb shelter to school sports days to her Pony Club days to local Gymkhanas to her charity work. It was Margaret's way; it was always Margaret's way and especially so with people from lower socioeconomic backgrounds because they were used to being led. Margaret was the organiser, the leader, the one in charge, the one they listened to, the one they followed, the one they obeyed. They all willingly fell in behind her. She was her true mother's daughter in that regard.

*

Following being reported by her Counsellor to his Controller for the unsanctioned recruitment of Blind Operatives, Margaret was summoned to the Organisation's Global HQ in Half Moon Street for a reprimand, or possibly worse. In her Counsellor's opinion she'd overstepped the mark and needed a "good carpeting". She waited for her turn to be admitted to the Controller's office. There were a lot of people in to see the Controller that day. *Surely they can't all be in for a reprimand?* she thought. Though there were eight people ahead of her Margaret was called in ahead of them.

"Follow me," was all the PA said to Margaret and, turning, he mince-walked ahead of her, knocking on the Controller's office door and opening it before being invited to enter. He obviously knew the ropes.

"Sit down. No, not there… there!" said the PA pointing at a chair by the wall. "Miss Rotheram, sir."

"Miss Rotheram? Ah, good, I've been looking forward to this. You've been making quite a name for yourself Miss Rotheram. Please don't speak," said the Controller while holding the flat of his hand toward Margaret in anticipation of her attempting to get her defence in early. "You seem to be, what some might call 'a loose cannon'. Would you agree? I said not to speak."

"If I can't speak then how can I answer your questions?" replied Margaret in her now signature tone of voice while holding the Controller in the icy grip of her pale blue eyes. He felt as if the temperature of the room had gone down a few degrees and cleared his throat.

"Now I see what they mean. It's clear to me that you're in need of something more to do. A challenge if you will. So, here it comes. Are you ready young lady? Effective immediately you are promoted to Counsellor. You'll take over as Counsellor for the Operatives run by your present Counsellor."

"May I ask why?"

"You tell me. Why do you think you're being given this opportunity?"

"In my opinion my Counsellor is…" Margaret hesitated as her Counsellor quietly slipped into the room just within the periphery of her vision.

"Go on Miss Rotheram, you were saying about your Counsellor."

"In my opinion my Counsellor is lazy, incompetent and ineffective and should be put out to pasture."

"Is that it?"

"Isn't that enough?" Margaret turned to stare at her Counsellor before continuing. "He's not doing the job that needs to be done. The job of Counsellor is a very important one as it controls front line Operatives and I don't feel… no, I don't believe… no, I know… that he has neither their respect nor their confidence; he certainly doesn't have mine. He needs to go and the sooner the better." Margaret crossed her arms and legs and turned to face the Controller again.

"What do you say to that old thing?" asked the Controller of the Counsellor.

"A bit harsh I'd say old chap. I've done my bit and I try my best and—"

"Stop blithering for God's sake Godfrey. Yes, Miss Rotheram, I agree with you, he's all those things and more besides but he's got more contacts than any other of my Counsellors. He's worth his weight in gold which is why I'm creating a special position for him and moving you into his shoes. Everybody knows exactly what he is and would probably have said the same thing about him as you've just said. The answer to my question though was simple and has nothing to do with your rationale. You displayed initiative and we applaud the use of initiative, when correctly applied of course. Do you feel you have an apology to make to Godfrey?"

"No, I don't. I stand by what I said and, what's more, if there are any more like him wandering around this place you need to create special positions for them too and move people into their roles who can do the job."

"I'll take your opinion under advisement. Now you two need to get together for a hand over of responsibilities. I hope that's not going to be too awkward for you after what you've just said about your former boss. He'll tell you everything you'll need to know for now, including when I want my reports and how I like them. And if you find you don't like the way I run things then, who knows, you might well find yourself sitting in my seat one day."

Next stop Controller, mused Margaret and smiled.

After barely two days with her former boss Margaret had extracted what information she needed to take over from him. She now had 120 Operatives under her plus her 32 Blind Operatives. Hers was a large Unit for the time as most had only around 100 personnel in total, including so-called PAs.

*

As a Counsellor, Margaret Rotheram was willing to listen to her Operatives' ideas but with no guaranty she'd implement them. Many ideas she did implement she gave credit for them coming from an Operative, though she never named them. This policy of anonymity proved useful when implementing her own ideas. Not that Margaret's changes were draconian but many were concerned with tightening up administration and nobody wants tighter admin as it leaves less wriggle room. She wasn't scared of putting controversial policies in place but like most people she wanted to be loved. She'd always been that way and was surprised to discover that Machiavelli disagreed with her; "It is better to be feared than loved," he wrote. He also wrote about people needing to understand that you knew how to be the opposite of kind. This fitted Margaret to a 'T'.

All Margaret's moves were being closely monitored by the Chancellor and reported up to the Mandarins. Just a single Mandarin latterly as all the others seemed to have become less involved for some reason. On the side-lines, Rex was watching and waiting for his moment to strike.

*

Margaret's reign as Counsellor was relatively short lived. It seemed no sooner had she taken up the position than a Controller vacancy opened up, which she was appointed to unopposed, thanks to Rex. In turn, Margaret promoted one of her deadliest Operatives, Lisette, to take over as Counsellor of what had become the best performing Unit across the entire Organisation. Margaret saw a good deal of herself in Lisette with the exception of the sex side of things which 'Lizzie' was reputed to take to extremes. Also, in Margaret's opinion, Lisette took far too many recreational drugs, but that might work to her advantage, she thought.

Not many Controllers die in the job but Margaret's had. Generally, once Controllers or Governors reach a certain age, or they lose their edge, they are put out to pasture in some role glad-handing big wigs or making deals or alliances for the benefit of the Organisation. Seldom does retirement result in premature death.

Rumours begun by an old school-style Governor, Sir Jeremy Hawksmith, spread like wildfire that Margaret had killed her Controller and as, he claimed, she had something on the Chancellor he had no alternative but to promote her into her dead boss' shoes. Margaret heard the rumours but did nothing to dispel them. She liked the notoriety. The Mandarins liked it too as it meant everybody was watching her and not noticing the things that were going on around them.

Yes, she'd been fast tracked but in truth she was outperforming her peers, *so why shouldn't I be given the opportunity to show what I can really do?* she thought. *Next stop Governor,* mused Margaret, toasting to her success and smiling.

*

Controllers, unlike Operatives and some Counsellors, do not hold down external jobs. The Organisation is their employer. Margaret, however, was used to working hard and so kept working for the Advertising/PR Consultancy she'd fought so hard for a partnership in. It seemed she was one of those people that the more she did the more she was able to do. Besides, her husband was the senior partner in the firm so she could come and go pretty much as she pleased. This didn't satisfy her Governor though. He demanded she quit her job as he particularly didn't like her working with her husband as he believed that she could find herself in a conflict of interests which might force him to '*act to protect the interests of the Organisation*'. A threat which Margaret did not take lightly.

*

After six months as Controller, one day, Margaret asked a question out aloud of nobody in particular.

"Am I not doing the job right?"

"Sorry? What?" asked Margaret's PA. "I didn't quite catch—"

"What the hell do these people do all day?" Margaret was doing her Controller's job standing on her head and was becoming bored and bored people soon become mischievous.

"Madame Controller, you have to keep yourself ready for when something happens. Don't you worry, something will happen and when it does then you'll be rushed off your feet."

I need a new PA, thought Margaret. "Where's Lisette?" she asked her existing PA.

"Let me check her diary. Ah yes, she's reviewing the lists of Potentials."

"Call her and get her to come in immediately. Is it unusual for a Controller to have two PAs?"

"Why do you ask?"

"I'm going to light a fire under this place to get things moving and to do that I'm going to need another PA."

"You're getting rid of me, aren't you?" whined the aging PA, her voice tinged with resignation.

"Not at all," Margaret lied, "Lisette is more used to my ways and with what I have in mind my PAs are going to operate more like a war council than bookers of restaurant tables."

As it turned out, the aged PA was perfect in the role of a War Council PA having served in SOE during WW II. She had operated behind enemy lines for over two years before being captured and tortured by the Gestapo. She'd been due to face a firing squad but was rescued just in the nick of time by advancing Allied soldiers.

*

Margaret's success caused consternation amongst the other Controllers as it was making them all look bad. In fact, she made the job look so easy. They weren't achieving similar results despite often having more resources. Margaret was the golden girl and each of the Controllers recognised the danger she presented.

*

A meeting of the newly formed Central Committee of Mandarins.
"I told you. She's everything I predicted she would be and more. She has them all looking over their shoulders so they don't have time to notice what is really going on," bragged Rex. Classic Mandarins, using the Organisation's own methods against it.

"What makes you think she'll cooperate when the time comes?"

"That's the beauty of it, we won't require her cooperation. She'll do all the hard work and then we'll make our move. By the time she realises what's going on it'll be too late."

"I'm still not convinced she's right for us. She's too headstrong, too arrogant and—"

"And ambitious. Don't forget ambitious."

"She was always ambitious and now she's power hungry. She'll do whatever it takes to become Madame Chancellor once we dangle the carrot under her nose." Rex checked reaction around the room before continuing. "We need to get her promoted to Chancellor and soon."

"It'll be risky. If we rush things—"

"Time is of the essence. If we don't act now we'll lose our advantage."

"What about the others? They'll be against what we're doing.

They have their own plans for the Organisation. They want to see a new structure at the top. One that isn't so autocratic."

"Actually, I agree with them on that point. It'll enable us to place people around her and report everything she does back to us."

"What if she decides to run things her own way?"

"We'll make certain conditions to her appointment. After all, we choose the Chancellor."

"But there are only four of us… we're in the minority. We'll be outvoted."

"I only need to change the mind of one of the others and then we'll be the majority. I'm sure that even I can change one little mind," said Max feigning modesty.

"We must be careful not to alert the others to what we're doing."

"I know for a fact that Allegra will be against our plans," said Sophia. "She's said as much," she added sealing the fate of the woman she'd hated for years. She'd been looking for an excuse to eliminate Allegra and this was her opportunity to do so without any repercussions.

"When the time comes, I shall deal with Allegra," said Max.

ALTCAR

Early one Sunday morning in May 1968, Sergeant Huggard called at the Frosts' house to ask Mary if Michael would be attending the various summer camps at Altcar with the Royal Tank Regiment. She shouted upstairs to ask him if he knew anything about this and why hadn't he told her about it if he did. "It costs a lot of money and we don't have any," Michael shouted back downstairs. Mary said they might be able to afford it as she had been doing overtime and was desperate to send Michael to Altcar with his Cadet mates. The real reason she was able to afford to send Michael to Altcar was that Joseph had been sending her money for the children but she used it to buy groceries and pay household bills. While she herself wouldn't accept money from her former husband she was happy to use money he sent for the kids to run the home. Classic Mary; independent, defiant and with her own unique logic. Money apart, Mary would make any sacrifice for Michael if she thought it meant him having friends, real friends, not the ones inside his head despite him having told her many times that they were not friends.

*

The Cadets congregated outside the barracks in Bootle as they waited for the coach to take them to Altcar. Walking toward them was a group of TA Soldiers who were going to Altcar for the Inter-Regimental games. As the two groups jostled to get the best seats on the coach Michael turned to look behind him and standing right there was Buckhead. They recognised one another instantly.

"Awright gobshite," said Buckhead, digging Michael in his ribs. "Look who it isn't? Fancy seein' you 'ere. Bet ye never thought y'd be seein' me again, did ye eh?"

"Do you know him?" asked Tommy Munroe.

"Yes. His name is Buckhead. We had a fight once."

"Jesus, he's massive. He must've battered ye."

"I knocked him out."

"Yeah, right," scoffed Tommy. "Anyway, he doesn't seem too happy with you so I'd watch me back if I was you, he looks a nasty bastard."

When the coach arrived at Altcar the Cadets were separated from the Soldiers and given their own area of the camp. A Sergeant yelled at them to, "Get a move on and assemble on the parade ground in five minutes."

Their first exercise of the day involved Cadets of various Battalions de-tanking and taking up defensive positions. Four Cadets at a time loaded themselves into a tank before simulating it being hit and rendered inoperable. For most Cadets this was their first experience of Thunderflashes. The bang they made frightened the life out of them. "They're as loud as grenades!" shrieked one Cadet covering his ears. Everything went well until the turn of the tenth group of Cadets, commanded by Leading Cadet Munroe. After de-tanking, instead of taking up defence positions, they broke cover despite orders not to engage with the enemy under any circumstances.

"I'm gonna shoot something!" Tommy yelled to the amusement of those around him. Following an heroic charge, Tommy leapt on top of the tank while making 'ta, ta, ta, ta, ta, brrrrrrrrrrrrr, pyoo, pyoo' machine-gun shooting noises and spraying his wooden SSMG around like a hose pipe. All the Cadets fell about laughing.

"Munwoe!" shouted a voice the Tank Cadets recognised. "Is that you Munwoe? Get down off that tank at once and come here! Put that Cadet on a charge Corpwal."

"Oh shit," snarled Leading Cadet Munroe more or less to himself. "It's Captain Jones. He's such a divvy."

"Listen to me," said a uniformed Officer the Cadets didn't recognise, "Captain Jones is a highly decorated Soldier and he's as tough as you're going to find anywhere. Just because he talks funny doesn't mean he is funny. He was formerly a Captain in the Royal Marines and has seen proper action!" Cadet Munroe shook his head in surprise. "So show some respect Mon Amie, okay?"

"Oui Mon Amie," replied Tommy saluting the Officer in the unfamiliar uniform to the utter delight and laughter of the Cadets.

*

Later that day, during the Cadets' target practice on the rifle range, Buckhead snuck up on Michael while he was shooting from the prone position and stood on his ankles, making him scream in agony.

"What are you doing to that Cadet, Lance Corporal? Are you trying to hurt him?" shouted the Officer in the strange uniform.

"No sir. I'm just making sure he learns to lay with his feet flat on the ground while shooting so he doesn't get himself shot in the heels, sir. He'll thank me for it someday."

"Well Lance Corporal that won't be today. Are you alright Cadet?"

"Yes sir."

"Can you carry on?"

"Yes sir."

"Then carry on Cadet." The Officer then whispered to Buckhead, "If you do anything like that again I will kick you in the bollocks so hard they'll appear as lumps on the top of your thick skull. Do we understand one another?" Lance Corporal Buckhead nodded. "Now

Cadet," said the Officer to Michael, "I noticed you're not a bad shot but you need to control your breathing when you shoot. Take a few deep breaths and when you're ready to fire breathe out completely and give the trigger a gentle squeeze. See how that works for you."

After giving his legs a good shake to sort his knees out, Michael laid back down. He breathed in and out a couple of times, let out a long slow breath, sighted the target and rapidly fired ten rounds.

"What's the hurry Cadet?" asked the Officer.

"I was running out of breath, sir, so I fired all the rounds so I could breathe in again." The Officer laughed at Michael's misunderstanding his advice; though he wasn't to know about Michael's respiratory problems resulting from his nana's old wives' tar treatment for whooping cough which was still giving him breathing difficulties.

"Perhaps I should have mentioned that you can breathe between shots. In future, take a deep breath then breathe out a little for each shot. Okay? If you haven't done that well you can have another ten rounds as I didn't explain myself properly." The target-sighter reported all ten rounds had hit the bullseye with less than a two-inch spread. *Very impressive*, thought the Officer in the strange uniform. "I don't think you need to shoot again, Cadet. By the way, what is your name?"

"It's Michael Frost, sir."

"Okay Cadet Frost, well done. Maybe I'll see you later. Dismissed."

*

Back in their bivouac, the Cadets were sitting around talking and generally messing about as they prepared to cook their evening meal.

"You lot, come with me," shouted a TA Soldier emerging onto the scene.

"What for?" asked Leading Cadet Munroe who was about the same age as the TA Soldier.

"Are you questioning an order, Cadet?"

"No, Corporal."

The Cadets were force marched over sand dunes in the direction of the sea and the stink of cigarette smoke.

"Well if it isn't Annie Oakley and her girlfriends," sneered Lance Corporal Buckhead when the Cadets arrived at a group of old Nissen huts near the sea shore.

"What's goin' on Buckhead?" asked one of the TA Soldiers.

"I owe this little turd a hiding," said Buckhead pointing at Michael.

"Get lost Buckhead, he's only a kid, leave him alone," shouted another TA Soldier. "I thought we were just gonna chuck them in the sea or somethin'. I'm not havin' anythin' to do with givin' a kid a hidin'."

"Well piss off then and don't forget to pick yer tampons up on yer way out." Several of the TA Soldiers laughed at Buckhead's taunt just to be a part of his TA gang. Pointing to the other Cadets, Buckhead shouted, "Youz lot can piss off back to the barracks and yer'd better keep yer gobs shut or I'll burst yez."

"Michael told me that he knocked you out once and I didn't believe him but I do now ye big chicken ye," shouted Leading Cadet Munroe from the front of the group of Cadets. "If you touch him you'll have to take us all on. C'mon lads let's burst him." The rest of the Cadets looked very unsure but knew they had to back Tommy and Michael up.

"Yeah!!!!" they screamed, their squeaky voices crackling as they prepared to attack the TA Soldiers.

"There's no need for anything like that," said the Officer in the strange uniform, appearing from out of the sand dunes. "If Lance Corporal Buckhead is so keen for a fight then he can fight me. But the proper way. You and I will meet in the boxing ring tomorrow at 0700 hours. Do you have any objection to that Lance Corporal Buckhead?"

"I've got no argument with you sir," grovelled Buckhead.

"Are you declining my invitation Lance Corporal?"

"Yes sir, I am," answered Buckhead, his voice barely audible. The TA Soldiers looked away, some in disgust and some in laughter.

"Did you really knock Lance Corporal Buckhead out Cadet Frost?"

"Yes sir."

"Do you think you can do it again?"

"Yes sir," repeated Michael. The Officer in the strange uniform regarded Michael for a few seconds before replying.

"I'm sure you could but now is not the right place or time. There's a regimental boxing tournament the day after tomorrow and, who knows, you two might get the opportunity to sort your differences out in the ring. Now, everybody return to the encampment. Immediately!"

That night the Tank Cadets were so agitated they couldn't sleep. "Nobody told us about no boxing tournament," was the main topic of conversation as Tank Cadets, unlike other Cadets, don't ordinarily box. They had a bad feeling about the 'day after tomorrow'. What they didn't realise was boxing wasn't compulsory and were in little danger of an angry Infantry Cadet rearranging their beautiful faces unless they volunteered to box.

"Hey Michael, do you really think you can knock that big turd Buckhead out?" asked one of the Cadets.

"Yes."

"He's really big though. How long ago was it that you knocked him out?"

"About four years ago."

"Was he big then?"

"Not as big."

"Well, anyway, I doubt they'll let a Cadet fight a Soldier so you should be alright. Night night."

*

The exercises the following day involved Red on Blue scenarios. The Tank Cadets didn't do very well as they weren't allowed to use Tanks.

"Are you looking forward to the boxing tournament tomorrow Cadet Frost?" asked the Officer in the unfamiliar uniform.

"What's that uniform, sir?" asked Michael.

"It's a French Artillery Officer's uniform which I usually wear when I take part in camps such as this. I'm just an observer. I have no authority here but I'm tolerated." Which was sufficient explanation for Michael.

The final day of camp began with Cadets and TA Soldiers taking on the obstacle course. It was a bit of fun but fiercely competitive. Once again, the Tank Cadets didn't cover themselves in glory.

"Before we break camp this afternoon," began the Camp Commander, "there will be the traditional end of camp boxing tournament. Any Cadet not wishing to take part please raise your hand now." The Camp Commander briefly looked around before continuing. "Good, that's everybody in then. Well done chaps." The Tank Cadets kept their hands down as they felt they couldn't raise them with everybody looking on.

"Right," shouted an NCO who was larger than an outhouse door, "those of you who've boxed before go to rings A and B, all others go to rings C and D." Michael was the only Tank Cadet who made his way toward rings A and B.

"Where the hell are you goin' Michael?" asked Tommy Munroe.

"I've boxed before so…"

"Yeah, I get it but why don't ye come with us, it'll be a laugh and ye won't lose yer good looks," joked Tommy to Michael's disappearing back.

As might be expected, Michael breezed through all his bouts; watched carefully by the Officer in the French Artillery uniform. Following the Round Robin, the remaining names were put into a hat for a pot-luck draw. Apart from Buckhead, nobody wanted to get drawn against Michael, the only remaining Cadet, as to do so would bring shame whether they be winner or loser.

"You have a very interesting style of boxing," remarked the Officer in the French uniform.

"I like to box that way."

"How long have you been boxing?"

"My cousin Timbo taught me to box when I was five."

"Five! And you've kept it up?" Michael nodded. "Have you boxed for a club?"

"I boxed for Penrhyn Street School and Timbo's boxing club until he went to jail. I just box for my Grammar school now and I learnt Karate at the Huyton Dojo. They do Kenjutsu there… I like swords. I fence for my school but I like Japanese swords best." This was a lot of information for an often monosyllabic Michael to spew out all in one go.

"Does anybody here know you've done so much boxing?"

"Sergeant Huggard does. He's the Policeman who takes us to Cadets."

Okay, thought the French Officer smiling to himself, *perhaps Lance Corporal Buckhead deserves his opportunity for satisfaction after all.*

Pushing the Lieutenant aside who was about to make the draw for the next round of boxing matches, the French Officer shoved his hand into the upturned Camp Commander's hat containing the names of the remaining boxers. "First out of the hat is… Lance Corporal Buckhead and he will be fighting… Cadet Frost of the Royal Tank Regiment." The Tank Cadets who'd joined the audience thought this was too much of a coincidence. There being an unwritten rule that whenever Soldiers come up against Cadets they go easy on them, everybody, except a certain few, expected the fight to be a bit of a farce as it's frowned upon if allowances aren't made when fighting Cadets in boxing tournaments.

As soon as the bell sounded Buckhead flew out of his corner and straight at Michael who simply back-peddled twice around the ring behind his jab. Unable to catch up with his opponent, Buckhead cried out in frustration, "C'mon you chicken bastard, come here where I can hit you," his annunciation being greatly improved by his gum shield. Michael, unmoved by this invitation, remained in his Southpaw stance waiting for his opponent to make his move. Buckhead advanced behind a solid jab but, being more a plodder than a boxer, Michael easily stepped inside Buckhead's lead and let rip with a left hook to the ribs. Taking a few steps backwards, he changed to orthodox stance and did the same to the ribs on Buckhead's left side. Both shots were delivered with such power and ferocity they made the audience wince. Buckhead then came swinging at Michael with everything he had. If he'd have connected with any one of the shots the bout would've been over. Having put everything into round one Buckhead was all out of steam.

When the bell went for the second round Buckhead stayed in his corner, making it look like he'd thrown the towel in. Everybody began jeering. As soon as Michael looked away Buckhead pounced, hitting him with good straight left jabs and finishing with a solid right cross; leaving Michael on the seat of his pants looking up at Buckhead who was jumping around the ring whooping wildly despite the boos of the crowd. "Four, Five, Six, Se…" Michael was back up on his feet before the referee could count seven. He slapped his gloves together, did a little hop, Timbo style, and moved towards Buckhead who, without Michael laying a glove on him, went down on one knee and took a count to the boos of the crowd.

Michael stood over Buckhead, fists ready, waiting for him to get up; he would not take his eyes off him again. Getting to his feet at the count of eight Buckhead reached out in an attempt to entice Michael into a glove tap to show there were no hard feelings. He declined the offer. With devastating speed Michael rained punches and combinations down on Buckhead from all angles. Once again, Buckhead went down on one knee and took a count which the referee decided was enough. Flattening his palms parallel to the canvas, and crossing them over each other three times, the referee indicated that the fight was over.

Buckhead foot-dragged his way back to his corner like a spoilt sullen teenager before slumping down on his stool. As soon as Michael's back was turned, Buckhead leapt up and ran at him. A scream from the crowd of "look out!" was shouted as Buckhead closed the distance to Michael. Hearing the warning shout, Michael rolled, Paratrooper style, to his right; just as he'd done many times as a Bridge-Dropper. Quickly setting himself into a Karate stance, Michael delivered a perfectly executed mawashi geri roundhouse kick to the left side of Buckhead's jaw. Lance Corporal Buckhead was out cold before he hit the canvas. The crowd gasped an "Oooooooooh" and then an "Ahhhhhhh" at the sight. Few of them had any idea what they'd just witnessed but the French Officer knew exactly what he'd seen. *A recruit? A Sentinel perhaps?* he thought.

The French Officer sidled up to Michael. "That was very impressive Cadet Frost, I can tell that you're a special fighter. A very special fighter indeed. Promise me, do not fight any more today. Tell them you're under orders not to continue in case you damage anybody. Okay?" Michael looked puzzled. "It's a joke. But seriously, no more fighting today. Okay? I shall see you again young man."

*

Robert Buckhead never amounted to much; he lived an ordinary life; worked hard; got married; had three children, all of whom turned out okay; was faithful to his wife; was a good dad; began reading books when he was forty and realised what he'd missed out on all his life. A late developer, Buckhead obtained an OU degree in philosophy. One night in May 2015 he was watching a News at Ten report about the abduction of Mikhail Morozov, a Russian émigré, by ISBJ extremists, outside the entrance to Swiss Cottage tube station in London. Buckhead felt sorry for him and thought about what Mr Morozov's family must be going through. He didn't recognise Morozov's face, or deduce that the name translated to Michael Frost in English, which was just as well for him that he didn't.

*

An Organisation conversation.

"How very good of you to be on time for once. How did things go at Altcar? Well? Do you have your report ready to hand?"

"My train was on time for once. Things went very well and, yes, I do have my report with me; thank you for asking!" snapped the French Captain.

"Very well, let's start with the Potentials."

"Okay. List A; most of them are making satisfactory progress, they're doing the right things and showing the right signs. A few are falling behind academically which, from experience, usually indicates they've plateaued so I doubt they will pass the next stage. I estimate we'll get an overall ten to fifteen percent yield, which is about normal."

"Are there any potential Doublers in list A do you think? There usually are you know, either one way or the other, which is fine by us but probably not so fine for some of the others."

"I have my suspicions about a Major in the Royal Tank Regiment."

"A Major you say? Not a Captain?"

"No, a Major. Next. I'm proposing to strike off between fifty and sixty percent of lists B and C." The French Captain paused for a comment. There being none he continued. "There was an unexpected bonus. A Cadet, name of Frost, with the Royal Tank Regiment."

"That regiment has done very well for us in the past. A Cadet you say? He must be too young for us surely? Are you proposing to add him to the lists? What's so special about him?"

"I think he may be suitable for list B, depending on how well he does academically. Apparently, he has a gift for languages, so who knows where he might end up? The Foreign Office? A desk in MI6? Other than that he's an absolute fighting machine, so, potentially, he could end up as a Sentinel."

"What's his background?"

"Nothing spectacular. Very ordinary really. He lives in a small house on a council estate in a place called Huyton in Liverpool. He attends a good Grammar school and represents his school in boxing and fencing."

"He sounds very ordinary to me. My instincts tell me not to allow this, but go ahead, convince me," uttered the Controller arrogantly. The French Officer read from his report.

"His full name is Michael Frost. He's a Grammar school pupil; excellent in mathematics and practically fluent in German and French and, get this… Russian too. He's boxed ever since the age of five and at a boxing tournament at Altcar last week I rigged the draw for him to fight an old adversary, a full-grown TA Soldier, who was big, muscular and aggressive. He never laid a glove on the boy until he cheated. After the fight, this Soldier went to attack Frost from behind. The boy instinctively rolled away and regained his balance before delivering a mawashi geri with such perfection that he KO'd the Soldier. It was beautiful to watch. I spoke with him after the fight."

"You did what! That's against protocol. I cannot emphasise enough just how risky behaviour like that is to us. You never know who's watching at places like Altcar. It's a recruitment ground for all sorts of organisations, including ours and yours."

"I do know that, Sir Ronald," replied the French Officer dryly, "but time was short as we had this meeting scheduled. I've done some checking into Frost's background and though he's not a typical prospect he has some remarkable talents. During my time I've recruited dozens of agents and I feel it in my bones that Frost will be a top recruit. I doubt he'll ever be an Intelligence Officer but he'll make a damn good Operative or a deadly Sentinel. I'm convinced of it. I'd stake my reputation on it."

"Fair enough, Monsieur Lefort, it's your funeral. I do hope you don't live to regret this decision of yours. He's your responsibility. Understand? I want regular six-monthly reports on him and if at any time things don't look right you must drop him. Don't get so close to Potentials in future, you know the rules and I will not tolerate… anyway, place him on list B for now. What's next?"

The French Officer's report continued for two hours.

"Well done Lefort, you're a damn good man. It's a pity you're on the other side so to speak. Do you think you'll ever convince the French Splinter to heal the wounds?"

"I genuinely hope so Sir Ronald. Do you think you'll ever convince your High Council to play their part?" The Field Marshall looked at the French Officer and grinned.

"Touché Monsieur Lefort."

*

An Organisation conversation.

"It's me. Have you reported to your MI6 paymasters yet?"

"I have, thank you very much."

"Where's my copy? It's late."

"Please, a little patience. MI6 isn't a lending library you know."

"An Operative there has already seen your report and she mentioned there's a new potential from the Royal Tank Regiment. She says he's a square peg and doesn't understand how he made the lists. Tell me about him."

"He's on list B as a potential. His name is Michael Frost."

"How old is he?"

"As you've had a briefing you already know how old he is."

"What's so special about this boy? He beat up a thug, so what."

"It was the way he did it. He destroyed him. His fighting style is unique… he has such raw strength, power and speed. Phenomenal. Very impressive. He's an A student in mathematics and fluent, or as near as damn it, I understand, in German and French and Russian. With his language skills I'm certain I can get him inside MI6. I doubt he'll ever make Intelligence Officer, he's not made from the right sort of stuff."

"What's next for him?"

"I'll start planting the idea in his head of him signing up."

"Where to? Not the guards I hope!"

"Of course not, I'll want him where I can keep an eye on him."

"So, the Royal Tank Regiment then?"

"Of course, where else? He'll do—"

"Are there any familial connections?"

"No, of course not. But talking about familial connections, what news on Count Bouvier bringing his son Albert into the French Splinter?"

"Very sad news about Albert, I'm afraid. He was found floating in a lake at his father's chateau the other day."

"Drowned?"

"No, crossbow bolt through his right temple."

"How did Bouvier take it?"

"Very badly, I hear, which is understandable, but he ignored the rules, which makes him a liability." The Controller carefully considered his words before speaking again. "The French Splinter has always thought it can just do as it pleases. But what it does affects us all. We regularly turn a blind eye to their antics, and acts of nepotism, but we will not allow dynasty building! The old Count still has young Hugo and presumably he won't ignore our warning. I mean, after all, he'll want to keep Hugo safe as he's fast running out of heirs to hand his little Froggy Empire on to. No doubt he'll retaliate by starting up a little war. They do come in handy from time to time though, don't they?"

"Is little Hugo going to be taken care of?"

"Oh goodness me no. If we take care of little Hugo then the Count will be a man who has nothing to lose and a man that has nothing to lose is a very dangerous man. In trying to protect little Hugo he'll suffocate him and then things will get interesting. Are you going back to your day job any time soon?"

"I am. By the bye, who's the Operative that you mentioned? I'm unaware of any female Operatives at MI6 who have ready access to reports at my level."

"You know the rules, Jones!" snapped the Controller. "One day you may rise high enough to see the curvature of the Earth itself but until then keep your head down and your arse up and don't ask stupid questions. Report on time in future. Goodbye."

THE ROVING AMBASSADOR

Margaret's life, it appeared, couldn't get any better. She was riding on the crest of a wave of success and her reputation in the Organisation was going from strength to strength. Many wondered how much farther she could go. True, the Organisation was a meritocracy, but it had been fifty years since the last Madame Chancellor and twenty since the appointment of a Madame Governor. In her opinion the Organisation was nothing more than a Boys' Club, "The Old Farts' Club", as she often referred to it as. "It's little more than a den of misogyny." She'd built her reputation on bringing about change and so she had it in her head to bring change to the very top of the Organisation itself, if she ever got the opportunity. *Why not? If I don't try I'll never know.*

Her ambitions apart, her new job just wasn't enough for Margaret. She was beginning to think that her desire had been misdirected. The upper half of the greasy pole of the Organisation wasn't turning out to be what she thought it would. She needed a new path, or maybe a return to an old path and then try another route. She'd relished in her work as an Operative because it was exciting, often dangerous, filled with intrigue and gave vent to lusts she didn't realise she had. When promoted to Counsellor she felt she was more of a nurse maid than anything else. Now that she was a Controller, well, life was positively dull. *Perhaps she was too young for the job?* she'd thought more than once, but not for the reasons her peers might think. The job of Controller was, in essence, an administrative role and she was a girl of action. Now, with everything set up and running on greased wheels, there was nothing for her to do that lit her fire. She no longer sprang out of bed of a morning and raced into work filled with enthusiasm determined to make the day count.

*

As Rex passed the door to Margaret's office he slowed his pace and glanced in at her before walking on. He then walked backwards past her door and glanced at her again, but this time with his eyes crossed. He walked to and fro, forwards and backwards, three more times. Every time he passed the door he pulled a different face at her. He looked so ridiculous it made her laugh.

Ever since Rex had moved in down the hall they'd seen very little of one another as she'd purposely avoided him. She never trusted him but he was always such wonderful fun to be around. He was very witty and humorous, so she couldn't help but like him in an odd sort of way.

"Now Margaret, I'm no trick-cyclist but you look depressed to me."

"Is it that obvious?"

"I keep on telling her to buck up," interjected Lisette.

"Yes, thank you Lizzie."

"What's wrong old girl?"

"Old girl?"

"Just a figure of speech, old thing. Come on, tell Uncle Rex what's wrong."

"No matter what I do it doesn't seem to make the slightest difference. Lisette, can you leave us for a moment and close the door behind you please." After Lisette had left the office Rex spoke.

"You are making a difference, a huge difference. Just look at what you've achieved."

"What have I achieved? I got promoted, so what."

"It's nothing to do with getting promoted you silly sod, it's what's happened to this place since you arrived. Look at them, they're like Rabbits caught in headlights. You're the tonic we've needed for some time now."

"Am I? I don't feel much like a tonic."

"We'd become too inward looking… stagnant. We weren't making any progress in peace talks with the Splinters and the numbers had plateaued; fallen actually in some regions in real terms. Since you arrived on the scene people are looking over their shoulders. They're making the efforts they should have been making for years. You've shown them it can be done and how to do it. They're all copying you Margaret."

"So what if they are? That just means they'll catch me up and then what? Eh?"

"They'll never catch you up because you're an innovator. They'll play catch-up forever while you lead them on to new heights."

"I want to go back to being an Operative… Uncle Rex." Margaret said 'Uncle Rex' like a coquettish little girl to tease and arouse him. "Is that possible? Can you fix that for me Uncle Rex? Can you do that? Hmmm?"

"It's been done before but I have another idea."

"Another one of your great ideas like the one that got me here in the first place?" Margaret replied caustically.

"Precisely old girl," Rex replied ignoring her tone of voice. "I have an idea for a role that will challenge you like never before. I'll need to talk it over with the Chancellor first and, if he's agreeable, then we'll have you in for a nice little chat."

"Shouldn't you discuss it with me first?"

"No," Rex answered and left Margaret's office whistling a tune she'd never heard before.

When Lisette returned to Margaret's office she asked what she and Rex had talked about. Margaret told her they'd talked about her going back to being an Operative. Lisette asked why she wanted to do that and Margaret replied, "I'm bored. Simple as that." Lisette said she knew exactly what Margaret was talking about as she was bored too, adding that if she did go back to being an Operative could she please put a good word in for her for the vacant Controller position. Margaret returned Lisette a straight-mouth smile that said it all. Lisette said she thought it unlikely that they'd just let her quit. Margaret insisted that she wasn't quitting, "it's a reassignment… or a realignment or whatever you want to call it." They talked about the conditions under which Margaret might return to being an Operative, what precedents there were and why succession planning in the Organisation needed updating. Margaret thought Lisette seemed to know an awful lot about the Organisation's policies for a Counsellor.

As it was nearing lunch Lisette asked Margaret if she fancied going to sit in Green Park to check out the talent. They laid down on the grass and stared at the rare blue sky. It'd been grey for months. While walking back to the office Margaret told Lisette that she'd made up her mind. She was going to move away from London and take up an Operative role in… she couldn't quite think where at the time but she thought it best to leave London; leave England perhaps. Lisette asked if her dark mood might be due to the miserable weather they'd been having lately. Margaret tutted and shook her head but smiled as she knew Lisette was trying to lift her spirits. They weren't friends exactly but the pair were as close as anybody could be in the friendless Organisation. They held hands crossing over Piccadilly from Green Park, each giving reassuring squeezes to the other. Back in the office Margaret typed her resignation letter.

As soon as the letter was finished Margaret walked down the corridor, straight past the Chancellor's PA and into his office. She didn't want to think about it in case she changed her mind, she just wanted to slap the envelope on his desk and stand there while he read it.

"He's not in," shouted the PA at Margaret's back.

"Where is he?"

"Out."

"When will he be back?"

"I have no idea. Whatever it is it wasn't in his diary. The Chancellor and Rex took off after he told him about his conversation with you." The PA thought he'd finished speaking but his anger got the better of him. "Look you, you might think you're the best thing since sliced bread but you need to show some respect and consideration for others. You think you can do exactly as you please and everybody has to lap it up. Well I think you're a shit. A selfish little shit. You've been handed everything on a silver platter but no, that's not good enough for you, is it? You've created mayhem here this past couple of years and now you want to walk away from the steaming pile of shit you created. You have no idea what the Chancellor has had to put up with because of you. Nobody likes you and they want you out but Rex thinks you're the next coming or something. To be honest love, I don't see it."

"Thank you for sharing your opinion but I am not to blame for the decades of neglect and mismanagement that has brought about the appalling state of affairs which—"

"Oh, put a sock in it. You need to take a good long look at yourself in the mirror, love. You don't know these people. You don't know what they've contributed. You don't know the sacrifices they've made."

"We all make sacrifices just to be here. I've left a letter on the Chancellor's desk. Please bring it to his attention as soon as he returns. I'll be in my office… waiting." The PA had gotten to her.

When Margaret returned to her office she asked Lisette to hold her calls and admit no one but the Chancellor's PA. Slamming the door behind her, Margaret sat facing out of her office window at the people in the offices of the building opposite. She wished she could turn back the clock on Rex's offer and pondered on the life she might have had.

*

A Mandarin and guests' conversation.

"Let's just let her go back to being an Operative. She's far too much trouble."

"People like her don't grow on trees you know."

"There are others."

"But they're not with us."

"Neither is she."

"She's young and an idealist and driven by ambition, all of which makes her perfect for our purposes. She's also very insecure. She'll jump at the opportunity of becoming Madame Chancellor when it's dangled in front of her. With the strings that will come with the job we'll have exactly what we want."

"Couldn't I just do it? There's really no need to go through all this palaver."

"If you do it it'll raise everybody's suspicions and then the Splinters will likely rally round to help them. The Governors must be removed before we can proceed, but not by you. It has to be by somebody else's hand and hers is perfect."

"But she wants to go back to being an Operative."

"Nonsense. She just needs a challenge, that's all. What's your plan Rex?"

"As you know, her vision is that the Organisation will become one again with the Splinters which she can't fulfil in her present role so I suggest we help her achieve her vision."

"How?"

"Haven't you been listening?" tsk tsked the Mandarin. "She wants to bring the Splinters back into the fold, which of course we do not want for a minute. So, what is your plan Rex?"

"We create a roving ambassadorial role for her. She can go out into the world to contact the Splinters and sound them out for a reconciliation. That should keep her busy until we're ready to make our move."

"Isn't that rather risky?"

"Granted, it doesn't come without its risks but knowing the conflicting ambitions of the Splinters she'll have her work cut out to get them round the same table."

"Then what?"

"We let time do our work for us as it always seems to. After a suitable period you'll resign and she'll win the vote to make her Madame Chancellor. She will see it as recognition for her efforts as roving ambassador. You'll need to set things up in order to—"

"Go straight to Chancellor without ever being a Governor? They'll suspect something. Can't we give it to Sir Jeremy Hawksmith? Let him have a go, I'm sure he'll—"

"Hawksmith is toxic plus his Faction is running its own agenda inside the Organisation."

"But," urged the Chancellor, "she's female, and far too young, too young by far, and a lot of the chaps won't like that. We haven't had a Madame Chancellor for many a year and—"

"It's always problems with you isn't it, Charles? Glass always half empty with you. We'll create a situation whereby she will be proposed and seconded to be entered into the race for the vacant Chair."

"A race? Why is it going to be a race? There hasn't been a race for hundreds of years. It always caused problems. Those who were unsuccessful were killed and the successful candidate slaughtered those Mandarins who hadn't voted for them. It was mayhem and it'll be mayhem again. No, we must not—"

"No? What do you mean 'no', Mr Chancellor?" The threat in the Mandarin's voice was palpable.

"Well, Herr Grodt, what I'm saying is races have caused problems in the past, that's why the Mandarins always choose the Chancellor. There's no race… no election… no competition. That's the way it's been for centuries for obvious reasons."

"In order for everybody to accept her she has to be seen to win a race. It's the only way."

"Please, Herr Grodt, consider Jem… Sir Jeremy again. At least let him be included in the list of candidates."

"Very well, Charles, I'll add him to the list of candidates. Happy?"

"What will happen to the unsuccessful candidates?"

"You need not concern yourself about that, they'll be looked after." The Chancellor failed to grasp the meaning behind Herr Grodt's words.

"As to our present predicament. Do you think you can talk her into her new role?"

"I won't need to, she'll jump at anything we put in front of her so long as it speaks to her ambitions and massages her ego."

"What about her PA? The young one, not the crabby old one."

"I think there's a certain amount of resentment and jealousy between her and her boss," lied Rex, "so I suggest we promote her to Controller once Margaret has officially vacated the role."

"That should be okay. It shouldn't be for very long anyway. Yes, we'll do that."

"Never mind her. What about me?" asked the Chancellor.

"There will soon be a vacancy on the Mandarin Council… perhaps even two." Herr Grodt paused to let his words hang in the air to allow their full effect to take hold of the Chancellor before continuing. "I always thought you'd make a good Mandarin, Charles," he lied.

The Chancellor's head was in a spin. "Me, a Mandarin? Oh yes, that will do nicely, very nicely." Charles felt much better about the plan now he'd practically been told he was getting a seat on the Mandarin Council. He'd go along with anything they wanted now.

*

When Jem, Sir Jeremy, was eventually told about Charles' pending retirement and the upcoming election for a new Chancellor, and that he was one of the candidates, he declined the Mandarin's proposal claiming that he was far too old for the job and that it should go to somebody younger; "someone with energy". His refusal surprised and shocked Herr Grodt, the Chancellor and Rex. None of them saw that coming. "Oh well," remarked Herr Grodt to Rex resignedly, "we'll have to put up with him for a while longer but not so the other four. I've made special arrangements for them on the big day."

*

On his return to Half Moon street, Rex went into Margaret's office despite Lisette telling him that she didn't want to be disturbed. As he passed Lisette, not for the first time, she asked him what he did, what his actual job was and for the same amount of times he tapped the side of his nose with his forefinger and whispered, "It's a secret." Like everybody else, Lisette found this side of nose tapping infuriating.

Rex didn't wait to be invited into Margaret's office, he simply popped his head around the door and told her to come with him to see the Chancellor. She asked if it was about her note. He asked, "What note?" but added it didn't matter and said they should have a chat first before going to see the Chancellor. Rex began by saying he had always thought very highly of her and that she shouldn't sacrifice all her good work by throwing away her career. He told her she needed to give serious consideration to a job offer the Chancellor was about to make her. She wanted to know what the job was and he told her that a position was being created especially for her that would totally occupy her time and energy. She was eager to know more. He whispered that the role was to help reunite the Organisation. Rex knew she'd be interested. He knew her better than she knew herself.

As soon as they entered the Chancellor's office the PA left the room, after having confessed all to his boss about his earlier outburst. He whispered a tearful apology to Margaret on his way out. The Chancellor sat swivelling in his chair fifteen degrees left and the same right from centre. He was fanning himself with the envelope containing Margaret's letter. He asked her if he should read her letter right then or wait until after he'd told her about an exciting new opportunity he'd thought up for her. Rex gave a grimacing smile at that one. She said she'd prefer to wait until after he'd told her what was on his mind. The Chancellor smiled at the way she put it. He liked her turn of phrase.

After the Chancellor told Margaret about the role he said he had in mind for her he asked if she needed some time to think about it. She said she did not. Accepting the job on the spot, Margaret moved swiftly to snatch her letter from the Chancellor's hand saying that there was no need for him to open it now. He looked at Rex and smiled. Rex looked at Margaret and smiled. She asked who'd be taking over from her. They said they hadn't had a chance to consider that question yet. The liars. Margaret suggested Lisette. They looked at one another and said in unison, "that's not a bad thought but don't say anything to her for the moment." They first wanted to ensure that Lisette would be beholden to them and not Margaret for her promotion.

The phrases that stuck most in Margaret's mind were; 'the role has an international dimension to it' and 'a unique opportunity to bring peace and stability to the Organisation'. *That will mean a lot of travelling,* she thought. *A lot of time away from the office.* That suited her perfectly at that precise moment. The way things were going with her marriage she imagined that would suit her husband too. She still loved him and he loved her as far as she could tell but them marrying was a big mistake, him being the way he was.

When Margaret returned to her office, she found Lisette tidying her desk, which was very unusual for her. She asked Margaret if she was still her boss. "Let's go for a chat. Why don't we pop over the road to the Ritz? Phone ahead and book a booth for two." Lisette looked apprehensive and asked Margaret if it was a drink of celebration or farewell; to which she cryptically replied that it could be considered to be a bit of both. As soon as they sat down in their favourite booth Lisette began.

"C'mon then. Give me the worst."

"I put my letter of resignation in today. Well, not so much resignation, more of a reassignment request."

"If you go I want to go with you, I can't stand being a Counsellor, it's so boring. I want to get back to active duty." Margaret knew exactly what Lisette meant by 'active duty'.

"I'll see what I can do. I'll probably need a PA for a new role," smiled Margaret smugly.

"What? You've got a new job… one that needs a PA? It's not Madame Chancellor is it?"

"Better. I'm going to be a roving ambassador with responsibility for bringing the Splinters back into the fold."

"I didn't know there was such a job."

"There wasn't until today."

"Be careful Margaret, it sounds too good to be true. No disrespect darling, but why you? You don't know anything about the Splinters."

"That's not entirely true. I've met lots of their Operatives. I even worked with one in Russia for a while."

"Yes, but this is different, this will be dealing with the heads of the Splinters and if stories about them are to be believed they're a pretty ruthless lot."

"I know. Fantastic isn't it? What a great opportunity."

"Aren't you scared? They could be setting you up."

"Why would they do that?"

"A thousand reasons, for example—"

"Lizzie, I could probably think up as many reasons as you for why this could be a setup but I'm going into this with my eyes wide open. This is something I've wanted to do for a long time. I can do it. I know I can. I'm sure I can. I'll need a PA of course. Would you like to apply for the role?"

"Apply for the role? Why you cheeky so and so." The friends, if they could be called that, laughed and toasted to their future successes.

*

The following day when Margaret entered her office Rex and the Chancellor were sitting waiting for her. She had never known them to be so early. They explained that as her new role would soon become common knowledge it was best if she left her post as Controller immediately. She asked who would be taking over from her. Margaret was surprised when they told her they'd already offered the role to Lisette. *Why didn't she call me?* she thought. Margaret said to the Chancellor that Lisette would make a good Controller before adding that she had her in mind as her PA. The Chancellor said that one PA wouldn't be sufficient in her new role and that four IOs would be reassigned as her PAs. *They're going to keep an eye on me and report back*, she thought.

Lisette entered the office wearing a sheepish expression on her face. The Chancellor announced they had already spoken to her about the job. Margaret said she "understood entirely" and asked Lisette when exactly had she been offered the job. She replied that Rex and the Chancellor had been waiting for her when she arrived at her flat the previous evening. They left the room, saying Lisette and Margaret had a lot to discuss as the handover should begin immediately. It was a very uncomfortable morning with neither apologising to the other for any misunderstandings or whatever they were. They both went their separate ways for lunch and continued the handover in a frostily professional atmosphere in the afternoon.

*

Rex phoned Herr Grodt to let him know that everything was in place and that Margaret would be out of the HQ and on the road within days. He was a little alarmed when Max told him that he intended to make contact with Margaret during her visit to the Italian Splinter. He wanted to ask why that was necessary but didn't have the guts.

THE OLD HUT DOWN BY THE SEA

The next Altcar summer camp came right on the heels of Michael's 'O' level exams and money, as ever, was tight in the Frost household. Mary was preparing to tell her son that they couldn't afford to send him away to Altcar that summer. She got herself in a real tizzy about it.

As per the previous year, Sergeant Huggard visited the Frosts to talk with Mary about Altcar. However, this time he arrived with some particularly good news.

"Hi Mary, it's that time of year again; Altcar summer camp!" announced the Sergeant brightly.

"Oh, hello Sergeant Huggard, I'll put the kettle on and make us a nice cup of tea. Biscuits? Sandwich?"

"Yes to both thanks luv." The Sergeant was on earlies and had missed his breakfast after sleeping past his alarm.

"Sergeant Huggard I'm afraid we don't have the money for our Michael to go to Altcar this year. The kids need shoes and—"

"Mary," the Sergeant butted in, "can I just stop you there luv? I've had a message from the administration offices at Altcar saying that Michael's subs have been paid by some foundation or other. Apparently, they do this sort of thing for kids they think deserve some help." Poor deluded Sergeant Huggard. He wasn't to know that Michael's subs were being paid by a Government department run by the Organisation masquerading, in this instance, as a front for a 'think tank'. As part of his continuing observation of young Michael Frost, the French Captain had arranged for the so-called 'think tank' to pay the boy's Altcar subs. Classic Organisation, spending other people's money for its own purposes.

"That's very kind of them Sergeant Huggard, but who are they? I know we haven't got much money but I like to pay my own way thank you very much," answered Mary defiantly.

"Please don't get upset now Mary luv, everybody around here knows you pay your way but this is different. It's like drawing out a lucky ticket. Y'know, like a raffle sort of thing and Michael won. It's not charity, it's something, I hear, this foundation does week in week out for loads of kids. Anyway, the details are in the post to you. The final decision is yours but it's a great opportunity for Michael. You have a think about it and when the letter arrives you can give your answer then. Okay? C'mon now Mary luv, that tea won't make itself y'know," said Sergeant Huggard trying to break the tension with humour though, in reality, Mary had already decided Michael would go to Altcar as it was free; she just wanted to put on a show of independence.

*

Everybody knows that at the end of every school year there's a limbo time when exams are over and pupils ask themselves, *Why am I still here when there's nothing to do?* To address this, teachers occupy the smaller children with finger painting, middling children with listening to music that some teacher brought in which isn't to anybody else's taste and the big kids are expected to occupy themselves. This is very dangerous. It's a time bomb waiting to go off!

"I know, how about we stage a boxing tournament?" suggested the school's boxing coach in a 'pre-planned brainwave' that had been suggested to him over a couple of pints in a pub a few weeks earlier by a generous stranger. The coach thanked the stranger for his suggestion and adopted the idea as his own.

"Yeah, why not," chorused an unenthusiastic teacher body.

"Good, I'll get in touch with a couple of boxing coach mates of mine and get it sorted. C'mon youz lot show a bit of enthusiasm, it'll be fun." Next, the boxing coach told the kids the plan.

"Look sir, we just want to get out of here and get on with earning some money for the summer holidays. Who's with me?" shouted Spike. All the students except Michael raised their hands. "What's wrong with you Michael, aren't you interested in earnin' a few bob?"

"I'm going to Altcar this summer with the Royal Tank Regiment."

"Are you still doing that? Why don't ye give it a miss and come with me and Jacko and the rest of the lads and earn a few bob doing gardenin' and cleaning cars and stuff. It'll be a laugh. C'mon."

"All in good time," interrupted the boxing coach. "First we'll get you lot boxing and then you can go and earn some money for the summer holidays." The boxing coach made his way to leave the Gym for a sneaky cigarette. "You lot do a bit of sparring while I… and don't kill one another while I'm away. Okay?"

What the boxing coach, not to mention the rest of the teachers, saw in arranging a boxing tournament was that it would be a great skive. Classic Teacher end of term stuff. After calling them up, the idea of an 'Inter-school Boxing Tournament' was leapt upon by all the other boxing coaches. It was so popular that it turned into a big event spreading over three days, maybe even a week. *Why haven't we done this before?* thought the teacher body. *What a great skive!*

The first of the boxing bouts were arranged for the next day and held at Michael's school. The outer doors of the Gymnasium were opened to allow students to peer in from the paved areas surrounding the building. All the real interest was in the big-boys' bouts, not least from an observer who'd come to check on Michael's progress. The observer sidled up to Michael and introduced himself as a boxing coach from London. He told Michael that he'd heard a lot about him and had come to watch him fight and suggested to Michael that he fought to win his fights on points so he could check out his form. "Are you okay with that Michael?" asked the bogus boxing coach. "Yes," was Michael's monosyllabic reply, as was normal for him.

The ringside was packed for Michael's first fight. "C'mon Michael. Show everybody what ye can do!" yelled the school boxing coach. The bout kicked off with a few range finders then Michael began throwing sets of light combination punches. As requested by the bogus boxing coach, he was trying to win the fight on points. Something happened to Michael during that bout. Boxing in that way gave him a warm feeling in his stomach. He enjoyed testing himself to see what was possible. It felt like he was floating outside his body looking down on the fight from above. This gave him a tremendous sense of power.

"What was that all about Frost, you div?" asked the school boxing coach at the end of the fight. "You were love tapping him. What's going on? Is he your boyfriend or something?"

"I fought to win on points."

"Well, don't arse around like that in yer next fight, a boxing ring isn't the place to go arsing around in because if you do you're going to get hit and nobody likes to get hit. Do they?" Michael shook his head. After the school boxing coach left Michael's side, the London boxing coach appeared next to him.

"Well done Michael," he crooned. "That was excellent but in your next fight take your time so you can show off your technique; use all your skills."

"But the coach told me not to arse around in case I get hit."

"Look Michael, nobody doubts your ability, you're the best boxer here but power isn't everything. Lead your opponents into traps, bring them in and let them out like they're on a piece of string. Control yourself, control your opponent and control the fight. You can do it Michael, I know you can. Now go and shadow box your next fight from start to finish in your head. Imagine how the fight will go in your mind. Win the fight in your head and then win it in the ring." Michael understood exactly what the London boxing coach meant.

An hour later came Michael's final bout. His opponent this time was a 'ringer' who, in reality, was an ABA champion boxer of twenty, though, with his baby face, didn't look it. He'd been specially selected by the London boxing coach to test Michael. As they danced and sparred around the ring, Michael admired his opponent's technique; mimicking in real time much of what he observed of his movements. Then, after a period of close-in fighting, the ABA boxer stepped back before throwing a sweet right followed by a left uppercut to Michael's jaw – one, two! Though he didn't hit the canvas, Michael felt groggy from the punches. His opponent didn't move in for the kill though. Standing off, the ABA boxer threw daisy drops over Michael's shoulders until he'd regained his senses. The bell sounded to end the second round.

"What the hell did I tell ye about arsing around, eh? You took two big punches there; are ye feeling okay to carry on son? It's not a real tournament ye know so it's okay if you throw in the towel."

"I will not throw the towel in," replied Michael in a grave monotone. "I haven't lost a fight in over four years and I'm not going to lose this one!"

"Michael, listen to me son, according to one of the other coaches he's an ABA champ and probably going to turn pro so do yerself a big favour and give it a miss. You've got nothing to prove here lad."

Michael wasn't listening to his coach, he remained staring coldly across the ring at his opponent. At the bell Michael jumped up off his stool, slapped his gloves together and did a little hop, Timbo style, before pumping the air with a dozen uppercuts before touching gloves with his opponent for the start of the final round.

"Good luck," mumbled Michael's opponent through his gum shield.

"Same to you," returned Michael while thinking, *Remember what the ref said – Defend yourself at all times.*

What Michael hadn't realised was that his opponent had been going easy on him up to that point but now it was totally on. The ABA boxer set about his business with combinations of body and head shots, but all from distance. Michael attacked in a Southpaw stance before switching to Orthodox and throwing his opponent off balance, forcing him to cover up from an onslaught. Both boxers regarded each other from behind high guards. Michael then dropped his gloves to his waist and body swerved, Muhammed Ali-style, the punches being served up to him. Using his phenomenal speed Michael closed the distance to his opponent to deliver a sickening uppercut to his solar plexus. Winded, the ABA boxer put a knee on the canvas. After a count of seven he got back to his feet and offered Michael a glove tap which he took as a mutual sign of respect. Recalling what the London boxing coach had said to him, Michael finished the third round by moving and controlling his opponent around the ring. At the bell both fighters held up each other's hands, declaring the fight a draw themselves.

"You had me in the second. Why did you back off?" said Michael through his gum shield.

"I've heard a lot about you and wanted the fight to go on. Y'know, see what happens. You can often learn more by stepping back than going in for the kill. I learned things today which will help me in the future. Thanks."

"Well done lads," said the school boxing coach wrapping his arms around each boxer's shoulders.

"Excuse me," said the London boxing coach interrupting, "do you mind if I have a minute with the boys?"

"Not at all, be my guest, pal. Who are you by the way?"

"I'm a boxing coach from London. I'm here to see how well my protégé is getting on." He carefully didn't say which of the boxers he was referring to.

"Hey, you're not nicking our lads to take them off down to that London are ye? They're better off staying here in Liverpool an' not swanning off down to that London," bleated the boxing coach.

"I have no intention of nicking your lads as you put it. Now excuse us please!" replied the London boxing coach firmly if not a little rudely. The school boxing coach walked away shaking his head and muttering.

"That was the perfect way to demonstrate your talents Michael. I think you could be a real prospect. What do you think of our Roberto here?"

"He's a great boxer. The best I've fought by a mile. His hair is very black." The London boxing coach snorted in surprise at the unexpected comment about Roberto's hair.

"You'll be seeing Roberto at Altcar."

"Which Regiment are you with?" asked Michael.

"He's not in a Regiment, he's going there to do some hand to hand combat demonstrations for the grunts."

"My dad's hair is black. His family are from southern Ireland. Are you from there too Roberto?"

"No, I'm from London but my parents are from Sicily."

"I've heard of Sicily."

"Yeah, it's an island in the Mediterranean near Italy. I've never been there but I hope to go one day. Maybe I'll box there, who knows. See you at Altcar Michael." Roberto and the London boxing coach left the tournament. They'd seen enough.

*

An Organisation conversation.

"What do you reckon then Roberto? Is he as good as he looks?"

"Better than good. He's got fantastic technique and hits like a sledgehammer. He's got a terrible strength inside him. My ribs are killing me. If he can do the business at Altcar I reckon he'll make a great Sentinel. I'm off back to my hotel room for a nice long hot bath. See you later for a big steak and it's on you after the pounding I took. By the way, stop calling me Roberto. I hate that name."

"You know the rules. No real names, so as far as I'm concerned, you're Roberto."

"Yeah, but keep calling me that name and you and me are going to fall out!" warned the Operative who had designs on becoming a Sentinel.

*

The coach trip to Altcar was more enjoyable than the previous year because there was no Buckhead on board. The Tank Cadets were bivouacked in a newly erected barracks. There were bunk beds everywhere. They raced one another to the far end to be the bad boys at the back of the room.

"I'm not sure about this setup," said Billy Smith. "Why haven't we got our own bivvy like last year?"

"Would you like a room in the West Wing your Lordship?" asked a Sergeant sarcastically. "Right you lot, put your kit bags on your bunks and be out on the parade ground in one minute; fifty-nine, fifty-eight, fifty-seven…" Once the Cadets were on the parade ground the Sergeant shouted, "Atteeeeeen'hun. Stand aaaat… ease. Stand easy. Sir, Soldiers and Cadets are fell in, sir," said the Sergeant.

"Thank you Sergeant, I'll take it from here." The Sergeant saluted the Camp Commander, did a brisk about face and joined his NCO compatriots. "Now listen up all of you. In an effort to keep Britain at the cutting edge of warfare we are going to be conducting exercises which will be new to some of you and, if that's the case, consider yourselves Guinea Pigs. The War Office has a concern about the country's state of preparedness for Nuclear and Biological warfare. The exercises you'll be undertaking will concentrate on Armageddon scenarios. Though the exercises will primarily focus on defence, naturally there will be offensive elements too. In all, there will be three scenarios staged as Red on Blue with Blue being the defence of the realm. The Cadets of the Royal Tank Regiment will play the part of the general public, or other non-combatant roles, attached to Blue teams; all except Cadet Frost that is." The Tank Cadets looked surprised but had enormous pride that not all of them were going to be playing the part of battlefield corpses.

Having introduced the exercises to the Soldiers and Cadets, the Camp Commander handed proceedings over to Major Finn for him to continue with their detailed briefings. The Tank Cadets weren't involved in the first exercise so they went to assembly point 'D' to see what Michael was up to. As they approached the Red team briefing zone to get a closer look a couple of Royal Marines Commandos wearing black balaclavas came at them from out of nowhere.

"Passes!" they demanded.

"What passes?"

"Okay you lot, hands behind your heads and keep them there. Got some spies here sir," said a Commando, presumably to an unseen Officer. They then kicked the Cadets behind their knees sending them crashing to the ground to let them know they weren't joking. "I told you lot, hands behind your heads and keep them there, I won't tell you again!" A rifle butt was brought down on one of the Cadet's backs to emphasise the point.

"Spies eh Corpwal? Is that you down there Munwoe?"

"Yes Captain Jones, sir, it's Cadet Munwoe here, sir, having his neck stood on by a big hairy arsed Commando, sir." The Tank Cadets wanted to laugh at Tommy's cheeky remark but thought it best not to.

"Let them up Corporal Roberts, I'll deal with them. Follow me Cadets," ordered Captain Jones. The Cadets knew it was all a big game but nevertheless it was very frightening having masked Commandos come out of nowhere and pointing guns in your faces. "You do realise that technically I could have you shot as spies? It would mean the end of the games for you and that would be a shame as we'd have no civilians to look after or corpses littering the streets. You Cadets play a vital role in all this. You might not think so but you do. If we don't make it real then we'll make mistakes when it comes to the real thing. Understand? Understand Munroe?" The Tank Cadets couldn't help but notice Captain Jones' speech impediment had disappeared.

"Sir, your speech impediment has gone sir. Are you cured sir?" asked Leading Cadet Munroe, causing the Tank Cadets to laugh.

"Gone? Weally Munwoe? Whatever do you mean? I have no idea what you're talking about. Now stay here and wait until you're called by your team leader and keep your noses out of things that don't concern you!"

"Yes sir, sorry sir and sorry for taking the piss out of your speech impediment… if you ever had one in the first place sir." Tommy Munroe had more balls than sense at times.

*

For the next exercise the Tank Cadets assembled at RVP 'B'. En route, they saw Michael in a briefing session with a group of Soldiers wearing uniforms they didn't recognise. An Officer was using a stick to point at a blackboard. *Just like being back in bleedin' school,* thought the Cadets.

The second and third exercises went according to plan, after which everybody assembled together in the debriefing zone. This was the first opportunity the Tank Cadets had to properly check out what was going on with Michael. They sat at the back and picked him out from amongst the Soldiers. He was sitting taking notes about what had gone well and what needed working on and receiving instructions of what he personally needed to improve on. *Funny,* the Cadets thought, *Michael looks like he fits right in.* In his Bio-suit he didn't look like a boy amongst men, he looked like a Soldier.

When the Tank Cadets got back to their barracks, the whole place was full of proper big rufty tufty Soldiers. They made their way to the far end wishing they'd chosen the bunks near the door.

"Hey, Cadet Frost. Well done today lad. If you sign up make sure it's for the Marines and not those cloak and dagger merchants," said a Corporal pointing to the SAS Soldiers who'd been on exercises with them.

"If the lad wants to try for selection then that's up to him. Don't let anybody pressurise you Frosty," said an SAS Soldier. Michael didn't appreciate being called 'Frosty' or anything else other than his given names.

"I want to join the Royal Tank Regiment when I leave school."

"Just saying though, if you do sign up then for Christ's sake don't be a grunt."

"Looking forward to tomorrow lads?" asked a SAS NCO of the Tank Cadets.

"Yeah!" they all said, trying to sound enthusiastic before asking, "What's on tomorrow?"

"Unarmed combat. They've got some kind of expert coming in."

Shiiiiiiiiit, unarmed combat! They won't want us to do that will they? thought the Tank Cadets recalling the previous year when the Camp Commander had asked if anybody wanted to back out of the boxing tournament, then realising they couldn't back out as they'd look like chickens in front of everybody. *At least*, thought Leading Cadet Tommy Munroe, *we'll go down swinging.*

*

A Cadets conversation.

"How come d'ye reckon that we're the only Cadets at camp?" asked James Hill of no one in particular.

"I know, weird isn't it?"

"I reckon they just needed a few of us to make the numbers up for the nuclear stuff. Y'know, bodies and injured people and tha'."

"Then why wasn't Michael with us then, eh?"

"Yeah Michael, why wasn't ye with us, eh? Just askin' like. No offence and all tha'."

"I don't know. They just told me what to do and I did it."

"Yeah, but why you do ye reckon they chose you and not somebody else?"

"Don't be so bleedin' thick Jamesey. Michael's different to the rest of us and if ye can't see that then you're thicker than I already think ye are," said Tommy Munroe.

"Are you lookin' for a fight Munwoe?" joked Jamesey bobbing around on his toes, sparring like a boxer. The Cadets fell about laughing.

"Seriously though Michael, I'd watch me back if I waz you. There's somethin' goin' on. But I'll be watchin' out for ye, don't you worry."

"Thanks Tommy, I'll be careful."

"Yeah, dead right Michael. Any funny stuff and we'll burst them," added a Cadet, whoever 'them' was.

The next morning as the Cadets were getting ready for their morning 'fun-run' in the mud they heard a Soldier cry out.

"Oh bloody hell… no!"

"What's up Simmo?" asked his mate.

"Some dirty bugger's pissed in me boots."

"Oh, that'll be the phantom slasher. Nobody knows who it is but he sneaks around the barracks in the middle of the night and pisses in boots. He's been doin' it for years."

"If I get me hands on 'im I'll cut 'is nuts off."

"He doesn't piss in anybody's boots," said Michael.

"What do ye mean?"

"He probably pisses into a cup and then pours it into boots."

"'Ow the bloody hell do you know that, eh? Are you 'im?"

"Don't be stupid Simmo, he hasn't been here when the phantom slasher's struck before so it can't be 'im can it? That's not a bad thought though Frosty. When did ye figure out that he pisses into his cup and then pours it into somebody's boots?"

"It's obvious. Nobody would risk pissing into a Soldier's boots in the middle of the night in case he gets caught."

"The lads a bleedin' genius. Well done Frosty. Now all we've got to do is find out who's been pissing in his cup."

"I doubt he's pissing into his own cup, he likely pisses in somebody else's cup," said Michael matter-of-factly.

"I wish ye hadn't said that Frosty," whinged a few Soldiers.

"Are there no end to your talents Michael?" asked Tommy Munroe. "Ye couldn't figure out the winner of the 4.45 at Haydock for me could ye?"

"No," answered Michael completely missing the joke as usual.

*

Before breaking camp the Soldiers had to attend a demonstration of hand to hand combat. Michael recognised the instructor. It was Roberto.

"Hello Roberto, you said you'd be coming here."

"Hi Michael, by the way, my name's not Roberto, that was just him over there messing about," he replied pointing at the man Michael knew as the London boxing coach.

"What's your real name?"

"I'm here incognito so call me Roberto for now. Okay? But only you. And not too loud."

"This is the final day of camp and I think you'll all agree it's been a tremendous success," said the Camp Commander into a microphone and pausing for applause which eventually came. "You can all be very proud of what you've achieved here over the past couple of days. Before we break camp we have a demonstration of hand to hand combat for you. The instructor has advised me that once the demonstrations start it'll be realistic to the point where maximum force will be used to subdue anybody who acts up. You all know what I mean by 'acts up'? Good. Enjoy the demonstration and afterwards we'll assemble on the parade ground for a speech from a very special guest speaker. Let the demonstration begin!"

Rows of benches had been placed around a single canvas mat. Standing in front of the mat was the person Michael knew as Roberto.

"Gather round, all of you. C'mon, quick as you like and take a seat. C'mon, get a move on!" shouted Roberto. The Soldiers wondered who this punk kid was who was talking to them like they were children. "Right then, now that you're all sitting comfortably we can begin. Can I have some hush?" shouted Roberto over everybody's heads. "I'm going to be giving a demonstration of hand to hand combat and I'll need some volunteers to lend a hand. I warn you that if you try anything off your own bat you will get hurt. Understand?" This remark drew disgruntled groans form the audience.

"Excuse me," said a Soldier raising his hand, "who are you? I don't know your rank or anything so I don't know whether to call you sir or salute you."

"It's not important who I am and as far as you lot are concerned Army protocol is suspended for this session. Okay? So no saluting or calling people sir or any of the usual Army bollocks. By the way, keep irrelevant questions to yourselves! Now, let's see who we have on the list." Roberto paused to peruse a list of names. "I understand that those on here have been specially selected because they're the best of the best. Let's see how you get on with me and I'll let you know how good you are." Roberto read out six names. Each of them had one thing in mind and that was to flatten this cocky little sod.

"First though, I'd like to invite Cadet Frost to come and join me on the mat." Michael heard his name called out but remained seated. "Michael, please?" said Roberto indicating that he should leave the audience and join him on the mat. "Now, Cadet Frost, you've been on exercises with this lot. How did they do? Any good?" The Soldiers were becoming more furious with Roberto by the minute.

"We worked well together and learned a lot from the exercises. They are good Soldiers and look after one another."

"Any favourites Michael?"

"I like Corporal Enis. He's a great shot. He won the shooting competition," said Michael earnestly.

"Well now, would you believe it? Corporal Enis is on my list. Lucky your name isn't Phil or Peter, instead of Mike, eh?"

"Yeah, dead lucky that. I've never heard that one before; yeah, good one," replied Corporal Enis sarcastically. His blood was just about boiling as he walked towards Roberto.

"Now pal, listen carefully. I'll speak slowly 'cause I know you northerners aren't too quick off the mark. We're going to start with the basics. This is a Commando dagger," he said to Corporal Enis of the Royal Marines Commandos. "Now be careful because it's very sharp. Fortunately it's sheathed so you shouldn't come to any harm when you handle it. I understand from your CO that you're a bit of a Judo expert so you should be able to handle a little chap like me even when I'm holding a knife. Right? Come and take the knife, Enis!" snarled Roberto. Corporal Enis was already like a coiled spring and he leapt the few feet between himself and Roberto in the blink of an eye but failed to grab anything but air. Roberto used Corporal Enis' momentum to throw him hard to the mat. He then put him in an agonising arm lock which he immediately released and sprang to his feet. "Now then Phil, sorry, Mike, it's your turn with the knife," said Roberto handing him the Commando dagger. Corporal Enis was up for this.

A Soldier in the crowd shouted to the Corporal for him to take the sheath off the knife and "stick the little gob-shite with it". Ignoring the shout, Corporal Enis crouched in the middle of the mat and beckoned Roberto to come to him. Roberto casually sauntered up close to the Corporal and when he was close enough the Corporal struck out at Roberto. The result was exactly the same as previous with Corporal Enis ending up in exactly the same agonising arm lock which was, once again, immediately released.

"What was Corporal Enis's mistake?" Roberto asked the crowd.

"He left the bleedin' sheath on the knife instead of stickin' you with it," shouted the same shouter-outer. The crowd roared its approval.

"No! Wrong! Corporal Enis wasn't thinking straight when we fought. The things I said messed with his head. I messed with all your heads. Remove the head and the body dies. Remember that if you don't remember anything else from today; remove the head and the body dies. Okay? Apologies for any disrespect or rudeness but I'm not here to be your mate. I'm here to teach you to be better at hand to hand combat which just might save your life one day. You're already good but if I started off by saying that you'd have coasted this session. When it comes to the real thing you have to be in control and the first thing you need to be in control of are your emotions, then you can control your enemy. Never ever ever get mad at anybody. It should never be personal." Roberto held the audience in his gaze before continuing. "Now, I'm going to go through some exercises with you; first I'm the attacker and then you're the attacker. Okay? Enjoy, and let's get to it." The Soldiers got to it with a vengeance.

*

Following the hand to hand combat class, several Soldiers came and spoke with Roberto about H2H training for them. Michael wanted to speak with Roberto too but he departed before he had the opportunity. As he walked away, Roberto was joined by a man known to him as Mike; he'd been the shouter-outer in the audience.

"You were bleeding rude back there!" said Roberto.

"It had to be realistic. Anyway, I got that lot right wound up didn't I?" replied Mike smiling a cheesy smile.

"Did you see the colour of Corporal Enis' face when he had the dagger in his hand? I thought he was going to bust a gut. Anyway, where are we meeting?"

"At some an old hut down by the Sea. The PPS to the Minister of Defence will be there so we'd better get a move on. She needs to be on the road before the camp spills out."

The two men made their way over the dunes toward the sea. Stealthily following them, at a distance of thirty or so yards, was Leading Cadet Tommy Munroe. Using the sand dunes for cover he kept the two men in sight. After a couple of minutes Tommy saw the men enter an old signals hut. He crept up to the hut and made his way round to the wall facing the sea so he couldn't be spotted from the sand dunes. He pressed his ear up against the wall and could hear those talking inside the hut surprisingly well. He picked out three distinct voices; two male and one female. The female was shouting at the two males.

"You have both acted in a most unprofessional manner!" screeched the PPS to the Minister of Defence. "A most unprofessional, risky and dangerous manner! I observed each of you talking openly to several Potentials you're here to observe! There are some here who are watching out for us and last thing we want to do is to attract their attention!"

"Relax, nobody has a clue who we are! Why would they? The problem with you is you're paranoid. People don't question authority, it's not what they do. They follow orders."

"I remind you, there are SAS, Paras and Commandos on the base and they can't be relied on to follow orders! They might already be suspicious of who we are! The brief I provided called for you to come here as an observer," she said pointing at Mike, "and for you to do a demonstration of hand to hand combat... not run a circus! You're encouraged, of course, to use your initiative but not in circumstances where it is inappropriate to do so, such as here." The PPS paused to light a cigarette. "In case it's escaped your attention, we're on an MoD facility. We might well be being watched right now! Might we not? I'm reporting you both for serious breaches of protocol and then it's up to others to decide your fates. Now, gentlemen, if you would be so good as to provide me your updates on the Potentials along with your recommendations. Your written reports must be with me within the week. Let's start with list D and work up to A."

At this particular camp there were four A list Potentials and eight others spread between the B, C and D lists. Tommy Munroe could hardly believe his ears when they began talking about Michael.

"Now to Michael Frost. He's honing his self-defence skills nicely and has developed a steely determination when going about his work. Academically there are still question marks over him but he's extraordinarily gifted at foreign languages, which is useful for obvious reasons. Something else, he's freakishly good with numbers. He's been top of his entire school in mathematics since the end of his third year. I recommend he remains on list B. Ma'am, there's something I'd like to add at this point."

"Carry on," said the PPS tapping her watch for Mike to get a move on.

"There's something about Captain Jones that's not right. Something's eating away at me but I can't put my finger on it."

"Well, 'Mike', if you come across anything concrete then bring it up at the next review; sooner if it's urgent. You know what I mean by urgent, right? Anyway, let's continue with the review. I can't afford to be here all day. We're all agreed, then, about Michael Frost? Good. He'll remain on list B for now but it sounds like he may make a damn fine Sentinel. Pity about his academic side but we can't all be Intelligence Officers, can we?" gloated the PPS in a smug, self-satisfied way.

With what was being spoken about inside the hut, Tommy Munroe knew this was not the place to be caught with his ear pressed up against a wall. He looked around the corner of the hut to check if the coast was clear. As he did so he thought he spied what he thought looked like the top of a balaclava bobbing above a nearby sand dune but convinced himself it was just his imagination. To be on the safe side, instead of heading north he headed south to make his getaway; he had to get back to the camp to tell Michael and Captain Jones what he'd overheard. Reaching the first sand dune Tommy looked around to check he wasn't being followed. All clear. Next, he climbed to the top of a massive sand dune to survey the surrounding area. His heart was racing. Then he thought, *Why am I hiding? What are they going to do to me on a military base surrounded by hundreds of Soldiers?* He really shouldn't have allowed himself this thought. It made him relax. As Tommy rolled to the bottom of the sand dune, he was knocked face first to the ground from behind.

A black sack was placed over Tommy's head and a couple of heavy blows were landed to his kidneys to remove any fight he had in him.

*

The door to the hut opened with a crash and a man wearing a black balaclava entered pushing Leading Cadet Munroe ahead of him.

"Saw him outside. He had his ear pressed up against the wall. I'm not sure how much he heard," said the man removing the black bag from Tommy's head.

"You're one of Cadet Frost's friends aren't you? Munroe?" said Mike.

"Yeah, that's right. What are youz lot doin' with Michael, eh?" sputtered a frightened but defiant Tommy Munroe.

"Tell me, Cadet Munroe, what did your piggy little ears hear while they were pressed against the wall listening to things that don't concern you? What did you hear us talking about Cadet Munroe?"

"Nothin'. Nothin' at all. The walls are really thick, I didn't hear anythin', honest."

"Really? Then why did you ask what we're doing with Cadet Frost?"

"How long do you reckon he was out there?" asked Roberto.

"Dunno. Maybe he followed you two here, so fifteen minutes… twenty?" said the man in the balaclava pointing at Roberto and Mike.

"Did you follow me and my friend, Cadet Munroe?" Roberto asked in a menacing tone.

"To be honest, I did. I thought ye might be goin' somewhere interestin' so I followed ye but I was only listen' at the wall for about ten seconds. I didn't 'ear much, honest. Swear on me brother's grave, I didn't 'ear much. In fact ye can't hear anythin' through these walls. Try it. You go outside and we'll talk in here and I bet ye won't 'ear a thing," said Tommy while crossing himself several times to convince everybody he was speaking the truth.

"I watched him for a good few minutes. He was at the wall all that time."

"Now Cadet Munroe, you started off by saying you didn't hear much, then you said you didn't hear anything. You say you were listening for ten seconds and he says he watched you listening for a good few minutes. What's the truth Cadet Munroe? Don't worry, you'll be okay if you just tell us the truth," said the PPS reassuringly.

"I 'eard yez saying 'ow yer watchin' Michael and 'ow it's a pity he can't be an Intelligence Officer an' stuff. And what about Captain Jones? Why are yez watchin' 'im? What's goin' on?"

"Cadet Munroe," called Roberto in a whisper.

As Tommy turned to his right to see who it was that had whispered his name, Roberto plunged an eight-inch stiletto dagger into his chest, piercing his heart. Instinctively, Tommy tried to grab hold of the hand holding the dagger to pull it out of his chest. He didn't want to look down. He didn't want to see that thing sticking in his chest. He couldn't help it. He had to look. After seeing the dagger Tommy went into shock and nearly passed out. He looked around at the faces of the people surrounding him. They looked back at him in silence.

As there was very little pain, and virtually no blood, Tommy wondered if he was going to be alright. He tried once again to grab hold of the dagger. With that, Roberto forced Tommy backwards, slamming him hard against the wall of the hut, forcing all the air out of his lungs. Being expert at his job, Roberto placed his free hand over Tommy's mouth to prevent him from calling out. Tommy tried to pull the hand from off his mouth as he couldn't breathe.

With his back pressed up against the wall, Tommy stared with frightened eyes at the four pair of eyes staring back at him. Still nobody was speaking. There was only silence and staring. Tommy's breathing became more and more shallow and laboured as mucus built up in his nasal passages. After Roberto removed his hand from Tommy's mouth his breathing changed to rapid panting. The panting was of the type which heralds the imminent end of a life.

Tommy's body became limp and yielding. He no longer needed restraining so Roberto let go of him. As he stepped away, Tommy fell to the ground and was finally able to grab onto the handle of the dagger but could do nothing with it. Roberto knelt and removed the dagger from Tommy's chest in one slow continuous movement. The colour had completely drained from Tommy's rosy, apple-cheeked face. All was still and silent in the hut. Roberto looked into Tommy's blue sparkling Liverpool-Irish eyes and watched as they turned milky and lifeless.

"Are you out of your bloody mind?" screamed the PPS to the Minister of Defence. "Are you? Granted, Munroe had to die but why do it here? Why do it now with the Minister still on site? You could've had him away and drowned him in the sea or thrown him under a tank. A post mortem will show he's been stabbed. Statistically speaking, not many people are stabbed with a stiletto and as you're rather prolific with that thing the authorities might start noticing a pattern. Arghhhhhhhh!!!" she screamed in anger and frustration.

"Right... let's assess the situation," suggested Mike. "The boy is due to attend the final parade, which is in about twenty minutes' time. The Minister of Defence is going to make a speech thanking everybody for their efforts in improving the country's preparedness for a nuclear attack... what a load of crap, we'll all be blown to pieces if that ever happens."

"What the hell are you talking about nuclear attacks for? Why bring that up now? We're standing in a hut with the body of a dead Cadet and you're waffling," screamed the PPS. Fingering her 9 mil inside her purse, she considered whether she should kill Roberto but concluded that would only make a bad situation worse. After the moment had passed, she continued, "I need to leave with the Minister before a search is mounted for the boy so you need to hide the body to buy us some time," she said pointing at Mike.

"Don't worry, I'll take care of it," said Roberto. "As soon as the Minister's speech is over make an excuse for him to leave immediately.

Say he's got an emergency back in London or something. Then get him into his car and drive straight out. The guards won't stop you, they'll just salute and wave you through. Nobody would dare stop the Minister of Defence on important business. Is he one of us by the way?"

"You know better than to ask a question like that," sneered the PPS. "And what exactly are you going to do to 'take care of it' as you put it? Blow the whole place up?" she barked.

"No I'm not going to blow the place up, I'm going to take care of it like I said I would." With that Roberto ordered the man in the balaclava to pick Tommy Munroe's body up and follow him to the sand dunes. *She doesn't know if the Minister's one of us or not. She's nowhere near as important as she likes to make out. She's a gofer just like me*, Roberto mused.

While most everybody else on the base was standing around waiting for the speech by the Minister of Defence, Roberto ordered the man in the balaclava to go get him a couple of Thunderflashes. Minutes later he returned holding two Thunderflashes.

"You might've grabbed a handful while you were about it! You needn't have been so precise!"

"You said grab a couple so I did!"

"Go back to the hut and make sure it's empty and anything that shouldn't be there isn't there including the PPS."

Once the man was out of sight, Roberto placed a Thunderflash in the breast pocket of Cadet Munroe's jacket and waited until the Minister's speech was over before setting it to detonate. A few seconds later, the Thunderflash exploded right over the stab wound in Cadet Munroe's chest. The explosion attracted the attention Roberto knew it would. He cunningly left the second Thunderflash laying on the ground right next to Cadet Munroe's body before making his getaway from the scene. The sound of the explosion expedited the Minister of Defence's exit from the camp.

*

It only took the search teams ten minutes to find the site of the explosion. The scene they came upon was shocking. A Cadet was lying on the ground next to an unexploded Thunderflash.

"You there, go and tell the Major and the Camp Commander what we've found, I'll stay and guard the body. There may be other explosives lying around so check if we've got anybody from Bomb Disposal on site." The Camp Commander ordered the whole area to be cordoned off and that the body was only to be approached after Bomb Disposal had given the all clear.

"How the hell did a Cadet get hold of a Thunderflash?" snapped the Camp Commander.

"We're looking into that sir. It appears the ammunition store hasn't been broken into so perhaps the Cadet obtained it earlier. Perhaps he intended to remove it from camp. It wouldn't be the first time somebody like him has stolen Thunderflashes," sneered Major Finn.

"Somebody like him Major Finn? Would you care to explain that remark?" asked the Camp Commander, himself coming from the same type of background as Tommy Munroe.

"Yes sir. It probably seemed like a good idea to steal a couple of Thunderflashes for a joke or perhaps he thought they were of value and he could sell them. It wouldn't be the first time that one of these light-fingered Cadets has stolen military equipment. Many of them come from troubled homes and are disposed to certain temptations. He even had an unexploded Thunderflash next to him when he was found. It's pretty clear what happened. He was obviously putting the Thunderflashes into his jacket pockets, primed one by accident and paid the price."

"I think you're jumping pretty quickly to conclusions Major Finn but I have to say I'm finding it difficult to put a different interpretation on things. Please keep me posted on developments and give me your written report by this time tomorrow. Everybody dismissed."

*

"Did ye hear what happened to Tommy?" sobbed Jacko.

"I know it's terrible isn't it? How d'ye reckon it happened?"

"They're sayin' he was stealin' Thunderflashes an' one accidentally went off in his pocket."

"That sounds like a load of rubbish to me. What d'ye reckon Michael? Do you think it was an accident or wha'? Do you think Tommy was nickin' Thunderflashes? Why would he do tha' eh? What would he do with them if he was nickin' them?"

"It's hard to set off a Thunderflash by accident," replied Michael matter-of-factly.

"Ay you Michael, why aren't ye cryin' eh? Why aren't ye cryin' like the rest of us, eh? Are you glad Tommy's dead, eh? What's up with you anyway?" Others joined in with Johno's verbal assault on Michael.

"Shurrup youz lot," shouted Jamesey. "Tommy and Michael were best mates so don't nobody go sayin' anything different. He's as sad as the rest of us so shut yer gobs and let's get out of here. I wanna go home. I tell yez wha' I'm not comin' back to this place ever again."

In fact most of the children never went to Cadets club ever again, let alone Altcar. In most cases it was their parents' decision to stop them going but in others it was their own decision. Michael, though, continued going to Cadets, even attending the remaining camps that summer after Altcar reopened.

*

Investigations concluded that Tommy Munroe stole the Thunderflashes and one of them had accidentally exploded in his breast pocket; give a street kid a bad name and it sticks. As intended by Roberto, the site of the stab wound made by his stiletto dagger was disguised by the explosion of the Thunderflash and as there were no suspicious circumstances the coroner recorded a verdict of accidental death. The marks left on victims' bodies by Roberto's stiletto often went undetected during post mortems and autopsies for a variety of reasons but mainly because the entry wound was so small. R.I.P. Leading Cadet Tommy Munroe.

*

Tommy's funeral was attended by family, friends, relatives, neighbours, old school mates, his colleagues from the docks and Cadets. The coffin was white as were the horses and the hearse that carried it, which was unusual in those days. The inside of the hearse was crammed full of wreathes. The family's floral tribute spelled out "Tommy" and was positioned leaning up against the rear window of the hearse so everybody could see it. Though Tommy's family were extremely poor they knew how to demonstrate their love and devotion by arranging an expensive funeral and buying expensive wreaths they could ill afford. The immediate family travelled behind the hearse in a black limousine; the first car that most of them had ever been in, and behind them was a procession of cars of the day, decked out with white ribbons and Everton FC flags and scarfs. It was more like a wedding than a funeral because the family were determined there should be no more sadness. But there was more sadness for the Munroe family. Two of Tommy's brothers joined the Army because there were no jobs on Merseyside in the early 1970s. On a day which was to be significant in Michael's life, they were blown up in a Republican ambush. One survived and one didn't. The survivor spent the rest of his life, such as it was, in a wheelchair. He married the nurse who had looked after him in hospital while he was recovering but she left him after his drinking became too much.

*

An hour after Tommy Munroe was murdered the Minister of Defence, his PPS, his driver and bodyguards were well on their way back to London.

"I wonder what all that commotion was back at the camp?" asked the Minister.

"I really have no idea Minister but I'll contact the Camp Commander and let you know," replied the PPS. She never contacted the Camp Commander nor did she mention the incident ever again. In answer to Roberto's earlier question, she had no idea if the Minister was one of them and to ask would prove fatal.

*

Just prior to the end of the autumn term of 1969, the school boxing coach approached Michael to sound him out about taking his boxing career to the next level; ideally with him as his coach. Michael dropped what the boxing coach considered to be a bombshell.

"I'm leaving school."

"What! When?"

"At the end of term."

"You can't do that."

"Mum needs me to earn some money. I'm going to join the Royal Tank Regiment."

"But Michael, what about your boxing?" implored the boxing coach. "And your education too of course. We need to see the Headmaster about this right away and put a stop to this nonsense."

The Headmaster wrote Michael a letter for him to hand to his mother, inviting her to come to the school to discuss matters. Mary, being rather deaf and not liking speaking with people she considered to be in authority, didn't go to the school to discuss Michael's future with the Headmaster. Instead, she told Michael that bringing money into the house was more important than school. Having no education herself to speak of Mary didn't value education, so in her mind it was better for Michael to go out and earn money to make life easier for everybody which is exactly what happened to Mary in her childhood home. Classic poverty trap behaviour.

*

Four days after Michael told the school he was leaving, an Army recruiting officer came to his house to discuss his application to join the Royal Tank Regiment with him and his mum.

"I want to join the Royal Tank Regiment," said Michael to the recruiting officer.

"I understand that son but I'll need to check to see where they're accepting new recruits at the moment." Michael hadn't considered the possibility that he couldn't join the regiment of his choice. "The important thing is to get you in the Army and then you can apply to transfer to whatever Regiment you want afterwards." Not understanding the way things work, Mary and Michael both signed the pre-enlistment documents. A few days later Michael received a letter asking him to report to the recruiting office in London Road in the centre of Liverpool.

"Good news son," said the recruiting Sergeant, "there's a place for you straight away in the Royal Regiment of Fusiliers. If you pass the medical you can be in within a fortnight."

"I want to join the Royal Tank Regiment."

"They're not recruiting right now but if you join the Fusiliers you can apply to transfer to the Royal Tank Regiment when they are recruiting. The important thing is to get you in and get the basic training out of the way."

"I'm a Cadet in the Royal Tank Regiment and I've been to Altcar twice so basic training isn't necessary for me."

"Son, everybody has to do basic training, even I had to do it and I was in the Cadets for five years before I enlisted. As I say, the important thing is to get you in and you can transfer to the Royal Tank Regiment when they're recruiting and I bet you'll have no trouble getting accepted as you already know the ropes. Take these papers home to your mum and get them signed and we can get things started." Michael took the papers home but had no intention of joining the Royal Regiment of Fusiliers.

During Cadets the following evening Michael spoke with Captain Jones about his predicament. He was pleased to hear that Michael was keen to enlist and as he knew the boy was on the lists thought he might be useful in building up his secret Faction inside the Organisation; Michael would be its fifth recruit. "You know what Cadet Frost? I think you'd make first-class tank crew. I might be able to pull a few strings for you. I'll speak with some people I know and get back to you. Don't worry, everything will be okay, I'm sure of it." The following day there was a knock on the Frosts' front door and a military motorcycle messenger delivered a recruitment letter offering Michael a posting with the Royal Tank Regiment. He showed the letter to his mum.

"Oh Michael, son, this is just what you wanted. Now are you sure you want to go? If you say yes I'll sign the forms and that'll be that. There'll be no going back!"

"I want to join the Royal Tank Regiment. P… p… please sign the forms Mum and I can go after Christmas," replied Michael still having trouble with the p word. Mary signed the forms and handed them back to the messenger. There was no going back for Michael now. His fate was sealed.

*

In the days leading up to Michael leaving home to join the Army there was more laughter and tears than the Frost household had known in years. Thomas in particular was going to miss his big brother and protector. Things between Thomas and Rose had never been great but now that Michael was joining the Army there was a change in her attitude as she became even more conspiratorial and confrontational.

'My little Queen', as Joseph called Rose, had made Thomas' life hell and with Michael leaving home he feared it was going to get worse in the future. Joseph believed everything his little Queen said and gave her whatever she wanted. In contrast, Michael and Thomas seldom got anything nor were they ever believed, much to the consternation and frustration of Thomas but not so Michael because he didn't think in such terms. As a result of Rose's lies and scheming, poor little Thomas was often punished for things he didn't do which made him extremely angry towards her and his parents. In later life, Rose was recognised by all those who knew her as a pathological, congenital and compulsive liar. Like all accomplished liars, Rose lived her lies so that they became real in her mind; thereby making her convincing in the telling of them. She could never get to Michael, though. No matter how much or how hard she tried she could never get to him. What Rose, nor anybody else for that matter, didn't know, didn't understand, about Michael was that he operated on a different level to almost the rest of humankind.

THE KISS OF THE MANDARINS

During the summer of 1969, Margaret was carrying out her Roving Ambassadorial duties between the Splinters when it hit her that she'd taken on an impossible task. "It's like herding a flock of cats! Whichever direction one wants to go the others don't!" Then she had a moment of inspiration; instead of trying to resolve differences through individual treaties, she'd invite all the Splinters to a reunification conference and deal with them collectively. She'd first suggest this to the Italians; if they could be persuaded then the others could too.

While thinking about her meeting with the leader of the Italian Splinter a distinguished-looking gentleman joined Margaret at her table in the hotel's restaurant. He didn't ask whether she minded him joining her, he just sat down and joined her. Margaret asked the man if he would mind finding another table as she was expecting company. His reply was simply to say that he knew she wasn't expecting anybody. *He's a hitman!* thought Margaret as she sat clinging to her seat in anticipation of being killed in some horrific way. Where were her so-called bodyguards? On closer inspection, the man didn't much resemble an assassin so she dismissed thoughts of imminent death from her head. If they were in her room, she thought, she would have access to a gun. She then thought about what circumstances could possibly lead them to being in her room. Then the stranger asked Margaret if they could go to her room to talk. She told him that there was no way they were going to her room 'for a talk'. *The cheek of it!* she thought. *He hasn't even offered to buy me a drink!* The stranger didn't seem to be put off in the slightest. He wrote something on a napkin and passed it across the table to Margaret. On it he'd written the name, 'Alice'. Realising this could not be a random act nor a chance meeting, she asked the stranger how he knew her name. He said she'd find out everything in her room. He stood and offered Margaret his hand which, in her state of astonishment, she took.

The moment they entered Margaret's room she went for her 9 mil while he sat down on the corner of the bed. The stranger wasn't fazed in the slightest at having a gun pointed at him. He remarked that he knew her to be a deadly shot but the noise from the gun would attract attention and so recommended that she not shoot him and listen to what it was he had to say. She asked what he wanted. He got straight to the point.

"I know why you're here. It's a very laudable thing you're trying to do. I applaud your efforts. I think the French Splinter were totally charmed by you, especially the Count. You may have won a heart there."

"Who are you? I'm not afraid of using this," said Margaret putting a pillow over the muzzle of her 9 mil. "You know my real name. Was it you who got the lawyer to write to my sisters telling them of my existence?"

"No."

"But that means you know about them otherwise your reply would have been different."

"I do know about Lilliana and Henrietta, of course I do. But they are not why I'm here. Please, I mean you no harm, there's no need to keep holding such a heavy pistol. Please, put it down. I'll sit over there if it will make you feel more comfortable."

"I'll keep hold of this if it's all the same to you."

"I've followed your career with interest."

"Do you know Rex?"

"Not particularly," he lied, "though what I have to discuss with you may involve him." The man casually glanced about the room before continuing. "I represent a group with special interest in the Organisation. Tell me Margaret, how do you think the Chancellor is chosen?"

"I've never given it much thought," she lied. "I imagine some kind of board of Governors meet to—"

"I don't mean to be rude but I must stop you there." Margaret noticed a slight German accent and a cadence in the man's speech which she recognised as typically German. "If Governors selected the Chancellor it would be disastrous as they would be beholden to those who voted for them; probably rooting out and killing those who hadn't." He paused to pour himself a sparkling water. "No, Margaret, it is we who elect the Chancellor."

"And who is 'we' exactly?"

"We are the Mandarins. We've been in existence for almost as long as the Brotherhood, or the Organisation as it is now called."

"Why are you telling me this?"

"Because, for some time now, we've been of the opinion that the Organisation has lost its way and needs somebody to put it back on the right road again. We believe that somebody could be you, Margaret."

"Me? That's ridiculous."

"Is it? Why?"

"But what if you decide it's not me? Will you kill me as you've told me things I shouldn't know?" The stranger laughed.

"Of course not," he lied. "There are many in the Organisation who know of our existence, it's just your turn to find out, that's all. Nothing to be concerned about. Promise," answered the stranger giving Margaret his best snake smile.

"You know my name but I don't know yours or indeed anything about you."

"That's easily rectified. My name is Maximillian Grodt, Max, and…"

Max spoke for the next hour and a half, pausing only occasionally to sip from his glass of sparkling water. He told her about the Brotherhood, the Organisation, the Mandarins, The 400 and how it all worked, or rather a version of how it all worked. Max said that if she was agreeable he would mentor her, as her sponsor, for her to become the Chancellor. She asked why her. He replied that from what he and his fellow Mandarins knew about her and her qualities they believed she could be Madame Chancellor, "with the right backing, of course." Max went on to say that the main characteristics that had attracted their attention were her integrity, her leadership skills and her passion for change and that change, more than anything, was what the Organisation was in dire need of. He said the Organisation must change in order to meet the challenges of the modern world around it. Max captured Margaret's imagination; it was as though he was wired directly into her. He'd researched his subject well and knew all the right buttons to push. He knew her past life and how she craved validation in a world run by men and he could put her where she needed to be to change that. Max gleaned from Margaret's responses that despite everything, despite all she'd said and claimed in the past, she was really only interested in two things; herself and power. In that respect she was no different from the male candidates for the job.

Max laid out his ideas on how the Organisation should be run in future. The main one being that it could no longer continue as an autocracy. "It needs a leader but not an Emperor," he said, adding that Margaret, as Madame Chancellor, would be all-powerful when it came to matters concerning the Organisation achieving its mission. "To avoid any misunderstandings, Max, what is this mission exactly?" asked Margaret naïvely. His answer shocked her. He told her that the Organisation had originally formed as a Brotherhood in the early fourteenth century with a mission to bring about the downfall of the Aristocracy. "But a Faction inside the Brotherhood, as we were called then, had, instead, the destruction of the Church as its mission." Margaret replied that she'd never heard of this Faction. "They're commonly called the ACF and are still in existence today… but we're not here to discuss those malefactors." Max continued as though nothing further need be discussed about the Organisation's past. "In future," he said, "the Organisation will be run by an inner council. Initially, it will necessarily be set up as a 'secret' inner council because its introduction will most likely incite dissent among the Governors."

"You will, of course, Chair the inner council and choose half its membership. We will appoint the other half." Margaret understood why the Mandarins were going to appoint half the inner council. If she proved incapable then the transition to a new leader would be much easier to accomplish but her second thought worried her more; it meant the Mandarins had people close to her who would be loyal to them and not her.

"What are the changes that need to be made?"

"I'd have thought it would be obvious to somebody like you." Margaret felt she'd disappointed her sponsor. "As you appreciate, change can only truly take effect if it's made at the very top. Hence your appointment. Its present leader is incompetent and needs to go. You'll need to get rid of most of the others."

"Get rid of most of the others?"

"Yes, of course, they must be got rid of. But don't worry, we already have replacements for eighty percent of them. You'll need to identify the other twenty percent. I suggest the structure of the regions remains unchanged for now, we'll just replace the leadership. It will need to happen virtually overnight for obvious reasons."

"Who are we talking about? Governors? IOs? Controllers? Their IOs?"

"You'll be provided with a list but, to set expectations, it'll be most Governors and a good many Controllers. At present there are no IOs, Counsellors, Operatives or Sentinels on the list."

"That's more than a thousand individuals. Wouldn't it be better if the present Chancellor did this so I could then—"

"Surely you must realise the answer to that question. He's part of the problem. He's the main reason we're being forced to act in the way we are. You were born to do this Margaret. I have the greatest faith and confidence in you and your abilities. You'll make an outstandingly good Madame Chancellor and with my help you'll be running the Organisation within months, perhaps weeks."

Max and Margaret talked for another hour before agreeing to meet again over the following days and again at her next destination, Israel. Margaret was more than a little disappointed after Max informed her that the post of President of a reunited Organisation was going to be somebody from the French Splinter called Christan Lefort. He promised to introduce Monsieur Lefort to her at the earliest opportunity at which time he felt certain she would agree with the choice he'd made. *He'd made?* thought Margaret.

*

The Mandarins have been in existence for almost as long as the Brotherhood has itself. During the early years they helped with the Brotherhood's European expansion. Shortly thereafter they became partners and, following a revolt, its rulers before being banished for conspiring against the mission, only to be brought back, albeit in a reduced capacity, because the Brotherhood couldn't function without them. From the last decade of the nineteenth century the Mandarins once again fostered ambitions to play a pivotal role and began building up numbers of followers. They grew exactly as the Brotherhood had grown, right under the noses of those they sought to destroy.

Throughout the centuries there were many attempts by the Aristocracy and the Church to destroy the Brotherhood but their efforts rarely went beyond a single generation. Anti-Brotherhooders were invariably rich and powerful so their offspring wanted to enjoy their lives rather than go waste them chasing shadows. They didn't possess the same energy or commitment as the Brotherhood and so it outlasted them all, generation after generation. The Church built up a head of steam in the fifteenth century but during the Renaissance, and following that the time of Henry VIII, it had other matters to attend to and so lost sight of what it mistakenly took to be a rag-tag collection of malcontents. By the end of the seventeenth century the Church had all but forgotten about the Brotherhood. From time to time, rumour of its existence rose but by then it was untouchable. Untouchable, that is, until Bonaparte. The Mandarins had backed him but he and they failed to gain control of the Brotherhood. Defeated, they slunk away to lick their wounds. It was fortunate for the Mandarins that Bonaparte kept their alliance secret. They tried time and again to conjure some plot to gain control of the Brotherhood but each attempt ended in failure.

Accepting their machinations were getting them nowhere the Mandarins decided on a more subtle, considered strategy in place of bloody conquest. To achieve this they needed time to rebuild their numbers. They were convinced a world war would tip the balance in their favour but they were mistaken. The person they believed would lead them to victory was exposed as a traitor by the Organisation and, given his position in British society, he had to step down otherwise his Regal family would not survive the scandal.

By the late 1950s or early 1960s the Mandarins had the numbers but they lacked a leader. Then, after one of them unexpectedly died, her son, Maximillian, came onto the scene. He was too reckless as far as the other Mandarins were concerned and time and again they blocked his plans by outvoting him. There being only nine Mandarins on the Council at the time, Max sought to increase their membership, gain a majority of support among the new members and enact his plans. This was a step too far for the Mandarin Council. Having no desire to see their power diluted they banished Max. He slipped into the shadows to plan his next move. After blackmailing two Mandarins, and with the others disunited, Max re-joined the Council after one of its number mysteriously disappeared.

At a bi-annual Council meeting, Max set out his plans for gaining control of the Organisation by first replacing its Chancellor with a patsy he knew from university. Five Mandarins were opposed to Max's plans while favouring their own candidates as the next Chancellor. This was a major setback and sticking point. The meeting broke up in disagreement and disarray. A week later, Max's candidate was found naked, bound and gagged and hanged in the 'dungeon' of a 'House of Correction for Naughty Boys'.

When Max later backed a female candidate some of the Mandarins laughed out loud. "What the hell is he thinking backing this young woman? She's not even thirty!" they said while claiming Max's candidate was also his mistress. He was furious at the allegation. Not for the first time, the Council meeting broke up without reaching agreement but this didn't bother Max; he now knew with absolute certainty who he could rely on for support. He was certain Rex had found the right candidate for what he had in mind. Max had no intention of returning to the discussion on the future Chancellor of the Organisation, he was simply going to go ahead with his plan while taking the opportunity to rid himself of some people he'd wanted to bump off for years.

*

In line with Max's plan, the Chancellor would soon retire necessitating the appointment of a new Chancellor, one with new ideas, Max's ideas. It was unknown for the post to be filled by anybody but a Governor but Max had a scheme to overcome any objections to Margaret Rotheram's nomination. He'd keep it simple and claim she'd been added to the list due to her outstanding performance as an Operative, Counsellor and Controller. "But she's not yet even thirty," they'd say, "she's inexperienced in the ways of the Organisation," they'd say. Margaret, for her part, hadn't yet seen the Organisation for what it really was, further convincing Max she was the ideal candidate to replace the current Chancellor. There's risk in everything people do and to combat risks contingency plans are put in place. Max's contingency plan was one of last resort; he would order his secret Sentinels to assassinate all the members of the Mandarin Council. He hoped he wouldn't have to do that because the fallout would be unpredictable and unpredictability is the last thing anybody wants, especially people like Max.

*

Margaret returned to London as soon as her meetings with the leaders of the Splinters were concluded. Among the first people she bumped into in Half Moon Street was Lisette. Their previous differences were immediately put aside as they'd missed each other enormously. They went for a drink in the Ritz to catch up. Margaret asked Lisette how her job was going. "I'm bored out of my mind!" she replied, which didn't surprise Margaret in the slightest as it was a very boring job but she added, "With what could happen shortly all that might change." Lisette wanted to know more but was told that everything would become clear in the near future and that she should sit tight for now. Lisette knew better than to press for an answer. She felt confident that if something good was going to happen for Margaret then it could work out well for her too.

*

The Chancellor came into the office one day and announced his retirement. He tried to recall Max's exact words but couldn't quite do so; he'd said something like, 'there would soon be some vacancies for Mandarins,' or something like that. People only ever hear the words they want to hear, especially when blinded by greed or ambition. The Chancellor had taken Max's words to mean that some Mandarins were about to be killed off. He didn't care because he felt sure that if he unwaveringly supported Max he'd be safe. He'd watch his back though, just in case. He'd be vulnerable with no Sentinels to protect him but *I have Max for that,* he thought. The Chancellor had no idea that the Mandarins had been building up their forces for some time and was surprised when Max said he'd be assigned a dozen PAs. *What for?* He had no real idea. Nor did he ponder where Max could have conjured up a dozen PAs, which he believed were really probably IOs or Sentinels. In any case, he expected them to protect him with their lives if necessary. The Chancellor kept saying the word over and over in his head; *Mandarin.* He couldn't believe it. No longer would he have to listen to all those whinging whining bastard Governors. He hoped his new PAs weren't whingers but with him as their boss what could they possibly have to whinge about?

*

A Mandarin Conclave.
"Are we all finally agreed on the candidates?"

"We are, but I still don't understand why are there four of them."

"As has been discussed, there used to be only one pre-ordained candidate but as we can't agree on a single candidate we have four nominees for Chancellor and whichever of them receives the highest number of votes wins. Simple."

"There is no recent precedent for multiple candidates but I see no reason why we can't proceed with a vote."

"In that case, do we all agree to proceed with the vote?" All heads nodded. "There being no dissenters let's put it to the vote. Each of us shall cast a single vote per candidate. Abstentions are not permitted. The winner will be the candidate who attracts the most votes. Brother and Sister Mandarins, please take your place in front of the—"

"One moment, what will happen to the unsuccessful candidates?" asked Allegra.

"They shall be removed from the Tabernacle by the Recorder

and placed in the ante-chamber of the Inner Temple to await the pronouncement of the High Council."

"What sort of pronouncement? None of us has been in this situation before and I want to know what will happen to the unsuccessful candidates."

"I have studied the ancient texts of the Brotherhood," interjected the Recorder, "they say, 'whosoever shall fail in his attempt in becoming the Elder Brother shall be taken to a place of solitude where he shall come upon a Sphairai and open his veins.' That's a rough translation," the Recorder admitted.

"That's from the old Brotherhood days, surely we don't intend for the unsuccessful candidates to do that do we?"

"No, of course not," interjected Max. "The High Council will determine the futures of unsuccessful candidates. They will be dealt with individually; for example, it might not be appropriate for some of them to return to their former post so we will agree where best to assign them. Rest assured there will be no leaving of people in dank chambers with a Sphairai for company," concluded Max trying to laugh it off; whereas he fully intended to have the three unsuccessful candidates killed after losing a vote they could not ever have won.

"I saw Sentinels entering the Temple," said Allegra. "What are they doing here? Since when have we allowed Sentinels to attend these gatherings?"

"Allegra, nowadays we each of us has our own Sentinels and some of them have been brought here to guarantee our safety."

"The Sentinels I saw entering the Temple were from the Italian Splinter."

"Being from the Italian Splinter they are neutral and will ensure everything is carried out according to our laws," said the Recorder. "Now, ladies and gentlemen, if there is nothing else you should now proceed with the vote. Kindly listen to the instructions." The Recorder unrolled an ancient Velum sheet and read from it. "You are to enter the Tabernacle one at a time. Inside you will find latticework booths separated from one another by a curtain. You are to leave a mark, called a Kiss, on the left cheek for 'no' or the right cheek for 'yes' on each candidate in turn. You are only allowed one Kiss per candidate. Is that understood?"

"Couldn't we just raise our hands to vote for whoever we want to vote for?" suggested Christoph de Heer, a Dutch Mandarin, leaving the remaining Mandarins shaking their heads in disbelief of his inane comment.

"After the Kisses have been checked and counted by me, as official Recorder, the result will be announced, also by me. The candidate with the most Kisses on their right cheek will be the new Chancellor. If there is a tie the Kissing will be rerun between those tying until we have a winner."

Inside the Inner Tabernacle were four latticework booths resembling confessionals, separated from each other by heavy curtains. The only light to see by was a single candle placed above the face of each candidate. Adjacent to the cheeks of the candidates were apertures through which Kiss marks would be made by the Mandarins. For the vote to be secret, the Mandarins drew up their hoods before entering the Inner Tabernacle, covering their faces before leaving Kisses on the cheeks of the candidates. The Recorder was in attendance to ensure the Kissing was carried out properly. Each Mandarin Kissed each candidate once, departing before the next was called in by the Recorder. Margaret was in the far left-hand booth and was last to be Kissed before each Mandarin exited through a maze of hanging black drapes.

In preparing Margaret for the Kissing ceremony, Rex told her she'd be tied naked to a crucifixion cross in the Mandarin's Tabernacle which brought to her mind fanaticised rituals of murderous cults as well as whether Max was telling the truth or not. It was a half-truth as all she wore for the ceremony was a thin black shroud as she sat in the near total darkness of the Inner Tabernacle. Sensing each shadowy figure pass in front of her, Margaret felt something touch her on either her left or right cheek. None of the candidates had any idea of the significance of the warm waxy crayon 'Kissing' their cheeks.

*

Kissing in the days of the Brotherhood.

Following the ending of the line of the Clay dynasty, Elder Brethren decreed that the Brotherhood would, thereafter, be ruled by a High Council and not an autocrat. It was then that the Kissing ceremony was introduced. In those times it was not carried out in a candlelit Tabernacle but surrounded by hundreds of Brethren in a forest glade or atop a lonely mountain at either dusk or dawn. As with the Roman Senate, the High Council could vote for a Dictator to rule the Brotherhood in times of great need.

The number of High Council members changed with time. Originally they had been thirteen but more commonly they were nine. Always an odd number so votes could not be tied as abstentions were not permitted.

Whenever a seat on the High Council became vacant, Brethren would be proposed to fill it from the various Factions. In such situations, there being an even number of living Elders, the oldest of all the Brethren would join the High Council for the Kissing ceremony. They would don hooded cloaks and one at a time Kiss each Candidate on either their left or their right cheek. The Kissing was observed by the Recorder who counted the number of Kisses for each candidate. Unsuccessful candidates usually took defeat honourably. However, some did not. Even though the High Council were hooded it wasn't difficult to identify who was who and on several occasions vendettas were undertaken by unsuccessful candidates, often resulting in the assassination of those who hadn't voted for them. In turn, this led to multiple vacancies on the High Council in a single year. As can be imagined, the deaths of so many of the High Council caused mayhem within the Brotherhood.

Oftentimes, those slighted by defeat would take revenge in one of any number of ways, for example, betraying Brethren to their ardent enemy, the Church. This was the Aristocracy's main source of information concerning the Brotherhood for nearly two centuries. It all changed when an Elder called Daniel Smythe was declared Dictator following the hunting down and slaughtering of over 200 Brethren and their families. Many suspected Smythe to be the informant behind the massacre in order to rid himself of debt. He changed the rules on Kissing to what they are in modern times. Henceforth, the Kissing was carried out in a barely lit Tabernacle. A Recorder made sure the Kissing was counted and carried out properly. It was Daniel Smythe who decreed that unsuccessful candidates would be killed so as to prevent vendettas fomenting or information leaking to the Church or the Aristocracy. Unsuccessful candidates were led from the Tabernacle by Sentinels to a chamber lit by a single candle where they found the same number of Sphairai awaiting them. The chamber door would be locked as would the door at the top of the stone stairs leading to it.

*

After the Kissing ceremony was over the Recorder, from beneath his hood, announced the numbers of Kisses for each candidate. When he finished he declared Margaret Rotheram, she being the only candidate to have received five right-cheek Kisses, as Madame Chancellor. Afterwards, nobody thought to ask about the unsuccessful candidates. All of whom Max immediately turned over to the Sentinels of the Italian Splinter. As they were being taken away on their final journey Max made the sign of the cross over each of them while whispering the Trinitarian. The Sentinels performed the same ritual over themselves and then their victims.

The ceremony that followed the Kissing lasted nearly two hours. Margaret thought it more akin to a coronation than the election of a leader of a shadowy organisation. After the ceremony was over she had to hand back the ceremonial robes and black shroud. She wanted to keep the shroud as a memento but the Recorder said it wasn't allowed, "Not even for an all-powerful Madame Chancellor," he said. "All-powerful Madame Chancellor," Margaret whispered to herself. An all-powerful Madame Chancellor! She liked how that sounded and would work toward becoming just that.

*

It was a beautiful sunny morning and as if the day couldn't get any better it was Charles' last day as Chancellor, his final day at the office in Half Moon Street. His main duty that day would be to announce his replacement. He couldn't wait to see everybody's faces when he named Margaret Rotheram. Then he'd pop a few Champagne corks, down several glasses of the bubbly stuff, eat some canapés, do some glad-handing around the room, make his farewell speech, in which he'd wish his replacement all the very best of luck in the world, and then wave goodbye as he left the building for the very last time. At least he hoped it would be the last time as he didn't ever want to see again the faces of all those whinging whining bastards he'd grown to hate.

Everything went according to plan. Charles especially loved the look on everybody's face when he announced that Margaret Rotheram was the new Chancellor. He wished he'd been allowed a camera but no cameras are allowed in the Half Moon Street office. Sir Toby Carlton almost had a heart attack on the spot as he'd been touting his friend, Lord Fitzroy, for the post. Fortunately for the old boy he hadn't made the final cut and so was spared the Sphairai. Lord Fitzroy announced he couldn't have been happier with Margaret Rotheram as Madame Chancellor because, according to him, the Organisation needed a good shake-up. He took hold of Margaret's hand firmly, earnestly congratulating her and swearing his support for her in everything she did.

"Well done old chap. You certainly fooled her," muttered Sir Toby.

"What the hell are you talking about old thing?" asked Lord Fitzroy.

"What you just said to… I'll shudder when I say it… 'Madame Chancellor'."

"Whatever do you mean you bloody fool, I meant every word of it. Damn fine girl. I'll back her all the way. I'd be proud to have a daughter like her. We need more of her sort… this place is becoming a morgue. A word to the wise Toby old thing, she might look like she wouldn't harm a fly but I wouldn't be so sure if I were you. Be careful old love. Take my advice. Retire before you're retired, old fruit." Lord Fitzroy departed Sir Toby's company as Sir Jeremy Hawksmith, a loathsome, hateful, despicable creature, came to join them.

"What was that all about?" asked Hawksmith.

"He's lost his marbles. He thinks she's… oh, I can't be bothered. I'm going to my club for a few. Care to join me old man?"

"I certainly would. Perhaps we might discuss the opportunities which always come about with change. I have a few ideas which we can both profit from."

"She won't last," said Sir Toby nodding toward Margaret. "Mark my words… she will not last a year."

Not if I have my way she won't, thought Sir Jeremy.

*

Two weeks later, the former Chancellor, now merely Charles Cavendish, was walking along Rue Phillippe-Plantamour in Geneva on his way to his swearing-in ceremony as a Mandarin. He hadn't given a moment's thought to the likelihood that for him to become a Mandarin somebody had to die. They could have retired but he hadn't considered that either.

As he neared his destination he noticed a man crossing the road just ahead of him. He thought he recognised the man's gait. As the man approached closer he saw it was Rex.

"Hello Rex old boy. What a coincidence seeing you here."

"Hello Charles old boy, nice to see you again."

"What are you doing here? Business? I'm afraid I'm out of touch with events so—"

"Yes, business. The same business as you as a matter of fact."

"What do you mean?"

"I am being completed today."

"Being completed?"

"I am being completed a Mandarin today. That's the term that they use. Being completed. Get it?"

"Oh, I see. So we're both being completed today?"

"So it would appear."

"How are things back at the—"

"Like you, I don't go there anymore. No, I decided the atmosphere was just too claustrophobic and womanly, if you know what I mean?"

"I do and I couldn't agree more." The pair arrived at their destination. "After you old man," said Charles opening the door for Rex to enter the building first.

"I wouldn't dream of it old thing, after you old man," said Rex for Charles to enter the building ahead of him.

Charles' first impression of the inside of the building was not very favourable. He thought it rather dowdy, dated, old-fashioned and shabby like faded glory. The lift wasn't working and according to the information board on the wall adjacent to the stairs their destination was the fourth floor. By the time they arrived at the office door marked MMD Inc. Charles was totally out of breath.

"Let me catch my breath for a moment before we go in old love. I don't want them seeing me wheezing like an old boiler."

"Of course Charles old thing, take your time."

As the pair stood waiting for Charles to catch his breath two men passed along the corridor and entered the room marked MMD Inc.

"I say, do you think we're in the right place old thing?"

"Oh yes, definitely. This is it. I was here only last week."

"I don't wish to be picky but the whole place looks a bit of a dump."

"Don't let appearances fool you Charles. The idea is to maintain a low profile," replied Rex utilising his customary tapping of the side of his nose with forefinger.

"Ah, yes, I understand. Well now, I've caught my breath so let us proceed inside." Charles walked into the room ahead of Rex. Once inside, the former Chancellor couldn't quite make out what was going on. The two men that had entered the room earlier were seated on a desk at its centre. It was the only stick of furniture in the entire room. "What's going on Rex…?"

"I have no idea," lied Rex.

"Mr Cavendish?" said one of the men in a soft Irish accent. Charles hadn't been addressed that way in a very long time.

"Erm, yes?"

"Are you ready?"

Ah, thought Charles, *this must be the start of the ceremony.*

"Mr Cavendish," said the other man quietly.

Charles turned to face the man that had spoken his name and, as he did so, the man thrust, with considerable force, an eight-inch stiletto through his sternum and into his heart. Charles looked down at the hand holding the dagger in shock and disbelief of what had happened. There was no fuss or commotion in the room and Charles felt very little pain. There was no blood apart from a small red dot in the upper middle of his crisp white shirt.

When Charles made to grab the stiletto, the man, who Charles took to be of Mediterranean origin, pushed him backwards, smashing him hard against the wall. He began feeling lightheaded and woozy. He looked again at the hand holding the dagger and then at the three pair of eyes staring at him. He opened his mouth to scream prompting the Mediterranean-looking man to place his free hand over Charles' mouth. He felt his knees go weak before they crumpled completely and he dropped to the floor. The Mediterranean-looking man knelt beside Charles. Raising his victim's head in the crook of his arm the assassin slowly slid the stiletto from Charles' heart causing blood to be pumped into his chest cavity and his blood pressure to plummet. Charles' vision became tunnel-like and sepia before going to grey and finally black. He wasn't quite dead. He could hear noises and speaking. His head hit the bare floorboards as the Mediterranean-looking man shoved it off the crook of his arm. It hurt more than the…

"You're gettin' really good with that thing."

"Who was he?"

"Don't ask any questions and ye might live longer. Well, that's what I heard anyway," said the Irishman.

"I need to be going now. You'll take care of this?" said Rex.

"Woah, woah, woah. Wait one moment 'auld fruit'," answered the Irishman in mock of an old Etonian accent. "Our orders don't include cleaning up here 'auld man'."

"Surely you don't expect me to—"

"Stop pissing around. Look fella, get lost, he's just having you on," said the Mediterranean-looking man.

"C'mon, I was just havin' a laugh with yer man. Did ye see the look on his feckin face though?" said the Irishman in playful mood. "I was just kiddin' with ye mate. Go on, get off outta here. Leave this to us. We don't mind gettin' a tip for a job well done though!" Rex took out his wallet and gave the men a bundle of notes so he could get out of the room and on his way to meet Max for his completion ceremony. He hoped he wasn't going to receive the same treatment as Charles had.

"What's five hundred Francs in real money?" asked the Mediterranean-looking man.

"Who cares? I was just havin' a bit of the craic with him like."

"We shouldn't really be doing things like that, Jack."

"What's wrong with ye? It was just a joke I was havin' with yer man. Anyway you grab the heavy end and let's do the necessary."

Roberto and Jack lifted Charles' body up off the floor and placed it on top of the desk. After removing all identifying items from the corpse they grabbed their carving knives and set to work. They estimated Charles would easily fit into two large suitcases for his trip to the landfill.

SITUATIONAL DETERMINISM

Margaret was admitted to the Half Moon Street offices by a security guard. He informed her that she was the first in though others were expected later. She was returning to work following the Yuletide holiday, not that it had been much of a holiday for her. Her inaugural AGM had been a disaster. The timing of the Chancellor's resignation meant Margaret had precious little time to prepare for it.

She'd wanted to delay the AGM until the end of February but Max insisted it had to be held in December. According to him, "changing the timing would be a bad thing" because "this was the AGM to announce her arrival… this was the AGM of change." Impatient to get on with his plan to destroy the Organisation, and despite previously reprimanding others for being too eager, Max made a huge error of judgement by insisting the AGM went ahead before Margaret was ready to lead it.

*

The AGM.

Not being a fan of smoking or smokers, Margaret banned all smoking during the AGM, especially cigar and pipe smoking as she associated this with the old farts' club. This did not go down well with them. Sir Jeremy Hawksmith, however, wasn't going to be told what to do by a slip of a girl and so lit up a cigar in the corner of an ante room. Nearby heads lifted like Meerkat sentries to see where the delicious cigar smoke smell was coming from. The rich aroma was too much for many and they pulled out their cigar cases. Before a second cigar could be lit an "Ahem!" came from the direction of the main auditorium. At the "Ahem!" the gathered knots of old farts parted like the Red Sea, leaving Madame Chancellor a clear line of sight to the smoker.

Standing at six feet three inches in her heels, Margaret swivelled her head Owl-like to glare at the rotund five foot five smoker with her piercing pale blue icy eyes. "Put! That! Out!" said Margaret with each clearly enunciated word spat out at one second intervals, each ending with a crisp 't'. Sir Jeremy Hawksmith stubbed out his cigar on a nearby saucer, throwing its remains into an ornamental fireplace. "Sorry old thing, old habits and all that," he muttered without the faintest trace of remorse in his voice.

That was the first time the Governors experienced Madame Chancellor's tone of voice and the glare from her icy pale blue eyes lowering the room temperature a few degrees. Something they would never forget.

By admonishing Sir Jeremy Hawksmith in the way she did, Margaret blamed herself for getting the AGM off to a bad start. It was her opportunity to announce 'her arrival on the scene' as Max had put it but she'd blown it. *Why couldn't I just have let it go?* she'd asked herself. *Oh well, I have a year before the next one. Yippee! That's if I'm still around in a year's time.*

Shortly after she'd reprimanded Sir Jeremy, Margaret bumped into a woman. The woman apologised immediately while pressing a piece of paper into Margaret's hand. She knew better than to read it out in the open and so went to the ladies' toilet. As she stood before the mirrors over the wash basins the woman emerged from out of one of the cubicles. Their eyes met in the mirror. Margaret reached inside her handbag for her trusty .38.

"I knew you'd come in here to read it. Wait a mo', I'll lock the door. We can talk without being disturbed. I don't think they've bugged this place yet so it should be okay." Before Margaret could say anything, the woman introduced herself. "I'm the new Control."

"I'm—"

"Don't be silly, I know who you are."

"The note makes no sense," said Margaret after glancing at it.

"It wasn't meant to. It was meant to bring you in here."

"What do you want?" Margaret cocked her .38, the click was audible.

"As I said, I'm the new Control…"

"I didn't know we had a new Control."

"Charles promoted me just before he retired."

"Charles?"

"Your predecessor, the former Chancellor."

"Oh, I see. And why did he promote you? Was he leaving me a surprise or was he simply looking after an old… acquaintance?" said Margaret accusingly.

"There was nothing like that going on between Charles and me. We'd known each other for years and over that time we confided in one another… probably more than was wise. He wasn't a very good Chancellor. He knew his limitations though and when the Mandarins began pressurising him he confided in me." There was a heavy knock on the door. "Look, we don't want to be discovered together in a locked loo. I just wanted to let you know that Charles did what he did to protect you. You can always rely on me." Fisted hammering replaced the door knocking. "Yes, alright!" shouted Control. "The latch must have slipped… one minute please!" Control handed Madame Chancellor a key. "You might need this one day. Charles said something about the Churchill Papers when he handed it to me. Remember, Madame Chancellor, you can always rely on me." Control departed the toilet, admonishing the persistent door knocker on her way out.

"What was that all about?" asked Madame Chancellor emerging from a cubicle.

"I became concerned when I realised you were alone in here with her," replied Margaret's undercover Sentinel nodding toward Control.

"Thank you Awhah. I can always rely on you to protect me." Awhah bowed and remained with Margaret while she washed her hands.

*

It's odd how things work out. It seems as if there's some kind of cosmic karma at play which shapes events and destinies. It's sometimes referred to as Situational Determinism. Others call it conspiracy paranoia.

Situational Determinism is the universal force which creates opportunities which would not have existed or otherwise arisen had you not been in the market for them. For example. You start a double-glazing company and the next thing you know is you're surrounded by double-glazing conversations, situations and opportunities which weren't there before you started your double-glazing company. That is Situational Determinism at work.

*

A Mandarin and invited guests' conversation.

"What's going on?"

"What do you mean 'what's going on'?"

"Don't play games with me, Rex. What's happening inside the Organisation with our protégé Madame Chancellor?"

"As you know I don't get in there very much these days but I heard that the AGM went appallingly badly for her. Sir Jeremy thingy is out to get her… so I hear."

"We can't afford for her to fail not after all the work that's gone into this."

"Then we'd better hope our little enterprise consolidates her position as Madame Chancellor and puts the Governors in their places."

"If you'd have done a better job in the first place we wouldn't be in this position!"

"Have you always been like this?"

"Yes, from a small child so I am told," snapped Max. Rex pressed a button on Max's desk activating a buzzer in the outer-office which was followed by a gentle tapping knock on the office door.

"That'll be Lara," said Rex.

"Enter!" shouted Max. A slender blonde female entered the room.

"Good morning," said Lara in her southern drawl way.

"Can you update us please Lara?" said Rex.

"Well, everything is in place. I just need to make the call. Hopefully she'll meet with me, so long as she doesn't still bear a grudge that is."

"If she doesn't agree to a meeting then I'll get involved… but it's better that I don't for obvious reasons."

"Both the CIA and the American Splinter are on board," said Lara.

"Excellent. When the time is right the details will be leaked to the Russians."

"They'll go crazy."

"That's what I'm relying on."

"They'll never agree to a deal involving the Americans."

"We should tell the Russians straightaway, they'll get to know something is going on anyway, they've eyes and ears all over Half Moon Street. The place leaks like a sieve."

"The Russians will find out in good time."

"On a slightly related topic," added Lara coyly, "I don't trust Lefort and when he finds out what's going on he'll run to his Froggy boss and then all hell will break loose."

"He won't say anything to anybody after he finds out that he's being put forward for the Presidency of a reunified Organisation."

"What? Him? He's a moron!"

"I agree. He's barely capable of tying his own shoe laces but he's well liked and is trusted by the Splinters so he won't appear such a crazy nomination. Everybody'll buy it, they'll never see it coming."

"I hope you're right. I'll stay close in case he decides to blab. Do I have your consent to sanction him… if the need should arise that is?" Max nodded his consent.

"What about the General? How's he holding up?"

"Variable," replied Lara. "He's panicky at the moment but so long as he's given the right medication he'll be okay. By the way, will he really be allowed to go to the US when all this is over?"

"That's not our concern. You can do what you wish with him after the goods have been delivered."

"He knows way, way, way, too much. We don't want him writing his memoirs. You know what they're like as soon as they get Stateside and think they're safe, they write a damn book. Folks everywhere love that sort of spy stuff."

"Let me think a while on that one but be prepared to deal with him Stateside… personally, I mean. We can't afford to have him wandering around Russia after the KGB start their witch-hunt. He'll crack for sure. Now, Lara, if you'd be so kind, leave us." Lara bowed and left the room.

"Where did you dig her up from?"

"Oh, I've known Lara for a long time now… she's a Doubler."

"Obviously. They're useful though aren't they?"

"They certainly can be at times. Speaking of time, you need to leave."

*

Lara, an Operative working for the American Splinter, had once worked with Margaret on a special assignment, and as she was, so-say, passing through London she called her on the pretext of being interested in knowing how she was getting on in her new job. Truth be told, Lara was as surprised as many at Margaret's appointment as Chancellor, even though she'd been impressed by her during their assignment and thought it possible that others might have been similarly impressed. But impressed enough to give her the top job? What Lara was unaware of was that Margaret had been marked out for greatness long before her appointment to the top job. A top job that came with conditions.

Lara suggested they meet on neutral ground for obvious reasons.

"Hi honey, thanks for seeing me," said Lara smiling. "Congrats on the new job." The two women hugged one another as a pat down and then performed the Kissy Kissy face dance ensuring not to touch cheek with lips.

"It's good to see you again, Lara," lied Margaret. "How are things in Moscow?"

"Oh, the usual."

"The usual? Can't we be open with one another?"

"Well, you know, you're Madame Chancellor and I'm an Operative with the American Splinter so what can I say?"

"I wonder then why you're here, Lara. Coffee?" Margaret wanted to get on with it as she was a busy woman now she was Madame Chancellor. That was the image she wanted to portray at least.

"Yes please. I wanted to sound you out on… a… an… opportunity."

"An opportunity? Why me? Why not your CIA or Splinter bosses? Isn't the American Splinter interested in opportunities?"

"They're both on board already but this opportunity can be so much more than they can do with it. You know how hard it is to get some people to listen?" Lara said pointing a finger toward the ceiling before realising her erstwhile co-assignmentee was now one of those her index finger was alluding to. She smiled in recognition of her faux pas.

"Black? No sugar? Right? You talk, I'll play mother."

"You know I've been running a Russian General for some years now? Right?"

"Old Vladimir? How is he?"

"The very same and he's fine, next time I see him I'll tell him you were asking after him." Lara took a sip of coffee. "You remember how it was whenever we wanted to shake the tree in Moscow? You wind up the clockwork KGB and off they go and pick up some somebody you want to settle a score with… or set hares running, or something similar. It always ends up the same way, though. Somebody dies. Usually by being so unfortunate as to fall from the tenth floor of some desolate Soviet tower block. Amazing how often that happens."

"They have no imagination."

"Well, we shook the tree just before Christmas…"

"Cruel timing."

"It was. We wanted the KGB to arrest Ilya Vakhnenko. He'd been a P in the A for a while so we wanted him off the streets. Instead, the stupid bastards arrested a whole bunch of people. Slaughtered them all, including Lyudmila Mikhailovich."

"Shame, I liked her a lot." Memories of the times she and Lyuda had spent together came flooding back to Margaret.

"That's when old Vladimir came a running. He thought the KGB might be onto him or perhaps one of those arrested might've squealed under torture and fingered him. He begged me to get him to the US as quick as possible. He wants to go to California, says he's tired of cold weather. I told him I'd have to check with the boys in the office. On my way to make the call it hit me like a bolt of lightning." Lara paused to see if Margaret was going to ask the obvious question, which she didn't. "So, when I got to the office I called home and told them my plan. It involved telling old Vladimir that my bosses didn't think he'd done enough to warrant the diplomatic shit-storm his defection would create if we gave him asylum and he'd have to do one last job for us if he wanted a ticket to the US. Want to hear what the job is?"

"What would you do if I said no?"

"I'd tell you anyway because I know you'll want to hear it. I told old Vladimir that if he wanted to leave the workers' paradise of the Soviet Union he'd have to help us expropriate some Soviet missiles. Not the old crap, the brand new stuff they've only just deployed." Lara was being economical with the truth about who'd instigated what. The former co-assignmentees discussed Lara's plan which called for wargames to be staged in West Germany within the next year.

"That's a very short time scale to make the necessary arrangements for an operation of that size."

"That's the beauty of it. My CIA bosses convinced the President that advances in Soviet military technology mean that NATO must be capable of deploying quickly and wargames is the best way for us to test our preparedness. The order for the wargames came straight from the White House. The President, of course, is unaware of the true purpose of them."

"It sounds terrific but why are you telling me all this?"

"There's always a chance that things could go wrong and so I need to play the CYA game. If it goes bad my head will be on the block with the CIA… and probably the US Splinter too. My career would be over and I'm not willing for that to happen."

"It might just be me but I'm not following you."

"Then I'll tell you about my second brainwave. I went to my Splinter boss and convinced her that the best thing for the missiles is that they end up in your hands. You could then sell them and neither the CIA nor the US could be accused of involvement in stealing Soviet missiles… obviously we'd want a cut." Madame Chancellor laughed at the preposterousness of the idea.

"Oh obviously! In summary, you want me to steal Soviet missiles? What makes you think I could pull off something like that?"

"Because they're going to be delivered right into your hands by the Russkies themselves. All you need to do is drive them away. I haven't got all the pieces worked out yet but we've got about nine months to come up with a final plan and if the worst comes to the worst we let the CIA take them. It would be a shame though to let hundreds of millions of dollars slip through your fingers. It could even be billions if there are any ICBMs in the haul."

The former co-assignmentees went into a huddle until one had to go catch a flight and the other had a meeting to go to, or so each claimed.

Madame Chancellor immediately recognised what this opportunity meant for her and her standing within the Organisation. A bagful of Soviet missiles to sell would certainly make the coffers look a lot healthier and the kudos of pulling off such a heist would cement her position in the Organisation. Success would snap everybody into line and she'd become an overnight legend. *Maybe an all-powerful Madame Chancellor.*

After her meeting with Lara was over, Margaret called Lisette and told her to come to her home at ten that evening for a confidential meeting. She had never entirely trusted Lisette but they had liked one another from the moment they met on a sanction job in Berlin. Assassinations often do that to people, they tend bring them together, just like they have between the Irishman and the Sicilian; plus it was no secret that Lisette would prefer it if the Organisation were run by a man. It was one man in particular as it happened but Margaret wasn't aware of that yet. But, given the situation, she had to trust somebody and it might as well be Lisette.

*

The Soviet Missile Heist, as it was to become known, began six months prior to Lara's meeting with Margaret. General V.V. Grigorovich of the Soviet Army HQ Staff, assigned to the Kremlin, who'd been a CIA informant for nearly all his military career, went into meltdown after most of his closest associates were arrested, tortured and executed by the KGB.

While General Grigorovich wasn't certain whether any of his erstwhile associates were traitors, he certainly was. The fact was they were dead and he didn't fancy joining them. Were they spies?

Were they traitors? Nobody will ever really know but what was clear was that the KGB was on the hunt. He's seen it many times before, it was the lazy old KGB putting the Cat among the Pigeons knowing something was bound to fly out. It always did. When things like this kicked off it was usually because somebody way up high on the greasy pole had been given a kick in the arse and was passing it down the line. It was the old, old, same old, story. Nevertheless, VVG, as he'd been called since his Cadet days, was of the opinion that it was high time for him to leave town. He was confident that he'd done enough to feather his nest in the West over the years and that as soon as he requested to leave the USSR the CIA would jump at the opportunity of such a coup. He was in for a shock though when Lara informed him that he simply hadn't done enough to warrant the diplomatic shit-storm his defection would create. "But," she had said, "I'll have a word with the boys in the office to see if there might be a way to get you to the USA." You see, the United States had wanted something from the Soviet Union for a very long time and VVG could provide it and Lara had been alert and cunning enough to recognise the opportunity VVG's defection presented. The timing could not have been better for Rex either.

What neither the CIA nor the American Splinter knew was that it was Lara herself who'd instigated the KGB hunt which had spooked VVG. Seizing upon the opportunity a terrified VVG presented, Lara put the Soviet General under pressure to commit one final act of treason to pay for his ticket to America. When she told her CIA and Splinter bosses about the plan to steal the Soviet missiles, which she attributed entirely to VVG, they loved it; doing things that way she would get credit no matter what the outcome; zero risk for Lara. Classic Tripler action; whichever way things worked out she'd win. Rex was very proud of his Tripler.

*

The Organisation, its Splinters, The 400 and every other clandestine organisation around the globe employ Agents, a.k.a. Operatives, some of whom work for more than one Agency, organisation or Splinter. They pull off what is called the old Double Header or, more rarely and more dangerously, the old Triple Header. Their existence is tolerated because they can be useful to all sides, for reasons of it being simply good business to keep your enemies closer to you than you do your friends. Doublers and Triplers walk a fine line between remaining useful and redundancy. Redundancy inevitably results in death. So why become a Doubler or Tripler? It's often not by choice – rather, its driven by circumstances.

Lara is widely known as a Doubler and is suspected of being a Tripler. She could be regarded as a Quadrupler if you count the Mandarins but she's only an occasional gofer for Max and so, officially, she's not really involved with them… kind of.

For obvious political reasons, the Russian Splinter couldn't be involved, or even implicated in any way whatsoever, in stealing the property of the people of the Soviet Union, but it was happy, as was the American Splinter, to benefit financially from the missile heist.

Soviet missiles of the mid to late 1960s were far superior to anything the West had at the time. The US government, of the time, were extremely concerned about the capability gap as the Soviets might launch a pre-emptive nuclear strike, leaving them with insufficient retaliation time. This is where VVG and the upcoming wargames, which were to be held right next to the East German border, came into the picture.

*

A secret message passed to Madame Chancellor from the Russian Splinter confirmed that they knew all about the Soviet Missile Heist and promised not to interfere, "But we will need a cut of the proceeds to bribe crooked officials inside the Kremlin," they claimed. *That was quick*, thought Margaret, *I wonder who it was that blabbed to the Russian Splinter? I bet it was... no, Margaret, don't jump to conclusions, make one more enemy and it could be all over for you. We'll bide our time and see where the leak is... and then plug it... plug it permanently.* It being inappropriate for Margaret to carry out that sort of thing, Lisette, Awhah and Cho came to her mind.

What was becoming noticeable in the Half Moon Street HQ was Margaret kept referring to herself in the third person causing some there to mock her by imitation and others to spread rumours that she was losing it.

*

To lay the groundwork for the missile heist, VVG created a great fuss inside the Kremlin about "intelligence he'd received concerning major American-led NATO wargames to be staged right next to their border with West Germany". He feigned outrage at the idea of America provoking his beloved USSR in this way. VVG insisted, however, that this was actually a great opportunity for them to spy on the West to understand their capabilities and to test their own preparedness for war by staging counter-war-games-exercises at the same time as the NATO wargames. "Our counter-war-games-exercises," VVG said, "will necessarily involve tens of thousands of Soviet troops, thousands of tanks and planes and many hundreds of missiles, enough to put the shits up the West!" The missiles were to be the latest generation of mobile SAMs and short- and medium-range ICBMs, perhaps even some long-range ICBMs.

The plan to steal the missiles had support at the highest levels. As far as Washington was concerned, it was a 'go'; they were going to steal at least a dozen or so missile carrier vehicles loaded with the latest Soviet missiles. Many at the top of the CIA thought it had all gone through too smoothly but nobody was willing to put the brakes on. They all signed on the dotted line for operation 'Soviet Missile Heist' to go ahead.

When Madame Chancellor briefed the High Council of Governors about the Soviet Missile Heist they were sceptical but nevertheless thought it was a game worth playing. "It could well be worth hundreds of millions of dollars and should level the balance of power around the globe, both of which will be good for us," claimed Margaret though her voice said otherwise.

*

So, the CIA was in, the American government was in, the Russian Splinter was in and, most importantly, the Organisation was in. The stage was set for the most audacious heist in history.

*

A Mandarin conference.

"Max, I tell you, she has got to go, she's alienated almost everybody around here. I'm telling you, she has to go."

"I told you Max. Didn't I say? She's a mistake. Let's remove her now before she does any more harm. Let's just accept that we made a mistake and move quickly to rectify it—"

"Nobody will be moving, removing or rectifying anything. She's only been in the job a couple of months. She's still finding her feet."

"Why didn't she postpone the AGM for a month or so? It wouldn't have mattered just this once surely. That was a real mistake… a huge misjudgement, on her part."

"I suggested that to her but she's so head strong. She insisted she wanted to go ahead with the AGM so that she could 'stamp her authority'," lied Max.

"Stamp her authority? I thought we were moving away from that sort of thing? Didn't we tell her a condition of her appointment was consensus management?"

"We did but the secret inner council isn't fully operational yet. Ladies and gentlemen, let us review the situation in three months and, during that time, rather than replace her, we should mentor her. Each of us has something to offer her, have we not?" The Mandarins nodded in agreement with Max.

As soon as the conference was over Max made his apologies to the other Mandarins saying he had another meeting to go to that he could not get out of.

*

A Max and Sentinel conversation.

"She must not be allowed to fail. If any of the others move against her they must be eliminated. Do you understand?"

"They're very well guarded so I'll be needing a little help," said the Sentinel in his soft Irish accent.

"Do you have anybody in mind?"

"Well, there's this little Italian fella who's not bad. Not as good as me mind you but good enough."

"Is he from the Italian Splinter?"

"Nah, he's one of the Organisation's own boys."

"A Sentinel?"

"He is but best you don't know too much. Knowin' what ye shouldn't might get ye into trouble if things go wrong. Just leave it to me and himself to do the business and you just sit back an' relax."

"I won't forget you if you..."

"Ye bet yer loife ye won't be fergetin' me Maxy boy!" returned Jack purposely employing a thick Irish accent and meaning every syllable of his implied threat. Max didn't rise to the bait.

"Get close to her, Jack. Make yourself indispensable. Do her bidding in everything. Do as she commands without question. Then, when the time is right, you'll have your revenge on them all."

"There's just the one I want, that's all. Just the one'll do for me!"

ON THE MOVE

After completing his basic training, Michael travelled to the Bootle barracks of the Royal Tank Regiment and reported to Captain Jones.

"So, Private Frost, how did basic training go?"

"It went—"

"Pretty boring stuff eh given the amount of training you've been through as a Cadet but I imagine you made some good mates? You make some of your best friends during basic training, you know. Funny how you come across them time and time again… you can always rely on them to have your back in a tight spot."

"I—"

"I have good news for you, Private Frost. As you're not part of a regular intake your induction training will be carried out at Altcar where you'll learn to drive a Chieftain and a Saracen APC… plus all the other tank crew duties… loading, aiming, firing, navigating. I imagine you'll end up as a navigator. During your training you'll be performing tactical battlefield exercises and so on. Any questions Private Frost?"

"No sir."

"Good. Then let's get you started."

"Thank you for getting me into the Regiment, sir."

"No need to thank me, Private Frost. When you were a Cadet, you created a good impression both at the barracks and at Altcar," grinned Captain Jones. "I think you'll be an asset to the Regiment but don't rule out applying for selection to other Regiments. I, myself, passed Officer Selection for the Royal Marines and saw action overseas."

"I'm just glad to be in the Royal Tank Regiment, sir."

"That's the spirit. The Army's a great life and you have your whole life ahead of you, Private Frost. Now go and pick up your kit and meet me in the parade yard in ten minutes and we'll get off to Altcar."

On arriving at Altcar, Captain Jones introduced Michael to Sergeant Morgan who showed him where he'd be eating, sleeping and assembling. All of which was unnecessary as Michael was already very familiar with the layout at Altcar but this was the Army and they do things by the book. Discipline within the Royal Tank Regiment is just the same as it is in the rest of the Army but being tank crew is different; it's a brotherhood and Michael had been in need of a big brother figure ever since Timbo was incarcerated. A close bond quickly builds between members of a tank crew and Michael, despite his many oddities, was no different.

*

While conducting a review of the lists with his Counsellor, Captain Jones reached list B and Michael's name was at the top.

An Organisation lists review.

"First on list B we have Michael Frost. Reading from Sergeant Morgan's notes, 'Frost finds it hard mixing with people though everybody seems to like him.' Sergeant Morgan describes him as 'a bit odd' and 'a bit of a loner' but it isn't holding him back at all," reported Captain Jones before adding, "Academically he's quite bright... he's clearly not a simpleton... he speaks several languages fluently and—"

"He's quite young so it could just be that he's shy," interjected the Counsellor. "It's also not so very unusual for people from his type of family background to have social limitations."

"He might be on drugs. Young people are on drugs all the time, aren't they?" proffered the London boxing coach. After a deep sigh Roberto spoke next.

"Just because Michael's a bit different it probably doesn't mean any of that. I think he's locked up inside his own head and doesn't work like the rest of us," Roberto said tapping his head, "but he's got real talent and we mustn't lose sight of that. People like him don't just grow on trees. Michael Frost possesses incredible fighting skills. I've fought him and I can tell you there's a terrible strength inside of him and we've all been in situations where that sort of thing has been the difference between living and dying. I say we get him through his tank training and see how he is then."

"I'm in agreement with our friend here. Frost remains on list B for now but he needs to be removed from Altcar as soon as possible," said the Counsellor.

"Why's that?" asked Captain Jones.

"It's to do with a posting I have in mind for him," was all the Counsellor would say. Captain Jones was unhappy with the reply and concerned with what might be in store for Michael. "Move on Jones, who's next on the list…"

After the meeting, as the group made to leave the old signals hut by the sea, Captain Jones held Roberto back by the arm.

"Is this where you stabbed Cadet Munroe? He was only a child. Who would have believed him if he'd spoken out? He was a good lad and loved the Cadets, it was his escape from terrible troubles at home. He had a real cheeky way about him. He was a good kid. Couldn't you have convinced him that what he'd heard was just a joke of some kind? He'd have forgotten all about it soon enough. Was it really necessary to kill him?"

"I don't know who you think you're talking to but you want to keep your nose out of things that don't concern you. Never question me like this ever again." It was hard to accept being spoken to in that way but Captain Jones kept his temper and walked away, leaving Roberto standing alone in the old signals hut down by the sea.

*

Following the lists review, Sergeant Morgan was ordered to take personal charge of ramping up Michael's training. They re-enacted famous Tank battles, debating afterwards what could have been done differently to affect their outcome. I say debated but it was more of a lecture Michael gave Sergeant Morgan. The Sergeant was astonished at Michael's knowledge of military strategy and wondered how he could have come by it.

"Sir, I need to talk with you about Private Frost. He has knowledge and understanding of military strategy which is way beyond anything I've ever come across. He's some kind of... I'm not sure what he is."

After a lengthy discussion, Captain Jones was left wondering what else he didn't know about Michael Frost and agreed with Sergeant Morgan that a visit to Michael's home was necessary in order to investigate his unusual knowledge. In the meantime, the Captain ordered Michael to be placed on administrative duties. Performing repetitive mundane tasks didn't faze Michael in the slightest; he just got on with things and being very efficient in everything he did earned him the nickname 'Robbie the Robot'. This type of work calmed the voices in Michael's head and kept the Demon at bay though it was always there lurking in the background... waiting... waiting.

While performing his administrative duties Michael's path crossed with that of Major Finn. The Major still had a bee in his bonnet over the day he'd been forced by Captain Lefort to allow the Tank Cadets to use sniper rifles for target shooting and since then he'd had it in for them.

"Do you remember me Private Frost because I certainly remember you and your Cadet chums? It was one of your lot who proved to be a little too light fingered and it cost him his life. He got what he deserved if you ask me..."

"Tommy Munroe was his name and it's not possible for a Thunderflash to go off in the way it was described."

"What do you mean, 'in the way it was described'?"

"The report said that Tommy must have primed the Thunderflash accidentally when placing it in his pocket. Have you tried priming a Thunderflash in that way Major Finn, sir?" Michael went on to use the exact words Major Finn had used in his report regarding the death of Cadet Munroe.

"How did you get a copy of my report Private Frost?" screamed Major Finn.

"I've never had a copy of your report sir."

"Then how do you know what it says?"

"I saw a copy on Captain Jones' desk, sir. It was upside down but I could still read it."

"You're just a little sneak aren't you? I'm going to speak with Captain Jones about his lapse in security and suggest a suitable punishment for you while I'm about it."

"But that doesn't answer the question, sir. How did Cadet Munroe prime a Thunderflash while placing it in his pocket? It doesn't make sense as it can't be done that way."

"Then he must have primed it before placing it in his pocket."

"That doesn't make sense either, Tommy wasn't stupid. If that Thunderflash was primed before it was placed in Tommy's jacket then somebody else must have primed it and put it there."

"What are you suggesting Private Frost? That Cadet Munroe was murdered? On a secure MoD site while there were over a thousand people here, including the Minister of Defence? Why would anybody want to murder Cadet Munroe? No, Private Frost, Cadet Munroe was a thief and got exactly what he deserved. I'll be speaking to Captain Jones about you this evening so be prepared for whatever might come your way. Dismissed."

An Organisation conversation.

"I've just had an extraordinary conversation with a Private Frost, a potential on list B."

"Extraordinary in what way?"

"He's convinced Cadet Munroe's death wasn't an accident."

"He can't prove anything. Just keep an eye on him and report back if—"

"Keep an eye on him? He must be removed."

"Major Finn, I am giving you a direct order, you are not to remove Private Frost, we've had a few too many 'accidents' here lately and it's beginning to attract the wrong type of attention."

Michael would need to tread very carefully around Major Finn in future.

Ten minutes later, Captain Jones took a call at his desk from a Counsellor. This was highly irregular as, passing through a switchboard, it could be monitored. During the call the Counsellor intimated that Major Finn wanted Private Frost to receive more than the reprimand that was due to him. The Counsellor then emphasised how vital it was for Michael to be fast tracked to keep him out of Finn's way. As soon as the call hung up, Captain Jones called out to Sergeant Morgan, "Sergeant Morgan, we need to bring our visit to Private Frost's home forward. We'll use some excuse to be off base tomorrow and drive to Liverpool together."

*

The following morning Sergeant Morgan and Captain Jones set off for the Huyton district of Liverpool. They hadn't contacted Michael's mother in advance because they didn't want to alert her. They wanted her responses to their questions to be unprepared. They planned to make it seem as though they just happened to be in the neighbourhood and were taking the opportunity to drop in for an informal chat about her son.

Before reaching the Frosts' front door Mary opened it. Her face was pale. She looked terrified.

"What's happened to our Michael? Is he alright? Where—"

"Please, Mrs Frost, there's nothing to worry about," interrupted Captain Jones. "Let me introduce myself." Captain Jones introduced himself and Sergeant Morgan and mentioned that they were in the area and thought it a good idea to take the opportunity to drop in on Mary as they would with the parents of any young recruit.

That's nice of them, thought Mary. Once the Soldiers crossed the threshold Mary offered them tea and biscuits. "Sugar?" she asked.

"That would be lovely, thank you Mrs Frost, two lumps please."

"I'm a bit hard of hearing love so you'll have to speak up," said Mary cupping a hand behind an ear. This expression of hers drove Thomas and Rose crazy. They told her to tell people she was deaf and not 'a bit hard of hearing' as people invariably ended up repeating themselves because they'd underestimate the extent of her 'hard of hearingness'.

"Mrs Frost," began Captain Jones.

"Call me Mary, love."

"Mary, you have nothing to worry about with Michael. He's getting on extremely well and already proving himself to be a good Soldier. I thought we might take this opportunity to find out a little more about your son, so—"

"I know what you're going to say. He's a bit… strange… no, that's not the word for it, but you know what I mean? He's a good boy and there's nothing wrong with him," Mary insisted. "He wouldn't hurt a fly." Which wasn't the best compliment she could've paid Michael; he was in the Army after all.

"I wouldn't say Michael was strange, I'd say he has some special talents and I was wondering where he might have acquired them. I understand from his file that he was a very good student and passed his exams in foreign languages with very high marks, the highest ever I believe."

"Oh, you're not going to send him to some foreign place just because he can speak foreign are you?"

"Mrs Frost, Mary, I can't tell you where your son will be posted but I can tell you that speaking a foreign language might mean he could be selected for special duties, perhaps in one of the Army's Intelligence Units for example. He'd be tucked up nice and safe behind a desk so nothing to worry about there," said Captain Jones wanting to calm Mary's concerns even if it meant bending the truth. Mary liked the idea of Michael having a desk job, nobody from the family had ever had a desk job before. She thought this real progress. The Captain continued, "So, Mary, tell me, what was Michael like as a child?"

A very proud Mary talked non-stop for an hour about Michael's childhood but omitted the bit about him seeing a Demon with the yellow eyes. They were interested in hearing that Michael didn't speak until he was three years old and how ill he'd been with whooping cough and how, "his nana saved his life by getting him to breathe in hot tar fumes." At the description of this old wives' cure the Soldiers looked at one another thinking the same thing; *Poor little sod, but that explains why he runs out of breath so easily during physical exercises.* Margaret mentioned Michael's boxing, fencing, Karate and 'stuff' and that she didn't like him fighting and she'd told Sergeant Huggard that he wasn't to speak to Michael about him becoming a professional boxer. From what Mary told them, nothing jumped out as to how Michael had acquired his knowledge of military strategy.

"Mary, did Michael have any hobbies? Did he read much at all when he was at home?"

"Oh, he was too busy for hobbies, he was always doing his homework or studying for exams or reading library books. I didn't understand half of it but some of his books are in the cabinet over there," said Margaret pointing to a typical, cheap, 1960s drop-front faux-wood bureaux with cupboards beneath.

"May I see Michael's books? See what he was reading?"

"Help yourself, I'll go and make us another pot of tea. Sandwiches?"

Captain Jones opened the cupboard doors to find the shelves crammed full of books plus pads and pads of handwritten notes. There were language books, books on mathematics, books on martial arts and… bingo, books on military strategy. Inside each of the books in Michael's little library were copious foot and margin notes, most written in what appeared to be a code of some sort. What neither man grasped was that the foot and margin notes cross-referenced, according to Michael's faultless logic, other books, not even necessarily from the same genre. Something they could not have realised was that all Michael's notes were made from memory; he didn't need to reread the other works.

There, in front of them, was the proof they were looking for. One book in particular was heavily annotated; *The Art of War* by Sun Tzu, a high-ranking Chinese general. Another book of interest it seemed was *The Book of Five Rings* by Miyamoto Musashi, a Japanese sword master and ultimate deadly duellist with the Katana. It was evident that Michael had researched military strategy and he was somehow able to apply his research in the real world without prior experience. Had Sergeant Morgan been paying more attention to what Michael said during his 'lectures' he would have noticed that he'd quoted word for word from highlighted texts in the books on the shelves. Captain Jones had been right to visit Michael's home and now he had to secure his future path. Mary re-entered the room.

"Sorry Mary, I must apologise, I've just noticed the time and I'm afraid we have to be making our way back to Altcar. Do you have any message for Michael that you'd like to give me for him?"

"Thanks love, that would be great." The Captain waited while Mary wrote out a four-line letter.

"There's just one other thing before I go," said Captain Jones.

"I know what you're going to say. He's always been the same. I don't know when it started but it doesn't stop him doing anything."

"Doesn't it?"

"No. He says he's not talking to himself, he says he's talking to…" Mary couldn't bring herself to say the word.

"Talking with who?" asked Captain Jones puzzled.

"He calls it his Demon… he can describe it and everything. It must've been terrible for him before not being able to talk about it but when he started talking about it we had to stop him because it was frightening all the kids away." The Captain stood open mouthed at Mary's revelation.

"Does he still see this Demon?"

"He says he doesn't. I used to catch him talking to It every now and again. There's nothing wrong with him just because sees things… we all see things, don't we? You won't kick him out of the Army because of this will you?"

"No, Mary, he won't be getting kicked out of the Army but I must have a talk with him about this Demon."

"Oh good Jesus, don't do that love, he'll know it was me who said something. Why don't you just keep an eye on him and if you see him talking to himself you can say something then and he won't know it came from me. He's a good lad."

"Actually Mary, I was going to mention about Michael sometimes not concentrating properly and I was wondering if you'd noticed it."

"Oh that? Yes, we noticed that a long time ago. If there's something coming up he seems to get excited inside and can't think of anything else. He goes from one thing to another depending on what's coming up next. We stopped talking about Christmas and Birthdays and stuff years ago and it seemed to work." Yet something else about Michael the Captain needed to consider.

"I must be getting back. Lovely meeting you, Mary. Goodbye." With that Captain Jones was gone.

After hearing of Michael's afflictions, Captain Jones was caught in two minds about what he should do. Should he abandon his plan to recruit Michael into his Faction of fifth-columnists, simply leaving the lad to get on with his Army life, or should he use the knowledge he'd gained to control the boy to his own advantage? He felt disgusted with himself for even having such a thought but without further consideration he decided to proceed with Michael's recruitment into the Organisation. His hatred of which was far greater than any feelings of guilt over the future of one small boy.

*

Back at Altcar, Captain Jones gave Michael the letter from his mum. It didn't say much, just the usual; "I hope you are alright and you are keeping well and you are having a good time and you are making some nice friends… " et cetera. The normal stuff that mums like Mary write to the Army sons they're missing. Mary couldn't write what she really wanted to because she didn't want to upset her number one son by pouring out her heart and telling him what was really on her mind and how much she wanted him to leave the Army and come home. Oh how Mary missed Michael being her ears. Her other children weren't interested in being Mary's ears.

Captain Jones told Michael to report to him after lunch the following day for a performance review. In the meantime he contacted his Counsellor to finalise approval to fast track Michael.

*

The following morning, as he waited for his review, Michael felt as if he had a worm in his brain. As Mary had told Captain Jones, one of his quirks was that if something was arranged to happen then he couldn't properly concentrate on anything else until it was out of the way. He'd been the same all his life. His parents never got Michael excited about Christmas or birthdays because of what it did to him. Captain Jones wanted to see for himself, hence arranging a review for the following day.

"What the hell's up with you this mornin' Frosty?" yelled the NCO going over the Tank skirmish which Michael and twenty-three other Soldiers were participating in. "You separated from the rest of the battle group… again! I'm going to have to write you up for this one, it's just too much. It beats me how you can be so good at some things and, quite honestly, so shit at others." The NCO noticed Michael swaying unsteadily on his feet. "Are you feeling okay Private Frost?"

"Sorry Corporal. I can't get my mind off seeing the Captain after lunch. I wish I could have seen him yesterday after he'd been to see my mum."

"He's been to see your mum, eh? How did that come about?"

"I don't know. I didn't know he was going." The Corporal put two and two together and got five. He surmised that Michael was getting booted out of the Regiment and the Captain had been to his home to prepare his family. He felt sorry for Michael as the early days in the Army can be difficult for recruits away from home for the first time.

"I see. Well, no need to mention this morning's… what shall we call it?… misunderstandings? to the Captain. Eh? I'm sure it'll all be okay," said the Corporal while thinking, *Poor sod's got enough on his plate and doesn't need me to drop him in it. Pity really, he's a nice lad and a great little boxer. Fingers crossed he'll be okay.*

Michael's review with Captain Jones lasted a mere ten minutes. During it, he said his only concern was Michael's concentration during team exercises. Then, as if as an aside, he mentioned putting Michael in charge of the Cadet exercises during the Altcar summer camps, followed by an even briefer mention that he was putting him forward for Royal Marines Commandos selection the following January, but Michael had to "keep that confidential". This meant Michael would have RMC selection on his mind for six months without sharing it with anybody and in the interim he'd have to perform as a Soldier in charge of Cadets over the Altcar summer camps. It was Captain Jones testing Michael's ability to keep his concentration while waiting for significant events to happen. He couldn't risk recruiting Michael if he was mentally unstable. The Captain resolved that if Michael made it through to the next year he would enter the final phase of recruitment into the Organisation. If he didn't, he'd be cut loose, remaining unaware of the Organisation and how close he'd come to a life of virtual, if not actual, slavery.

"How'd you get on with the Captain?" asked the Corporal.

"He put me in charge of the Cadets for the summer camps," replied Michael, trembling.

I know what his game is, thought the Corporal. In his mind he assumed Michael was being set up to fail so that his discharge from the Army wouldn't reflect badly on those who'd recruited him. "Well done Private Frost, that shows the Captain has faith in you," the Corporal lied. "I'll act as your observer and be the responsible NCO for reviews and live firing exercises."

"Thank you Corporal Welsh, that would be great." This interaction was overheard by Sergeant Morgan who reported it to Captain Jones.

"Keep an eye on things Sergeant. I don't know why Corporal Welsh is involving himself in this but we need to find out. Be careful not to do anything to arouse suspicion. A dead Cadet playing with Thunderflashes is one thing but the death of a Soldier will be an altogether different matter. Look into Welsh's background, discretely of course, and if anything suspicious turns up we'll deal with him."

From here on in, anybody getting close, or even trying to get close, to Michael would come under scrutiny. Henceforth, just simply being around Michael was a very dangerous place to be.

*

Overhearing things, as Sergeant Morgan had, can be very useful. Imagine, though, a world where you never, or seldom, overhear anything. How much poorer your understanding of the world about you would be if that were the case. Now imagine a world where overhearing, or even just everyday speech, manifests itself as an indistinct cacophony and the louder the talking the less is understood. Add to this an absence of alternate communication channels, a lack of education because your schooling was interrupted by the war, abject poverty preventing you from accessing help and an uncompromising attitude of denial, defiance and independence and there you have Mary and there you have the environment in which Michael Frost grew up. Communication was extremely limited in the Frost household and was the main reason behind Michael's unexpansive conversation style. However, giving lectures, such as on Tank battlefield strategies, is an entirely different matter and then Michael becomes a verbal torrent, fluidly sharing the knowledge he has inside his head. He'd learned to be careful though with his sharing over the years. Regurgitating information, uncensored and uncontrolled, had pushed people away from him in the past. From his earliest times he'd learned that sharing information, especially about his Demon, resulted in legs slapped red. As far as Michael was concerned, communicating just for the sake of it was a bad thing.

While overhearing is an everyday part of communication it's important not to solely rely on it or place disproportionate emphasis on it, which was Sergeant Morgan's mistake. Looking into Corporal Welsh and observing the interactions between him and Private Frost took up a lot of the Sergeant's time during the Altcar camps of 1970. But it wasn't a total waste as Sergeant Morgan got a front row seat to observe the remarkable talents of Michael Frost and he got to know what an asset Corporal Welsh was to the Royal Tank Regiment, which was the best possible outcome for all concerned.

*

The first of the Altcar summer camps would commence in just four days. As usual, most of the Soldiers stationed there were either temporarily posted elsewhere or assigned Cadet Camp duties, which most of them hated.

In the lead up to the first Cadet Camp, Michael was noticeably agitated which was exactly what Captain Jones thought would be the case. Also, he'd arranged for an inexperienced, newly commissioned Lieutenant who was unsure about a career in the Army, to be assigned to oversee Michael's exercises. The first meeting between

Lieutenant Hunt and Private Frost was awkward because one of them didn't want to be there and the other had things on his mind.

Despite not understanding what was required of him, Lieutenant Hunt ordered Corporal Welsh to assemble the Cadets and for Michael to fall in behind them. Classic newbie Officer; when in doubt, fall back on your training in an attempt to pull yourself out of a hole but, no matter what, don't ask anybody below you what's going on. Consequently the Lieutenant assumed control and started barking out orders in an effort to demonstrate he was in charge.

"Excuse me Lieutenant Hunt, sir," whispered Corporal Welsh, "I think you'll find Private Frost is in charge of running the exercise, I'm the observer and my role is to review the outcome of the exercise and you're the Officer responsible for guidance should it be required… sir."

"Of course Corporal, I was just setting things up," stuttered the Lieutenant. "Erm… carry on Private Frost," ordered Lieutenant Hunt.

"Yes sir," yelled Michael, marching to the front. "Squad!" he shouted, "Squaaaaad… 'shun." The Cadets came to attention. "Squaaaaad… stand aaaat… ease. Stand easy." said Michael calmly and so soothing the voices inside his head. "This morning's exercise is de-tanking into a holding defensive position as described on the blackboard behind you. Don't look, you'll be told when to look!" shouted Michael. "After I've gone over the exercise with you you'll take up your positions. The exercise is blue only so no vests are required. Right Cadets, gather round the blackboard."

"But sir, we're not Tank Regiment, sir," complained one of the Cadets.

"If you're on the battlefield are you going to hold your hand up and tell everybody you're excused because you're not in the right war?" answered Michael tartly.

"No sir."

"I'm not 'sir', I work for a living," said Michael having heard this before from some old lags. "You'll address me as Private Frost. Is that clear to everyone?"

"Yes, Private Frost, clear," chorused the ranks of Cadets.

Michael went over de-tanking and the taking up of defensive positions with the Cadets. A simple exercise and one he'd done dozens of times before. Focusing on the job in hand all his thoughts and anxieties about the future were pushed from his mind. This didn't go unnoticed by Sergeant Morgan. Following the exercise the Cadets assembled for a review, identifying what went well and what needed working on. The usual stuff. They'd got the basics right which was the important thing. However, they got into disarray with some scenarios; for example, cover for 'dead' Cadets thus leaving gaps on flanks et cetera. Overall, Corporal Welsh gave a favourable review but warned them that things were going to get tougher. Classic Army behaviour; gee you up for what lies ahead.

To Corporal Welsh's surprise, Lieutenant Hunt wanted 'hands-on' involvement in the exercises but he obviously couldn't take orders from subordinates. This was risky for the Lieutenant as the Army frowns on such arrangements. It regards them as symptomatic of weak leadership. In the Army's view the Lieutenant had been stuffed full of leadership at Sandhurst and he should be exercising it.

Lieutenant Hunt wanted to be 'hands on' so it was agreed that he would act as an additional observer, providing feedback direct to Cadets. To make things interesting, Lieutenant Hunt and Michael held separate briefings for the Red and Blue teams and then switched after each exercise to re-run them using alternate strategies. This proved to be fun for the Cadets and stimulating for the Lieutenant, the Corporal and Michael. By the end of the Altcar summer camps they were working as a close-knit team, holding twice-daily sessions where they decided how they were going to stretch the eager Cadets who especially loved the inter Regimental competitive elements to the exercises. The Lieutenant was actually enjoying being in the Army and thought he might have found his niche.

*

Time flies by and in a blink of an eye for people who are busy. The Altcar summer camps were too quickly over and Sergeant Morgan delivered his report to Captain Jones in which he concluded there were no security risks in the relationship between Private Frost and Corporal Welsh.

"It appears Private Frost brings out the best in people according to your report Sergeant. Your early comments about Lieutenant Hunt were quite disturbing but it seems he took up a proper leadership role toward the end of camp."

"Yes sir, and he appeared impressed by Private Frost's knowledge of military strategy. I believe he found his company quite stimulating. He's certainly a very different Officer to the one who walked in here six weeks ago."

"Quite so. His father was concerned he wasn't fitting into Army life and so pulled a few strings to get him here so I could have a good look at him. I think he's turned a corner and I've told his father that there's now a good chance his son will make a decent Officer. As for Private Frost, I don't want to put the mockers on it but I think we've cracked it. He absolutely thrives on pressure. Could it be that simple? It seems that when he doesn't have a second to think about future events he focusses fully on the here and now." The Captain paused to retrieve some documents from his desk. "I've decided to send Private Frost to Germany to join the Seventh Armoured Division. We've a few of our people there who'll be able to keep an eye on him. I don't intend telling them about Frost's interesting way of dealing with events and see if they notice anything unusual about him. For him, this posting will be a mixture of being bored out of his mind to being stretched every which way during the upcoming wargames. There's a big exercise coming in November being run by our American cousins which means, no doubt, it'll be the usual cockup. Tell Private Frost I want to see him will you please Sergeant."

"Sir, Sergeant Morgan said you wanted to see me?"

"Yes Private Frost, come in and stand to attention in front of my desk. You did quite well during the summer camps though I got the impression you were coasting towards the end. That simply won't do Private Frost, it simply won't do! The Army has high expectations of you as do I and any slacking off is frowned upon. Do I make myself clear?"

"Yes sir," replied a confused Private Frost.

"You relied too heavily on involving others in things you were responsible for. Do you know what I'm referring to Private Frost?"

"No sir."

"You formed a cosy little triumvirate with Corporal Welsh and Lieutenant Hunt. Didn't you?"

"Sir, I can't give orders to a superior rank and the Lieutenant wanted greater involvement and I… I… I don't know sir, I didn't know what to do so I went along with it. I didn't see the harm."

"You went along with it. You didn't see the harm. Exactly! Exactly Private Frost. You were under my direct orders to run the Cadet exercises. You were made the Soldier responsible so I could assess your leadership capabilities. Do you understand?" Before Michael could answer Captain Jones held up his hand to silence him. "You were not ordered to form a cosy little Mother's club and have nice little tea parties with Lieutenant Hunt and Corporal Welsh. How am I to assess your progress if you abdicate your responsibilities? You've wasted six weeks of my time as far as I'm concerned so now I'm left with no other choice than to have you transferred to the Seventh Armoured Division of the British Army of The Rhine, BAOR. You'll remain on active duty there until RMC selection in January. In future, Private Frost, when an Officer gives you an order and that order is countermanded by another Officer you're to report that to the original Officer. Do you understand? You may answer, Private Frost."

"Yes sir."

"You know Private Frost, you don't seem to appreciate what a tremendous opportunity you're being handed here. Grasp your opportunities with both hands Private Frost. You leave for Germany in three days' time and until then you'll remain on camp. Dismissed."

Interesting, thought Captain Jones, *there was no reaction whatsoever no matter how I spoke to him. There was no outward sign of the impact of anything I said. It's as though it's all just words to him.* Sergeant Morgan returned to the room.

"Sir, is there anything else or shall I stand down?"

"Sergeant, you've noticed how Private Frost is a man of very few words unless he's… to use your word, 'lecturing'? He an entirely different person regurgitating facts from inside his head but otherwise you can't get more than a couple of words out of him. Another thing for me to consider in the world of Michael Frost I suppose. I hope he turns out to be worth all the effort I'm making for him."

"If you don't mind me saying so sir, you're putting your head well and truly on the block for that boy."

"Sergeant Morgan, we all have to take some risks in life – the bigger the risks then often the bigger the rewards. But thank you for your concern. Carry on."

LARA'S GAME

The American-led NATO wargames were just a couple of months away. Madame Chancellor had finalised the plan for the missiles heist and Lara was acting as intermediary between the CIA and the American and Russian Splinters. Discovery of Lara's connection with the latter being a surprise to Margaret.

Lara reported to Margaret on the respective positions of the Russian and American Splinters, as well as that of her official employer, the CIA. She told her that the Splinters had offered to 'lend a hand' with the heist, if she so desired, on the basis of 'disposable assets'. Margaret often found Lara's use of American English grating if not downright irritating.

"For goodness' sake, Lara, say what you mean; you mean the Splinters want to loan me Operatives and they don't care whether they return in one piece."

"That's what I said," replied Lara. Margaret couldn't be bothered arguing and so continued the discussion.

"I'm keeping the detail of the plan to myself... largely."

"Largely to yourself? What does that mean?"

"It means exactly what I said," replied Margaret with a touch of mischief in her voice. "I need to build some bridges so I took several Governors into my confidence. Chief among them Lord Fitzroy, Sir Stanley Lucas, Sir Toby Carlton, Michael London, Sir Jeremy Hawksmith, Sir Christopher—"

"Hawksmith? Really? He's the last person I'd trust."

"Why so?"

"According to the American and Russian Splinters he runs his own Faction."

"I know," replied Margaret coolly while wondering how Lara and the Splinters knew. Both women realised their mistakes as soon as they'd spoken. "You know what they say, Lara, friends close, enemies closer." Lara thought that might also mean her. "Keeping Sir Jeremy close means he'll be aware of what's in it for him and will use his considerable resources to ensure the success of the operation."

"I think you've made a big mistake, Madame Chancellor, a very big mistake."

"Too late now, what's done is done but I take your concerns seriously so I'll keep an especially close eye on him. I'll assign him a couple of PAs."

"I wouldn't do that if I were you. He'll know they're really Sentinels put there to sanction him on your order. Just go with the hand you've dealt but watch out for any funny business."

"How long are you in London for?"

"A few days."

"Where are you staying?"

"Why, the Ritz of course."

"Lovely. Dinner and a club afterwards? It'll be just like old times."

"Love to."

*

The American and Soviet Splinters both wanted twenty percent of the proceeds of the missile heist for their non-interference. Margaret negotiated this down to twelve and a half percent on the basis that she would cut them in on future revenue streams, which there always were with the Organisation because that was how it operated. Once an organisation became involved with the

Organisation its Operatives would infiltrate it, often in the guise of consultants. Once bedded in, the consultants become part of the fabric of the host and in some cases become the host. Classic Organisation: both parasite and host, but mostly parasite.

*

Back in Russia, VVG was holding up quite well, more especially so after Lara told him that he wasn't on the KGB's list. According to her, she "knew about these things". She was invariably right about such matters as she had Doubler insiders just about everywhere, including the Kremlin and the Organisation, all the way up to a seat on Madame Chancellor's secret inner council.

A Faction conversation.

"According to her bloody majesty, the missile heist is set for the penultimate day of the wargames. The plan is to conceal their escape by mixing with military vehicles heading back to their bases. It'll be virtually impossible to pick them out during the inevitable search for the stolen missiles," said Sir Jeremy blowing smoke rings from a fine Havana cigar.

"Who'll be taking part?"

"A list will be provided at the next meeting, so she says. She plans to use only British personnel. She says it's not that she doesn't trust our German brothers and sisters, it was just the way the team was chosen. But I seriously doubt that!"

"I'll leak this to my German contacts in case they don't know already."

"Don't do that, old thing. If the German operation already knows then it'll blow up in your face and if they don't then Madame Chancellor will know she has a leak at the top table."

"Then why are you telling me this?"

"I'm keeping you informed, Geoffrey, that's the way things work. Something you might be able to help with though, old love, is the British listening post monitoring the east/west border. If they happen to come across anything concerning the job it could prove useful. We might be able snatch the missiles for ourselves before they're spirited out of Germany."

"I'll see what we can do but do let me know if anything changes. I'll make sure Lefort is assigned to the British, just in case."

"Lefort? Really? Are you sure about that? He's got fingers in too many pies for my liking and he's really only interested in himself and his own career."

"Do you know anybody else like that, Jeremy?"

"Very funny, Geoffrey, very funny. Let's keep in touch and do let me know if your chaps come up with something at the listening post. For the avoidance of doubt I'm referring to the one run by MI3 in Bielefeld… MILR I believe they're called. Tread carefully old boy, we don't want another cockup like the one last year."

*

The missile heist team had in fact been chosen months earlier and was already ensconced in West Germany. Madame Chancellor had no intention of keeping the Germans away from the party. It would be rude not to invite them as it was being held in their back yard. She was keeping the details of the heist to a select few while spreading disinformation to see if it turned up where it shouldn't as she was convinced she had a Doubler inside her secret inner council, perhaps two. The German and UK operational Units of the Organisation historically got on particularly well together. Recently, though, they'd had a huge disagreement about whether the ball crossed the line in the 1966 World Cup final.

*

In the weeks prior to the Soviet Missile Heist, Lara kept especially close to VVG in case he got the jitters. Which he did of course just about every other day. He flip-flopped between plan A, "confessing all to his bosses and hope for mercy"; to plan B, "running away to Israel"; to plan C, "ending it all". He favoured plan B as with a surname ending in 'vich' he felt he'd be given a warm welcome in Tel Aviv. Lara just rode the storm of VVG's panic attacks until they blew themselves out. Occasionally she'd say to him that if he didn't stop his whining she'd transmit an easy intercept message back home naming him as an informant. This threat kept VVG quiet, for a few days at least.

Lara was keeping a watchful eye on more than just VVG. She was constantly monitoring the plan, wanting to know whether there'd been any changes. Madame Chancellor was puzzled to understand what was in it for Lara for her to run the risks she was. She'd posed this question to her in several different ways and had always gotten the same response. Lara said she was an American patriot doing the best she could for her country. She believed the Soviets to be dangerous, unpredictable gangsters who presently had the upper hand in the arms race and she wanted to level the playing field.

"And, presumably, you're doing yourself some good out of this?" asked Margaret leaning over Lara to take a cigarette from a pack of Marlboroughs. She invariably smoked on such occasions.

"You know Margot, there really is no such thing as altruism, everybody's out for themselves at the end of the day... but I do hate those goddamn Soviets," mumbled a doped-out Lara. Madame Chancellor wondered exactly what Lara meant by "everybody's out for themselves at the end of the day". The remark concerned her.

"What do you mean?"

"Nothing. Come here!"

I'm just putty in her hands, was Margaret's final thought before dropping off to sleep.

After what Lara had said Madame Chancellor kept an especially close eye on events. If she saw anything she didn't like she'd press the red button, stop everything and bring her people home. How prepared she was to actually do that Margaret wasn't sure as more than anything she wanted the heist to be a success to prove her worth to the Organisation and show everybody she deserved to be Madame Chancellor. In the back of Margaret's mind, though, the Soviet Missile Heist seemed just too good to be true. She felt something was not right about it, like she was being set up to fail. *But by who? The Mandarins? The Factions? Hawksmith? Max? Rex? Why put me where I am in order for me to fail?* She concluded it had to be the Mandarins because of her disastrous start. *But what if…* Margaret told herself that she had to stop thinking this way and to get on with the job, there was no going back now. At times she felt out of her depth but her inner need for validation kept pushing her forward.

By September all the pieces were in place. All they had to do was wait for time to take care of everything as it always seems to. Let things alone, sit tight, and don't attract attention. Just wait. The trap was set and the key was to spring it at exactly the right time. The one thing they were short of was fluent Russian speakers. The Russian Splinter offered to help out and were put on standby as it would be extremely difficult sneaking Soviet citizens into a British MI listening post, or relaying them information, with the danger that anybody caught would go to jail for a very long time. The answer was to get Russian-speaking Operatives seconded to MI3, and quick.

*

With the clock ticking, Sir Jeremy Hawksmith was moving his own pieces into place. His contingency plan was simple; if he couldn't have the prize he'd spoil Madame Chancellor's party by letting the French in on the plan. He was determined to destroy Madame Chancellor, and the Mandarins too, whom he'd hated ever since being made aware of their existence.

*

Michael was making his way to BAOR HQ at Bielefeld as the storm clouds of fate gathered over him.

WARGAMES

The British military transport plane carrying Michael landed at Bielefeld Flughafen. His posting had been changed at the last minute by Captain Jones to the HQ of the 1st Division of the British Army of the Rhine [BAOR] Bielefeld, a long way from Soltau where the Seventh Armoured Brigade was based. He had decided to send Michael to an HQ unit in order to isolate and unsettle him as a test of his emotional stability.

On arrival at divisional HQ, Michael was assigned administrative duties where he was able to utilise his German and, to a lesser degree, his Russian language skills which, once they became known, attracted the attention of MI3 who then snapped him up. The first thing Michael noticed about MI3 was that everybody was referred to as 'chaps'.

This unforeseen development greatly concerned Captain Jones. He'd underestimated Michael's language skills and now the spooks had him, *Damn!* The Captain knew he was in deep trouble. If he lost Michael to Military Intelligence that would be a huge blunder on his part. He'd have to give some serious thought to how he could put a spin on the situation otherwise the last four years he'd spent infiltrating the Organisation would have been for nothing.

*

On joining MI3, Michael was assigned to the Soviet desk of Military Intelligence Liaison – Russia; MILR. The Unit was responsible for monitoring activities along the whole of the East German border. This elite group within MI3 were impressed by Michael after he cracked an encrypted message in his head because, "I had some time on my hands." They'd been trying to crack the cipher for four days without success.

When MILR came across the messages they had the characteristics they looked for in a Soviet military intelligence cipher despite it not conforming to the regular format. The fact that Michael had cracked the cipher in his head was 'noteworthy', everybody thought. "Noteworthy? Noteworthy!" exclaimed the Russian desk section leader. "It's a-bloody-stonishing. Give him more to do!" After forty-eight hours the messages ceased and were replaced by a broadcast cipher, the origin and nature of which eluded the MILR chaps. It was as though the sender knew the original cipher had been cracked and had changed format.

Michael became immersed in his MILR cipher cracking duties, becoming more and more lost in his own world of thoughts. He was like a machine, ultimately cracking dozens of ciphers. Weeks drifted by. His trance-like state continued until mid-October, when it was interrupted by the preparations for the American-led NATO wargames.

*

The call Captain Jones was expecting came while he was at home on weekend leave. Since he now had no family, his Controller knew he would be home alone.

"It's me."

"I'm okay to talk…"

"I know. I believe congratulations are in order! That was a master stroke placing Frost in Bielefeld HQ. MI3 took to him in hook, line and sinker! Well done old chap. Getting him recruited by the MI3 spooks fits perfectly with what I have planned for him." Captain Jones' Controller took credit for Michael's recruitment by MI3 with his Counsellor who in turn took credit with his Governor.

"I thought it best he work for an MI unit for obvious reasons. That sort of background will work well for him and us in the future. It might even get him inside MI6."

"Good thinking, if a little risky, but no risk no reward, eh?" replied the Controller not totally convinced by Jones' reasoning.

"Quite," said Captain Jones agreeing with his Controller. He needed to change the subject. "As an aside, something I've been meaning to ask you for a while. Why do we use ABCD designations for the lists, they seem a little simplistic."

"They're meant to be old man. On the one hand, those carrying out reviews can easily understand the status of those on the lists and, on the other, ABCD designations are used by Secret Services around the world. We're playing the old imitation game. In the event that somebody comes across our lists, they will assume we're MI6 or whoever and in their moment of uncertainty we disappear. It's happened before and it'll happen again the next time somebody trips over us by accident." The Counsellor was enjoying the sound of his own voice and so lectured Captain Jones for ten minutes before getting back to business. "I'm planning on removing your sleeper status. With your background it won't look odd when you're recruited, once you're placed in the right area that is. And, believe me, you will be placed in the right area and the right people will know to watch out for you. You understand what I mean don't you Gareth?"

He's feeding me disinformation to see where it turns up, thought Captain Jones. "I do indeed. I expect I'll be hearing more from you soon then?"

"Yes, all in good time. But for now, you need to get close to your primary targets and study the briefs you'll be receiving on France and Northern Ireland. I'm not a hundred percent certain where you'll be placed yet as we've had a few unfortunate losses recently. Once again, well done on getting Frost on the MI ladder, I'm sure that will look good on his record when we move him into our world." The phone line went dead without any goodbyes.

It was obvious to Captain Jones that the Organisation was testing his trustworthiness and would check if the information he'd just received turned up where it shouldn't. As for his Controller telling him that he had plans for Michael, that was a big surprise. *What could they possibly have in store for somebody like Michael…? He isn't even operational yet,* he thought. As Captain Jones had his thought he knew that whatever it was it wouldn't be good news for the lad; a feeling of guilt ran through him. He could've reported Michael as unsuitable during lists reviews and he would have been cut loose and allowed to get on with his life oblivious to the existence of the Organisation. Deep down, the Captain believed Michael simply wasn't well enough equipped to deal with the world of the Organisation. He'd kept quiet about the lad for his own purposes; making him feel deeply ashamed of himself.

Captain Jones was completely at a loss to understand why plans had been made for somebody like Michael. The Organisation had lots of people they could use for just about anything he could think of, *So why Michael?* He wouldn't have had to look far for the reason why Michael was soon to be put in harm's way. The boy really shouldn't have spoken to Major Finn about Tommy Munroe's death in the way he had. A high-level Organisation conversation was had and the outcome was not favourable to Private Frost's prospects of having a long life.

*

After the format of the messages changed to what was clearly a bespoke cipher, they increased in frequency as though reaching a crescendo, a conclusion. MILR decoded parts of messages but they didn't make sense. They were confident that their decoding was correct which could only mean that they were missing a piece of the 'broadcast'. Analysis of the decrypted sections of the messages indicated that somebody was expecting something… expecting what? What were they expecting? To be met? To be… the MILR analysts were guessing and the more they guessed the more confusing, bizarre and unlikely their guesses became.

Just before the wargames commenced, Michael's assignment at MILR was suspended and he was moved into a role performing translation duties for the Wargames Chiefs of Staffs. Who would ever have thought that this lad from the slums of Liverpool's docklands would end up in the big boys' tent? This plum posting, however, was nothing to do with chance.

*

The main site for the wargames was an area just north-east of Göttingen, between the American base at Bad Herzfeld and BAOR HQ Bielefeld. This location was purposely chosen for being close to the border with East Germany so the Soviets could have a good look at what was going on. It was all a big game; a chance for NATO to show the 'Russkies' just how much trouble they'd be in if they ever crossed the border and invaded West Germany. The Russians, however, were ambivalent about such shows of strength as they believed that NATO's forces were no match for them.

During the Cold War, had the forces of East and West come into conflict, the Americans and their allies would've been slaughtered due to the sheer weight of numbers of men and armaments the Soviet Union could pour into a theatre of war in the blink of an eye. The forces of the West were a very poor second to the forces of the Soviet Union at the time. NATO needed something to help even things up. A missiles heist perhaps?

*

While working for the Wargames Chiefs of Staffs, Michael became a leading member of the translation group. His language skills had improved enormously since his posting and now he was working alongside native speakers of various languages. His French was fluent so he picked up Italian very easily and, unlike most people, he didn't struggle with Finnish. Not being NATO, the Finns were there but not there, so to speak. Michael's colleagues thought it was creepy how quickly he picked things up. They didn't dislike him but they never sought his company. Not that Michael noticed.

During the early days of the wargames, a colleague of Michael's back at MILR passed copies of the bespoke ciphers to him via attaché cases marked 'Top Secret' in red letters. A note inside the most recent attaché case read, "The chaps still haven't cracked the broadcast cipher, it's proving very tricky to tie down." It went on to say that MILR were looking forward to welcoming Michael back when, "Those silly games are over!"

*

During a Chiefs of Staffs strategy session, a French Lieutenant made a comment which grated with Michael. The Lieutenant was giving his theories on a Red on Blue on White exercise, which Michael fundamentally disagreed with. A discussion ensued between the Lieutenant and Michael which went on for over a minute when a British General intervened.

"What's going on? What are you speaking with the Lieutenant about Private?" asked the General.

"Sir, the Lieutenant hypothesised a strategy concerning the exercise which I cannot agree with."

"Agree with? Surely you mean you can't translate?"

"No sir, I can translate perfectly well what the officer said but I don't agree with it." Several officers let out snorts of derision at Michael's impertinence. "The Lieutenant's strategy is fanciful, the only successful outcomes from similar scenarios have come from

Armies prepared to sacrifice the White forces." Michael provided examples of what he was referring to and stated he could provide more if required. After whispering something to his aide-de-camp the General responded.

"Very interesting Private but, in future, if you could just translate what the Lieutenant says that is all that is required of you."

"Yes sir," replied Michael without any ill feeling about being put down as such things simply didn't register with him.

As soon as the debriefing session was over most of the Officers left the tent. The majority of those remaining had already forgotten what Michael had said but some had not.

"What did you think of that extraordinary outburst by the Private?"

"I wouldn't call it an outburst exactly, he seemed perfectly calm and rational and I found what he said rather interesting and, unless I'm mistaken, entirely accurate."

"But to sacrifice the very people you're supposed to be saving?"

"That wasn't the Private's point. He was stating, from a historical perspective, outcomes of similar scenarios. He was not saying we should go around sacrificing people willy-nilly. Don't you agree General?" A French General joined in the conversation.

"I do and, as you said, it was rather interesting what the Private had to say. I thought it was uncalled for though. I don't know what he expected to achieve by speaking out in the way he did."

"Are you saying Soldiers shouldn't show initiative?" interjected a German Major in accent-less English.

"Not at all, I just think there's a time and a place for that sort of thing and this is not it. I welcome Soldiers showing initiative, however, these are wargames exercises and the Lieutenant would have learned more had he given his comments uninterrupted by the Private. We could then have quizzed him about his proposed strategy. It wasn't appropriate for a Private to enter into a debate with the Lieutenant, he should simply have translated what he'd said without offering an opinion. Don't you agree?"

"I wonder, would we really have taken the time to 'quiz' the Lieutenant? I believe it more likely that we would have thanked him and instantly forgotten about what he'd said, but having the Private comment in the way he did the matter has stuck in our heads. Well, it stuck in mine at least."

The remaining group went their separate ways.

An Organisation conversation.

"Where was that Private before he joined the wargames?"

"I understand he was at MILR. They've asked if they can have him back after the games are over."

"Was he with a regiment prior?"

"Yes sir, the First Royal Tank Regiment."

"He appears well up on military strategy. The White sacrifice scenarios appeared to me to be a blending of Napoleon and Alexander amongst others. Unsurprisingly, for Tank Crew, there was a bit of Monty in there. Surely he can't be that well read about such things? Can he? He's a Private for goodness' sake."

"I could contact his CO for more information about him, sir? From his security review I understand when he enlisted with the Royal Tank Regiment they weren't actually recruiting at the time. He'd been a Cadet beforehand so they must have gotten to know him and thought enough about the lad to pull a few strings."

"That's not so unusual, we've all done that for a good man."

"Indeed, but on passing out he didn't actually join the Regiment. Instead he was posted to Altcar and remained there until his posting to BAOR. Shall I mention anything in particular to his CO about this, sir?"

"If you would. It seems this Private leads a bit of a charmed life and I'd like to understand why. Relieve him of translation duties immediately and send him back to MILR if they're so keen on him. Keep me posted on what you get back from his CO. Carry on."

"Yes sir."

The aide-de-camp was already intimately familiar with Private Frost's background. He'd been advised about Michael's posting in advance by his Counsellor. A report about the translation incident was passed up the line until it got to a point where the lines crossed and was then fed down another line to end up with Captain Jones' Counsellor and then the Captain himself. This wasn't an unusual occurrence as messages about the Organisation's assets get transmitted hundreds of times a day around the globe. It was a totally manual system, ripe for modernisation when the computer age eventually arrived. The system was simple and effective, though hardly Stalinesque in size and thoroughness. As there aren't many layers in the Organisation it's easy to keep tabs on situations such as Private Frost's posting and several interested parties were now keeping tabs on Michael Frost, which was not a good situation for him to be in.

*

An Organisation conversation.

"It's me, I need to talk to you about Private Frost's most recent incident. Have you read the daily sheet on it? I am extremely nervous about this odd fellow. I was against bringing him in at the start but I was persuaded to act otherwise. I should have followed my instincts. It seems he simply doesn't have anything between his brain and his mouth to stop him blurting out all manner of things. Unless you're able to provide me with a good reason as to why we should keep him on I shall cut him loose. He'll be none the wiser about us, particularly after you move on, which I have to inform you is imminent."

"I think we should persist with him until after RMC selection and decide then."

Hmm, yes, we could send him to Northern Ireland if it all goes wrong. All sorts of things can happen to a stupid Soldier over there, thought Captain Jones' Counsellor. "Okay, fine, I'll give him until after RMC selection and see how he is then."

"I understand MILR want him back so that should keep him out of trouble for a while. When it's time for RMC selection I'll refuse any requests for Frost's MILR secondment to continue." Captain Jones paused to check consent, but typically the Counsellor remained silent. "I'm thinking of allowing Private Frost some home leave at Christmas. That will act as a natural break between Bielefeld and the next phase. What do you say?"

"I wouldn't go so far as to say I say anything. His leave arrangements are your affair. Once he goes for RMC selection then there's no turning back. He either makes it or we cut him loose," said the Controller while his head said, *He'll be sent to Northern Ireland and dealt with there.* As usual, the call ended without any goodbyes.

Following this conversation, Captain Jones, once more, felt guilty for keeping silent about his concerns over Michael. He was putting his needs to the fore without any regard for Michael's safety or wellbeing. He could cut him loose now and let him get on with his Army life. *It could be a good life for him,* he thought not for the first time. Captain Jones hated himself but he hated the Organisation more.

*

An Organisation conversation.

"I've just had a conversation with Jones. He's so very, very, slippery that one. What's with him and the boy Frost?"

"I'm certain he's a Doubler... Jones I mean, not the boy... too young," replied Major Finn in military staccato speak.

"There's no doubt in my mind that Jones is, as you say, a Doubler but why are you so keen to see the boy come to harm? Northern Ireland is a brutal place to send anybody, especially somebody like him."

"He's not right for us and, besides, he knows too much of the wrong sort of thing."

"What does he know?"

"He knows his little friend was murdered at Altcar. He said as much to me and now this fiasco in Germany. He's always attracting the wrong sort of attention. I'm certain MI3 is looking into him."

"MI3 looking into somebody like him? Rubbish! What else is there about him you don't like?"

"He's protected beyond his worth. Lefort once said—"

"And there we have it, there we have it! It's the old Lefort thing again. That vendetta is more likely to be the end of you than it is of him. Let it go, Finn! I'm warning you, let it go!"

"It's nothing to do with…"

"Don't waste your breath, Finn, it's already agreed that Frost will go to Northern Ireland when the time is right; if he lasts that long that is. There are one or two who'll be going there with him to share his fate. I'm late for my next meeting." The call came to an abrupt end. The Controller's next meeting was with his barber.

*

While Michael was waiting for his orders to return to MILR he noticed that the attaché cases had stopped arriving. Going by the contents of the most recent of them the chaps back at MILR were close to solving the puzzle of the broadcast cipher. *Hopefully I'll return in time to put the final piece in the puzzle.* Unusually for Michael, he crossed his fingers at that thought.

CRACKING THE CODE

An Organisation conversation.
"Is everything arranged?" asked Lara.
"Yes."
"Any changes to the plan?"
"None."
"Good. Do you have enough people or do you need me to find you some?"
"We have enough. A couple more Russian speakers are going to be joining us."
"When will you do it?"
"Soon. Perhaps within the next forty-eight to ninety-six hours."
"I see. Still don't trust me?"
"As I always say, Lara, if you don't want somebody to know something then you don't tell them. It's for your own good. You know that."
"Are they under orders to use maximum prejudice should the situation prove necessary?" Madame Chancellor hated the way her erstwhile co-assignmentee abused the English language.
"You mean; 'are they under orders to kill if necessary'…"
"That is exactly what I mean."
Then why didn't you say so? thought Margaret. "The answer to your question is 'yes they are' but we're going to try and avoid that sort of thing at all costs. It's bad enough that we're going to steal

the property of the good citizens of the Union of Soviet Socialist Republics, we don't want to go killing them into the bargain."

"Hopefully it won't come to that. In other news…" Lara paused to ensure she had Madame Chancellor's full attention, "Vladimir is taking some time away from work. He's not holding up too well. If he gets any worse I'm sure he'll have a heart attack."

"I hope not, Lara, I truly do. It's vitally important that Mr Grigorovich does not suffer a heart attack," replied Madame Chancellor in a tone of voice that lowered the temperature of the room. "That sort of thing is very bad for business. You must do all you can to ensure that everything goes smoothly with Mr Grigorovich and he gets to spend his autumn years soaking up the California sunshine. If he's sanctioned that will turn others against us all."

"Madame Chancellor!" responded Lara in feigned shock. "What are you implying? I assure you that I'll do my best to ensure that Mr Grigorovich remains in the land of the living," lied Lara.

*

Before Michael re-joined MILR, sealed orders arrived directing him to report immediately to a forward operational unit. When he arrived there he recognised Major Finn and the French Captain but nobody else. They ignored him and he did likewise in return. Following a conversation between the French Captain and another Officer he left the camp without speaking to, or acknowledging, Michael, who didn't think this behaviour strange as he'd acted similarly in the past. A General then stood on an elevated platform at the front of the encampment.

"Quickly now, all of you, take a seat," barked the General. "Some of you don't yet know why you are here. You are going to be carrying out a mission inside East Germany. Its purpose is to acquire certain Soviet hardware. During the mission, many of you will be disguised as Soviet Soldiers. I'll now hand you over to Major Finn who will give you the details of the operation and the part you'll be playing in it. I needn't tell you what a great honour it is for you to have been selected for this mission and I'm sure you'll all acquit yourselves extremely well. Good luck everybody. Carry on Major Finn."

"Thank you, sir. First things first, do not discuss this operation with anybody, not even your COs, and that applies equally after the operation is over. I cannot emphasise enough that secrecy is paramount. Once the mission has commenced those playing the part of the Soviet forces will remain in character throughout. The aim of the mission is to ambush a Soviet convoy…" Those in the know thought all the dramatic scene-setting ridiculous. Had they understood the circumstances of several of the actors and the intentions of Major Finn they would not have held that opinion.

After outlining the overall plan, Major Finn split the men into four Units for each of them to go over their parts in the ambush. Following the briefings everybody was brought back together and told where and when to rendezvous before being dismissed. On their way out of the camp, sealed orders were handed to several Soldiers, including Michael. They were their written permissions to be relieved from their normal duties so they could travel to the rendezvous in time to take part in the raid.

*

Arriving back at MILR Michael went to his office, sat at his desk and picked up where he'd left off without missing a beat. In his mind it was as though he'd never been away.

Michael's colleagues were extremely glad to have him back as there'd been a significant increase in Soviet activity since the wargames had begun. The Soviets knew their communications would be monitored and so took the opportunity to transmit highly offensive messages about the allied forces. The crudest messages were transmitted in plain English, German and even Russian. The chaps thought many of the messages were quite humorous. All the messages were routinely copied between the various Soviet staffs.

These communications were bread and butter to MILR. They helped in their decoding activities as they got to know the habits, phrases, cadence, idiosyncrasies and idioms used by those originating and passing the messages. All intelligence is useful intelligence no matter how trivial something might appear to be.

*

The moment Michael sat down at his desk, Ronald told him that Clifford had gone on leave at short notice a few days earlier saying it was something to do with a family emergency, according to Victor that was. *No wonder the attaché cases stopped arriving*, thought Michael. It was very bad timing as far as MILR was concerned as following Michael's secondment to when Clifford departed the broadcast cipher went into overdrive and had stopped only a day ago. MILR had planned to have a review session to go over what they'd learned about the cipher but it was called off by Victor who told them that MI3 were running with it. Later that day all Soviet chatter stopped completely, nothing whatsoever was coming over from the other side of the fence.

The following day, Michael handed his orders to his supervising Officer and off he went. He hated being late and had left in plenty of time.

*

As has been mentioned, while Michael was at the wargames he'd been receiving attaché cases from Clifford Coley at MILR marked 'Top Secret' containing the latest information about the broadcast cipher. The final attaché case Clifford planned to send to Michael was intercepted so he never got to know just how close Clifford had come to cracking the whole thing wide open.

After working around the clock for days on end trying to crack the broadcast cipher, Clifford Coley had a stroke of genius. He hypothesised that perhaps it wasn't a broadcast cipher after all but a proxy two-way 'conversation'. Such conversations usually indicated there was a traitor in the network. Clifford went searching for the other side of the conversation. It didn't take him long to find it. He took messages from one side of the conversation and shuffled them with messages from the other side of the conversation like splitting a deck of cards. He then further hypothesised that the conversation would likely contain common words or phrases, perhaps taken from a book known to both parties. It's virtually impossible to crack such codes. *They're probably transmitting a predetermined message… but about what? What the hell is it they're saying? What's it all about? Is it a just another Russkie joke to tease we chaps?"*

Clifford pored over the coded messages; matching transmission times he constructed the thread of the conversation. It became clear to him that several transmissions were segments of a single message. Interspersing them, Clifford became convinced the conversation was a script. *Both sides seem to know what to say and what to expect, like in a play… the book could be a play.* Things now started to make more sense. *The conversation must concern something which has been previously agreed*, thought Clifford. He deciphered several words which ran throughout the conversation; raid… Soldiers… strength… east west… border… weapons… escape… destroy. *Are the Soviets planning to invade West Germany?* So many numbers too. *What do they mean? Are they dates? Size of invasion force? Number of battalions? Co-ordinates?* Clifford needed help, but where to go? He'd start with his supervising NCO, Victor. Then at least there'd be more brains on the job as his brain was very tired.

"Are you positive?" Victor asked.

"I'm as certain as I can be, but then again I'm so tired who knows what I'm looking at. That's why I need fresh eyes and more brains on the job. Whatever this is it seems to be coming to a conclusion… a finalisation… or whatever," mumbled Clifford as if rambling. Victor pretended to be deep in thought. "What's more,

I've been sending Private Frost updates using TS attaché cases, so let's see what he thinks. He's good at this sort of thing, after all he cracked the code before they changed the cipher."

"Hang on, Clifford, we should hold back on that a bit. You know, get our thinking straight before we go setting hares running. Who else knows about the work you've been doing?"

"Well, nobody really; except Frost of course."

"This smells of espionage to me; bespoke ciphers, unexplained numbers and the mention of weapons. Maybe you're right, maybe the Russkies are planning an attack. I wonder who's sending the messages and who's receiving them and where the transmission locations are. Have you managed to pinpoint anything?" Clifford shook his head. "We'll need to get tracking on the job. What do you think?"

"I'm too tired to think. I need some help."

"I think you need some sleep. Give me what you've got so far and I'll carry on while you get your head down. I'll wake you if I find anything interesting." Clifford went to his bunk and Victor left the camp to find a public phone.

Two hundred yards from the main gate was a Café Bar with a public phone in the corridor next to the toilets. Victor dialled a series of numbers, waited for a confirmation tone and then dialled another series of numbers. After receiving his instructions he returned to camp and got on with tracing the point of origin of the west side of the signals. As Victor was more technical than analytical he quickly obtained a good guesstimate of the location. There was only one building in the vicinity so that had to be the point of origin. After a quick drive out there Victor was convinced that he was on the right track and immediately got back on the phone to his Counsellor.

A Doubler conversation.

"What do you think?"

"It's only a matter of time before Coley works things out and if this is what we think it is then there can be only one course of action."

"Shall we send somebody?"

"Yes, I can't afford to be involved. I'll order Coley to take some R&R. As soon as he's off the base he's yours to deal with. How long before you get somebody here?"

"We already have people close to you. They'll let you know when they're ready for Coley. Expect a call within the next four hours. Call me if the situation changes."

A Faction conversation.

"Have you seen the daily sheets?"

"No, I leave that sort of thing to others and let them bring me titbits, which, I imagine, is precisely what you're about to do," replied Sir Jeremy, his interest piqued.

"There's been an event."

"An event? Where?"

"Bielefeld. It appears somebody on the Russian desk in MI3 has cracked the code for the missile heist."

"Heist is such a vulgar expression; call it an appropriation in future. Were we common criminals it would be a heist or a robbery but, as it's political, appropriation is more appropriate. Continue."

"The sheets say an Operative there has requested a clean-up of an MILR Agent… apparently he's the one that cracked the code. It goes on to say that he, the Operative, has located 'the point of origin'. I have no idea what that means but thought it would be of interest…"

"Pull the Bielefeld sheet and bring it to me before anybody else has a chance to read it."

After digesting the entire contents of the Bielefeld sheet, Sir Jeremy Hawksmith believed the time was right to strike. He went with Plan B, "Better to have somebody else do the dirty work and leave me to clean up the mess… everybody'll think I'm a hero." He called Count Bouvier, leader of the French Splinter, and informed him of Madame Chancellor's plan to appropriate Soviet Missiles and sell them off to the highest bidder while sharing the proceeds with the American and Russian Splinters. The Count, a long-time enemy of Sir Jeremy, scoffed at his news but said he would be interested to know more. Sir Jeremy could tell the Count was sceptical and so told him that his proof was about to be delivered to a remote farmhouse for interrogation. He suggested the Count 'swap out' the interrogation team for Operatives of the French Splinter.

"What have you got to lose, Maurice old love?"

"Okay, give me the details."

"Once you're convinced it's all kosher I'll give you everything you'll need to know to grab the missiles for yourself."

"Why are you doing me this favour?"

"Oh, you know, Maurice old thing, burying the hatchet and all that."

"You must really hate her to betray her in this way."

"Maurice, I love the Organisation and I'm determined that neither she nor those heathen Mandarins shall destroy it."

*

When Victor returned to MILR all was quiet. He went through Clifford's files, carefully removing everything connected with the work he'd been doing. He was just about to wake Clifford when he noticed a red TS attaché case pushed right underneath Clifford's desk. The slip in the address window was to Private Michael Frost at 'Wargames HQ'. Victor opened the attaché case and read what Clifford had written about progress on the work he was doing. *Well, well, well, that won't do at all, dear Clifford,* thought Victor as he tore up the note and, removing the contents, he placed the TS attaché case back in the rack alongside all the others.

When Victor told Clifford he'd tracked down the source of the west side of the conversation he was ecstatic with joy. He was not quite so ecstatic, however, after Victor told him that MI3 had taken over the case. He claimed that he was as unhappy about it as Clifford was but there was nothing either of them could do about it. In fact, MI3, he told Clifford, were already aware of the transmissions but thanked him for all his work before confiscating everything and ordering them both not to disclose anything to anybody. Additionally, Victor said, they were very concerned about the amount of time Clifford had put into the case and ordered him to take a week's leave. Clifford went into protest mode but Victor said that, reluctantly, he had to agree with MI3; he needed to take some leave.

"A tired Clifford is not what the service needs," said Victor, followed by, "After a good rest you'll return refreshed and ready to get on with things again."

"When does my leave start?"

"Immediately. They're so concerned about you that they're sending somebody to make sure you obey orders."

"What about Private Frost? I've been keeping him updated on events."

"Don't you worry about Private Frost, Clifford, I'll see to it that he's informed about what's gone on. I already sent him the attaché case you had under your desk."

"Oh thanks Victor, you're a pal. Where will I be leaving from by the way?"

"That all depends on you and where you want to go. If you want to go back home then you'll be on the next transport out of Bielefeld but if you want to do a bit of travelling around dear old Deutschland then you can be dropped off at a railway station or even driven to your destination if it's close by. Entirely your choice, Clifford. In fact, there's your taxi now."

As Clifford placed his case in the boot of the taxi he felt a scratch on his leg for which the taxi driver apologised. Seconds later he passed out cold. The taxi driver looked around before stopping and taking a small leather pouch from his jacket pocket. Removing two phials from it, he first injected Clifford with a prototype sedative followed by a second injection to stabilise the experimental drug now flowing around inside Clifford's body. The drugs combined to put Clifford into a coma which he would only come out of once injected with the antidote drug. The taxi driver propped Clifford up in the rear seat of the taxi and held him in place by pulling the seat belt tight across his chest.

The taxi drove to an isolated farm where Clifford was injected with the antidote to bring him around. Still woozy from the effects of the sedative, Private Coley was questioned about the coded messages he had been working on. He spoke openly about his work, saying he didn't really understand very much about the messages except to say they were a conversation and not a broadcast and his supervising NCO, Victor, was about to look into them but MI3 had taken over the file and were keeping it to themselves. "Must be big," commented Clifford stupidly. "I say, you seem to know a lot about the work I've been doing, you must have a…" He stopped speaking before he said the word 'spy'. Clifford's interrogators injected him to put him to sleep.

As he came to, Clifford awoke to find two strangers staring at him. *They must've arrived while I slept,* he thought. They were speaking French to one another and as Clifford's French wasn't bad he asked them what they wanted and said he was perfectly willing to co-operate fully. He was confident that as he was such a small fish he would probably be dropped somewhere in the countryside when they were done with him; co-operating would get him released most quickly being Clifford's logic. They didn't ask him any questions. *Perhaps they're waiting for somebody to arrive before the questioning starts.* That thought filled Clifford with dread as this inquisitor might be a professional and… he was letting his imagination get the better of him. *Calm down Clifford, calm down, it'll be alright.*

The night being very cold, Clifford asked his captors for an extra blanket and somewhere to lay down as his lower back was seizing up sitting on a chair for so long. They injected him. When he woke the following morning he was lying on a cot bed with a couple of blankets thrown over him. His shoes and socks had been removed. After eating breakfast Clifford was jabbed again and that was the last he ever knew. His captors had misplaced the phial of stabiliser and so, unable to stabilise the experimental sedative, Clifford slipped into a coma. After eventually finding the stabiliser, the men tried to revive him. Over the next thirty-six hours they injected Clifford with various amounts of the sedative followed by the stabiliser and then the antidote. At times Clifford appeared to come round but he never regained consciousness. Eventually his heart just gave out. He'd been given far too many strong drugs in so short a time it had been too much for his body to take. The kidnappers went into a state of panic. They were supposed to keep hold of Clifford until after the missile heist operation was over and then drop him off near Bielefeld for the French Splinter's future use inside MILR.

One of the men drove to a nearby phone box and called his Counsellor about the mishap with Private Coley. The Counsellor ordered the man to send Private Coley back to where he came from.

*

In a wood outside a military camp on the outskirts of Bielefeld a German Shepherd guard dog pulled its handler towards a clump of bushes. When the guard drew closer his eye caught a reflection bouncing off his torch beam. Then another. Then another. *Looks like a row of buttons,* he thought. It was a row of buttons. He got on his radio and called for assistance. It was a body he'd found in the beam of his torch.

The area where the body was discovered was quickly cordoned off. A military vehicle with a generator arrived to provide the Bielefeld Stadt Polizei with light to conduct their grim tasks. The body was photographed in-situ and the whole area examined before it was removed.

Going by his uniform, the dead Soldier was British, though no ID was found on the corpse or at the scene. He appeared to be around twenty-five years of age with strawberry-blonde hair and stood at around five feet eleven inches tall, or one metre eighty centimetres according to the Bielefeld Police scene of crime log. He appeared to have been dead for a couple of days though it was unlikely he'd died where he'd been found, leading to the early presumption that he'd been placed in the wood so his body would be discovered. He wasn't wearing shoes or socks though his jacket was buttoned up. It was the reflection of the torchlight bouncing off Private Coley's jacket buttons that had caught the guard's attention.

Officers from British Military HQ were summoned to identify the body. An out-of-uniform Officer recognised it as being that of Private Clifford Coley, an analyst with MILR. He called the camp CO to one side and whispered to him that the body was one of his men. Considering the work performed by MILR the CO called his Officers together and told them that they were to return to camp. "Under no circumstances are you to discuss the night's events with anybody. This situation is highly classified and I will not tolerate idle chatter, gossip or speculation as to what happened to this unfortunate Soldier. Dismissed."

A British Army conversation.

"What was he working on?"

"Oh, you know, the usual stuff," replied Major Finn casually.

"Stop the secret squirrel bullshit and tell me what he was working on!" roared the CO.

"Apart from his intercept duties he was working on some unusual messages with another Private called Frost."

"And where is this Private Frost?"

"That's the thing. As soon as he returned to his desk following a secondment with the Chiefs of Staffs at the wargames he left camp and nobody has any idea where he went," lied Major Finn.

"Were Coley and Frost friends?"

"I believe so. Why, do you think Private Frost might have had something to do with Private Coley's murder?"

"Murder?" gasped the CO. "Oh yes, it might well be murder."

"We won't know until Private Frost is questioned whether he had anything to do with this. When he shows up don't alert him, just let me know," said the Major.

"Of course, anything to help our friends in MI3," replied the CO sarcastically.

Major Finn reported the evening's events to an 'on-duty' Controller, requesting her permission to sanction Private Frost before he exposed them all to danger. The Controller approved Major Finn's request to sanction Private Frost. "To be sure of cutting out the whole lump we should include the NCO too… he's a Doubler who's rather lost his way." The Counsellor approved Victor's sanction also. Major Finn was having an excellent night.

*

Given the nature of Private Coley's work, the British Secret Service contacted their German counterparts to obtain a total news embargo about the discovery of a body outside a military base. Each thought it likely that Private Coley had met his end at the hands of foreign agents, a matter which needed investigating. This required Private Coley's body to be held on ice until after investigations were completed, which could take years. His body might never be released at all. Perhaps he would ultimately be listed as a missing person, like so many unfortunates are around the globe every year.

*

Clifford Coley's body was dumped where it had been due to a misunderstanding between the Operative and his Counsellor; he being Belgian and his Counsellor French; hardly surprising, therefore, that there was a breakdown in communications. The Counsellor hadn't wanted to attract unwanted attention and so ordered the Operative to return Private Coley's body to his home town – after all, he was meant to be on leave, hence, "Send him back to where he came from." This was a humanitarian gesture on the part of the Counsellor as it meant Private Coley's parents would be able to grieve their dead son. His parents went to their graves not knowing what had happened to their lovely boy.

THE SOVIET MISSILE HEIST

It was an audacious plan conceived by Madame Chancellor herself, or so she claimed when briefing her Congress of Governors on the 'Soviet Missile Heist'. She hoped they would name it Madame Chancellor's Soviet Missile Heist. She'd even thought of calling it by that herself.

Shortly after news had broken of the NATO wargames, Madame Chancellor claimed to have had a flash of inspiration along the lines of; "let's get the Soviets to hold some wargames of their own at the same time and have them bring their shiny new missiles to the party. When they're close to the border with West Germany we'll snatch them and sell them on, making billions for the Organisation!"

In was a simple plan, she said, but the Devil is in the detail and Madame Chancellor was not a detail person, "I'm an ideas person." She'd leave the detail to others. The Organisation has long maintained that simple plans are best, less to go wrong. The fly in the ointment of this plan was that the missiles would be surrounded by tens of thousands of Soviet troops, thousands of Soviet Tanks and protected by hundreds of Soviet jets. As soon as the missile carriers came under attack they'd simply put out a call for help and that would be that. Game over. But the Organisation wasn't going to be put off when there were hundreds of millions, if not billions, of dollars at stake. They had to go for it. They'd let the CIA make all the running and then step in at the last minute and steal the prize from right under their noses. They'd played and won this game before.

*

Ever on the lookout for opportunities to create mayhem, the Organisation regularly appropriated one country's assets to sell on where they'd do the most good or harm, depending on the desired outcome. All to keep the global hate-pot bubbling and prevent people from looking around and seeing what was really going on.

*

Things started off well. The American-led NATO wargames began right on schedule. The Soviet counter-war-games-exercises began right on schedule also. The CIA made their plans to snatch the Soviet missiles and the Organisation made its plan to relieve them of their prize. Then things started going off the rails.

A chronology of events:

The Organisation went on high alert as somebody inside MILR, a Private called Michael Frost, cracked VVG's bespoke cipher. What was concerning was that Private Frost was a potential on list B. This set alarm bells ringing back at Soviet Missile Heist HQ; "What is this Frost character up to? Is he a Doubler?" they asked.

Private Frost then went on secondment as an interpreter working for the Wargames Chiefs of Staffs at Wargames HQ. While there, he got involved in an argument with an Officer over military strategy which ended up being reported on the daily sheets. As far as the Organisation was concerned, attracting this sort of attention is never a good thing, especially so for a potential on the lists; "Frost is attracting far too much attention. Something needs to be done about him," they said.

After Private Frost joined the wargames, an Agent, called Clifford Coley, began work on cracking the new code. According to information received he almost succeeded when he went missing. It was known that Private Coley's supervising NCO is a Doubler, possibly working for the French Splinter. He was suspected of being involved in Private Coley's disappearance. Intercepts at Control confirmed Private Coley was being held by Operatives of the French Splinter. Private Coley's body then turned up in some woods outside a military base. Private Frost is a suspect in Private Coley's murder. "What the hell is going on? Did anybody order a sanction on Private Coley? Who's this Frost working for? What the hell is going on?" they asked.

A Major Finn requested permission to sanction both Private Frost and Private Coley's supervising NCO, "a renegade Doubler working for the French Splinter." Major Finn's request was initially granted but was later overturned by a Governor who said he has plans for Private Frost. The same Governor claimed Private Coley's supervising NCO is a Doubler working for the Israeli Splinter. "This is getting messy, very messy indeed, we need to make a decision. Somebody needs to go and tell her?" they said.

On top of everything else that was happening, worrying news arrived from Moscow that VVG had gone missing. He hadn't been seen for over forty-eight hours. A possible Tripler, known as Lara, had activated all her assets in an effort to locate him but they all came up empty. If VVG had left the country he must have gone out via the back door. "This is now even more messy. Is it a go or a no-go? Who'll tell her?" they asked.

In summary: the Soviet Missile Heist cipher had been compromised; an Agent working at MILR had been abducted and murdered, possibly by a potential on list B who might be a Doubler; VVG was missing and it was possible that the French Splinter knew of the Organisation's plan to snatch the Soviet missiles. There was nothing else for it, Madame Chancellor had to be informed. Out of fear for their careers, none of the planners wanted to tell her about what was going on so they went to the person widely regarded as her second in command, Lisette. She listened carefully to what they had to say and to their recommendation that Madame Chancellor 'red light' the operation and bring everybody home. Lisette's reply was unequivocal, "The operation remains green. All of you, keep your nerve, we've been in worse situations than this and come through okay." Though none of them could think of any worse situations they dared not cross Lisette with the reputation she had for 'dealing' with people who disagreed with her.

*

Lisette briefed Madame Chancellor on the things she wanted her to know. The French Splinter possibly being aware of what was going on was of enormous concern to Margaret. "They could make things very tricky," she confided to Lisette. On Madame Chancellor's orders, Lisette asked Captain Lefort if he could use his influence to persuade the French Splinter not to get involved in the Soviet Missile Heist by promising them a cut. Their hatred for the American and Russian Splinters was well known and, as expected, they rejected the offer. The French Splinter was not in the mood to negotiate as it was confident it could snatch the missiles for themselves having moved considerable numbers of Operatives into north-eastern West Germany. Unfortunately for the French Splinter it was just that, a Splinter, and besides, twenty percent of its Operatives were Doublers. They would have to be extremely fortunate indeed to get anything at all out of this venture. Many Governors were angry at the Count for not accepting Madame Chancellor's offer.

*

With just hours to go before the Soviet Missile Heist was due to be carried out, VVG turned up at an Embassy gathering for the Promotion of Agriculture and Equipment; Cold War code-speak for a spy to spy get together. Lara sidled up to him and asked where the hell he'd been. She said she'd been worried about him.

"Worried about yourself more like," replied VVG displaying more backbone than he'd shown in years.

"What's gotten into you?" mocked Lara.

"I want to take somebody with me to America… and it's not negotiable."

"Otherwise?"

"Otherwise a message gets sent and the whole thing's off."

"It'll mean the end of you."

"So what? I have no future without Anya."

"I'll have to speak with the boys back home to see what we can do."

"No deal. You have the authority to do it, I know you do. Get me and Anya on a plane for America this afternoon or the whole thing goes up in smoke." Lara agreed to VVG's demand.

I'll deal with you Stateside you little shit! she thought.

"There's something you need to know," muttered VVG from the side of his mouth.

"Another little surprise?"

"Yes, but you'll like this one."

"Go on."

"One of the missile carriers will be hot."

"Hot?"

"Yes hot. It means it'll be carrying missiles loaded with atomic warheads." Lara almost fainted with shock and fright. She then went pale and shaky.

"Are you…" Lara, dazed, couldn't complete her sentence.

"The carrier to look out for is number four. That changes the game doesn't it?" smiled a cocky VVG.

"But that's not what we…" said Lara breathlessly.

"Too late. Do you want the missiles or don't you? If not I can make a call." Lara thought frantically for a moment about who the nuclear missiles might be sold to. She'd let Madame Chancellor know without delay so the decision would be up to her.

"Okay Vladimir, it's still on for now but it may be called off later."

"What do I care, Anya and I are going to America."

VVG walked away from Lara to glad-hand with the rest of his fellow 'delegates' at the embassy gathering for the Promotion of Agriculture and Equipment.

*

As the time for operation 'Soviet Missile Heist' drew ever nearer, the normally ice-cool Madame Chancellor was displaying signs of nerves. Lisette told her not to worry, that everything was going to be okay especially as she'd just heard that VVG had shown up again.

"I didn't know he was missing," whispered Margaret.

"He wasn't missing as such, he was just playing a last-minute game of brinkmanship. Nothing to be concerned about, Lara has everything under control."

"Classic Vladimir. I hope she's not planning on doing anything foolish to him."

"Of course not," lied Lisette. "In fact I think he's probably already in the air and well on his way to America by now."

"Anything else."

"Funny you should ask." Lisette handed Margaret a coded message from Control. "This was couriered over a few minutes ago; for your eyes only, apparently." Madame Chancellor knew the cipher off by heart. The contents of the message made her face flush and her heart race. "Everything okay?"

"Couldn't be better, darling," replied Madame Chancellor breathless with excitement.

"Good, then what say we have a nice little drinky poos?"

"Celebrating early is unlucky."

"It's not a celebration, it's more of a heart starter or nerve settler or whatever you want to call it… Brandy?"

"My favourite."

"I know. And I know where you keep the good stuff."

Margaret and Lisette sat drinking until it was time for them to go to the operations room. They entered hand in hand like two giddy gals from Margaret's old school. A chair had been placed for Madame Chancellor at the centre of the situation monitoring table. Lisette made room for herself next to Margaret by shoving all the other chairs a little closer together. Governors raised an eyebrow but Lisette's attention was elsewhere.

The tension inside the operations room was palpable as Margaret's anxiety spread to infect everybody. She knew this was it; it was make or break for her. If the heist went well it would secure her future at the top of the Organisation; she didn't want to think about what would happen if it did not go well. To appear confident, and to reassure all those around her, Margaret stood, looked about the room and made a short speech telling everybody what an auspicious day this would turn out to be for the Organisation. Then, looking over her shoulder, Margaret noticed two members of her secret inner council, neither of whom she'd invited to join her in the operations room. As she turned to face forward again she saw Lisette patting the breast pocket of her jacket. She let the jacket fall slightly open to show Margaret a black webbing shoulder holster in which nestled a Browning 9 mil, Lisette's weapon of choice. She looked at Margaret, gave her a little smile and flicked her eyes toward the two uninvited guests. Madame Chancellor shook her head almost imperceptibly and whispered, "Maybe later, let's see how the heist goes first."

*

While Margaret and Lisette were waiting in the operations room for things to get started, just over 500 miles away Michael arrived at the rendezvous point where he fell in with the rest of his Unit. Michael's Unit were to dress as Soviet Soldiers, flag down the convoy of missile carriers and convince its Commander that the road ahead had been compromised by NATO forces. The more the bogus Soviet Unit thought about it the more ridiculous it sounded. Their orders were clear though; once the encounter began they were to remain in character throughout.

The bogus Soviet Unit advanced into East Germany through a hole smashed in the east/west border fence. Michael examined the marks in the ground around the hole in the fence and thought, *a Centurion tank did this.* He felt as proud as if he'd been driving the tank himself. A hundred yards inside East Germany, the bogus Soviet Unit team leader gathered his men around him and flattened a map of the area on the ground.

"Right, chaps, we are right here…" said the bogus Soviet Unit leader pointing to a grid box on the map.

"Shouldn't we be speaking Russian, sir?"

"Quite right, Corporal. From now on we're to only speak Russian." The bogus Soviet Soldiers nodded in agreement.

"Private Frost, you have the best Russian accent so you'll approach the convoy leader and engage him in conversation as per the script. You've learned the script I assume?"

"Yes sir."

"Word perfect?"

"Yes sir."

"Good man, Frost, I'm sure you won't let us down."

"I won't, sir," replied Michael in his matter-of-fact way.

"The ambush itself will be carried out by American Special Forces acting in concert with covert operatives of the CIA so be sure to give a good account of yourselves… we don't want to look like a bunch of chumps in front of our American cousins."

"But sir…"

"Yes, Corporal?"

"Sir, why are the Yanks involved?"

"Orders, Corporal, orders." None of them knew it was always going to be that way.

The bogus Soviet Unit made its way to the ambush RVP and gave a signal, which was acknowledged. With credentials given, received and returned correctly, those hiding in the undergrowth made themselves known to the bogus Soviet Unit.

"Any problems getting here?" asked the bogus Soviet Unit leader.

"Nope," replied the American Special Forces Commander. "The hole in the fence, won't that attract attention?"

"Not at all. We shorted out the alarm wire from one insulator to another to maintain the circuit. It's been checked, no alarms went off. Nobody has any idea we're here."

"Shall we go over the plan one more time?"

"Good idea." Everybody took up their positions.

Michael never got nervous or anxious but this situation set off something inside him. As his vision became tunnel-like he concentrated hard to try and prevent the Demon from forming. To focus his mind, Michael retreated into his memory palace but it was too late. There It was, the Demon, slashing with Its razor-sharp claws to get at Michael. It ripped open a hole in the silver ether and poked Its slavering maw through, Its yellow eyes shining bright, rotting flesh hanging from Its filthy fangs, mucus dripping from Its nostrils. It screamed inhuman screams with the effort It was making to break into Michael's world. He knew It wanted to take him away to Its world. Michael believed that if the Demon ever touched him he would die. He didn't know why he believed that; he just did.

Michael looked at the people around him. He couldn't hear what they were saying but he could guess by the way they were looking at him. He had to regain control of himself, he'd done it before and he hoped he could do it now. One of the Americans grabbed him and shook him by the shoulders, pulling him around and shouting at him, asking him what was wrong.

"It's nothing," replied Michael, "it's just a headache… I get them… I'll be okay." As Michael spoke he could feel the heat of the Demon's breath on the back of his neck; close at first but getting further away with every breath It took. It was going, he didn't need to turn round to confirm it, he knew It was going… going… gone. Michael had learned from childhood not to mention his Demon visions because they scared people away. The parents of his little friends didn't want their children playing with the 'weird boy who spoke with the Devil'.

"What the hell's wrong with him?"

"What's wrong Private Frost?" asked the leader of the bogus Soviet Unit.

"It was just a headache but it's okay now, it's gone. Look. Everything normal," smiled Michael. He'd learned that smiling put people at their ease but his smiles, or rather his attempts at smiling, had the opposite effect.

"Jesus, that smile would crack a mirror," whispered one of the bogus Soviet Soldiers.

"Did he have some kind of seizure?" asked a concerned American. "I've seen people have seizures before and he looked like he was having one… especially with that smile of his."

"Private Frost is a bit of an odd-bod but he's not… dangerous." The bogus Soviet Unit leader regretted the use of the word 'dangerous' immediately he uttered it.

"That's it, replace him with somebody else," called out a CIA Agent.

"I told you, I'm fine. I'm really the only one who has a convincing Russian accent so unless you want to abandon the exercise you have to trust me." The calm way in which Michael spoke mesmerised everybody. Some thought he seemed to glow. The CIA Commander said he had the final decision and it was that Michael would speak with the Russian convoy leader, "and that's final."

After several rehearsals everybody was wondering where the Soviet convoy had gotten to. It should've been with them by then. The Commander became concerned that the hole in the fence had been discovered and that thousands of Soviet Soldiers were out looking for them when a rumble of half-tracks was heard coming through the woods. Everybody took up their positions. The welcoming committee stood in plain sight in a clearing warming themselves around a small fire, a kettle was dangling from a metal tripod.

All the players were in place. VVG had directed a dozen missile carriers to the co-ordinates he'd transmitted to Lara in his final message. The CIA had ensured that radio jamming covered the area where the missile carriers were to be snatched from. Additionally, they'd deployed experimental equipment designed to render navigation instrumentation ineffective; plus they'd removed road signs as the convoy was from the Urals and consequently in totally unfamiliar territory.

The point where the missile convoy was to be brought to a stop was less than a kilometre from the border with West Germany. As the convoy approached, the welcoming committee of bogus Soviet Soldiers casually swaggered along the dirt road toward it swigging hot steaming Tea from Soviet issue metal mugs while holding up the palms of their hands signalling it to stop. They acted so casual and natural. And why shouldn't they? They were being covered from the surrounding undergrowth by dozens of heavily armed Special Services Soldiers in case things went wrong.

Michael approached the lead vehicle. A window was wound down and an Officer asked Michael what he wanted. He asked to speak with the CO. The Officer told him he was in command. Michael told the Officer that the road ahead had been 'compromised' by the NATO wargames. The Officer wanted to know what Michael meant by that. He replied, "All I've been told is NATO Soldiers 'accidentally' demolished part of the border fence and entered East Germany. After they'd been discovered they ran like cowards back to the West but some of them might still be around." The Officer asked what all this had to do with him and his convoy. Michael said that the NATO forces had possibly laid mines and the road ahead wasn't yet cleared. The Officer looked distrustfully at Michael but he wasn't fazed by the Officer's glare.

"You'll have to turn around."

"But we don't know the area. In fact," confided the Officer, "we are lost. Can we just stay here until we get our bearings?"

"No, that is not possible."

"Why not?"

"You know what it's like. They don't tell you anything," said Michael nodding his head toward the bogus Soviet Unit leader.

"Can I speak with your Lieutenant? Why isn't he telling me about this?"

"He's Ukrainian," replied Michael. The Officer returned him a knowing nod. "You know, this isn't so good for us either. We've been roped into this because our Unit intercepted the radio messages from the NATO troops. We shouldn't even be here. We should be in our nice warm barracks drinking Vodka… but you know what these Ukrainians are like," said Michael nodding toward the bogus Soviet Unit leader. "He's after a promotion," he whispered.

"Typical bloody Ukrainians," sneered the Officer.

"Why don't you and your men join us in a nice hot mug of tea and we'll gather round the map together to see where you need to go?"

"Why not!" replied the Officer, ordering his comrades out of their vehicles to join him around the map.

As soon as the Soviet Soldiers got out of their vehicles they were overpowered by the American Special Forces Soldiers waiting in ambush for them. It was all over in seconds. The Soviet Soldiers were tied hand and foot in a tight circle for warmth. Michael was surprised to see the Soviet missile carriers being driven away by people he hadn't noticed earlier. *Where did these people come from?* he thought. Michael heard from general chatter that they were specialists brought in to drive the missile carriers away "to a place of safety". None of them had any idea what that meant. A man appeared next to the radio operator, grabbed the handset and spoke into it, saying, "The Fox has jumped the Dog," before ripping the handset from the radio transmitter. "What are you lot hanging around for? Get gone!" The bogus Soviet Unit didn't need a second invitation to run back through the hole in the fence.

Following the ambush, the Special Forces ground team gave one another congratulatory pats on their backs before leaving East Germany by punching multiple holes through the border fence and setting off alarms in a dozen guard stations in the process. This action was designed to alert Soviet border guards to the plight of their comrades who'd been left tied up on the freezing cold forest floor.

*

The Soviet Soldiers who had, "cowardly surrendered the property of the people of the Union of Soviet Socialist Republics without firing a single shot," were condemned as anti-Soviet saboteurs, wreckers and traitors and sent to the Lubyanka for 'debriefing'. After enduring days of torture, during which they confessed to whatever their interrogators wanted them to confess to, they were all executed by being made to kneel in a tiled room, they being the easiest to wash down, and shot once through the backs of their heads. Their bodies were chopped up and flushed into Moscow's sewage system via the Lubyanka's toilets.

*

In the operations room in Half Moon Street the radio message confirming the success of the Soviet Missile Heist was received with cheers of relief. "Don't celebrate too soon," cautioned Madame Chancellor. "They still have a long, long, way to go before they're out of the woods." She thought her turn of phrase amusing. After a moment's pause, Madame Chancellor spoke to Control, telling her to signal the Operative leading the Soviet Missile convoy and order her to abandon the plan to leave West Germany by the northern route and proceed with plan B instead. In keeping with protocol, the Operative called back on another channel and asked to speak with 'Wolf 2', who, for this mission, was Lisette. She returned the correct credentials to the Operative and received confirmation that she would comply with the change of route.

As Lisette hung up the radio handset, the two uninvited secret inner council members scampered from the operations room. Margaret cast a glance at Lisette; no words were necessary. She sprung from her seat in hot pursuit of the men while affixing a silencer to the business end of her 9 mil. She came across them making a call from an office they shouldn't have been in. Lisette waited in silence for the call to connect and as soon as it did she moved from the shadows; phutt, phutt; phutt, phutt. Lisette always double tapped to make sure of a kill. As the traitors lay bleeding on the floor, Lisette stepped over them, picked up the telephone and said, "It's me." The call hung up with a click.

Lisette reported to Madame Chancellor that the traitors hadn't had time to pass on the information about the change of route. They had their suspicions about who it was on the other end of the call with each naming Sir Jeremy Hawksmith. Later that evening, Madame Chancellor and Lisette concocted a plan to make sure that the spoils of the Soviet Missile Heist wouldn't fall into anybody else's hands.

A Faction conversation.

"I just received a call from Dante. Unfortunately, he didn't have time to pass on his message. Before I hung up I heard the voice of that scrawny little bitch, Madame Chancellor's lapdog, Lisette. Given her reputation I can only assume Dante and Salman are dead."

"I'll get confirmation."

"Do that, I don't want any loose ends; dead men tell no tales. I could guess what the call was about but I must be certain. I believe she's changed the plan regarding how the missiles will leave West Germany. Who knows, she might even have a nice little hidey-hole for keeping them there. We need to find out what's happening."

"Weren't you invited to the operations room old man?" scoffed Rex. Sir Jeremy cast him a venomous glance. Right then the phone rang. Sir Jeremy's PA picked up the receiver.

"Hello… no he's not… I see… I'll pass the message onto him as soon as I see him… yes… yes… you are welcome… yes… goodbye."

"Who was that?"

"That, sir, was one of Madame Chancellor's so-called PAs, name of Cho. She said Madame Chancellor has called an emergency meeting of the Council of Governors regarding the Soviet Missile Appropriation project. Will you go?"

"Of course I'll go. I'll have to. What choice do I have? If those two morons aren't dead after all I hope they kept their mouths shut!"

OUTFOXING THE FRENCH

Madame Chancellor's meeting of the Council of Governors for the Soviet Missile Heist was held in the operations room. When they arrived she looked like the Cat who'd gotten the cream. Lisette was at her right hand, eyeing all those around the table with her trademark dead-eye blank stare. She let the front of her jacket fall open to show her shoulder holster packing a matt black Browning 9 mil. Several Governors objected to Lisette being armed. Madame Chancellor replied that it was regrettable but necessary as two 'spies' had been uncovered in the operations room during the 'execution' of the Soviet Missile Heist. The Governors didn't like the way Madame Chancellor said the word 'execution'. One of them asked what had become of the spies. Lisette answered, saying they'd been "retired". The Governors shifted uncomfortably on their seats. They wanted to look at one another to check reactions to Lisette's news but dared not in case they gave away a 'tell'.

"I am happy to report, ladies and gentlemen, that the Soviet Missile Heist," beamed Madame Chancellor hoping it would soon be called Madame Chancellor's Soviet Missile Heist, "went off without a hitch. At the present moment, the convoy is speeding toward a secret location before being driven out of the country. And on that point the exit route has been changed for security reasons." The Governors guessed that Madame Chancellor's 'security reasons' had everything to do with the two spies Lisette had reputedly recently retired.

"What route will they now take?" asked Sir Toby. Madame Chancellor had already decided to tell the Council of Governors some vague details of the new route that the missiles were to leave West Germany by and did just that.

"I assume we have cover along the new route?" probed Sir Jeremy Hawksmith.

"I decided against having cover as it might attract attention. I received intelligence that the French Splinter is on the prowl in the area so the lower the profile the better."

"They are going to be mightily upset if they come away empty handed," scoffed one of the Governors.

"Precisely. Now, to business. It's not going to be easy selling stolen Soviet missiles so I propose they remain off the market for at least six months to give the situation time to cool down." The Council of Governors nodded agreement with Madame Chancellor's proposal; the missiles wouldn't be offered for sale until the following summer.

"So long as you're able to report the financial outcome at next year's AGM?" added one of the Governors keen to make sure of her bonus.

"That is my intention, Clara, though I will, of course, announce the success of the Soviet Missile Heist at this year's AGM." This caused murmuring between the Governors. "Now before you jump in, I realise that announcement will pose a few problems but I want to build up trust with the Governors for me to pass some changes that I'm going to make to the running of the Organisation." At the mention of 'changes to the running of the Organisation' the change-averse old-fart Governors looked around the table at one another.

"What might these changes be, old girl?" asked Sir Jeremy.

"They aren't yet finalised," lied Margaret. "I don't want to start a rumour mill so let's leave it until the AGM itself." The imminent timing of the AGM made the Governors nervous. Sir Jeremy's spies on Madame Chancellor's secret inner council had previously told him what the changes concerned and he had plans to thwart them.

But, inconveniently, his spies were now dead and he wondered from where he could recruit their replacements. He had even considered making Lisette an offer she'd be crazy to refuse. But as he thought her to be on the crazy side of insane he reconsidered.

After the Council of Governors broke up, Sir Jeremy sought out Margaret to offer her his services in brokering the disposal of the Soviet missiles, "on the best possible terms," he assured her. She said she appreciated his kind offer and when the time was right she'd "get him involved". He recognised that as weasel-word-code for "you're not getting anywhere near the missile deal". Sir Jeremy, being desperate to communicate news to the French Splinter that the exit route had been changed, bowed to Madame Chancellor and left Half Moon Street to put in place the next piece of his plan to remove her.

*

A Faction conversation.
"It's me," said Sir Jeremy.
"Go ahead," replied Major Finn.
"Have you heard that the convoy has a new escape route?"
"I have and you'll be pleased to know I have a map of it." There followed a long pause.
"And?"
"Well now old chap, what's in it for me?"
"The usual… now stop pissing around and give me the map."
"You forget, I'm in West Germany, old man."
"Then give it to Lefort so he can pass it to—"
"I need to talk to you about him."
"What about him?"
"As you are aware, several of those involved in the missile heist were to be dealt with and left on the eastern side of the border but instead Lefort spirited them away. Something needs to be done about him," said Major Finn in the hope his nemesis would finally get what was coming to him.

"Indeed, he needs to be taught a lesson but he's far too prominent a figure to just go bumping him off. Why don't we, and by 'we' I mean you, exact revenge on his family. He has a twin sister I believe?"

"I'm not going anywhere near her! She's a bigger psychopath than Lisette. The last time we…"

"Yes, yes, very interesting, Finn, but time's a wasting, I'll get the Count to sanction her. Now give me the route of the convoy so I can pass it onto the Frogs. They'll grab the missiles and Bouvier will owe me one."

Major Finn gave Sir Jeremy details of the new escape route. He even suggested a place he favoured for an ambush to take place. The call ended with the sharp click of a telephone receiver being slammed down. Minutes later Sir Jeremy called Count Bouvier to tell him about the change of route to get the Soviet missiles out of West Germany. At the end of the conversation Sir Jeremy mentioned that Captain Lefort had 'transgressed once again' and suggested his twin sister, a Madame Lefebvre, be sanctioned to teach him a lesson. The Count, though apprehensive, agreed to the sanction though it was later abandoned after four Sentinels went missing while on a mission to carry it out.

*

The plan Major Finn had alluded to during his conversation with Sir Jeremy involved the corralling of a group of 'blacklisted Operatives' and executing them close to where the ambush had taken place. They would be discovered on the eastern side of the fence wearing Soviet uniforms, carrying no IDs and having been shot with Soviet bullets. This would have had the appearance of Soviet Soldiers having shot them and thereby possibly saving the lives of those who'd been executed for not guarding the convoy. Funny how things work out.

An Organisation conversation.

"Boss, you do realise that by now the French Splinter will know all about the new route the missile convoy will be taking, don't you?"

"Of course I do Lizzie darling, that's why we're going back to plan A. Get your coat on, we're going to pay Control a visit."

"I don't trust her," said Lisette pouting like a teenager.

"Don't worry Lizzie darling, you're still my favourite," laughed Madame Chancellor pinching her bum cheek. "Give her a call and tell her to meet us outside her office in ten minutes."

When Madame Chancellor and Lisette arrived outside Control's office she was on the pavement waiting for them. They walked to a nearby safe house. Margaret radioed the Operative who had led the Soviet Missile Heist and ordered her to revert to plan A. She sent a signal back to London requesting the confirmation key. The key sender this time was Control, for obvious reasons. The key was accepted and the Operative reverted to plan A. At the same time Control passed details of how one of the missile carriers, number four, was to be separated from the rest and transported to the UK.

*

It wasn't until long after the American Special Forces Soldiers and their CIA 'observers' arrived back at the RVP that a CIA Agent noticed there weren't any missile carriers where he expected them to be. "Maybe they got lost along the way," joked a Major whose laughter wasn't shared by any others in the camouflaged compound. From the time of the ambush to the assault teams arriving back at the RVP was one hour and fifty minutes. They'd been kept waiting an hour and thirty minutes for the top brass to arrive before the debriefing commenced. It was an hour after the debriefing session had ended when the CIA Agent noticed the missile carriers weren't where they were meant to be. By this time, the missile carriers and their shiny new missiles were being resprayed and having their decals altered.

*

Operatives of the French Splinter were waiting in hiding along the route they'd been assured the stolen missile convoy would take. The ambush location was perfect. It was on a sharp bend, meaning the vehicles would need to slow right down in the lead up to it. Just beyond the bend was a wide trail leading off into a forest, ideal for hiding the missile transport vehicles. There was a slither of moon giving just enough light to aid the ambushers. The lead Operative of the French Splinter Ambush Squad was dreaming of the plaudits, and the millions of francs, coming his way.

The French Splinter had been given to understand there would be minimal personnel travelling with the convoy; twelve drivers plus a few guards; so, unlikely to be more than twenty Operatives in total. Despite their superior numbers and having the element of surprise on their side the French Splinter wanted to avoid a firefight. They felt confident the Organisation's Operatives would throw in the towel as soon as they'd stopped the convoy and shown their numbers.

It was a long cold night they spent waiting for the convoy. In the small wee hours a single motorcyclist cruised slowly around the bend in the road at the ambush location. As it came to a halt on the gravel verge between the forest and the road, four members of the French Splinter Ambush Squad emerged from the trees adjusting their clothing, making like they'd been attending to a call of nature. The motorcyclist dismounted and put the machine up on its stand.

"Please, gentlemen, don't go to all the trouble of putting on an act on my behalf. I'm here to deliver a message to your commander." The leather-clad motorcyclist removed her silver, black-visored crash helmet and shook out her waist-length blonde hair. It was a wig but a very good one and chosen for a purpose. The hair shaking out was all that was needed to distract the four men. Knowing men were always randy, no matter what the circumstances, or the danger, men are always ready for sex, the hair shaking out was her way to distract them.

"What are you talking about?" replied one of the men, walking toward the motorcyclist with a jaunty swagger for the amusement of those hiding in the trees. He moved close to her. That was all she needed. The Operative grabbed the man by the arm, spun him around and, putting an arm lock on him, placed the muzzle of a neat little .22 against his temple and shouted into the forest.

"I am not alone," she lied, "I am here to deliver a message to your Commander. I know what you are doing here. The convoy isn't coming this way. It's already long gone on its way out of Germany."

"Who are you?" shouted a voice from the forest.

"I don't talk to trees, show yourself." A man emerged from the forest. "Are you the Commander?"

"I am. What is your message?"

"I bring a message for you from Madame Chancellor. I am one of her personal Sentinels so you will appreciate how important this message must be." The motorcyclist whispered her message into the Commander's ear while pressing her .22 hard against his testicles. The Commander looked totally deflated after receiving the whispered message.

"So, what do we do now?" he asked.

"We all stop shivering and go home. Okay? No shooting of messengers. Okay? I'm going to turn around and ride away. My associates are watching and if anything bad should happen to me then all hell will break loose."

"You have my word that nothing will happen to you. You are very brave coming here under such circumstances. Madame Chancellor is very lucky to have someone like you… or perhaps she doesn't value your life?" The Sentinel returned the Commander a smile.

"Of course she values my life," she replied, followed by a low hiss-whispered thought as she turned away, "You stupid man."

It was vitally important that the French Splinter dispersed quickly because, according to the messenger, American Special Forces were on the lookout for the stolen missiles. If they came across the French Splinter hiding in the forest then the outcome would have been disastrous and Madame Chancellor didn't want that. She didn't want the Count's Operatives slaughtered, especially as eight of them were Israeli Doublers.

*

The post mortems, recriminations, allegations, accusations, counter-allegations and finger pointing began even before the French Splinter had finished covering their tracks at the ambush location. They wouldn't be getting the massive payday they thought they were going to get. The post mortems, recriminations, allegations, accusations, counter-allegations and finger pointing continued for several days. Order was only restored following a phone call between Madame Chancellor and Count Bouvier.

"Count Bouvier, Maurice, thank you for taking my call."

"It's always a pleasure to speak with you Madame Chancellor… Margaret," he replied. They had a long-established mutual admiration for one another since they'd met during her time as a roving Ambassador. She had always loved the way he said her name.

"I know how disappointed you must feel right now but you must realise I had no option after you turned down what I considered to be a very generous offer."

"I didn't like the terms of the offer. You know how I've long despised the Americans and the Russians. It wasn't the Organisation I was set against, I hope you understand that?"

"I do Maurice, I genuinely do. But I had no choice. The whole thing was set up by an Operative of the American Splinter and when the Russian Splinter got to know of the project there was no way I could deny them their cut, for obvious reasons."

"It turns my stomach that these criminals are going to be rewarded. They abandoned the mission after Bonaparte. They are traitors to the cause." In truth the Count was being more than a little disingenuous and duplicitous.

"Maurice, you're well aware of my desire to reunite the Organisation. If we fight over money, of all things, then all my hard work… all our hard work… will have been for nothing. You must realise that Maurice?" Not answering Madame Chancellor's point the Count changed the subject.

"What about Lefort? I understand he had a hand in betraying us." Margaret was surprised at the Count's assertion and wondered what really lay behind it as it was untrue. She considered for a moment how she should respond. Should she support the man who was being touted as President elect of a reunited Organisation, a job she coveted and wanted for herself, or should she abandon him to his fate at the hands of the French Splinter? She so nearly chose the latter option before replying to Count Bouvier.

"Maurice, if we use words such as 'betray' then the situation can't improve and will, in all probability, get worse. I believe that Lefort is a good, honest, honourable man, I'm sure deep down you know that. He's liked and trusted by all the Splinters and I believe he could possibly be the right person to become President of a reunified Organisation. What he did he did for the greater good… need I say any more?" Margaret's carefully chosen words confirmed Captain Lefort's guilt in the mind of the Count.

"Margaret, there has to be another way of achieving peace than electing somebody like Lefort President."

"There might well be, Maurice, but I can't think of one right now," she lied, "I believe Lefort is the best chance we have for peace." Margaret paused for effect. "You know what I'm going to ask you next don't you Maurice?"

"I believe I do."

"Then please promise me that you will not seek revenge on Lefort or harm any of his family."

"As a favour to you I will forgive Lefort but I will not forget what he did. No harm will come to him or his family from me or anybody in my Splinter. Is that good enough for you Margaret?" Though the Count gave this assurance he wasn't in control of all of those who wanted revenge on Lefort for the Soviet Missile Heist ambush fiasco.

"It is. I love the way you say my name, Maurice. I always have." The call ended with blown kisses and warm goodbyes.

Madame Chancellor now had Captain Lefort right where she wanted him. If he was successful in becoming President she was certain she could make him her puppet. She just had to let a little time go by before proceeding with her scheming.

MR FLASK'S GAME

During his journey back to Bielefeld, Michael's driver reminded him of the need for total secrecy over the Soviet 'exercise'. She told him that he was never to speak about it with anyone. "Anybody at all… ever!" she emphasised. Michael asked about those who'd driven the vehicles away. She looked at him coldly. He sensed danger and promised not to say anything to anybody about the Soviet exercise… ever. She thanked him for making his promise and patted his knee.

As soon as Michael was dropped off at his barracks he was arrested and taken away by MPs. Observing Michael's arrest, the driver called Control to let her know what had happened. She said she wasn't sure why Michael had been arrested but assumed it had to be something to do with the Soviet Missile Heist. Panicked messages were sent flying around the members of the Council of Governors.

An MP Officer told Michael that he was under arrest on suspicion of the murder of Private Coley and he was taken to an interrogation room. No sooner had Michael sat down than Major Finn entered the room and sat behind a desk in front of him. The door opened again to admit a Corporal and another man who sat down quietly behind Michael.

"You can leave us," said the Major to the MP. After the MP had closed the door, Major Finn asked, "Private Frost, why did you murder Private Coley?"

"I had no idea Private Coley was dead. I did not murder Private Coley," replied Michael in a more monotone voice than usual.

"I understand that you and he were working on some secret squirrel thing together and you went missing right before his body was found. Are you saying it's all just a coincidence?"

"I did not murder Private Coley." Michael's reply was barely audible.

"Private Frost, let me introduce you to this gentleman," said the Major. "This is Mr Flask, a former Naval Commander, now with the MoD."

"Thank you Major, I'll take it from here." Major Finn was visibly put out at Mr Flask's taking over the proceedings. "Frost, what can you tell me about this person?" Mr Flask carefully placed a black and white photograph of a pretty young blonde female on the desk in front of Michael.

"She works in the post room in our building."

"Is that all you can tell me about her?" Michael thought for a moment.

"Her Russian is good enough for her to work in the translation section. I once wondered if she was really Czech."

"Did you mention your suspicions to anybody? Your CO perhaps?"

"I didn't have any suspicions. I just noticed her Russian was very good."

"How do you know how good her Russian was, Frost?"

"Because my Russian is very good."

"You say your Russian is 'very good', just how good is it?"

"My vocabulary needs improving but otherwise I am fluent."

"Fluent in Russian at your age and with your background? Really? Do you speak any other languages, Frost?" asked Mr Flask fully knowing the answer to his own question.

"I speak German and French and since working as a translator for the Chiefs of Staffs my Italian is now very good and I've picked up some other languages."

"Why are you so interested in foreign languages?"

"Studying languages occupies my mind."

"Studying languages 'occupies your mind' you say? What are you Frost? Speaking all these languages I'd say you're some kind of spy."

As Mr Flask spoke the word 'spy', the Corporal stood and placed his hand on the holster of his revolver. Major Finn was getting jittery; this was not how he expected the situation to play out. He'd allow things to continue but if matters got out of hand he'd have Mr Flask removed from the base. Michael, however, was the epitome of calmness.

"You seem very relaxed considering you have a Soldier standing behind you with his hand on his gun," said Mr Flask nodding toward the Corporal.

"I doubt the Corporal would shoot me."

"Just in case you're wrong about the Corporal I suggest you keep very still. Where were we? Ah yes. You knew somebody working at MI3 spoke excellent Russian and in your own words thought her Russian was so good that it attracted your attention to the point where you doubted she was really Czech. Did you ever meet with or speak to Miss Janak, real name Lyudmila Tarasova, outside of work?" Michael looked puzzled at discovering the mail room girl had two names and that he might meet her outside of work. For what purpose he could not imagine.

"I only spoke to her when she delivered mail and I never met her outside of work. I had no reason to."

"Well Frost, I suspect you and Miss Tarasova, a known Soviet Agent, were in this together. Do you see where this is going? So, I'll ask you, Frost, are you a spy?"

"You never mentioned anything to me about a spy ring," grinded the Major through clenched teeth. Mr Flask ignored him.

"Answer the question Frost; are you a spy?"

"I'm not a spy and I only spoke with… the female when she delivered mail to me at my desk."

"Tell me Frost, do you know who killed Miss Tarasova? Did you kill her?" The Major's eyes widened as Mr Flask hadn't shared this information with him.

"What's going on here Flask? You were going to question Private Frost over the murder of Private Coley not the murder of a Soviet spy. Any more surprises and I'll have you thrown off the base." At this, the Corporal unclipped the cover of his holster and placed his hand on the grip of his revolver.

"What's going on, Major, is Frost couldn't have murdered Private Coley because he was with the Chiefs of Staffs at the time Private Coley was killed. I'd say having a handful of Generals as witnesses is a cast-iron alibi. I am here to investigate the murder of Lyudmila Tarasova, a Soviet spy working undercover at MI3. Is that clear enough for you Major?" There being no response from Major Finn, Mr Flask continued. "Frost, who killed Miss Tarasova? Was it you?"

"No," replied Michael. Mr Flask waited for more but nothing more was forthcoming as Michael had answered the question to his satisfaction.

"No? Is that it? Is there nothing else you'd like to add?" Michael shook his head. "Are you curious to know the circumstances surrounding Miss Tarasova's murder?"

"No."

"Well, you might be interested if I told you that your French chum, the one who masquerades as an army Captain, Christan Lefort, is implicated in this murder as well as that of a virtually identical murder of a female near Göttingen a fortnight ago… while you were there working for the Chiefs of Staffs."

"I read about it but there was no mention of the death being a murder."

"Well Mr Frost, she was murdered and she and your Miss Tarasova were both killed with the same weapon."

"How was she murdered?" asked Michael feebly, his vision becoming tunnel-like. He knew what was coming and he hoped he could cope.

"She was stabbed with a long thin weapon… probably a stiletto. They were execution style murders the type of which is the trademark of an individual yet to be identified but who is possibly your French friend. Or at least he knows who it is as perhaps do you."

"I don't know anything about any murders."

"Really Frost? Miss Tarasova was found in her apartment the day after you left Bielefeld to join the wargames. She'd been dead for over twenty-four hours. She was found naked and there were signs that she'd been interfered with." Flask checked for any reaction from Michael. There were none. "She'd been stabbed… the weapon pierced her brain. The coroner almost missed it as the entry wound was so small. Death was instantaneous. And of course we know that you were in the vicinity at the time of both murders. Like blondes do you, Frost? Do they excite you?" Michael hardly understood a word Mr Flask said as his tunnel vision became more pronounced and his hearing echoey. "Tell me Frost, I hear that you're a bit of a dab hand with swords. Is that so, Frost?" Struggling to stay within the reality of the room Michael was becoming more and more detached from the interrogation.

"I was on… my school fencing team… I boxed… I studied… self-defence at the Dojo in… I box…" Michael ceased his rambling. Through the tunnel of his vision he found himself staring into the yellow eyes of the Demon as it ripped its way through the ether to enter Michael's world.

*

Before Michael's mutism passed he thought it entirely normal to see visions of Demons and that everyone could see them. After his mutism passed he told his parents about them and was puzzled to understand why they couldn't see what was right in front of them. Joseph shouted at Michael telling him never to mention the Demons ever again. He tried and tried not to talk about them but it was hard for a small child to keep all the horror locked up inside.

Over time he mentioned them less and less until finally he was alone with them. As he grew, Michael began to understand that the creatures weren't real but when he was young he couldn't distinguish them from reality. People thought he was disturbed as he shouted and argued with them. He vividly remembered the changing looks on their faces as he told them of his visions.

*

"Are you okay Private Frost? Would you like something to drink? Some water? Tea?" asked Major Finn suddenly concerned by how strange-looking Michael had become.

"What the hell are you up to Frost?" yelled Mr Flask. "What are you looking at? Are you playing games with me boy?"

"I was momentarily distracted but I'm okay now," said Michael despite the Demon ripping at the very air to get at him.

"You were saying Frost how you are an expert in self-defence." Which he hadn't said.

"I said I have studied martial arts. I have become a competent student."

"A competent student? Is that all I wonder? But to go on with the murders of the female in Göttingen and the Soviet spy in Bielefeld. They were both killed with a long thin-bladed weapon, probably a stiletto… which is just a short sword when you think about it. The female in Göttingen was stabbed through her left temple with the weapon mincing her brain. Miss Tarasova was stabbed under her chin and as with the other female the blade continued into the brain. Both died instantly. Investigations already carried out link you and Lefort to both murders. What have you to say for yourself Frost?" The Demon was snarling at Michael, rotting flesh hanging from its broken fangs.

"I had nothing to do with the murders. I've known Captain Lefort since Cadets. I can't believe he would harm anybody."

"A Soldier who wouldn't harm anybody? That doesn't even make any sense, Frost. Your French pal is probably responsible for far worse than involvement in murdering a couple of spy tarts. Oh, didn't I mention that the other female was a spy too? Is it commonplace, do you think, to have pretty young blonde girls swanning around the place, cosying up to people on the Russian desk? That means you Frost… that means you!" screamed Mr Flask pointing an index finger at Michael. "C'mon Frost, the game's up son. You'll feel better if you make a clean breast of it by confessing. Tell me everything you know about the murders of two pretty young blonde spies. Who knows, perhaps you didn't even know they were spies. Perhaps you just like murdering pretty young blonde girls who reject you. I understand the other female and your French chum were at it. How did that make you feel, Frost? It must have made you angry, he's old enough to be her father for Christ's sake. C'mon Frost, tell me, tell me you did it!"

"I didn't know the women were spies. I didn't murder Miss Tarasova and I can't remember anything about the night the young lady in Göttingen was murdered. I blacked out and I…" The room went silent at this revelation. They had him; he'd admitted blacking out and that was enough for them to arrest Michael.

"Major, dismiss the Corporal. Don't worry, I've got Frost covered," said Mr Flask patting a .38 special concealed under his jacket.

"Corporal, leave us."

"Yes sir. Shall I post a guard outside?" The Major looked at Mr Flask who nodded and he did likewise to the Corporal.

Once the Corporal left the room the atmosphere changed. Michael was given a drink and a biscuit. With the relaxation of the tension the Demon began to melt away back into its own world. Mr Flask now spoke quietly and calmly, almost paternally.

"You know you're in a whole lot of trouble, don't you Michael? You do know that don't you son? You know that even if you had nothing to do with those spies or their murders I'm going to have to arrest you and take you away. This is serious stuff you're involved in, son. You'll have to be locked up while matters are investigated and there's no telling how long you'll be in prison. There are always complications when military personnel are investigated while civvy criminal investigations are going on at the same time. I think it's probable that you'll do a couple of years behind bars on remand before your trial even begins. A shocking waste if you ask me." The mere mention of being locked up in a cell at the mercy of the Demon and His horde was too much for Michael to take and his evaporating tormentor took full form again.

No! yelled Michael inside his head. *No!* he silently mouthed into the Demon's visage.

"Of course, that all depends on whether or not we can reach an agreement. I can tell you, Michael, the Major here thinks you're probably innocent, or if not entirely innocent then not as involved as I think you are. But there's always a shadow of doubt in everything, isn't there Michael?" Michael's eyes were fixed on the Demon. He gave no reply. "Well, there is. Okay? I tell you what I'm prepared to do for you Michael. I'm going to give you a choice about what happens to you next but bear in mind that once you make your decision there's no going back. No going back. Do you understand, son?" Still no response from Michael. Mr Flask continued regardless. "Somebody with your skills and abilities might serve some useful purpose while any misunderstandings are cleared up. You could put all the training you've received to good use."

"Yes indeed," agreed the Major whose demeanour had similarly changed since the Corporal had left the room. "You can take up a secondment with Mr Flask, very much as you did with MI3, and then join your Regiment when it's over, if you wish to that is." Major Finn ended his sentence with a nervous little laugh.

"So what's it to be then Michael? Get dragged off to prison or do something useful while this mess gets sorted out. If you're innocent, as you say you are, you won't want to spend time in prison will you because… what is it they say, 'there's no smoke without fire'? Time to choose Mr Frost, time to choose!" Even though Michael hadn't heard most of what Mr Flask had said he'd picked up on the basic choice. He knew he couldn't spend time in prison locked up with the Demon for company.

"What is your offer?"

"You go on secondment to an active Unit… probably overseas."

"Where overseas?"

"That needs to be decided but let's start close to home; Northern Ireland perhaps. How does that sound?"

"I need time to think about it."

"That doesn't work for me Mr Frost. I need to leave here in the next hour and I need to know if you're on board or you're on your way to prison. Time's up Frost. Choose." Michael had no real option.

"Okay."

"Okay what? You're with me or you're off to prison?"

"I'm with you."

"Listen carefully, Mr Frost. Once you accept this offer there's no going back. Do you understand, Mr Frost, there's no going back after you sign on the dotted line?"

"What do I need to sign? Shall I—" Mr Flask held up his hand to silence Michael; he opened his briefcase and took out a number of forms.

"These are the documents that you need to sign. There's no need to read through them they're just standard MoD forms saying that you're going on a secondment for a year. That's all Michael, only a year. It's a good deal don't you think?"

"Captain Jones said I could take some home leave at Christmas and then go for selection with the Royal Marines… just like he did."

"I don't have a problem with that Michael. In fact that'll work out better. You can go home for Christmas and be with your family and then go for RMC selection in February. What do you say Major Finn?"

"Perfect," said the Major smiling a snake smile.

"One more thing Michael, you mustn't tell anybody about our deal… anybody at all. Understand? Promise?"

"I promise." After Michael signed the forms he was booted out of the interrogation room.

"What'll happen next?" asked Major Finn eager to learn what the future had in store for Michael Frost.

"Just as was said, Major Finn. Frost will take some leave over Christmas… then he'll return here for a short time and then go on selection with the Royal Marines."

"Then what?"

"Then what? To be honest with you, I don't know," lied Flask and Major Finn knew it.

"There's something going on with Frost and Captain Jones, don't you think?" said Major Finn taking another opportunity to poison Captain Jones' water. "I bet they're in cahoots together—"

"I'd love to stay and chat but I must be on my way," interrupted Mr Flask rudely. "Goodbye Major Finn, we will probably never meet again but if we do then we're to ignore one another. Got it?"

"Goodbye Flask. See yourself out," snarled Major Finn. Mr Flask left the room with neither man offering the other a hand shake.

*

Michael wandered back to MILR as if nothing had happened. Such events didn't register with Michael as they would with most other people. After arriving at his desk Michael was quizzed by the chaps about his hush hush wargames assignment. "Was he a spy?" some asked because many in their world were spies. "Not a chance" was the general consensus as he was regarded as not right in the head. Michael worked, ate, slept, got up and did it all again. He was like a machine. When not on duty, Michael was often observed sitting on his bunk staring at walls talking to himself. Had those observing him been aware of what he was seeing as he stared at the walls in the lonely barracks they would have been very concerned about his state of mind.

"Hey Michael, how do you fancy coming along to the pub tonight?" asked an MILR chap. The invitation was not an act of comradery. He was eager to find out more about Michael and getting him sozzled could loosen his tongue.

"I don't drink," replied Michael.

"You can have a coffee if you don't fancy a beer. C'mon, come out and let off some steam. You never know, you might meet a nice German bird." In truth, none of the chaps had any luck with the local girls.

"You should go Michael," said a familiar voice. "It'll do you good." The chaps dispersed as none of them trusted Captain Lefort.

"Why were you in a German Major's uniform at the wargames? Did you get a promotion?" The French Captain laughed; he thought Michael had made a joke.

"No Michael. But to return to the point at hand, you should go to the pub tonight with the others. I'll be there and it'll be nice to catch up with what you've been up to," replied the French Captain despite knowing full well Michael's every move over the past few years.

As soon as they were off duty the MILR chaps changed into their civvies and set off to the newly opened Sergeant Pepper's beer garden. They were laughing and chatting and stopped occasionally to turn their backs to the wind and cup their hands to light a cigarette.

"Fancy a ciggie Michael?"

"I don't smoke."

"Don't drink, don't smoke, what do you do?" The MILR chaps smirked at the answers to that question running around in their heads.

"Hey Michael, tell me, are you getting yer hole anywhere then?" This question drew sniggers from the chaps.

"Where would he be getting his hole then, eh? He never goes anywhere. Unless you mean he's shagging old Fruity Boy Williams?"

"He's a good lad and doesn't go in for that sort of thing," teased one of the chaps in an attempt to get the others off of Michael's back though he didn't care either way.

Arriving at Sergeant Pepper's it felt good to get out of the wind especially as it had just begun sleeting. Bielefeld's weather reminded everybody of Manchester. A couple of the chaps made their way to the bar and got drinks on trays and brought them to a table the others had commandeered.

"That was lucky gettin' a table so quick. We got everybody beer with schnapps chasers, all except Michael, we got him a Coca Cola and a schnapps for the cold. Cheers!" The chaps downed their schnapps and got stuck into their litre glasses of beer. Within minutes of their arrival the bar filled up with Soldiers. "There's that bloody Frog over there staring at us." The chaps turned to look at the French Captain who beckoned Michael to join him.

"What terrible weather, so much rain and wind. You'll notice I'm talking about the weather which I know you British love to do," laughed the French Captain alone. "So, Michael, you joined the Army. I hoped you would. You'll make a great Soldier. What is that you're drinking? Schnapps? Let me get you another." The French Captain caught the attention of a beautiful, blonde waitress who took their order. "What a beautiful girl. She's around your age Michael, maybe a year or two older. I can't say I'd be too happy about her working here if I were her father." The waitress returned with a bottle of red wine and two glasses of Schnapps. "Thank you. I haven't seen you here before."

"No… I go the University… sorry, my English." Michael and the French Captain engaged the waitress in a brief conversation in German.

"What a delightful young lady. You should see if she has any free time and maybe get to know her better. Salute!" The pair downed their Schnapps in one and despite the Captain saying how terrible German wine was it seemed to taste okay to Michael whose head was becoming dangerously disordered. He'd clearly not learned his lesson from Göttingen as he couldn't resist alcohol after he'd gotten the taste for it.

The French Captain became concerned after noticing the effect alcohol was having on Michael and so decided he'd had enough. As they stood to leave a stampede began to claim the seats they were vacating. In the commotion Michael was knocked to the floor, attracting the attention of the waitress to see if he was okay. This was the opportunity one of the Soldiers was looking for.

"Hey gorgeous, I'm not feelin' too good meself so maybe you can come and help me for a bit? What do you say?" slurred the Soldier.

"Shut up Harry and leave the girl alone. Don't pay him any attention love he's from Essex."

"I'm not botherin' you, am I darlin'?" asked Harry grabbing the waitress by an elbow and pulling her toward him. Once in close proximity Harry attempted to kiss the pretty young waitress.

"Young man, if you don't let her alone I'll be forced to teach you some manners," said the French Captain in his best put-on Franglais accent.

"Ooooooooo, listen to the Frog. Get back to Frogland you, or I'll…" That was all the Soldier had time to say before Michael acted. It was unheard of for him to instigate a fight but he'd felt such a rush of raw aggression and acted on it. His attack was swift and decisive with a cross shot to the jaw followed by a straight strike with the heel of his hand to the chest of the Soldier which laid him out flat.

It's fortunate that blow wasn't to the point of the nose, otherwise we'd have a dead Soldier on our hands, thought the French Captain. "That's enough, Michael," shouted Captain Lefort sternly.

Next thing, three Soldiers jumped the French Captain from behind. In an instant Michael planned and executed his attack. He first pushed against some nearby Soldiers to clear some space. Some other Soldiers made to join in the imminent scrap but thought better of it once they saw Michael in full flow. In seconds, he landed a dozen punches and kicks and, once finished, he stood stock still in a Ko Kutsu Karate stance over the prostrate bodies of the Soldiers, ready to resume his attack should it be necessary. The French Captain casually took Michael by the arm and they left the bar without making eye contact with anybody. Classic move; people who do not make eye contact are harder to recognise in the future.

"How could that drip Frost do something like that?" mumbled one of the MILR chaps. They were all open-mouthed speechless by what they'd witnessed.

"I've never seen anything like that in my life. Have you?"

"I saw a film once where they did that sort of thing but I thought it was all fake. Did you see how hard he hit that bloke? I thought he was going to start on the rest of them and then it would've really kicked off."

"I say chaps, we should leave. It's not good for MILR to be involved in stuff like this."

There was someone there that night at Sergeant Pepper's with orders to get close to Captain Lefort. She got an unexpected bonus witnessing the fighting talents of Michael Frost. *Something interesting to report back to my Counsellor,* she thought.

*

On their way back to the barracks, Michael confided to Captain Lefort that he'd been interrogated by Captain Finn and a 'Mr Flask' and that he was under orders not to tell anybody about it. Before Captain Lefort could say anything Michael continued.

"After the Soviet exercise I was driven back to camp by a woman who told me never to speak about it to anybody. I think we stole Soviet missiles." Under normal circumstances, people who make such dramatic statements show some outward signs of concern but not so Michael; it was all just words to him.

"Are you sure, Michael?"

"I'm positive." Captain Lefort needed to change the subject.

"Tell me, are you feeling okay after your interrogation by Mr Flask and Major Finn?"

"Yes. Mr Flask believes you murdered at least one of the women they questioned me about." Captain Lefort was stunned by Michael's revelation and wondered why somebody like Flask would make such an allegation.

"Michael, you need tell me everything that went on with Mr Flask."

Michael recounted the whole interrogation verbatim though Captain Lefort thought he was just giving a highly detailed verbal report, one which he was very impressed by. In those days they would've called Michael's gift 'photographic memory' but it was more than that. His gift worked for and against him, especially when his Demon came to call.

"Michael, you must promise me not to mention today's events or anything about the Soviet exercise to anybody unless I give my permission. Okay?"

"I promise," replied Michael without a second's hesitation.

The two men continued their walk back to the barracks in total silence, which suited them both for different reasons.

*

Getting the Soviet missiles out of West Germany was simplicity itself. The Organisation knew that for several days before the end of the wargames, units would be making their way back to their home bases at different times to avoid clogging up the roads, which would've been bad for PR.

Immediately following the heist, the missile convoy drove to a farm where a pre-fabricated drive-through workshop had been erected in readiness to receive the missile carriers and their cargo. Each vehicle entered the workshop, conveyor-belt style, and came out the other end after a quick respray and decked out, ironically, as 'Red' forces and bearing the insignia of an obscure AA unit. The outline of each vehicle had been altered by the use of camouflage webbing. The missile convoy drove to the nearest Autobahn junction and headed north toward the docks at Hamburg. All along the route they received horn toots and thumbs up signs from other military vehicles, which they returned. They also received some double-take looks with some Soldiers even engaging them in open window shouting conversations asking what sort of vehicles they were driving as they didn't recognise them.

"They're the new ones from Canada. Everybody'll be driving them soon," was the rehearsed response. The convoy drivers received dubious looks at the Canada claim but who was going to challenge a rolling convoy of twelve NATO-decaled vehicles? Not the Americans because they wouldn't want to spark an embarrassing international incident on the open highway and not the Soviets out looking for their property because the last thing they would want is publicity about the 'loss' of property belonging to the people of the Union of Soviet Socialist Republics. At government level the Soviets had already requested their property be returned to them by whoever had appropriated it as not to do so was not only theft but an act of war. The Organisation was confident that once the convoy was hiding in plain sight on a public road they were home free. Who could stop them now?

A cargo boat was tied up waiting at the furthest end of a quiet wharf after unloading its consignment of cheap wooden toys manufactured in the People's Republic of China. As military vehicles had been coming and going around Hamburg docks for months a convoy of twelve vehicles attracted little attention. As soon as the first of the missile carriers passed through the dock gates the cargo boat made ready by dropping its aft loading ramp. Eleven of the twelve vehicles drove straight on board and were secured within minutes by the dozens of Operatives crewing the boat. Within twenty-five minutes the boat was underway. The pilot guided the vessel out of Hamburg's busy port. He returned to his launch with the customary lack of recognition familiar to all Operatives of the Organisation.

The twelfth missile carrier, designated number four, was directed to a nearby ship which was bound for England. Dockside cranes lifted it up and carefully placed it on the deck where it was immediately secured and then covered by tarpaulins. The Organisation, or rather Madame Chancellor, was now a nuclear power; the only nuclear power at the time that was not a country. The ship left Hamburg without loading any further cargo on board.

On its return voyage to China, the cargo boat made several stops en route to deposit personnel, equipment and boxed-up cargo containing various parts from the Soviet Missile Heist booty. The main drop was in France of all places, stashing the bulk of the booty right under the noses of the French Splinter. Classic Organisation, hiding in plain sight.

*

After Sergeant Pepper's closed that night, the pretty blonde waitress made her way along the main road in the opposite direction to Bielefeld's student quarter. Within a hundred metres a car pulled alongside her; its passenger side window was already wound down. A quiet-spoken man in the passenger seat asked her for directions to the airport. As she leaned in toward the window of the car to point in the direction of the airport an eight-inch stiletto dagger entered the underside of her chin just behind the jawline and continued on into her brain. Death was instantaneous as her body crumpled like a handkerchief beneath her. Their orders were to leave the body at the scene as a message to whichever group had been so foolish as to ignore the orders of Count Bouvier not to harm Captain Lefort or his family.

"Shame," muttered Roberto, "I hate to see beauty destroyed."

"Are you some kind of a pouf or what pal? It's backs to the wall in future when you're around mate," sputtered the driver in a soft Irish accent. "Let's see if anybody else is around. We'll drop yer man off at the barracks first though."

The pretty young blonde's mission was to make contact with, and make herself available to, the French Captain. She wasn't in fact German, she was French, a Sentinel in the French Splinter and a KGB Doubler. Her orders were to get close to the French Captain and obtain information from him about the whereabouts of the Soviet missiles as a Faction within the French Splinter had not given up on getting their hands on them. It would have been unlikely that the French Captain would have divulged anything to the pretty young waitress during pillow talk in which case she was to kill him Black Widow Spider style. Classic French Splinter, sex with everything.

Foul play in the death of the waitress was not suspected despite an eight-millimetre wide scratch, hidden in among the mud splatters on the neck and face of the victim, being found on the underside of her chin. Nobody thought this significant. Nearly all Roberto's work goes undetected, with the deaths of his victims being put down to natural causes because the entry wound of a stiletto is so small and the slice through the brain is almost impossible to pick up during autopsy. He literally gets away with murder.

*

In the days following the missile heist life was extremely boring at MILR. Nothing whatsoever was happening, everyone had gone silent. "They're not even sending us the usual insults! Anything to break the tedium," whined several of the chaps. Being an insular bunch, MILR weren't keeping up to date with BAOR communiques, including those concerning its annual inter-Regimental games. They were, however, keeping up with the news about the 'pretty young waitress' who'd been found dead on the night they'd seen Michael in action. Typically for those in the world of spying, some of the chaps speculated she might've been murdered. Some of them even speculated that Michael might have had something to do with it as he'd gone missing later that same night.

"Hey Frosty, that girl who was found dead a few days ago, it turns out she was the same girl you had a fight over in Sergeant Pepper's."

"I didn't have a fight over the girl. I got pushed to the ground and got angry."

"That's not the way I remember it; you got the hump when the Soldier boys started getting funny with her. In fact it was after one of them—"

"I told you!" Michael uncharacteristically snapped. "I got angry because I got pushed to the ground." He walked away lest he got angry again. Due to the effect alcohol had on him he could barely remember the fight at Sergeant Pepper's, it was as if it had been somebody else who'd been doing the fighting and he'd been an onlooker. Since that night, the voices in his head were ever present and his visions were adding to the disarrangement of his mind.

*

The Soviet Union regularly used beautiful women to infiltrate governments and Intelligence Agencies alike. Despite knowing this was how they operated the honey trap worked time and time again. Countermeasures were put in place to mitigate this simplest of ways for Soviet spies to get close to government officials but they were never very effective because, in the final analysis, people are people with all their failings.

The vast majority of people working for Intelligence Agencies perform repetitive mundane tasks every day of their spy lives. Many of these dreary people work in areas of interest to hostile governments, the Organisation, Splinters and other clandestine Societies which makes them targets for blackmail, bribery and, most of all, receiving the attention they believe they so richly deserve from beautiful women, or handsome muscular men. Individually, these people do not shake the world; in truth, they barely brush up against it, but they have access to materials that can shape world events. All around the world there are tens of thousands of secret squirrels imperceptibly micro-adjusting states of affairs in one direction or another before returning them to their original position when the political climate tips in that direction once more. It's not a lot of work to return things to the status quo as they were never moved very far anyway.

To spice up their lives, these people have been known to purposely get close to people they know they shouldn't get close to in order to add excitement to their mundane existences. Perhaps it's their imaginings getting the better of them, making them giddy and go doing silly things. Some, of course, have pastimes which are career limiting, or career enhancing, depending on who you happen to bump into in the steam rooms of Mayfair, Belgravia or Covent Garden. Sexual deviancy has often been the crack foreign agents seek to exploit to get them into places they are looking to penetrate.

*

The annual BAOR inter-Regimental games required that every Regiment, including MILR, put up four boxers. Michael was an obvious choice given his performance in the bar fight at Sergeant Pepper's, with three others drawn from a hat. MILR had never won a single round let alone an actual bout. One of the chaps looked into the confidential records of the opposition boxers and was surprised to find that four of them were Australian SAS on a black flag mission. The chaps knew what black flag missions were and speculated on what the Aussies were there to get involved in. Most of them thought it would probably have something to do with Northern Ireland. Loose talk about the chaps snooping on the competition for the inter-Regimental games got back to their CO who carpeted the whole unit with a severe reprimand, while secretly applauding their initiative and ingenuity.

The day before the games, the chaps went to the Gymnasium to practise boxing when in walked the Aussie SAS Soldiers. Each took to different areas to work out with punch-bags, speed-balls and skipping ropes. One of them was shadow boxing when Michael joined him. The Aussie laughed and asked what a 'Noddy Commando' was doing there. Michael shouted over to the chaps asking them what a Noddy Commando was. They replied saying it was a derogatory term for chaps from MI3, including MILR. Michael didn't care, he just got on with his shadow boxing.

"Hey Ocker, will ye look at that! A bloody Noddy Commando who can shadow box!"

"Streuth, what next! What's yer name, mate?"

"Michael Frost."

"Well Frosty, you look like yer can handle yerself a bit, fancy yer chances tomorrow or what? Wanna a little side bet?"

"My name isn't Frosty, it's Michael Frost, and I don't gamble. My dad told me only to gamble with money I'm prepared to lose and I'm not prepared to lose any money because I send it all home to Mum."

"Hey Blue, he's a mummy's boy!" The Aussie Soldiers laughed but their laughing didn't last after Michael went into top gear.

"Hey mate, you're not allowed to do any of that kicking stuff."

"I know, I'm practising. I won't kick you when I'm in the ring unless you cheat."

"Cheeky little bugger! Tell yer what mate, glove up and let's have a bit of a spar, wha'd'ye say, Cobber?" The chaps had seen Michael in a bar fight and were keen to see what he could do in the ring.

"Okay," was Michael's classic one word reply.

The makeshift ref told the boxers to defend themselves at all times, "no low blows, no head butts and break when you're told." They touched gloves. The Aussie went to his corner and quickly spun round to surprise Michael but he was standing in the middle of the ring waiting for him. Advancing behind a solid jab the Aussie backed Michael onto the ropes and was about to hammer him when he slipped under the Aussie's guard, turned around and pummelled him against the ropes. After thirty seconds of absorbing punches the

Aussie went down on one knee and declared the sparring over. When he left the ring his advice to his mates was, "bet on the Pomm!"

As Michael left the Gymnasium the French Captain sidled up alongside him. He asked Michael what the hell he thought he was doing. He replied that he was practising for the inter-Regimental games. The French Captain told Michael he was never to box publicly without his permission. Michael replied that he had his CO's permission. The French Captain said that he'd find that permission would be withdrawn. Wanting to give Michael a plausible-sounding explanation for his demand, the French Captain told Michael that he was a rare talent and if he attracted the wrong sort of attention it could prove dangerous for him, "in the world you are now in," which Michael wrongly took to be the world of MILR. Unusually for him, Michael protested, saying that other chaps were boxing so why shouldn't he, to which the French Captain said that the other chaps were not boxers and they'd get slaughtered in the ring as they always did. "If you box tomorrow Michael you will win easily. None of these people are in your league. They will see you fight and they will ask questions and we don't want that." Michael wasn't convinced by what the French Captain had said but he had faith in him and so he withdrew himself from the MILR boxing team much to the annoyance of the chaps, though his CO didn't object.

Michael and the French Captain silently parted company before reaching the MILR building. Oddly, it seemed to Captain Lefort, it was in fact Major Finn who'd alerted him to Michael's latest reckless act. With what was in store for Michael he didn't want him attracting any more attention to himself than he already had. He also, of course, reported the incident in the Gymnasium to his Counsellor who passed the report down the line to Captain Jones.

THE SENSEI

Right from an early age, Michael was noticeably different to other children. Once he'd learned not to talk about his Demon, they didn't mind playing with him but they found him odd, not least because he never laughed or cried or spoke unless it was absolutely necessary.

Growing into adulthood, Michael's differences became more and more stark. He wasn't interested in drinking, dancing, football, going out to night clubs or, more concernedly, getting together with girls. These lacks of interests meant he stood out from the crowd. His behaviour made people around him suspicious of his nature and unsure of how to deal with him as they had no common ground. Generally speaking, people didn't dislike Michael but the older he got the more people wanted to distance themselves from his peculiarness.

It was detrimental to the Organisation's need to remain in the shadows that Michael attracted the wrong sort of attention from above. He was marked down as a potential liability. Some wanted to help Michael blend in while others wanted to cut him loose, while still others, such as Major Finn, wanted him dead. Captain Jones covered up for Michael for his own purposes, believing he might be useful to him at some point in the future. Feelings of guilt caused Captain Jones to suffer great anguish about what he'd consciously chosen to do, or perhaps what he'd chosen not to do, about Michael. He could have cut him loose before he got in too deep but he covered up for Michael for his own selfish reasons. Over time, they would each pay the price for this.

*

An Operative monitoring Michael became concerned for his wellbeing after observing him sitting alone on his bunk in the dark talking to the walls. She'd have been more concerned had she been witness to the visions Michael saw while staring at the bare barrack room walls. Acting on her own initiative, the Operative enrolled Michael in a martial arts club at a local American base. It was only a few weeks until he returned to the UK for Christmas and she didn't want him attracting any further attention.

As soon as his shift finished, Michael ran to the American camp. He was shown around the Dojo by a Sensei of Japanese American parentage. He was interested to hear of Michael's experience in the martial arts and was surprised to learn that they included the Katana. Michael told the Sensei how he'd adapted his European fencing style to incorporate Japanese swordplay. The Sensei suggested Michael join a Kenjutsu class. The instant Michael picked up a Bokuto he felt warm inside causing the Demons to melt away. After a few minutes' observation, the Sensei could tell Michael was more than a mere competent student.

After the class was over, the Sensei talked to Michael about the Sensei in England who'd taught him Japanese swordplay. Michael told him how he'd introduced him to the straight Katana to complement his European fencing style.

"That's very interesting. I myself own a collection of Katanas, including a very ancient straight Katana which you might like to practise with some time. I hope to see you here again. The club meets three times a week and we have weekend workshops to focus on particular aspects of martial arts. This weekend we're going to be concentrating on Kendo. Come along, you might find it interesting."

"I will."

During the evening, the Sensei had noticed Michael watching students taking part in other classes and how his body mirrored their actions, like he was learning them. Furthermore, it seemed that after observing the students Michael was able to anticipate their moves and then shape his body to counter them. The Sensei himself possessed the rare martial skill of misdirection of his own movements to put opponents off balance but thought Michael's anticipating the movements of others a whole other matter. He resolved to keep a close eye on Michael Frost.

With Michael's time happily and fully occupied, the last few weeks in Bielefeld before his Christmas leave flew by.

*

Michael's flight to England, the coach journey to Liverpool and bus ride to Huyton was delay after delay. He eventually arrived home at 4 p.m. on Wednesday 23rd December 1970. Schools had already broken up for the Christmas holidays and waiting at home for him were his mum and Thomas. Mary was there because she now worked in the kitchens at the local school and so had the same holidays as the children. Queen Rose was nowhere to be seen. "What do I want to see that weirdo for?" was what she'd said before leaving the house at 9 a.m. that freezing cold morning.

In the time that Michael had been away, Rose had turned into the Drama Queen from hell with any little thing setting her off on a moody. She'd become expert at creating situations to make herself the centre of attention. People who behave in this way are usually hiding something as their antics are merely distractions. Queen Rose was creating a smoke screen to hide the fact that she was 'borrowing' heavily from Mary with neither of them telling anybody about the so-called loans. It was 'their little secret'; 'anything to keep the Drama Queen happy' was Mary's approach because she could no longer take the verbal abuse. Even so, the borrowings weren't enough for Rose. She'd taken to pocketing any money she found lying around the house. The stage was set for Joseph's 'Little Queen' to grow into her life role of thief, serial scrounger and pathological, compulsive and congenital liar.

Even before Michael got to the front door it flew open and Thomas rushed to greet him. He launched himself into his big brother's chest, hugging him as hard as he could. "I've missed you our kid, I've really missed you…" Thomas began telling Michael everything he could think of as they slowly crept their way sideways into the lounge. While the boys were talking, Michael saw Mary out of the corner of his eye, standing there by the fireplace just watching her boys through tears of happiness.

After a meal of mashed potato with mushed up corned beef, the evening was spent filling Michael in on family matters which usually meant catching up on the dead pool. The Frost family was very large and as both Mary and Joseph were the youngest of their respective families there was always some older sibling, aunt, uncle, second whatever thrice removed who had died and so the usual confusing conversations were had about, "Do you remember your Aunty *so and so*?" "Yes." "Oh, you do!" "I do." "Oh Good, well *he's/she's* dead." Though most people would hardly remember the names bandied about, Mary was always astonished at how Michael was able to remember all the relatives and the individual events of their lives. Nobody else she knew could do that.

Queen Rose showed up at nine that evening.

"Look what the bleedin' cat's dragged in!" were Rose's words on seeing Michael.

"Hello Rose, how are you?" he asked. Michael had learned that it was polite to ask how somebody was.

"Never mind 'ow I am, ye weirdo. You know you're not sleepin' in your old room don't ye? It's my room now ye know?"

"I'm sharing with Thomas."

"Good, now where's me tea, I'm starvin'?" Taking Queen Rose to one side Mary asked her not to be so rude. Five pounds discretely changed hands on the promise of pleasantness during Michael's stay.

"Are you going to meet up with your school mates while you're home son?" Mary asked.

"I don't know."

"Why don't you get in touch with Allan Grice or Robby Garcia or Eddie Shearon, you always got on well with them?"

"I'll see them if I have time." Mary knew this was Michael speak for he wouldn't meet with them. She worried about him not having any friends. Mary had long ago realised that Michael was different to other children; they found his behaviour off-putting so the friends he did have needed his, and her, close attention.

"Yeah, see how it goes then son." There was a loud knock on the door. "Jesus tonight and tomorrow!" exclaimed Mary nearly jumping out of her skin at the booming sound. Before anybody could answer the door the big square face of Timbo Mulhall was at the lounge window.

"Lerrus'in will yez? It's freezin' out 'ere." When Timbo walked into the lounge he grabbed Michael and gave him a play head butt on his forehead, "Stitch that!" joked Timbo. "Well, 'ow are ye our kid? 'Ow long are ye 'ome for?"

"Six days."

"Ace, lots of time for bevvyin'. Let's shoot out to the Farmer's for a quick one."

"He's not going anywhere tonight Timothy Mulhall and don't you go getting him into trouble while he's home. He's in the Army now and he can't afford to get into trouble."

Timbo, Thomas, Mary and Michael made arrangements for the following days. Queen Rose took her tea upstairs not wanting to hear anything Michael or "that jailbird," as she called Timbo, had to say.

*

The boys slept in on Christmas Eve morning. Michael hadn't slept so late in over a year. They didn't do much during the day, they just lazed around the house stoking the coal fire, drinking tea and eating sandwiches stuffed with hot, fat, chips covered in brown sauce.

At seven o'clock that evening Michael and Thomas met up with Timbo outside the Farmer's Arms pub. Following his Schnapps and Wine session at Sergeant Pepper's, Michael was staying away from alcohol.

"C'mon Michael, one Christmas drink won't hurt ye!" urged Timbo but Michael wouldn't be swayed and stuck to lemonade, which Timbo spiked with a double Vodka. Thomas, however, eagerly downed a pint of beer with a whisky chaser. He knew that Michael disapproved of him drinking at fifteen but as it was Christmas anything went according to him. The pub landlord knew Thomas was underage to drink alcohol but landlords in pubs like the Farmer's Arms turned a blind eye because everybody knew everybody and if there was any nonsense parents got to know and then the underage drinkers were for it. "Have ye kept yer boxin' up our Michael?"

"I haven't but I've started at a Dojo in Bielefeld."

"Good for you our kid, it sounds like you're fittin' right in. Tell ye wha' Michael, when ye leave the Army don't come back here, it's dead. There's nothing' goin' on 'ere, I'm tellin' ye. Get down to that London or somewhere but don't waste yer time comin' back here."

"Piss off Timbo tellin' our Michael not to come back to Liverpool. An' what's it got to do with you anyway?" snarled Thomas. Only certain relatives could talk to Timbo that way and get away with it.

"Same advice goes for you Thomas. Leave Liverpool as soon as ye can. I'm off to Southampton in February and I tell yez wha', I'm not comin' back 'ere again. No chance!"

"What rubbish are you talkin' about now Timbo," shouted Baz formerly of the Sparrow Hall Gang as he entered the pub. He, Timbo and four others had served time together in Walton nick for robbery. "Still hangin' out with yer weird family I see?" Timbo and Baz moved away from Thomas and Michael for a little chat together. It was business, or so Timbo said.

"I hate that Barry Grogan," mumbled Thomas. "He duffed me up once," he whispered in confidence to Michael. When Timbo and Baz returned to the bar Michael was ready with a question for Baz.

"Did you beat my brother up?"

"Just messin' about like. Nothin' serious. It was a long time ago anyway. Nothin' to get yer knickers in a twist about mong boy."

"What did you call 'im?" asked Timbo.

"Just messin' about, Timbo. Jesus, I can't say anything without you or your weird relatives gettin' the 'ump."

"You shouldn't have beaten my little brother up," warned Michael.

"Listen plums, you wanna watch yourself, I've been to prison, d'ye know what I mean?"

"Baz, listen, I told ye before and I'll tell ye again, our Michael'd burst you with one hand tied behind his back so my advice to you is to keep that hole in the front of yer face shut because it's gonna get ye into trouble." But Baz wouldn't be told.

"Alright then plums, you and me outside, now!"

"Baz mate, it's Christmas Eve and nobody's goin' outside with anybody… I'm tellin' ye… okay?" With that Baz pushed Timbo out of the way and drew a six-inch flick knife from his pocket. The pub fell silent.

"Don't be an idiot son, put the knife away," pleaded the barman but Baz's blood was up. He'd wanted to fight Michael all those years ago but had been denied and now was his chance to cream one of Timbo's relatives and he was determined to take it as vendettas between street boys run long and deep. Thomas was terrified at the sight of the knife but Michael was completely calm. His calmness disconcerted Baz.

"Ye know I stabbed somebody don't ye?" screamed Baz trying to strike fear into Michael's heart but it had no effect. "What's wrong with you ye freak? I've got a bleedin' knife here not a… bunch of… daffodils." A few old timers in the bar tittered at Baz's words. "Do ye think I'm jokin'? Do ye? Is that wha' it is? Is that why yer actin' not scared? Think I'm jokin' do ye?" shrieked Baz.

"I'm going to take your knife off you and stick it in you," replied Michael in his calmest monotone. Baz knew he had to act before fear overtook him. He came lunging forward, knife in hand. Michael dropped him with a leg sweep. With Baz face down on the floor Michael jumped on top of him. Grabbing hold of the hand with the knife in it, Michael turned Baz's wrist agonisingly against the joint and then slowly, very slowly, he moved the knife towards Baz's throat. His eyes were wide with fear.

"Timbo! Timbo! Get yer weird cousin off me. I'm not messin' about, I mean it, get this weirdo off me!" shrieked Baz in fear and pain.

"Michael, whatever ye do, do not stab Baz! D'ye hear me? I mean it cousin. Don't stab Baz! Yer'll be in a cart load of trouble if ye do!"

Michael couldn't hear Timbo or anybody else nor was he aware of anything or anybody around him as he was already in the grip of his tunnel-vision terror. All he could see was a writhing Demon morphing with Baz as a scaly creature. Staring unblinkingly, Michael slowly pushed the knife into the creature's throat, making a three-quarter inch wide slice in the bristly skin under Baz's chin. The cut wasn't very long or very deep but it was long enough and deep enough to draw a lot of blood. Michael held Baz in an icy dead-eye stare. There was no emotion, he felt no mercy, no pity, no compassion nor empathy. He felt nothing at all. He just did what he did and as calmly as he sliced Baz he picked himself up off the floor, put on his overcoat and made for the door. Timbo was aghast at the level of cold-bloodedness shown by his cousin.

"Michael, ye just stabbed Baz and yer actin' like nothin's 'appened! The Police'll be here in a minute so we're gonna have to get you away from 'ere!" yelled Timbo who then turned and addressed those in the pub. "Listen youz lot, if any of yez say anythin' to the Police I know who ye are and I'll be back to pay yez a visit so keep yer gobs shut, okay?" Then to Baz he said, "If you grass our Michael up I'll cut yer plums off. Don't forget Barry Grogan, I did time in Walton nick because none of us grassed yer up after ye stabbed that bloke. I'm warnin' ye Baz, yer'd better keep yer gob shut 'cos if yer even whisper our Michael's name…" Timbo dragged his forefinger across his throat leaving Baz in no doubt about what would happen to him if he grassed Michael up. Then, to Thomas and Michael, Timbo yelled, "C'mon youz, let's ge' yez oura 'ere."

The lads casually made their way to a nearby bus shelter. Timbo was confident that nobody would grass them up, partly out of the fear of him and partly because being a grass on a council estate in Huyton was a dangerous thing to be. When the bus arrived they went on the upper deck so Timbo could have a cigarette, "to calm me nerves."

"Warrever yez do, don't mention a word to yer ma about tonight. I gorra say Michael, you frightened the life out of me when you stuck that knife in Baz's throat. Is this what the Army 'as done to ye?"

"He hurt Thomas."

"Did the Army teach ye tha', eh?"

"I've never done anything like that before."

"I'm glad to hear it an' now's not the time to start. Wha' ye don't realise, Michael, is the family are dead proud of ye. Ye went to Grammar school, ye didn't end up in jail, ye joined the Army an' yer mum says yer doin' great. Yer a great boxer, not as good as me like," grinned Timbo giving Michael a friendly punch in the arm to lighten the mood as he could see the concern building in Thomas' eyes. "So don't be an idiot. Keep yerself ourra trouble for yer ma's sake. Okay?" Michael nodded and Thomas did as well.

*

After Timbo dropped his cousins off at home he headed back out. Later that evening he bumped into Baz Grogan, who'd not been cut as badly as everybody thought he had. He was in the company of a couple of other former members of the Sparrow Hall gang. They shook hands and swore never to talk about that night in the Farmer's Arms ever again. Though Baz said he'd had enough of fighting that evening Timbo kept his eye on him and the other former members of the Sparrow Hall Gang in case they decided to give him a beating for what had happened to Baz at the hands of "Timbo's weird cousin". Timbo was wound as tight as a spring and ready to drop them all without notice.

*

As it was still early, Mary, Michael and Thomas settled down to watch classic Christmas Eve TV, eat mince pies and drink lemonade. At eleven-thirty in pranced Queen Rose with three of her friends.

"Mum, I've got somethin' to tell ye," announced Queen Rose. "Our Michael was in a fight in the Farmer's Arms an' he stabbed some lad in the neck an' now he's dead." Mary thought it was just one of Queen Rose's sick jokes.

"What? You're not serious are you Rose? Michael, do you know what she's on about son?"

"Somebody called Barry Grogan pulled a knife on me and I supposedly stuck it in him. He's not dead." Michael thought this sufficient explanation. Long tired of Michael's fighting ways Mary began sobbing deeply.

"See what yer've done to Mum now, eh, ye weirdo? Yer've really upset 'er. You shouldn't 'ave come 'ome. Yer not wanted 'ere so sod off back to the Army now or I'm gonna phone the Police on ye." Roses friends didn't like that idea one bit.

"You know what happens to grasses around 'ere don't ye girl?" said Thomas. "If you grass our kid up I'll make sure everyone knows ye did it and I'll tell everyone at yer school too."

"Are you threaten' me Tommy no mates? Don't you even think about bleedin' threaten' me ye little freak or I'll tell everyone how ye play with yerself in bed."

"Listen Rose, we're goin' 'ome now, see ye tomorrow," said Rose's best friend. "By the way, if ye grass your Michael up we'll never speak to ye again. Everyone knows Barry Grogan is a shit, an' I heard it was 'im who pulled the knife on your Michael an' he got wha' 'e deserved. I'm warnin' ye Rose, don't you dare grass your Michael up!" A tearful Mary closed the front door behind Rose's friends, returned to the lounge, threw her arms around Michael and whispered into his ear.

"For God's sake son, please don't you ever do anything like that ever again; promise me now son, promise me you'll never do anything like that ever again or you'll end up in jail just like your cousins." Michael promised. Another classic Christmas in the Frost household.

*

Mary was up at 7 a.m. on Christmas morning preparing roast turkey, roast potatoes, sprouts, carrots and gravy. Joseph was back on the family scene and he and Mary seemed to be getting on well. Thomas told Michael that he thought they were going to remarry. Like most people in the north of England at the time the main Christmas meal was eaten at around 1 p.m.

Queen Rose didn't crawl out of her pit on Christmas day until the meal was on the table. She took her seat, ate her food and stomped off back to her room in a massive sulk. She didn't like not getting her own way over calling the Police about Michael stabbing Barry Grogan. Being the spoilt brat that she was, Rose did her best to create a bad atmosphere in the house and ruin Christmas for everybody but she failed miserably.

Boxing Day and they all sat around watching telly together while various nosey neighbours and relatives dropped in to get news of whether Mary and Joseph were going to remarry. Timbo came by at five o'clock. Margaret took him aside for a word about the fight on Christmas Eve. He set her mind at rest, "Honest a God, Aunty Mary, it was 'ardly even a scratch that our Michael gave him, he's done worse shavin' 'imself, an' anyway I went out with 'im later on that night. Honest, Aunty Mary, he's okay; so stop worryin' will ye?" Mary wasn't totally convinced by Timbo's story but as the Police hadn't shown up and Timbo had met up with the lad later on then all was probably okay.

His Christmas leave over, Michael kissed his mum goodbye at the door and she watched his back disappear around the corner, the idea of never seeing her son ever again not entering her head. And why would it? Before Michael's departure, Queen Rose had one of her more poisonous outbursts, saying that she hoped he'd end up getting sent to Northern Ireland and being killed there. She told him that nobody wanted him to visit anymore but were too polite to say it to his face. She said that Joseph hated him and always had because he was a weirdo and that he'd told her that if she'd have been born first then they wouldn't have had him or Thomas. Michael knew that if what Rose had said to him ever came out it would hurt the entire family. Thomas overheard everything and waited his time to use it.

*

On his return to Bielefeld, Michael went and sat at his desk and carried straight on with his work as if he hadn't been away. The chaps were talking about what they'd gotten up to over Christmas. A couple of them asked after Victor and were told by the section Captain that he'd been transferred, "at short notice. It was all rather sudden." One of the chaps asked Michael what he'd gotten up to over Christmas. He'd been prepped by Timbo and Mary not to say anything to anybody about the Barry Grogan incident, so he didn't. "I watched telly with my family," was all he said. *Typical northern peasant,* thought a few of the chaps. As soon as his shift was over Michael raced to the American camp. The Dojo was open but there was hardly anybody there as many of the Soldiers had not returned from their Christmas leave.

"Come on in Michael Frost, it is good to see you. How was your Christmas?"

"Okay."

"I'm the only Sensei tonight so we'll start by warming up and then spend a couple of hours doing whatever everybody wants to do. What would you like to do Michael?"

"You said you have some Katanas. Can we use them… p… p… p… please?" he said still having difficulty with the p word.

"Hey everybody. Listen up," shouted the Sensei over the general hubbub. "Michael here has asked if we can have a session with Katanas. Anybody up for that?" The group's response to the Sensei's question was a selection of various American-style whoops.

"Good choice man," said an American Soldier slapping Michael on the back harder than he was comfortable with. The Sensei took a set of keys from beneath his gi, strode over to a tall metal locker and sprung open both doors in dramatic style.

What the students saw before them was an array of what were clearly top-notch Katanas. Each Saya had a high-shine, deep-lacquer finish in either black, dark red or dark green. They were things of startling beauty while exuding awesome, almost mystical, power. The Sensei picked a Katana from the locker and, grasping it in both hands, he fractionally separated it from its Saya. Then, with a flourish, he pulled the Katana free. The Ha of the blade shone like cracked diamonds in the glare of the fluorescent lights. The blade was etched with the story of the life journey of the first Dragon.

"This is a Katana," said the Sensei slowly and deliberately, as though speaking to a class of children. "It is very sharp," he said while he mimicked touching the blade with a finger and pretending it hurt. "Ouch!" yelled the Sensei comically; the students laughed. "Have any of you ever used a Katana before?" Four students, including Michael, raised their hands. "Before the rest of you can touch my beautiful Katanas you need to show me you're competent with a Bokuto. You'll find them in the locker at the other end of the Dojo; go get one each and come back to the mat." The students sighed thinking it was all just too good to be true that they would actually get to use a real Samurai Katana.

The Sensei got the 'experienced' students to carry out some basic exercises with a Katana so he could assess them. After seeing them perform, he felt each was capable of wielding a Katana without cutting or slicing through anything they shouldn't.

"Okay guys, you did well, now go get some straw bundles and stands and place them around the mat. I'll demonstrate some cuts which I want you to copy." The group placed a half-dozen tightly bound straw bundles on stands around the mat. The Sensei then lopped the top four inches off each straw bundle before returning his Katana to its Saya with a dramatic flourish. As he did so, the Sensei wiped the blade with his fingers, symbolically removing any blood. In his actions, the Sensei appeared unhurried but each student knew they'd have had no defence had this been a real duel. "I want you to inspect the cuts I made. You should note that the angle of the plane of each cut is flat. That's good technique. Now, I want you to strike a straw bundle and afterwards examine the plane of the cut for evenness. Your starting position is with both hands on the handle with the sword positioned above and behind your head. Aim to lop off the top four inches." Each student approached a straw bundle. Two cut the straw bundles at an angle of thirty degrees and two parallel with the floor, a much more difficult cut to execute properly. The Sensei inspected each cut with each student. "No bad cuts. Good. Very good. Let's move onto combination cuts."

The Sensei demonstrated several combination cuts. Each student went in turn. They had to move along a corridor of straw bundles cutting the top off each of them. If Michael could be in seventh heaven he was in it now. He didn't want the session to end. After the Sensei called the students together he took Michael to one side and told him that if he wanted to use the Katana again he was only to ask. As he left the Dojo that evening, Michael practically levitated all the way back to the barracks.

*

There were less than two weeks to go before Michael was to leave Bielefeld. Normally the internal mechanism for him dealing with time would be racing ahead to his RMC selection but not so this time. Thoughts of Katanas pushed everything to the back of his mind.

For his remaining sessions at the Dojo, Michael was first in and last out. The Sensei once again noticed how he was very good at mimicking the movements of others and he mentioned this to him. Michael told the Sensei that, from an early age, he'd mimicked people in boxing and then later, when attending Grammar school, sword fencing. He mentioned the first time he'd mimicked the Huyton Sensei's movements with a Katana and how it had made him feel inside. Finally, Michael told the Sensei that he could mimic movements during actual combat as though he was outside his own body observing and directing the fight.

The Sensei was curious to know just how far Michael's mimicking could go and so he invited two sword masters to the Dojo to give a demonstration in the artful use of the Katana. The students that particular evening had come to the Dojo expecting to train as usual but instead they were asked to sit around the Dojo mat for a "demonstration by some specially invited guests".

The sword masters arrived like a whisper dressed all in black. Their masks had black mesh covering the eye gaps. Their Katanas and Sayas were likewise black. The only thing that wasn't black was their sclera which reflected in the Dojo lights through the mesh of their masks. They moved to the centre of the mat and stood back to back, Katanas in hand and angled toward the ground. Their stillness rendered them like statues.

"Students," cried the Sensei, "I've invited along two very special guests to give a demonstration in the art of the Katana. After the demonstration… time permitting [groans from the students], we might practise using Katanas. Any questions?" The Sensei paused but there were no questions, just a sea of stunned, eager faces. "Okay, first, let me tell you this… most real Katana fights last less than a minute. They are usually won by a single strike due to one of the combatants making a mistake. Strikes on human beings from Katanas often end in death through the loss of a limb, or beheading or the severing of a major artery or, more usually, disembowelment. You only get one chance in a Katana fight. So students, it goes without saying that it's most important that you're never on the receiving end of a Katana strike." The Sensei laughed at his little 'joke'. Introduction over the Sensei described the exercises his guests were going to perform and for the next ten minutes the audience sat in stunned mesmerised silence at the awesome power of the Katana in the hands of people who were deadly experts in their use. The demonstration ended in a ballet of slashing Katana blades on the straw bundles. The sword masters made virtually no sound whatsoever.

After the demonstration the Sensei's guests politely bowed and made their way out of the Dojo without uttering a word. They didn't appear to hurry but they were gone in the blink of an eye. The Sensei asked Michael what he thought about what he'd seen. His reply was typical and typically brief. "I have a lot to do to be like them."

It was now the students' turn. The Sensei split them into groups to practise strike techniques on straw bundles. When it came to Michael's turn he sauntered, almost arrogantly, head down, round shouldered, along the alley of straw bundles to the far end. He turned and took up the stance the Sensei's guests had taken. Standing stock still for ten seconds before grasping the Katana in both hands, Michael ran as a blur down the alley of straw bundles, striking each of them in turn.

His choreography was identical to that of the two sword masters, something only the Sensei picked up. The students in Michael's group applauded him which attracted the attention of the other students who asked what all the fuss was about. "C'mon man, do it again," cried one of the students. Michael did it again. His choreography was identical to his first set of strikes to the microsecond and millimetre. The Sensei walked forward and inspected the cuts. They were identical to the first set of cuts; perfectly flat and in the same plane.

"Well done Michael," was all the Sensei said to him. "Now, can you all please return to your groups and continue practising." As Michael was leaving at the end of the session the Sensei asked if he'd enjoyed the demonstration.

"When I was observing their movements it became apparent to me that one of them was a woman."

"Absolutely correct," replied the Sensei astonished. "Well detected. See you on Saturday?"

"See you on Saturday. I leave Sunday."

*

Michael's sleep that night was, as usual, visited by the same visions and terrors which had haunted many of his sleeping hours since childhood but they were getting worse and becoming more frequent and he didn't know how much longer he could stand their company. No, not their company; how much longer he could stand their existence or his own if it came to that.

*

The Sensei wrote Michael a letter which he handed to him before he left for England. In it were the names and addresses of people in the Sensei's Martial world who could help him along his journey through life or perfect his Martial skills. The letter included the

Sensei's thoughts on what lay behind Michael's gifts and an offer for Michael to contact him anytime he needed help from somebody who didn't want anything from him in return. The Sensei recognised that Michael was special, if not unique, and knew from long experience that people like Michael are all too often exploited and seldom in control of their own destiny.

When the Sensei reached the sanctuary of his Sect's Temple, he swore an oath that he would keep Michael from the harms that he knew would be waiting for him on his path through life. All Michael had to do was reach out to him at any dark time and he'd use his considerable resources to help and protect him. That was the Sensei's sacred vow which he sealed with blood and prayers to his ancestors.

IT'S ONLY FORTY-FOUR!

During her opening address at the Organisation's 1970 AGM Madame Chancellor feigned modesty over the success of the Soviet Missile Heist. And with the promise of profits to come, she had the Governors worshipping at her feet. She still kept hope that, over time, the Soviet Missile Heist would become known as Madame Chancellor's Soviet Missile Heist. At the end of her opening address, Lisette read out messages of congratulations from those unable to attend the AGM, as well as from Splinter leaders. Lisette milked the messages for all they were worth, ad-libbing and enhancing certain passages to increase the magnitude of the compliments.

As she peered down from the top table, the all-powerful Madame Chancellor held certain Governors in the gripping gaze of her ice-blue eyes for what to them must have seemed an eternity. Her gaze conveyed an unspoken message. It was left up to the recipients to decipher the meaning of the message.

Madame Chancellor's lengthy 'state of the union' speech touched on the changes she had in mind for the Organisation; "Nothing drastic," she claimed. Her audience weren't to know this was just the entrée. While wrapping up at the end of the day, Margaret mentioned, almost as an aside, her previous role as Roving Ambassador would continue and in due course she'd announce the appointment of a President of a reunited and reformed Organisation. She smiled coyly and said, "No, no, no, I don't mean me, of course, though I'm grateful for your confidence in me." The Governors waited with bated breath; Madame Chancellor then announced the name of Christan Lefort as 'potentially' the future President of a reunified Organisation, "In the fullness of time." Those who knew her and those gifted with the ability of reading between lines sensed that Madame Chancellor had other ideas.

*

Taking her seat for the evening meal to mark the end of the AGM, beneath her napkin, Lisette discovered an envelope addressed to 'Madame Chancellor'. After deeming it presented no danger to her boss, she passed it to her. Margaret recognised the handwriting. Picking up her glass of Champagne she wandered into the ladies' toilet, this time checking to make sure she was alone and locking the door behind her. She was bubbling inside with excitement.

Dear Madame Chancellor,

Very many congratulations on a truly outstanding year.
  You have made me feel so very proud.
  Your success is vindication of my decision to back you.
  Many challenges lie ahead but I'm confident you will rise to each and every one of them.
  I wish you a very Merry Christmas and a happy and successful New Year.

Yours, Maximillian

"That's it?" whimpered Margaret. She felt deflated. She felt she deserved more than this.

*

In the early months of 1971, Margaret increased the speed of implementation of her, or rather Max's, plans to reform the Organisation. She was regretting having so readily agreed to the terms of her appointment and was beginning to resent Max's constant interfering. In her moments of greatest anger she recalled what the Recorder had said after denying her the thin black Tabernacle shroud as a memento of her coronation. He'd said, "not even an all-powerful Madame Chancellor can keep the black shroud as a memento." When he'd called her that it sent a shiver spiralling like a helter-skelter down her spine. 'All-powerful Madame Chancellor' – she liked the sound of it then and she liked it even more now.

The job of Chancellor came with more strings than she now felt she could accept. Philosophically, she agreed with many of the conditions imposed on her by the Mandarins. For example, she still agreed, in principle, with the removing of the old farts and that the Organisation had to be run by an Executive Council not an Autocrat Chancellor. She agreed with many other of the imposed conditions… in principle now admittedly. But having been called an all-powerful Madame Chancellor she found the images those words conjured up in her head too intoxicating to ignore. She thought, *More than anything, I want to be…* She dare not finish that thought.

*

Getting rid of the old farts wasn't going to be easy. They'd run the Organisation for centuries and, so they thought, were running rings around Madame Chancellor. But not for long, no not for long. The countdown had begun and nothing was going to stop it.

*

Max was keeping so close to Margaret that she felt she'd lost his confidence, that perhaps he thought he'd made a mistake by making her Madame Chancellor and was thinking of replacing her despite the success of the Soviet Missile Heist. She had to have it out with him and resolved to broach the subject of his meddling in the running of the Organisation during their private 'one to one' session.

Four days later, unannounced as usual, Max turned up at Half Moon Street and, as usual, he and Margaret went to the Park Lane Hilton for their 'one to one'. The view from the window of the penthouse suite overlooking Hyde Park was magnificent.

"Do you like the view Margaret?"

"You know I do. I've seen it many times before. Remember?" she replied frostily.

"I see," said Max recognising the coolness of her mood. "I think a view is important. Views can make the soul soar. Perhaps this is the opportune moment to mention that I've arranged for new offices overlooking St James' Park. The building has ten floors. I assume you'll be taking the top floor as your own? It has a—"

"Stop it, Max! I don't need candy, okay? Let's get straight to it. Every time I turn around there you are looking over my shoulder! I get the feeling you're regretting my appointment."

"What? That's nonsense! Whatever gave you that idea?"

"You did. You're always here… giving me *'little talks'*… changing things! It seems I never get anything right, according to you. You want things done your way but I'm the boss and I'm here every day so I do what I think is right. Do you want me to call you before I make a decision?"

"I see. I think you misunderstand my motives. You're not the finished article yet Margo but you soon will be, especially after you remove the old guard. I helped you to get the job of Chancellor because you are the future of the Organisation. In you is the person I believe will make the Organisation great again. Your predecessor couldn't do it but I believe you can. I want you to achieve the vision we share for the Organisation. Look, I'll back off and let you have the space you need to do things as you see fit. Okay?"

"Thank you Max, I appreciate that. Now, what did you want to cover this time?"

"I believe the time is now right for removing the old guard… but perhaps…?"

Margaret could tell by the cadence of Max's speech, the tone of his voice and the movements of his body that it was going to be sex before their little talk this time.

*

She hadn't wanted it to happen but after them meeting in Italy while she was a roving Ambassador she became infatuated with Max, with his arrogance and confidence. They became lovers on the second night and their affair continued as she travelled to meet with Splinter leaders. It wasn't unusual for her to be with a man like Max, her so-called husband was considerably older than her, but that was a whole different situation. She was beginning to regret their affair. She'd wanted to break it off many times but, she thought, *now is not the right time.* Besides, she wasn't having sex with anybody else and she needed to feel wanted and wanted to feel needed. She found Max attractive in a great many ways and very, very, very, much liked sex with him. Before her appointment as Madame Chancellor she wondered if, one day, they might take things further.

Whenever Max turned up out of the blue, it gave her a feeling inside that nobody else had ever given her before. She sometimes couldn't wait to get to the hotel and wanted to lock her office door and… but he always stopped her. He said it made things cheap. She agreed and disagreed. She agreed that it was cheap but sometimes she wanted to feel cheap. She disagreed because it was passion driving her lust and if the moment passed unfulfilled then it could never be recreated. *How can it be cheap?* she'd thought many times over. They never had sex in her office which was one of her life regrets at the time. Whenever she had such thoughts she realised she was more like Lisette than she liked to admit.

Max was extremely rich, which always helps, but he was powerful and Margaret found power more sexy than money. He was handsome and in good shape and was an astonishingly good dancer. She'd noticed how men who were good dancers were also good in bed and Max was the best dancer she'd ever met. Her husband wouldn't have minded if she found somebody else but it seemed that somebody was not going to be Max. But the sex was always good.

*

Margaret woke from her post-coital nap. As she did so she saw Max's hand in the half-light closing the door – perhaps that was what had woken her? Before the bedroom door closed completely she caught a glimpse of a room service trolley in the lounge. They always had Champagne afterwards and by the looks of things there was tons of food on the trolley this time. *How on Earth are we going to eat all that?* she thought. Hearing voices, and assuming Max was on speaker-phone or the TV was on, she wandered naked into the lounge.

As Margaret entered the room she saw three Mandarins sitting on the sofa. They didn't seem surprised to see her which meant that this was something Max often did or he'd told them they were 'having an affair'. She hated that hackneyed phrase. Darting back into the bedroom, Margaret dressed without showering, tousled her hair with her fingers to give it some body and wiped off her smudged makeup onto the bedsheet. When she returned to the lounge everybody was eating. Max had made up a plate for her of her favourite things and placed it, along with a glass of Champagne, on a small side table at the end of the sofa which she assumed was her place and so she sat down in it.

"Madame Chancellor," said each Mandarin with a slight bow of acknowledgement. Despite her embarrassment, Margaret didn't offer up an explanation.

"Good afternoon… or is it evening? Did you all have a good…" Margaret didn't bother finishing her sentence.

"I was only saying to Madame Chancellor earlier today, wasn't I Margaret, that it's time to get on with the changes we agreed as a condition of her appointment."

"Firstly, Madame Chancellor, may I ask whether the secret inner council is in place and, if so, how is it operating?" asked Béat.

"It is and it's operating very well and—"

"Secondly, we need to discuss the timing of the removal of the old guard. Béat, can you provide us with an update please?" said Max in a businesslike way.

"Certainly Max. The replacements for Controllers and Governors that we are responsible for have been selected and, I believe, Madame Chancellor has selected most of the ones she's responsible for choosing. In total we're about eighty-five percent of the way there." Max and Béat had actually recruited all their candidates many months earlier. Their pretence was all part of the game. "I've made copies of the latest lists and timings of those to be replaced and alongside their names are those who'll be replacing them. The blanks mean we've yet to choose a suitable replacement." Béat handed out sheets of paper with the names and dates on them. Some names had asterisks next to them. "We should be ready to make our move by the end of the year… which means Madame Chancellor can make the announcement of the changes at the AGM. All we need do ahead of time is brief the Sentinels on their targets." Had Margaret heard Béat correctly?

"I beg your pardon, Béat. What did you just say about Sentinels and targets?" Margaret was still a little sleepy and wondered if she'd heard Béat correctly. If he'd just said what she thought she'd heard him just say then it could only mean one thing with Sentinels involved.

"I don't understand how I can make it any more clear for you, Madame Chancellor. When you agreed to get rid of the old guard what did you think it meant? Some of them, for obvious reasons, need to be gotten rid of permanently, hence the forty-four. It's only forty-four! Which is about four percent." After some counting on his fingers Béat confirmed, "Yes, it's four percent... approximately."

"There's a huge difference between getting rid of somebody and... what do you mean, 'it's only four percent'? These are human beings we're talking about!" screamed Margaret.

"Please, leave us, all of you," ordered Max while passing Béat a bunch of keys. "Go to my Kensington home, I'll meet you all there after I've finished up here."

He has a home in Kensington? thought Margaret. *Then why do we always meet...?*

Margaret had always suspected Max was married, though they'd never spoken about it, but now the reality of it hit her it stung. The other Mandarins packed up their papers, picked up their briefcases and left the room.

"Margaret... you yourself said that a slighted person will seek revenge." She couldn't recall if she'd actually used those exact words but she recognised the sentiment. "There are Controllers and Governors who are just too dangerous to keep around once we make the changes. They will never accept you or the changes you're making. You cannot make the changes and allow them to remain alive. They will return to destroy you."

"There has to be another way, Max. Couldn't we just retire them... over time? Leaving the more difficult ones until last. You know, if they know they're on their way they might jump of their own accord. Most of them are looking forward to retirement... I'm sure they'll go quietly." Margaret knew she was talking nonsense; *"leave the more difficult ones until last,"* how could that ever work?

"Margaret, you know as well as I that people like them never really go away; do they Margaret? You know they don't. They leave behind tendrils which work as well as any poison. If there was another way we'd take it," he lied. "You know this change has to be made. It will be difficult and painful at first but once it's over then it's over. The Organisation is dying, Margaret, and only you have what it takes to save it."

Max had her there. She was convinced that she was the right person to change the Organisation and she believed that if it didn't change it would indeed die. Max stood and put his hands behind his back as though he was about to give a lecture.

"Margaret, do you know the origin of the Organisation?"

"Yes, of course I do."

"There's no 'of course' about it, Margaret, not all the stories can be true, can they? The Organisation was started by two Esquires, brothers, over seven hundred years ago. Back then it was called the Brotherhood. They formed following the slaughter of the Holy Order of Knights whom the brothers served." This was one of the origin stories Margaret had already heard but thought it best to let Max continue talking; *you never know what you will learn while others are talking.* "The Knights were murdered on the orders of King Philip the fourth of France, rather than repay the money he owed them. The brothers escaped the massacre and from that day forward their goal was to wipe out the Aristocracy."

"Aristocracy like you Max?"

"I am certainly no Aristocrat, Margaret. But to continue; Philip, being a devout catholic, and with nobody in those days doing anything without the consent of Rome, he sought permission from Pope Clement the fifth to wipe out the Knights. Now, it just so happened that Pope Clement also wanted the Holy Order of Knights gone, he thought they had grown too powerful, and so he gave Philip consent to slaughter them… on payment of a large tribute, of course. After the brothers fled to England they sought the protection of King Edward but he was betrothed to Philip's daughter, Isabella… do you see how helpless they must have felt against the power of the Aristocracy… and their familiars, the Church? It was in fact the Church which continued to pursue and persecute them in their own land. I won't bore you with the details of everything that has happened over the past seven hundred years but as the Brotherhood grew so did its ambition. After many failed attempts to expand their Society they realised they'd have to align themselves with the old families of Europe… the European Aristocracy. How ironic. Their greed and their lust for power led them away from their mission to destroy the very people who were now their partners." Max paused. "You've heard of the ACF?"

"The Anti Church Faction?"

"Indeed. It is one of the many Factions which exist inside both the Organisation and its Splinters. The ACF was formed in the earliest days of the Brotherhood by those who saw the Church as the real enemy. They hated the Church, branding it *'the Familiars of the Aristocracy'*. Many of the original Brethren were pious men and so the ACF had to remain hidden and were careful who they recruited. They were very nearly destroyed by our saviour, Bonaparte. If only he'd succeeded," Max lamented with a sigh.

"What do you mean by that? Bonaparte's treachery nearly destroyed the Organisation!"

"It was not the Organisation back then it was still the Brotherhood and Bonaparte was no traitor, he was a visionary!"

"The history lesson is all very interesting but…"

"You know who said *'the only thing we can be certain of for the future is what we can learn from the past'*?" asked Max.

"Of course I do."

"Then do you reject him and his teachings?"

"Of course not."

"Bonaparte followed his teachings and had he succeeded we wouldn't have the mess we have today. There would be no Factions, nor any Splinters… there would only be the Brotherhood."

"No Factions except the ACF, I think… which I assume you're a member of?"

"Margaret, I swear to you my Angel, I am not ACF," said Max sanctifying himself and Margaret with the sign of the cross.

"Then what are you Max? What are you really? You're a Mandarin, sure, but what else are you? What else are you Max?"

"I am merely a man with a dream, Margaret," replied Max, smiling inside in admiration of his deceitfulness. "Only you can turn the Organisation once more into a Brotherhood. Only you can return it to its path. There is still much work to be done to destroy the Aristocracy and you… you are the one, the only one, able to lead the Brotherhood back to its true course. Help me, oh big one, you're my only hope!" pleaded Max with uncharacteristic grammatical clumsiness and awkward stuttering cadence. Margaret thought Max's plaintive entreaties fanciful and so ignored them.

"But the Aristocracy are not what they were, Max. Nowadays, they are just a bunch of inbreds doomed to live out their lives festering in mouldy old family piles. Most exist outside normal society and so count for nothing."

"Not so, Margaret, you are wrong. The Aristocracy is still the power behind everything. They are the leaders of industry, banking and commerce… they are the politicians… the governments… they are the tyrants, the dictators… they are the Governors of the Organisation! With them it's 'Sir' this or 'Lord' that; would-be Aristocrats with ambitions of becoming the real thing and with the money the Soviet Missile Heist will bring them they will be one step closer to achieving it. Sir Jeremy Hawksmith has been out to destroy you from the very beginning. He's still out to get you but will wait until after the Soviet missile money is safely in the bank before he makes his next move. Moreover, membership of the ACF is growing year on year. By the way, you don't have to look too far for one of the ACF's leading acolytes… you know who I'm talking about?" Margaret made no sign. "Lisette. She's key to the ACF because she's so close to you. My advice is to keep her close… for obvious reasons." Margaret wondered whether Max was telling her the truth about Lisette.

If she's ACF how does he know? Margaret asked herself. The answer came to her straightaway. *He has his own people inside the Organisation. They're probably all around me.*

"If all I've said doesn't convince you, then just think about the upcoming generation of Aristocrats and the one after that and the one after that… the present generation is well educated, well connected, especially in the banking world, and they're already running the family businesses. Now, consider for a moment the French Splinter; it's run by a true Aristocrat… Count Bouvier. He was so arrogant as to think that he could break the rules and build a dynasty."

"His eldest son paid the price for his mistake."

"We must get things back on track and where better to start than with the Governors. They are the foundations on which the Aristocracy depends for its success."

"Some would say that the Governors are the foundations of the Organisation."

"Rotten foundations, Margaret, rotten foundations!" uttered Max shaking his head. "You need better, stronger, more loyal, foundations, ones that won't let you down when you need them. Did you know that Hawksmith told Bouvier about the route the Soviet missiles were to take out of West Germany?"

"I had my suspicions and so I played a game of double-shuffle. I had him believe the exit route had—"

"It's okay, I know what happened," interrupted Max. His offhand remark gave rise to thoughts about the loyalty of those involved in changing the escape route.

The former lovers talked and argued throughout the night and into the next morning. By the end, Margaret understood that the forty-four were destined to die and that the assassinations would go ahead with or without her. She said she needed time to think. Max said she'd had all the time she was going to get and now was the time for action. "They're dead anyway so why sacrifice yourself," Max had said at some juncture. She took that to mean she wouldn't be allowed to walk away from being Madame Chancellor. She had her Sentinels but doubted they'd be enough to protect her. Besides, from what she'd deduced, some of them were bound to be loyal to Max. Margaret steeled herself and told Max that she'd do as he'd asked but inside she hoped that she could find another way before the killing began. Max replied that it wasn't as he had asked, it was as she had agreed to do when she took the job. He was right; it was as she'd agreed to do when she took the job. There was no going back.

Before Max left Margaret sitting alone in the hotel suite, he told her to push ahead with selling the Soviet hardware straightaway. "You'll need money in the campaign chest for the fight ahead."

*

As Madame Chancellor entered the building in Half Moon Street she passed some of those on the list of the condemned. She would have to preside over their deaths or face the wrath of the Mandarins. Making her way to the lift, everybody gave a slight bow of the head as a sign of their fealty. On entering her office, Margaret saw Lisette perched one-cheeked on the corner of her desk going through her in-tray.

"Hey, don't look at me like that, I'm allowed to do this sort of thing now I'm on your hush hush secret council," joked Lisette. "I hope you don't mind me saying so darling but you look terrible. Truly terrible. Are you feeling alright?"

"No Lizzie, I'm not feeling alright but I don't want to talk about it right now. It's something I have to deal with but I may need to discuss it with you at some point."

An eavesdropper was alarmed at what Margaret had said but would wait to see how the situation developed. Lisette put an arm around Margaret and guided her like one would an elderly or infirm person to her chair. She fetched them both a cup of coffee into which she tipped a large snort of brandy from Margaret's secret stash. "Cheers," they said clinking their coffee cups together. Margaret stood and beckoned Lisette to sit with her on a leather sofa in the corner of her office. She told Lisette they were going to be on the move soon to new offices overlooking St James' Park. While she spoke Margaret wrote a short note asking Lisette not to react but she thought the room might be bugged and they would talk properly later about what was worrying her.

When they spoke later, Margaret left out the part about her having to slaughter forty-four Governors as part of a deal she'd made with the Mandarins. She'd leave that topic for another time, she thought.

CUTTING THE STRINGS

During the six-day war, when Israel ruled the skies flying American jets, the Arab nations realised their Soviet jets weren't up to the job. They urgently needed to reset the Balance of Power [BoP] in their favour and the stolen Soviet missiles were just the ticket. Even American jets couldn't outfly a Soviet SAM. Arab nations at the time claimed to be pro-Soviet but in reality they played the Americans off against the Soviet Union to gain whatever advantage they could over Israel, their unloved and unwanted neighbour. The problem for the Arabs was that the Soviets never provided them with the latest technology and were always playing catch-up. Classic Soviet partnership/friendship.

Accordingly, by the time the Organisation was ready to sell off the proceeds of the Soviet Missile Heist, there was no shortage of potential customers.

When disposing of the missiles, the Organisation was mindful not to tip the Balance of Power too far in any one direction as to do so, as history had taught it, could produce undesirable outcomes. That would not do at all; that's not what the Organisation is about; it needs to be able to go about its business unnoticed, just as it had done for centuries. One of the ways it remains unnoticed is by ensuring that people don't have time to raise their heads and look around to see what's really going on. An age-old, tried and tested way the Organisation achieves this is by creating societal strife through stirring up economic, religious, racial and intercultural hatred. Additionally, it creates balances and imbalances through backing conflicting political, industrial, financial, terrorist and trades unions organisations, all of which is aimed at pulling society this way and that. Sometimes it even starts wars to achieve its ends. All this intriguing and interfering is not cheap, so the proceeds from the Soviet Missile Heist would greatly help the Organisation work its mischief through replenishing its depleted coffers.

To maximise its RoI, while maintaining the BoP, the Organisation broke up the Soviet missiles, and their launchers, into various lots for sale based on technology and not the ability to obliterate enemies. Accordingly, guidance systems, warheads, missiles [SAM/ICBM] and launchers were sold as separate lots.

The Organisation weren't simply going to make complete weapons systems available. That would not do at all; that's not what the Organisation is about. It understands that people, as well as nations, who just acquire things, do not appreciate them. "The worthwhile things in life have to be worked for." Therefore the Organisation in arranging the missile lots made certain that there was no possibility of any one nation simply plugging in their purchases and firing them. A sudden burst of weapons advancement like that would shatter the BoP, especially between the lower-order nations. The BoP must change slowly otherwise all-out war is inevitable. Besides, if the Organisation sold complete working missile systems the Soviets would simply put pressure on the buyers to return their property to them and nobody wanted that, especially not the crooked high-ranking Soviet officials working in the Kremlin. Therefore the lots for sale were structured in such a way as to give the purchasers a teeny-tiny leg up on the weapons-race-ladder. That's it. In reality, that was all there was on offer. This approach facilitated long-term revenue streams as the Organisation supplied consultants to assist their customers' missile-launching ambitions.

The 'Missile Technology Sale', as it became known, was conducted menu style. The nations of the eastern Mediterranean were offered SAM technology. Where to offload the medium-range ICBM technology was proving problematic from the perspective of not wanting to start WW III. Problematic, that is, until the Chinese, the Soviets and the Americans came to the table. The Soviet stance was initially to demand their property be returned to them. All of it with nothing whatsoever missing. No negotiation. Doublers operating inside the Kremlin helped dilute these demands which resulted in the Soviet leadership ultimately accepting the offer made to them, leaving the way clear for a bidding war between the two other super-powers.

*

Whenever conducting business, the Organisation is always on the lookout for long-term revenue streams. This often takes the form of consultancy contracts to go along with deals they make. Eager for such additional revenue opportunities, Madame Chancellor, despite her having previously side-lined Sir Jeremy Hawksmith, agreed to meet him over lunch to discuss his ideas.

"Thank you for agreeing to meet me Madame Chancellor," said Sir Jeremy in his best toadying public schoolboy voice.

"While we're at lunch you should call me Margaret."

"Certainly... Margaret."

"I take it lunch is on you?"

"Of course... besides, no cash is allowed in my Alma Mater's club, everything has to be signed for." Sir Jeremy's old university club was situated on Pall Mall. Its dining room was a throwback to the 1920s including its atmosphere, decor and the behavioural standards for members and staff alike. The lunch menu was handwritten with ink on shabby dog-eared card which looked like it hadn't been changed in years.

"Do you come here often?" enquired Madame Chancellor holding the menu with the very tips of her fingers and wishing her nails were longer. Perusing the fare she couldn't believe her eyes; it was like that from her own school days; mash potato, two veg, meat and gravy with spotted dick and custard for pudding. Sir Jeremy caught her expression.

"It's Monday you see; roast potatoes Tuesday and Thursday and mash the rest of the week. We could go elsewhere if you prefer?"

"No, it's er… perfectly fine. I'll have the mash, veg, meat and gravy, thank you."

"Spotted dick and custard for pud?" prompted Sir Jeremy in upbeat fashion.

"Let's see after the main course. Do they do wine by any chance?"

"I'm afraid not. It's tap water at the table. We can go and sit in the comfy chairs in the member's area for a glass of wine before lunch if you like?" Margaret could see Sir Jeremy got his starchiness from his strict schooling. She almost felt sorry for him.

"No thank you Sir Jeremy—"

"Please… Margaret, as you've been so gracious as to allow me to use your name please call me Jem. Mummy called me that… Mummy's little Jem, she used to call me." Madame Chancellor wished he hadn't told her that as it made her gag.

"Is it safe to talk here?" asked Madame Chancellor as the tables were rather close together.

"Perfectly. They're mostly deaf. All that weekend shooting I should imagine."

"Well… Jem… what's this idea of yours you want to speak with me about?"

"You know how we're always angling to increase profit?" Madame Chancellor expected Jem to continue but he didn't, he was waiting for her to say '*yes*'.

"Yes."

"Well, here's one for you." Despite earlier assurances of them being able to talk freely, Jem leaned forward, lowering his voice to almost a whisper. "We sell off the," he silently mouthed the word '*missiles*', "at knock-down prices to our Arab friends on the basis that they cut us in on their oil revenues in perpetuity. They won't care, they just see oil as an accidental blessing bestowed on them from beneath desert sands."

"How much revenue are we talking about?"

"In the long run it'll be worth billions to us… billions and it will never end… so long as the oil doesn't dry up of course."

"Have you worked out the figures?"

"Yes and the best part is the more oil they sell the more money we get. You know what that means?"

Here we go again, thought Madame Chancellor. "Yes," she replied, "we somehow create increased demand for oil and benefit as a result." Mummy's little Jem hadn't thought of that.

"Precisely so," he whispered. Then a thought occurred to him. "And, what's more, we can start the odd war here and there to manipulate the market." Madame Chancellor hadn't thought of that.

"Exactly what I was thinking. Tell you what, Jem, let's not bother with lunch, let's go for that glass of wine and talk some more."

Even as Margaret and Jem were discussing how to make the most out of the missile haul, she could hear Max telling her about him selling her out to the French Splinter. This was unforgiveable but she'd let him set everything up, do all the hard work, and then, when he was done, she'd… she wasn't sure what but he'd have to go. As they were finishing their discussions, Sir Jeremy told Margaret about a 'near thing' in the run-up to the Soviet Missile Heist. He told her that a Potential, working at MILR, cracked the secret code, "And that led to the French Splinter finding out about your Soviet Missile Heist, Madame Chancellor," lied Jem not knowing Margaret already knew of his treachery. During the telling of his tale, Sir Jeremy mentioned the name of the Potential concerned. "He's called Michael Frost, I believe, a real nuisance, always attracting the wrong sort of attention. But don't worry, Margaret, I have plans for young Mr Frost. He's expendable and I know just the place for him." She didn't know why but that name, Michael Frost, struck

Margaret somehow. *What is it about that name?* she thought. It felt, deep down inside her, as though she'd known it all her life.

*

Implementing Sir Jeremy's scheme, the Organisation sold half the SAM technology to a consortium of Arab nations at a bargain price in consideration of a 'modest share' of their global oil revenues in perpetuity. This was later amended in favour of a split between oil and real estate. The Arab nations were delighted. And why not? Oil was just a happenstance of geography which had turned them into nations of billionaires. Property they purchased as a result of their oil revenues was thought of in likewise terms. The remainder of the SAM, ICBM and short- and mid-range missile technology was sold to the USA, which is how they caught up with, and then passed, the Soviets before the end of 1972. It's so very much easier improving on an idea. The USA provided the Israelis with SAMs and short- and mid-range missiles through the back door. *Favours beget favours,* thought Sir Jeremy in anticipation of rewards to come. Everybody was happy… even certain Soviets.

The Soviet Missile Heist was an outstanding success. The venture netted the Organisation billions of dollars, and they were receiving oil, and then real estate, revenues from their Arab BFFs, plus their consultants were burrowing in like tics into the very fabric of each nation. Margaret's star was in the ascendency.

After distributing the missile technology evenly amongst Arab and non-Arab nations, the Organisation set about pitting neighbour against neighbour, brother against brother, religion against religion. These nations became so preoccupied with watching their so-called enemies, they had no time to lift their heads and look around to see what was really going on, which is exactly how the Organisation likes things to be. Classic Organisation, spreading fear, hatred, death and destruction while remaining hidden in the shadows.

Following the sale of the proceeds of the Soviet Missile Heist, the Organisation's balance sheet hadn't looked so strong in decades. Governors were rubbing their hands in anticipation at what was coming their way.

*

Thus far, Margaret hadn't shared the details of the deal she'd made with the Mandarins when they appointed her Chancellor but if she didn't confide in somebody soon she'd lose her mind. *Lisette? What about Lisette?* Margaret thought Lisette was probably the best person to share her burden with despite not trusting her entirely. She hadn't shared with her so far because, she'd thought, *That's what they'd expect me to do!* Who then could she confide in who the Mandarins would never think of watching? It could only be Control.

Margaret resolved to contact Control. Believing the HQ in Half Moon Street could be bugged, she ordered Lisette to get the whole building swept for bugs. She asked her boss where she thought she might find somebody to check the building for bugs at that time of night. Margaret replied that was her problem, "I just want it done. Okay!" Lisette, in fact, had such a person in her little black book; 'Peter'. He arrived at Half Moon Street shortly after 11 p.m. and checked the whole building for bugs. He said he'd stake his reputation on there being none; he'd searched high and low, checking every potential hiding place for bugs and found nothing. Thinking he might prove useful in the future, Lisette kept Peter on the payroll as her 'Communications Consultant'.

The following day, to be on the safe side, Margaret sent Awhah and Cho to Control's office with orders to meet her at the Organisation's new HQ opposite St James' Park that afternoon. Then, if she could hold her nerve, Margaret would open up to Control over her deal with the Mandarins and her dilemma concerning the 'removal' of the Governors. Truth be told, when Control saw Awhah and Cho entering her office she thought they were there to eradicate her and reached for a 9 mil in her desk drawer but before she could grab it Cho kicked the draw closed. Fortunately, Control withdrew her hand in time.

*

Margaret was just about to slip out to meet Control when she heard Rex's voice outside her office door. *What the hell is he doing here today of all days?* she thought. Though Margaret was the boss, she still didn't know what Rex actually did. He came and went as he pleased and always gave non-committal answers to questions such as, "What the hell do you do Rex?"

"Is that you out there Rex?" shouted Margaret over Lisette's head.

"It is. Coffee?"

"I'll make it," offered Lisette with a sickly sweet smile. "You go on in and I'll bring it to you."

"Thank you Lisette for inviting people into my office. I'll have a coffee too while you're about it."

"Don't mention it boss, that's what I'm here for; to serve your every need," Lisette replied sarcastically. Rex entered Margaret's office wearing a serious expression.

"Margaret, I have something important to tell you but let's wait until after Lisette has served our coffees."

"Something important? Does that mean you're finally going to tell me what it is you actually do? I mean to say, I'm only Chancellor after all so it's about time I—"

"I said something important, not something secret," Rex replied with his customary tapping irritatingly on the side of his nose with a forefinger. Margaret wasn't in the mood for Rex's nonsense and told him so. As usual, he was indifferent to her remarks.

After Lisette served coffee she left the office, closing the door behind her, leaving the pair to their discussion. Rex looked toward the door to make sure it was fully closed.

"I have some news which affects you in your position as Chancellor," he said as easily as if he were wishing her a good day.

"Go on," replied Margaret, casually reaching under her desk to locate the hatched handle of her .38.

"Max died late yesterday evening," said Rex with an air of indifference. Margaret swooned with the shock of the news. "Here, please, take a tissue," offered Rex. He waited until Margaret recovered herself before continuing. He wondered if her tears were genuine. "Max wasn't a well man… but we all thought he had at least another decade left in him." Margaret was waiting for one of Rex's poor-taste jokes but none came.

"How did he die? What was the cause of death?" asked Margaret with deep suspicion in her voice which Rex recognised.

"There's nothing untoward. He'd had liver problems for years. Surely you, of all people, must have known that? It seems he suffered massive organ failure brought on by Sepsis. There'll be a post mortem, of course, and as soon as its results are known I'll tell you exactly what they say."

"Where is he?"

"I'm afraid I can't say…"

"Rex, I mean it, where is he?

"Margaret, you know I can't answer that question for obvious reasons." Rex sipped his coffee, lowered his bifocals, and squinted at the erotic Mongolian Horsemen prints around the office walls. "I believe you are aware of the closeness of the vote that elected you Chancellor? With Max gone your support is split fifty-fifty at best. Some of them may change sides and remove you. I'll do what I can but—"

"What if I wish to step down as Chancellor?"

"As you appreciate, that isn't an option old thing; you understand why, I'm sure. I'll do what I can but if things look like they're going badly I'll warn you and then at least you can rally support around you. I advise you keep your Sentinels close at hand."

"Some of them are Doublers. Maybe I'd be better off not

having them close if the worst should come to the worst?" suggested Margaret. Rex handed her a list. "What's this?"

"The names of Sentinels who are Doublers. I recommend you don't do anything about them for the time being but if things go against you then you know what you must do; kill them all. I have to go. I'll keep in touch. Ta ta."

Rex downed his coffee and left Margaret to her thoughts. He walked into his office just down the hall, locking the door behind him. Though he shouldn't have, Rex called his Opus Dei Controller from an insecure line. He reported what he'd spoken to Margaret about and hung up. Coincidentally, or perhaps not, Rex's Controller at Opus Dei was the same as Lisette's. While mainstream Churches had long ago forgotten about the Brotherhood, and reincarnations such as the Organisation, Opus Dei alone had not and wrote secret covenants into its constitution concerning the total destruction of the Organisation, its Factions and Splinters.

*

With Max dead, Margaret's head was in a spin; she felt vulnerable, weak, defenceless. Not knowing what to do or who she could trust, she told Lisette about Max's death, then showed her the list Rex had given her of Sentinels who were Doublers. Lisette looked it over, every so often shaking her head while making irritating tsk tsking sounds. She pointed to the second name on the list and remarked that she doubted Andrea was a Doubler. To silence Lisette, Madame Chancellor pressed a finger against her lips to which Lisette said, "My Communications Consultant, Peter, has checked everywhere. I'd stake his life on there being no bugs," then adding that she'd stake her life on the list being phoney. Going over the list together they were sceptical about half the names on it. Lisette reckoned Rex was probably a Doubler and so couldn't be trusted. Margaret believed he could well be but would play along with him for the time being.

Lisette went to her office to make a copy of the list. In fact she made four copies, posting three of them. Minutes later she returned to Madame Chancellor's office. "Don't ask how, darling, but I acquired a pair of snazzy-looking chromium plated Brownings the other day. They'll come in handy if somebody decides to take matters into their own hands. I'll give them a good clean before I hand them over to you. Don't want any misfires, now do we?" Margaret told Lisette to put the guns in her desk drawer after she'd finished cleaning them as she was going out for the day. Lisette asked where she was going but Margaret tapped the side of her nose with a forefinger and left. *Oh please Christ, don't tell me I'm becoming Rex!* thought Margaret in horror.

*

Walking to her meeting with Control gave Margaret time to think; time to absorb what Rex had told her. She knew from experience that when people in her world died suddenly it only ever meant one thing. Now she had to consider what opportunities Max's death presented. Margaret's thoughts next turned to changing her deal with the Mandarins; she could make things more to her liking. Though time was short, she was confident she still had time to save the lives of the forty-four. Margaret shook her head, smiled and gave a snort of derision. Here was she… Madame Chancellor… whose ambition it had always been to remove the old guard and now here she was trying to save the lives of the 'old farts club'. *What next?* she pondered. *Perhaps I'll take holy orders*, she thought mockingly. If what Max had told her was partially true, four Mandarins were for her and four against. She determined to keep Awhah and Cho close and in future have them and Lisette at hand wherever she went.

*

When Margaret arrived in front of the Organisation's new offices opposite St James' Park, she found Control waiting for her. She was intrigued to see what Control's reaction would be to the news of Max's sudden death and of her idea of saving the old guard. Crossing her fingers, Margaret hoped she could trust Control to keep their discussion confidential. If, after their conversation, she felt unsure then she'd... no, she wouldn't kill Control, she'd pay the price herself, she'd take her punishment. After all, it was she who'd decided to confide in Control and if that was a mistake then Control should not have to pay for it. That's the way Margaret wanted things to be from now on.

They took the lift directly to the tenth floor as Madame Chancellor was eager to see her new suite of executive offices. As they exited the lift there was an area which would be perfect for her new PA, Cressida. With Lisette now on her secret inner council Cressida would take Lisette's place as her PA. Unlike Lisette, Cressida wasn't promiscuous nor did she overindulge in recreational drugs. Lisette had always executed her PA duties perfectly but there were some aspects of her private life which caused concern, and not only with Margaret.

Control was experienced enough to know that there was more to this meeting than just having a look around the new offices. *She could have done that with anybody so why me?* she thought. Control asked Margaret if she had anything particular on her mind... anything that she wanted to discuss with her. "Are you unhappy with the way I'm carrying out my duties as Control?" she asked. Madame Chancellor told Control she was far from unhappy with her and then, taking her courage in both hands, took a deep breath before beginning her tale.

Margaret started by telling Control about Max's sudden passing and how upset she was by it. "Are you being serious?" Control asked. Margaret said she was and asked Control why she'd asked such a caustic question. She told Margaret of certain events in Half Moon Street that had occurred over the previous fifteen years, adding that she knew Max was a member of a group calling itself the Mandarins who were always trying to take over the running of the Organisation. Control said she believed they would have succeeded had it not been for the vigilance of the Governors. She agreed with Madame Chancellor that most Governors were a crusty old-fashioned bunch but they wouldn't take nonsense from anybody and had sent the so-called Mandarins packing on three occasions to her knowledge. Madame Chancellor told Control it was they who'd appointed her Chancellor. She said she'd heard rumours that it was they who appointed the Chancellor but thought them to be a myth and that she had always thought it more likely it was the Governors who appointed Chancellors.

Madame Chancellor asked Control why she used a deprecating tone whenever she mentioned the Mandarins; "the so-called Mandarins" as she'd referred to them. She replied that everything connected with them seemed to be tainted by treachery and deceit. She apologised to Madame Chancellor if she felt she was speaking out of turn and that she meant no disrespect to her or her position. Madame Chancellor assured her that she was in no way speaking out of turn, telling Control that she valued her openness and frankness and as the conversation proceeded each felt they'd gained the other's trust and confidence. The two women continued their discussion about the Mandarins while continuing with the inspection of the Organisation's new HQ, cementing their new-found fellow feeling, if not friendship.

"Madame Chancellor—"

"Margaret, please."

"Margaret… there's another group you should be aware of and I only mention it because Lisette is a member. They are known as the ACF and, according to Charles, they've been around for as long as the Organisation itself."

"Really?" replied Madame Chancellor sounding surprised. "What about them?"

"They are a Faction dedicated to the destruction of the Church… it's a long story."

"You must tell it me one day."

"I will. Before Charles left he told me that they are looking to take control of the Organisation. He said that they feel the time is right to take power."

"So Charles knew all this and did nothing?"

"No, not nothing. Remember the key I gave you? Well, he said it's all connected. That's what he told me."

"Connected how?"

"I don't know and now he's gone missing I doubt I'll ever find out but I feel it's very important. I'm sure it was the only thing that kept him alive all these years." Control knew Charles' suddenly going missing meant he was most likely to be dead.

"Well, do think on it some more and if anything occurs tell me."

"I will of course but what will you do about Lisette? I don't trust her, especially now that Charles is missing and Max is dead; though in my heart of hearts I feel Charles is dead too," said Control with sadness and a few tears.

"I'll keep an eye on Lisette. Do you really believe Charles is dead?" asked Margaret disingenuously as she knew the game.

"Yes I do, I genuinely do," answered Control giving Margaret something to ponder.

Arriving at a café on Trafalgar Square, Margaret and Control took a table at the back away from the window. She casually asked Control if she'd ever heard anything concerning Max and herself. Control said she had and that she hoped it wasn't true. Margaret understood and asked her how she could possibly know such a thing. Control replied that Rex had told just about everybody in the building about her and Max's affair. Now Margaret understood why some Governors rumourmongered about how she'd gotten to be Chancellor. Control asked Madame Chancellor if she felt favourably toward the Mandarins because of her affair with Max. She thought for a moment before replying, "That could be the case," without making eye contact. After finishing their coffees they left separately.

*

Following her meeting with Control, Margaret was in two minds as to what to do next; *Should I go back to the office or go to Soho, get drunk, and see what happens?* As it was still daylight she went to the office. *Next time Soho!* she thought as she entered the building. When she opened the outermost doors to her office suite she was surprised to find Lisette sitting at her desk.

"What are you still doing here? Don't you have anything better to do… or a home to go to?"

"Please, Madame Chancellor, whatever you do, don't thank me for all the effort I put in," Lisette answered sarcastically. "Or for the superb job I do for you. Not to mention looking after you by putting two fabulous chromium-plated Brownings in your desk drawer. They look super! Want to see them?"

"I do but first I need a stiff drink."

"Brandy?"

"Perfect."

"I'll get us them," said Lisette inviting herself to join her boss in the snifter. As she poured the drinks Lisette reached inside her handbag to retrieve a hexagonal blue bottle complete with rubber pipette. She put two drops of clear liquid into each glass, hesitating momentarily before adding another drop into each glass; *That'll do the job*, she thought smiling. "Cheers," said Lisette clinking her glass against Margaret's.

"Cheers Lizzie. Hmmm, that's better. Now let's go and see those guns you got me!" Margaret swigged her glass empty; slamming it down on the desk it shattered.

The two women ran like giddy, excited schoolgirls into Margaret's office where Lisette pulled open the desk drawer. Grabbing both pistols she offered one to Margaret and in doing so leaned forward and kissed her half on the cheek and half on her lips. It was an awkward moment.

"Check the weight. Check the balance," said Lisette spinning the guns around her fingers by their trigger guards. "Aren't they just the most beautiful pair you've ever seen? Let's check ourselves out in the mirror while we hold them. I'm going to be holding mine like this." Lisette struck a pose like a Bond girl. The clear liquid was taking effect as they sputtered a laugh, spraying each other with brandy spittle.

"What if somebody comes in and sees us acting like idiots?" asked Margaret.

"Then we'll shoot them right between the eyes!" crowed Lisette in a cackling laugh.

Margaret and Lisette stood back to back admiring themselves in the huge, gilt-framed, over-mantle mirror; guns held upright in front of them in both hands. They looked like they were straight out of a poster for a James Bond movie. The deep bevelled edges of the mirror somehow seemed brighter and more rainbow bejewelled than usual to Margaret. She imagined the gilt moulding of the frame flowed like liquid gold. Everything appeared more vital to them both.

Feeling loose tongued, Margaret said, "You know Lizzie, Max's death could be my salvation." She went on to divulge how she'd been deceived by Max and the Mandarins. She hesitated to tell Lisette about having to kill forty-four Governors but it came out eventually. Lisette's reply was that Margaret must have been so very eager to get the top job not to have seen something like that coming a mile off. Madame Chancellor agreed with her. She'd long believed that the shock and trauma of her discovering the truth of her past life had driven the need for validation in her new life.

"You're right, Lizzie. I was blinded by ambition and the thought of having all that power. But now I have a chance to put things right… do things my way. The right way. The fair way." Lisette laughed.

"Steady on now old girl. You don't think this will all just suddenly be okay; just go away because Max is dead, do you? What, just like that?" said Lisette clicking her fingers together but making no sound. "C'mon, Margaret, that's very naïve of you, it'll never happen."

"What do you suggest then?" snapped Margaret irritated at being spoken to in that way; after all, she was Madame Chancellor.

"If you look, even for a second, like you're not going along with them then you're a dead woman. This place is full of Doublers," said Lisette looking around, "and I suspect that at least two of your so-called secret inner council are spies, feeding everything back to their bosses; whoever they might be!" whispered Lisette giving Margaret a knowing wink. "What we need is a plan. Tell you what, and don't think badly of me for saying this, there are some Governors who need to go… permanently… if you know what I mean?" Lisette glanced a sly glance Margaret's way to check how she'd received her implied suggestion.

"I'm ashamed to say, Lizzie, that I've come to the same conclusion myself. After the Mandarins first told me about having to kill forty-four Governors, the next thought that jumped into my head, after I'd gotten over the initial shock, of course…"

"Of course darling," slurred Lisette, her approbation accompanied by a sicky mouth burp.

"My first thought was that I'd be glad to see the back of Sir bloody Jeremy bloody Hawksmith and his bloody cronies! Am I a terrible human being Lizzie?"

"Yes, darling, but you're forgiven. I'm joking. I'm joking!" added Lisette, laughing at her boss' hurt expression.

"Okay then Lizzie, let us see, then, who have been naughty boys and girls. Let us see who has been using my Organisation for their own purposes. Let us see who has been empire building and intriguing. Let us see who the conspirators are who have been corrupting my beautiful Organisation. Then we'll make our own list!"

"And then what?"

"Then what? We'll deal with them, that's '*then what*'."

"We'll deal with them? Who's this '*we*' by the way darling?"

"You're right as usual, Lizzie. There is no '*we*'. There can be no '*we*'. I must deal with them. Me… on my own… alone… as usual. The all-powerful Madame Chancellor must deal with them. She'll deal with them all alright!" The more Margaret spoke, or thought, of her self-proclaimed title the more she liked it. "*The All-Powerful-Madame-Chancellor!*"

"To the archives!" yelled Lisette like a mediaeval battle cry.

"What?"

"To the archives! That's where we'll find the evidence you're looking for. You know? Who's been doing all the this and all the that… you just said so yourself darling, just now. Intriguers? Empire Builders? Remember? It'll all be in the archives. Make your own list you said."

"Oh yes," replied Margaret sounding vague and spaced out. "Oh yes, good one Lizzie… good one. To the archives!" cried Margaret.

*

For three days in a row, Margaret and Lisette worked tirelessly sifting through the archives; checking, validating, rechecking, revalidating, discussing, agreeing, disagreeing. They gave the benefit of doubt where they could until a final list was arrived at. During their delving, Lisette was in charge of sustenance. Three or four times a day she added a couple of drops of the clear liquid from the hexagonal blue bottle to Madame Chancellor's drinks and, most times, her own too. She knew what her Opus Dei controller required of her and though she didn't think of herself as a Zealot, Lisette was prepared at that moment to be a martyr in the destruction of the Organisation.

The final list had eighteen names on it. Margaret and Lisette each feigned shock and being appalled at the number and resolved to look at the list again one final time before signing it so the deed could be done. At the top of the list was Sir Jeremy Hawksmith, "Mummy's little Jem, that's what his mummy used to call him you know, Lizzie; Mummy's little Jem," howled Madame Chancellor like a Macbeth Witch. There would be no going back for Sir Jeremy, he was doomed.

As they collected up the paperwork strewn about Madame Chancellor's office, to deposit it once again into the archives, Lisette suggested a celebratory brandy.

"Oh, yes please darling, that'll go down a treat!" exclaimed Margaret smacking her lips together though she almost refused the offer as it seemed to her that she was somehow already intoxicated.

"I'll pour us each a large one… special treat," crooned Lisette smiling.

Out of sight of Madame Chancellor, Lisette dripped eight drops of the clear liquid from the hexagonal blue bottle into both glasses, knowing full well that such a dose would put them both into a coma, from which they would not recover, in next to no time. Though dedicated to Opus Dei's cause, Lisette reflected that such a sacrifice as she was about to make would be the last desperate act of a Zealot and, after pouring both drinks away, she refilled the glasses; this time putting only four drops of the clear liquid in each of them.

After gulping down her brandy, Madame Chancellor walked toward the large, gilt-framed, over-mantle mirror at the far end of the office. After squinting at it from just a few inches away she hopped one-footed across to the other side of the office to admire it from there.

"Lisette darling, have you noticed anything funny about that mirror over there?" asked Madame Chancellor pointing an uncontrolled, unreliable finger in the general direction of the gilt-framed mirror.

"No darling, no, I haven't. I have not. Why? What's wrong with it?"

"It's beautiful. The frame is like a river of gold… river of gold, it flows so… and the rainbows… the rainbows are beautiful. Can you see the beautiful rainbows darling?"

Margaret collapsed into Lisette's arms. Laying her carefully on the floor, Lisette kissed Madame Chancellor tenderly on her cheeks.

"It has to be done," said Lisette distractedly but firmly.

"Yes, it has to be done," agreed Margaret, her voice thin and ethereal.

"When will you do it?"

"I don't know… I don't know," replied Madame Chancellor vaguely.

"Why not do it after the AGM. That's the best time to do it."

"Okay, right after the AGM. That's… that's the best time to do it," said Margaret, winking at Lisette with one eye then the other.

"Are you sure you can trust Control?"

"Yes, I'm sure."

"If you're found out they will show you no mercy."

"Yes, no mercy for Margaret. Poor Margaret. I'll be shown no mercy," replied Madame Chancellor, laughing for some reason.

"Oh darling, what a year it's been darling."

"Yes, what a year it's been…" repeated Madame Chancellor, her voice sounding eerily disembodied.

"You really shouldn't have chastised Sir Jeremy…" laughed Lisette. "But no; no regrets darling, you must have no regrets. I don't half fancy a ciggie!"

"You're right as usual Lizzie darling. The dressing down I gave Sir Jeremy Hawk-bloody-smith set everybody against me. I shouldn't have done it. I think they're scared of me Lizzie," whimpered Madame Chancellor, her voice trailing off as her eyes took on the appearance of a small frightened child.

"Yes, but that's a good thing, darling, that's a good thing. It is better to be loved than feared… no, no, no, that's not right…" Lisette laughed at her misquote. She had another go. "If you cannot be both then it is better to be feared than loved; yes, it's better to be feared than loved."

"But there must be a little love darling otherwise they'll never—"

"You pulled off the biggest heist in history… ever!" The women chinked glasses, smashing one of them in the process. "You have the Governors worshipping at your feet like yappy little dogs." The women toasted chinking glass against bottle, shattering the remaining glass. There was blood but neither of them noticed it flowing. "And you have the papers."

"The papers?"

"Yes darling, the papers. Where are they, darling?"

"Where are they, darling?" replied Margaret Parrot-like then laughing.

"You know where they are, don't you?"

"I know where what are?" replied Madame Chancellor tapping the side of her nose with a forefinger.

"Where are they, darling?"

"They're here," replied Margaret in the voice of a naughty little schoolgirl.

"Where, darling?"

"Here… in London," replied Margaret thinking about something completely different.

"Where in London, darling?"

"At Control."

"Control?" queried Lisette.

"What about Control?" replied Margaret confusedly. Lisette seethed believing the Churchill papers were stashed away in the basement at Control.

They'll be impossible to get at, Lisette thought almost lucidly. *That's why she put them there you idiot!* screamed her inner voice. "And now, darling, you must prepare yourself for your next great challenge; the Governors. Timing is important."

"Yes, timing is important."

"At the AGM then?"

"Yes, at the AGM," agreed Madame Chancellor, her voice ethereal and metallic.

"All who look upon you will fear and love you."

"Yes, they shall love me," gasped Madame Chancellor breathlessly.

"And in their weakness you will pity them."

"I shall pity them in their weakness," she choked.

"Max is dead and the others are nothing without him."

"Max is dead and the others are nothing without him," she rasped.

"They'll run for cover."

"They'll run for cover," repeated Madame Chancellor, her voice barely audible.

"And you, you'll finally be the all-powerful Madame Chancellor... just like you always wanted," spoke Lisette dreamily, barely able to keep her eyes open.

I shall finally be the all-powerful Madame Chancellor... just like I always wanted, repeated Madame Chancellor inside her head.

"Sleep darling, sleep. It'll be our time soon. Sleep," whispered Lisette spooning her mistress.

End of the first instalment.

EPILOGUE

As agreed with Mr Flask, Michael Frost arrived at CTCRM Lympstone to train with the Royal Marines Commandos in January 1971. The thirty-two-week course introduced him to every aspect of land and sea warfare. Before his arrival at Lympstone Michael's abilities were already leaning toward him becoming a Sentinel and during his PRMC training those observing him moved Michael to list D as his talent for killing developed. For different reasons, this is precisely what Captains Jones and Lefort did not want to happen to Michael.

During his early days at Lympstone, Michael struggled to keep up with the rest of the potential recruits because he lacked stamina due to his nana's old wives' remedy for curing whooping cough but his fitness and endurance improved and by week twenty he was a virtual machine.

The other potential recruits at Lympstone didn't dislike Michael but they didn't like him either. He'd never really had any friends and Lympstone was no different. There was something about Michael that kept people at a distance. An incident during one of the exercises didn't help matters.

Michael and five other Potentials were taking part in a four-day survival and evasion exercise on Dartmoor. The aim of the exercise was to evade capture and arrive as a team at the final checkpoint. Michael's group were making their way to the last checkpoint when they heard the sound of dogs barking close by. Having hardly slept, they were exhausted. Carrying a 50lb Bergen added to their fatigue. As pursuers and dogs closed in on the group it crossed their minds to ditch their Bergens, find cover and make a fight of it by trapping their pursuers in a crossfire. Not a bad strategy plus it showed initiative. However, being so exhausted, they weren't thinking straight and consequently they continued on their course hoping to somehow outrun the men and dogs.

The sound of the dogs' barking suddenly got a lot nearer. Unexpectedly, from out of the dark, four dogs, which had broken free of their handlers, came on the recruits from behind. There were shouts of "dogs, dogs, dogs; dogs loose" from the handlers with some also shouting for the Potentials to lay down and remain completely still and whatever they did they "must not hurt the dogs". Fat chance, they were huge. Being on Dartmoor, the scene brought images of the Hound of the Baskervilles to the minds of the group. Instead of laying down, Michael walked toward the dogs and as they drew near they ceased barking and slowed their pace.

One of the dogs, after sniffing at Michael's boots, moved off into the dark while the others came and laid down on the ground, looking up adoringly at him, their tongues lolling out of the sides of their mouths and their heads tipped to one side. At first, everybody was astonished by what they had witnessed but became concerned and then frightened as they stood in the dark and stormy landscape conjured up by Dartmoor. When the handlers approached their dogs to reclaim them they bared their teeth and growled; making lunges at them before returning to lay at Michael's feet. He looked at each of them in turn and without a word from him they reluctantly re-joined their masters.

Everybody took a few minutes to gather their wits and their bearings. The pursuers, their dogs and the Potentials made their way to RVP four where they were loaded into trucks and taken back to CTCRM Lympstone. There was very little chatter during the drive back. Nobody knew what to make of what they'd witnessed that night but the events did nothing to enhance Michael's reputation or endear him to his comrades. After that night, Michael came under even greater scrutiny as rumours spread that he must have had some kind of chemical on him which incapacitated the dogs, subduing them and putting them into some kind of trance. Nobody had any explanation for what had happened except perhaps that it was the dogs' sixth sense about Michael which pacified them. A report was sent up the line about the *'Dartmoor Incident'*. It ended up with Major Finn and he, Captain Jones and a Controller were at furious odds with one another as to what to do about Private Frost. "Just say the word and I'll see to it that he has an unfortunate accident," pleaded Major Finn. "No!" was the answer that came back from the Controller. *Why are they protecting him? Why!* screamed Major Finn inside his head.

Michael was due to pass out from Lympstone in two weeks and as much as he could look forward to anything he was looking forward to seeing his mum, dad and Thomas who were travelling down from Liverpool for the ceremony. Back in Liverpool the whole family were proud of Michael and they all chipped in to help pay for Mary, Joseph and Thomas to go to Lympstone and have a night in a guest house so they could celebrate properly.

What Michael couldn't know was that the *'mission'* he'd been selected for by those who ran Mr Flask had been brought forward and he was to leave Lympstone immediately. Mr Flask and an Irish Sentinel known as Jack Lynch arrived at the camp to remove him. They were taken before the camp CO. He knew he had no choice but to cooperate. Michael was ordered to report to the Medical Officer who told him that he'd been selected for a posting in Africa and needed to be injected with a vaccine which, in fact, was a prototype sedative. As soon as Michael was unconscious, Mr Flask handed the stabilising drug to the MO to inject him with it.

Michael was carried to a black Ford Cortina Mk III, strapped into its rear seat and driven away.

"Where's the lad off to then?" asked Jack Lynch.

"Your old stomping ground," replied Mr Flask.

"Christ! Who the hell has the lad upset for him to be sent there?"

"We're to ensure that—"

"I hope ye weren't thinkin' of havin' me takin' him there? I'm not too welcome in the old country these days."

"Don't worry, Paddy, you just drive. I'll direct you."

Jack wasn't happy at being called '*Paddy*' but he'd let it slide for now.